D0206049

Dear Reader,

Get ready to be whisked away to the color and pageantry of exotic India, where a noble hero with hidden secrets finds the passion of the one woman who can redeem him—all in the pages of this debut novel from brand-new Pocket Books star Meredith Duran. Even the story of how we found The Duke of Shadows *is romantic. This fabulous tale was the winner of the Gather.com First Chapters Romance Writing Competition, where the top prize was guaranteed publication by Pocket Books. But in order to understand just how thrilled we were to find this extraordinary romance, you'll have to read it yourself!*

Lauren McKenna
Executive Editor
Pocket Books

HER FATE RESTED IN HIS HANDS. . . .

She looked up. The shadows veiled him from her, but she could feel his presence all along her skin. Heat, and vibrancy, and that restrained, careful power. She had seen how the Anglo-Indians watched him as he passed through their drawing rooms, how their manner swung between sycophancy and contempt. He would have to be restrained around such people, especially when he could—if he liked—crush them so easily.

His face lowered to hers, so close that she felt his ragged exhalation against her lips. "Emma, you can trust me with your life. But I am not your brother. You cannot trust me in this."

"I have no brother," she said softly. "Nor mother, nor father, now. If I trust you with my life, I trust you with everything I have."

Something changed in him—a sudden focus to his silence, or the abrupt suspension of his breath. "Oh, you foolish girl." He carried her hand to his face, placing it against the rough stubble on his jaw. Caught by the sensation, she barely noticed as his hair brushed by her chin. And then he laid his lips into the curve of her neck.

The Duke of Shadows

MEREDITH DURAN

Pocket Star Books

New York London Toronto Sydney

The sale of this book without its cover is unauthorized. If you purchased this book without a cover, you should be aware that it was reported to the publisher as "unsold and destroyed." Neither the author nor the publisher has received payment for the sale of this "stripped book."

Pocket Star Books
A Division of Simon & Schuster, Inc.
1230 Avenue of the Americas
New York, NY 10020

This book is a work of fiction. Names, characters, places, and incidents either are products of the author's imagination or are used fictitiously. Any resemblance to actual events or locales or persons, living or dead, is entirely coincidental.

Copyright © 2008 by Meredith McGuire

All rights reserved, including the right to reproduce this book or portions thereof in any form whatsoever. For information address Pocket Books Subsidiary Rights Department, 1230 Avenue of the Americas, New York, NY 10020

First Pocket Star Books paperback edition April 2008

POCKET STAR BOOKS and colophon are registered trademarks of Simon & Schuster, Inc.

For information about special discounts for bulk purchases, please contact Simon & Schuster Special Sales at 1-800-456-6798 or business@simonandschuster.com

Illustration by Craig White

Manufactured in the United States of America

10 9 8 7 6 5 4 3

ISBN-13: 978-1-4165-6703-5
ISBN-10: 1-4165-6703-8

For Shelley,
who insisted that I try again.

Acknowledgments

Thanks to the denizens of Treeview-on-Florence (a.k.a. the Plotmaster and the Voice of Sanity), "Roasty Toasty" Monroe, AKT, LFL, Anu, Maddie and her CD burner, Kristen and the crew at Gather, Megan McKeever and everyone at Pocket Books.

And my utmost gratitude goes to Lauren McKenna, who is everything I could have hoped for in an editor, and then some.

Prologue

"I WON'T."

Her own voice sounded strange to her. Hoarse and low. So much salt water she'd swallowed. Her nose and throat burned, as if scrubbed out with lye. She coughed weakly. Beyond the hull of the overturned rowboat, the waves danced in an endless line to the horizon.

Just let go.

Her fingers flexed. The feeling in them came and went. Red and chapped from the sun overhead, they had clutched for hours now at the underside of the captain's gig. She had managed to get her torso up onto the hull. For a little while, a man had clung to the other side—a fellow survivor, who had jumped from the bow of the steamer just before it sank. He'd thought he might be able to right the rowboat, once the sea finally calmed.

In the end, he'd not even had time to scream. A wave

had come, and she had fought to hold on; when she surfaced, sputtering, he was gone.

So silent, in his wake. Water slapped into her back. A fish splashed. But no birds flew this far out to sea. The sky was blue and empty, fiercely bright. Her eyes smarted to look upon it.

Could she not let go now?

She swallowed. Her arms ached, and also her stomach, from coughing up water. But the thirst was surely the worst part. So suddenly the storm had struck. Masts cracking. Mama screaming.

Mama and Papa waited for her now below.

The ocean waited too. It sulked sluggishly beneath the tropical sun; slipping into it would not be so hard. The heat felt like a warm hand pressing on her back, urging her down and away. No trace of the great ship remained; no one surveying these flat, empty waters would suspect what had passed here. No one was coming for her.

But her hands would not let go.

She stared at them. Mama was particularly fond of these hands; pianist's hands, she called them. "Turpentine will ruin them. Use gloves when you paint, Emmaline. Do not ruin your hands before your wedding."

What a strange thought Emma had found it, this idea of being wed. "I am hoping for a great adventure," she had told the captain last night at dinner. Later, in their quarters, her parents had upbraided her. She was going to Delhi to be married; she must not speak of the journey so lightly. Her intended was a man of some import. She must comport herself accordingly.

A tear fell onto her bare arm. Hotter than the sun, saltier than the sea water, it smarted down her blistering skin. Always those same, gentle words. *You are stubborn, my dear. We must guide you in this. You are drawing attention; your remarks were unseemly.* So gently her parents scolded her. So gently they despaired of their wayward, indecorous daughter.

The man had said the boat could be flipped. He had planned to do it himself. If one man could do it, could one woman manage?

On a deep breath, she pulled herself up higher on the hull. Her arms shook and burned from the strain as she inched her hand down the far side . . . farther, farther now . . .

But the distance to the gig's other lip was too great. Her strength failed her, and she slid back down with a grunt.

Back to where she'd begun. She closed her eyes.

The tears came faster now, but she would not let go.

Part One

One

Delhi
May 1857

JULIAN FIRST NOTICED HER BECAUSE SHE LOOKED SO bored. Waiting for the Commissioner's arrival had put him on edge. He stood at the top of the room, half attending to the feverish chatter around him, his eyes fixed on the door. Rumors in the bazaar daily grew darker, and it was clear to him now that if Calcutta would not act, the local government must. Tonight he meant to exact a promise on that account.

He became aware of the woman gradually. It was her stillness that drew his attention. She was leaning against a wall, not ten feet away. Though several people surrounded her, sipping negligently at their wine and laughing, she seemed somehow apart. Tired of it all. Her eyes, which had been resting vacantly on the space over his shoulder, focused on him. They were a penetrating blue, and gave Julian a start. He saw that she was not bored at all, but unhappy.

She looked away.

He spotted her next in the green room, after the Commissioner slipped out of his grasp. "After dinner," the man mumbled, "if you truly insist on mixing business with pleasure, I would be most, most honored to speak with you." When Julian wheeled away in abrupt, frustrated dismissal, he discovered her behind him, the wineglass halfway to her lips. Again their eyes met, and she lowered the glass.

"Sir," she said evenly, bobbing a shallow curtsy. Something in her tone indicated she'd overheard the tail end of his argument with Fraser. He opened his mouth to respond—after all, the lady had seemed to be waiting for him—but she had already retreated in a swish of cornflower silk, and he was not in the mood for a chase.

He began to wonder about the coincidence when she drifted after him into the garden. Was she following him? In London he might have felt some faint, predatory stirring of interest—he enjoyed women, particularly those who spared him the trouble of pursuit—but he had a policy of avoiding memsahibs. Their husbands were rarely understanding, and they themselves tended to be so bored by life on a British station that passing love affairs quickly inflated to their entire reason for being. There was also an absurd set of ideas circulating about him in Anglo-Indian circles, variations on the theme of exotic Eastern eroticism, and he'd long since grown weary of it.

But she did not, in fact, seem to know he was there. She paused at the edge of the lawn, one hand coming to her throat, and seemed content to stand there, an abstracted look on her face. A breeze came over the grass, and her fingers loosened, letting the shawl flutter around her shoulders. Fleetingly, her pale lips curved in a smile.

Again, he was struck by the impression that she stood at a great remove from the scene around her. Curious. He studied her more closely, finding nothing of special note. Her hair was an unremarkable color, a curling, sun-faded dun that, in conjunction with her pale skin, made it seem as though all the energy of her being were focused in the brilliance of her deep blue eyes. A very odd sort of beauty, if a beauty at all. He wondered if she had recently been ill.

The thought made him impatient with himself. She was young, no more than twenty-two or -three years, with smooth white skin that bespoke a typical memsahib's routine. What was there to wonder about her? She would spend her days closeted in a bungalow, reading or at needlepoint. When the monotony began to wear, she would take heart in her zealous belief that the English way of life was the only one of merit in the world.

She muttered something beneath her breath. Despite himself, he leaned forward. He could not quite make it out. Surely she had not said—

With a violent gesture, she splashed her wine into the bushes. "Pig swill," she said clearly.

The garden was not cool, but it was quiet. Emma turned her face into the sultry breeze and let her eyes drift shut. Had Mrs. Greeley been speaking the truth? Either way, the woman must have been surprised at Emma's impassive reception of the news. It was unpleasant, of course;

one didn't often learn that one's betrothed was conducting a torrid affair with a married woman. But the act seemed entirely in keeping with the person Marcus had become since their engagement.

Perhaps it was this land that had changed him so. Emma had been here only a few weeks, but already she sensed that India had taken hold of her: loosening her tongue, widening her eyes. Even now, when her mind should have been racing with the implications of Mrs. Greeley's words, the gentle swaying of the trees and the parrots twittering in the branches above distracted her from thought. The night air mantled her bare shoulders, thick and warm, so richly perfumed with night-blooming jasmine that she wondered if she would carry the scent back inside with her.

A bullock lowed in the distance. She felt a brief stirring of pity, imagining he was confused at the excess of liberty granted him by the native culture. As to why the cattle were encouraged to wander through the streets, Marcus had told her that the Hindus believed them to be some sort of deities, but he hadn't been able to elaborate. Marcus was often impatient with details.

This party, for instance. He should have told her, given her some warning regarding the people she would meet. Within five minutes it had become clear that Delhi society was no friend to her, that news of the shipwreck and her "dishonorable" rescue had tainted local opinion. Instead he'd let her march inside like a lamb to the slaughter, encouraging her to mingle with the sharp-tongued harpies whilst he conferred with the Commissioner.

All this, and then to discover he was having an affair with the hostess!

Well, it was clear that whatever they did when alone together, Marcus had not reviewed Mrs. Eversham's wine list for her. *He* was possessed of impeccable taste. With a scoff she tossed the remnants of her Bordeaux into the shrubbery. "Pig swill!"

The quiet laugh startled her, and she gasped, squinting into the shadows. "Who's there?"

A form emerged from the trees, offering her a toast from a silver flask. "Pig swill indeed," he said, and lifted the pocket-pistol to his lips for a long swallow.

She relaxed slightly at the Oxford drawl, which complemented a deliciously low, rough voice. "Pray do not relay my sentiments to our hostess, sir." *Or perhaps do,* she added silently.

Another step brought him full out of darkness, and she caught her breath. It was the man from indoors—the one with whom she had nearly collided earlier. Once again, his height took her off guard. He was taller even than Marcus, and a full head over her own considerable height.

His eyes were a luminescent green-gold, catlike as they reflected the faint light spilling from the bungalow. They watched her as though he waited for something.

"Are we acquainted?" she blurted out—knowing very well they were not.

He gave her a faint smile. "No."

When he said nothing more, she arched a brow, returning rude stare for rude stare. At least, she hoped it was rude, for she suspected she might be ogling him. The man was unnervingly handsome—like something from a fever dream, brilliant and fierce, skin touched by gold and hair so black it absorbed the light. Earlier, indoors, she had found herself looking at him, thinking his face begged to be sketched. It would take only a few economical strokes—sharp, angular slashes for the cheekbones, a bold straight line for his nose, a fierce square for his jaw. Perhaps his lips would take more time. They were full and mobile, and saved his countenance from sternness.

He was very tanned. Doubt flickered through her mind, quashed as she considered his starched cravat and elegantly cut tailcoat. Of course he was English. The lazy grace with which he held himself made her aware of her own unmannerly slouch. She straightened, lifting her face toward the stars.

"A lovely night," she said.

"Pleasant weather," he agreed, eliciting a startled laugh from her.

"You must be joking!" she said, when he tilted his head in question. "It's dreadfully hot."

"Do you think so?" He shrugged. "Then I suggest you withdraw to Almora. The hill stations are quite popular this time of year."

His reference to the tradition of retreating to the Himalayan foothills during the hot weather sounded almost contemptuous. "You don't plan to go?"

"Business holds me here."

"Business. You're with the Company, then?" Most everyone she had met so far was in the employ of the East India Company, either as a civil servant or, like Marcus, as an officer in the army.

But he appeared mightily amused by the idea. "Dear God, no. I see my reputation does not precede me."

"Oh, is it very bad?" The question was out of her

mouth before she could reconsider, and she blushed as he laughed again.

"It's even worse."

When she realized he wasn't going to elaborate, she ventured to continue. "You'll have to tell me about it yourself; I've only just arrived in Delhi, you see."

"Really?" He sounded surprised. "I didn't know they raised chits like you in England."

"Chits like me?" She frowned. He had settled back against a tree trunk and was smiling at her indulgently, as if—suddenly it came to her—she were some three-year-old who had just shown him a neat trick with her doll. "Are you being insulting?"

"I meant you seem to have some spirit."

"You *are* being insulting," she decided. "To me and England both."

"Well then." He sighed and rolled his shoulders; his coat fit closely enough to reveal the ripple of arm muscles beneath the fabric. She wondered what he had done to acquire them; it was not at all the fashion. "Now you've discovered the first part of my reputation. I am considered terribly ill-mannered."

"But I knew that the moment I saw you! A gentleman would refrain from drinking spirits in the presence of a lady."

His brows rose. "And a lady would not call her hostess's wine—what was it? Pig swill, I believe?"

Her laughter was reluctant, but genuine. "All right, you've found me out. I'm a black sheep as well. Really, it's a wonder my intended will have me."

"Paragon of virtue, is he?"

"Not quite," she said dryly. "But they'll forgive him

just about anything." The conversation was utterly inappropriate, of course; but she had forgotten how good it felt to joke and be silly with someone, and to be spoken to without those ever-present undertones of pity and speculation. "In fact, someone inside just called him the Darling of Delhi."

"He sounds dreadfully dull. Do I know him?"

"Oh, you must. This party is in honor of us, you know—of our engagement." His sudden stillness made her frown, and she searched his face, concerned that she might have embarrassed him. "If you don't know who the party's for, I promise not to tell."

"Oh, I know." His voice was very soft now. "That would make you Miss Martin."

"Indeed! And now you must tell me your name, so I won't be at a disadvantage."

His cat's eyes moved over her shoulder, and he smiled again, this time rather unpleasantly. "Here comes your betrothed," he said, and took a deep swig from the flask.

"Emmaline! There you are!"

She turned back toward the doors, shielding her eyes from the light. "Marcus!" He was yanking his cravat in place, and she wondered acidly if he hadn't been waylaid by their hostess somewhere between the Commissioner and the garden. "I was taking some air," she said. "Flannel is horribly ill suited to this climate."

Marcus stepped into the yard. "I hardly think that's appropriate for public discussion," he said severely. "And I did warn you about the weather, but you insisted—" His voice died away as he stared at her companion. "What in blazes are you doing here?"

"Lindley," the man said curtly. "A pleasure."

Marcus made a rude noise. "I'm sure I can't say the same. I had no idea Mrs. Eversham was so indiscriminate with her guest list."

Emma glanced rapidly between them. The stranger's expression was perfectly neutral; Marcus, on the other hand, was glaring and breathing like a bull. "Marcus, really! This gentleman—"

"Knows he is not welcome," Marcus said. "Not anywhere I am, and certainly nowhere near my future wife. I would suggest you leave now, *sir.*"

The man shrugged. "Of course." Slipping the flask inside his jacket, he sketched a shallow bow. "Accept my congratulations on your betrothal, Lindley. Miss Martin is utterly charming."

"You soil her by speaking of her," Marcus snapped. "Beware lest I call you out for it!"

Now she was truly alarmed. Something about this man—perhaps his slight smile at Marcus's threat—made her think he would be more than a match for her intended. "Gentlemen, this is absurd!"

"Come with me." His hand tightening cruelly into her forearm, Marcus all but dragged her back into the bungalow.

Inside, the sudden brightness of numerous lamps and candelabras made her wince. She pulled Marcus to a stop at the edge of the crowd, beneath one of the giant fans hanging from the ceiling. Its starched chintz streamers were wilting in the humidity. "I cannot credit your behavior," she said. "How could you behave so loutishly!"

"How could I?" Marcus pulled her around to face him. "Do you know who that man is? *Do you know?*"

"Stop shaking me!" She yanked her arm from his grip. The strong, sour odors of wine and sweat were rising from his skin. Maybe he had overindulged tonight, but that was no excuse. "What has come over you?"

"That is my cousin," he managed, his face purple. "That is the half-breed who would have the dukedom instead of me."

"That—" She stopped, understanding. "*That* man is Julian Sinclair?"

"One and the same."

She turned away from him, staring blindly toward the dancers. Marcus had written to her of his second cousin, Julian Sinclair. Sinclair's father, Jeremy, had married a Eurasian, a woman of mixed English and native descent, when he had thought his brother the Marquess would have the dukedom. But within a short period, the cholera had killed Jeremy, and the Marquess had died in a hunting accident. That left Jeremy's young son as heir to the dukedom—Julian, whose blood was one-quarter native.

Now Julian Sinclair was grown, and his grandfather, the current duke, had made sure through every legal means that his grandson would follow him in the succession. But Marcus could not accept the idea that a man of mixed blood might inherit the title, when Marcus, pure-blooded English and in line after Sinclair to inherit, might himself wear the strawberry leaves so well.

"He didn't seem Indian," she whispered to herself.

"Of *course* he didn't!" Marcus exploded. "The Duke has done everything in his power to assure it—Eton, Cambridge, a seat in the Commons. But while a man can ape his betters, he can't change his blood. The proudest title in Britain is to go to a half-breed mongrel!"

She looked back to him, stunned. "Marcus, you sound so . . . hateful."

He stared at her, his mouth thinning into a grim line. "Is that so? To think, you've been here only five days, and already you're starting to pant after the natives. What would your parents say?"

She winced. A servant was passing with a tray of wine; she reached out and snared a glass. "That is cruel."

"Cruel but true. Even in death, they knew the honor of being Martins."

She took a deep swallow of the wretched Bordeaux and shut her eyes. Again and again it returned to haunt her—this image of her parents' faces, so small and pale as the ocean closed over them. The pain of their deaths did not fade; most nights, she still awoke weeping from nightmares of drowning with them. Only a miracle had guided her to the gig on which she had floated for almost a day; only God had given her the strength to cling to it as the hot sun beat down and she despaired of ever being found.

She set the glass on a sideboard and looked directly at him. The atmosphere was close and torpid, and sweat was trickling down her nape; strange, then, that she felt so cold. "You think it would have been more honorable to let myself drown?"

After a mute, stubborn moment, his face softened, and he reached for her hands. "No, my dear, of course not."

But she wondered. After all, he could play with his precious honor all he liked, risking it with his conspicuous philandering, his exorbitant gambling debts. But to have that honor tarnished by a woman! Surely it must irk him, to risk being made a laughingstock by upholding a betrothal with a woman of questionable reputation—a woman who had arrived in India sheltered not under the watchful gaze of her mother and father, but by a crew of rough-and-ready sailors. Those sailors had saved her life, but Anglo-Indian society was wondering if they hadn't robbed her of something even more important: her virtue.

Naturally, the fact that her betrothed's virtue was completely and publicly compromised was of no import at all.

She lifted her chin. "Oh, I was only speaking with him, Marcus. Do let's forget it. There's no need to look so grim."

Marcus exhaled. His eyes began to search the crowd beyond her shoulder. "I'm wondering why he hasn't been thrown out by now."

"Perhaps because he's the Marquess of Holdensmoor?"

He slanted her a sharp glance. "I'm not in the mood for your cheek, Emmaline. And for your information, the man's a threat to the Crown. He's been stirring up talk of a possible insurrection, trying to goad us into abandoning Delhi. Thinks our native troops might turn on us."

"Gracious! Might they?"

He waved a dismissal. "It's treason even to think it. No, of course they won't. We give them the bread their families eat in the morning. Just because of some silly nonsense at Barrackpore—"

Yes, she remembered that. It had been all the talk in Bombay upon her arrival in the port city. A sepoy, a native soldier, had turned on his British officers. He had shot two of them before he was stopped by his superiors; what had been so alarming, if she recalled correctly, was that none of the other natives had attempted to disarm him.

"He does have a point," she said. "It's a bit troubling."

"It was one isolated incident in more than two hundred years on this continent. And the man was directly hanged. We'll have no more trouble along those lines, I assure you."

"But if Lord Holdensmoor is partly native, perhaps he has heard something—"

"Emmaline!" Marcus wheeled to face her. "Yes, the man is part native, and for all I know, he's trying to scare us out of Delhi so the natives can take it back! In fact, I believe that is *exactly* what he is up to, and I have told the Commissioner so! Now cease your ignorant speculations and make yourself pleasant for your host."

"My *host*? Do you mean the one you're cuckolding?"

All color bleached from his face. Oh dear. Blond hair didn't look so well on skin that particular shade of green. "What did you just say?" he asked.

"So it's true." Nausea rolled through her stomach. "Well. I suppose you're going to tell me you still love me anyhow."

His eyes, such a guileless shade of blue, searched her face. "Of course I do."

She managed a smile. "Yes. We have loved each other quite a long time, haven't we? Since we were born, I believe."

"Since forever," he said, with an admirable show of sincerity. "And whatever rumors you hear to the contrary, there is no woman in the world for me but you. Some people are jealous, you see, and they would spread vicious gossip in order to harm me—"

"I know," she interrupted, and then stopped, swallowing hard when her voice would have broken. How sad to realize that she could no longer believe a word he said. "Marcus, I think I'd like to leave now."

He considered her for a moment, then gave a short nod. "Of course. But I will call on you at the Residency tomorrow. We'll discuss this, and you'll see, my dear. These lies—you must simply set them from your mind."

"Naturally," she murmured. "If you'll find Lady Metcalfe for me?"

She leaned back against the wall, watching him push his way through the congratulatory crowd as he went in search of her chaperone. Even though his back was turned, she knew every gesture that he made, sensed every smile that crossed his face. Such was the familiarity of twenty long years—decades of their families plotting to bring them together, arranging their betrothal, choosing the names of their unborn children. The Martins and Lindleys had never known that the only two who would live to fulfill their dream would be the very two who had never been quite as enthusiastic as the rest: the bride and groom themselves.

She closed her eyes, turning her head to press her cheek against the cool bungalow wall. The windows rattled in a strong gust of hot wind, and the candles flickered with the inrush of jasmine and darkness. Strange, how the night called to her so sweetly, promising a lovelier, more innocent place. Yes, India seemed to draw out her very soul. Perhaps that was why she felt so bruised inside—as though her defenses had been laid bare, allowing a terrible melancholy to settle in her core.

Surely she wasn't grieving over Marcus? She had

abandoned her childish dreams of romantic love three years ago, the first time she'd learned of one of his many paramours. She'd been heartbroken then, but her mother had explained quickly enough: marriage was not about something as illusory and fleeting as love. It was about alliances, partnerships, the continuation of the family line. Marcus's grand and crumbling estates would be consolidated with the vast Martin wealth, and the two of them would create a dynasty that would compensate for her mother's failure to produce male issue.

So, what, then, could account for this sudden foreboding? It slid like a shadow between her and the brightly lit room, leaving her with the odd conviction that she stood apart, watching a great panorama like those they sometimes displayed in the British Museum. This room seemed like Pompeii before the volcano eruption, or Rome before the fall: a civilization on the edge of disaster.

A shiver slid over her, and she glanced away, starting as she found herself locked in a vibrant emerald gaze: Lord Holdensmoor, coming in from the gardens. His face was expressionless as he stared at her. In defiance of both Marcus and her own gloomy reverie, she offered him a smile.

His own was rakish and swift, the effect of it on his aloof, aristocratic features dazzling to behold. And then he too was gone, his tall, broad form swallowed up by the crowd in a cloud of crushed silk and waving peacock feather fans.

Two

HAVING SPENT HER FIRST WEEKS IN INDIA COMPLYING with the unspoken agreement that everyone would behave as though they'd never left England, Emma had arrived in Delhi determined to see something of the country. But Lady Metcalfe, the Resident's wife and her *de facto* hostess, had a pronounced fear of the native culture, and refused to go into the bazaar. "Couldn't I just read aloud to you?" she had suggested this morning. "I have a new copy of *The Pilgrim's Progress.*"

Emma could not bear to spend another day reclining in that airless bungalow. Mama would have advised her to make calls, to accompany Lady Metcalfe on her constitutional through the *maidan*, or to meetings of her sewing circle at the club. But the very prospect made Emma feel breathless and slightly ill. So it had been since her arrival here. The cloying concern of new acquaintances seemed to stifle her. She did not know how to answer the questions she saw in their eyes; increasingly, she could not even be bothered to try. Her mind wandered during small talk. She trailed away in the middle of conversations—unsure of what she had been saying, indifferent about continuing.

Marcus made excuses for her. He told his friends that she was recovering from the long journey, and the shock, and her parents' death. All true, of course. But that did not explain her impatience, or her restlessness. She could not pinpoint the source of the feelings, much less guess what might assuage them. Of course she was fortunate; of course she was grateful; truly she was blessed to have survived. But surely not so she could pass the rest of her life in chatter about amateur theatricals and last season's races?

And so Emma had graciously declined Lady Metcalfe's offer, and then scandalized the woman by enlisting her ayah, a Hindustani woman called Usha, to guide her into the native quarters. When the streets in Chandni Chowk became too narrow for the carriage, Usha offered to lead her on by foot. And so they were maneuvering now down a crowded lane, Emma stepping carefully to avoid cow dung and bits of shattered clay from discarded teacups. On their left rose a white marble temple, where worshippers were ringing deep-throated bells suspended from the ceiling. To their right, a line of women in brightly colored silks paced past, slim brown arms arced upward to balance the sacks on their head. Their bangles and belled anklets flashed in the sun.

Emma had never seen a more disorganized or colorful

scene in her life. The watercolors she'd bought in Bombay would not prove sufficient to capture anything here; only rich, vibrant oils would do. With any luck, her cousin in London had already dispatched the pigments she'd requested; otherwise she might have to hunt down the vivid, textured material used in these charming street banners. The one over the brassware shop, for instance—a picture of a blue-skinned god, beckoning passersby with his many arms.

She sighed. Marcus would throw a fit if she went searching for the local paint. He already disapproved of her "little habit." "You draw the most inappropriate things," he'd said yesterday, after flipping through, then tossing aside, the sketchbook she'd been keeping. She knew better than to defend herself. Flowers; pastoral scenes; children: these were the proper subjects of a lady's work. Fakirs, mahouts, and everything interesting were reserved for gentlemen, who produced *real* art, not decoration.

"Memsahib, is the sun bothering you?"

Emma came back to herself with a start. "No, Usha, I'm perfectly well. It's just all so . . ." A movement over Usha's shoulder caught her attention: a white cow was lumbering by, a necklace woven of marigolds looped around its neck. Her lips twitched. A most glamorous beast, this—and clearly of some importance, to be moving with such brisk purpose. A laugh escaped her. "It's marvelous, Usha. This place is remarkable."

Usha offered a shy smile in return. "In the *gali* there is less sun. Shall we go?"

They threaded their way through the foot traffic and into a quieter lane leading off the thoroughfare. The houses here, "havelis" Usha called them, were stacked up against one another, with windows covered by latticed screens of red rock that projected over the street, so the footpath below was shaded. The screens were very effective at blocking the eye from the interior; it took Emma a long moment to realize that there was a woman standing on the other side of the particular screen she was staring at. The lady's face was covered with a veil, making her appear on casual glance to be a curtain.

Emma touched her maid's wrist. "Usha, that woman's face—why is it covered?"

Usha's eyes tracked upward. "Oh—it is purdah, mem. Mussulmans and also Brahmins, the wives and daughters of our priests, cover their faces to show they are—" She paused, searching for the word. "To protect their *izzat*, their honor."

"Even when inside?"

"Whenever they can be seen by strange men."

"And how do they see when they go outside?"

"One can see through the veil, but a woman in purdah does not leave her house often."

Emma nodded slowly, looking once more to the woman at the window. Did she see them as well? Was she curious about who they were, where they were going?

Emma might have told her that it did not matter. Indian or British, so many women were confined to their houses at this moment. Some of them seemed to like it, and were reading *The Pilgrim's Progress* for the fiftieth time. "How do they bear it?"

"They do not wish to bring shame to their families, mem."

Yes. Of course. How well she recalled the strained

look Marcus had worn when he first realized how she had managed to reach Bombay. As if the fact that she had been rescued by a freighter could invalidate the miracle of her survival! As if regard for others' empty opinions were more important to one's honor than one's own conduct. "It's not really fair to us, is it?"

"To us?" Usha studied her face. "But mem can come and go as she wishes, no?"

Emmaline opened her mouth to deliver some lighthearted reply—and a sharp blow landed on her back, sending her stumbling into the side of a building. She turned and found her arm in the grip of a squat, florid man in army uniform.

"Hello there, missus," her captor said slowly, in a thick Hertfordshire accent. "Nice day for an outing, isn't it?"

"Let go of me!" She tried to jerk away. He laughed, his breath rancid in her face.

"What's a nice memsahib like yourself doing all alone in the bazaar?" he asked, oblivious as she fought to slip her hand free from his hold on her glove.

"I am not alone—I am with my maid!"

"Her?" He glanced contemptuously at Usha, who, she was horrified to see, was being restrained by the man's cohort. "A native ain't no proper chaperone."

"And you are no proper gentleman," she snapped. "Assaulting a female!"

"I ain't assaulted you yet," he sneered, and his other hand dug up under her bonnet to hook into her chignon, yanking her head back. "Ain't such a bad idea, though. Don't know as any real lady would be out consorting with the natives, giving 'em ideas like you was."

"That's what she was doing," the other man agreed in

an ugly, eager voice. "Givin' the blackies all the encouragement they need, parading herself in front of 'em like she was one of 'em."

"Of course, Harry, I heard me that we received a new shipload of doxies for the officers' mess. Could be that she's one, eh?" He thrust his hips up against her, crushing her crinolines; she twisted aside and his teeth closed on the tender skin of her neck.

"You pig!" She wrested her arm out from between them and slammed her elbow into his face. With a roar, he threw her sideways, and she slammed into the ground on her forearms, her bonnet flying off. Stunned, she fought for breath. *Get up, get up!* On a gasp, she forced herself over.

"Foul-mouthed witch! Harry, watch me teach this one a lesson!"

A metallic click sounded from behind her. Her attacker froze. "Hell," he muttered, and backed away a pace.

"Don't move," a cool voice recommended. "Not if you value your life."

She recognized the crisp accents. Sucking in a mighty breath, she pushed herself upright. Her elbows felt as though they'd been dipped in fire. Hauling her skirts out of the way, she shoved her bonnet onto her head and clambered to her feet—whence she gave the swine who'd held her a sharp shove for good measure. His eyes narrowed, but he said nothing. She pivoted.

The Marquess of Holdensmoor stood before her, one of his arms extended to aim a pistol between the ruffian's eyes. He swept her with a cursory glance before returning his attention to the soldier.

"Your name?"

The man swallowed audibly. "I weren't trying to harm her, sir, I jest thought—"

"I asked your name."

"We thought she was a light skirt!" the other man burst out, pushing Usha away from him. "No lady goes around Chandni Chowk all alone!"

"Enough from you," Lord Holdensmoor said. He sounded rather bored with the situation. "I don't think the Company would miss a soldier or two. Or perhaps you would like to explain to Colonel Lindley how you came to molest his betrothed."

"Colonel—" The man who had attacked Emma went white. "Jesus Christ." The other man moaned agreement.

The Marquess scoffed and deprimed the pistol, lifting it away from them. "Run," he said flatly. "If I see you again, I'll kill you."

As the men ran off, he turned to her. "Are you all right?"

"Yes." The steadiness of her voice bolstered her; she spoke again just to hear it. "Yes, I'm fine."

He nodded, turning to Usha. *"Aap theek hain, na?"*

The woman gave a rapid speech in Hindustani. A faint, humorless smile crossed the Marquess's face. To Emma, he said, "I'm afraid your ayah is not impressed with me."

"With *you*?"

"With my failure to shoot them."

"Just so," she retorted, and sagged back against the wall. Her poor elbows! She clutched them to her and shook her head. Her teeth were suddenly chattering. "Just so," she whispered.

A warm touch, someone's hand on her shoulder,

brought her head up. The Marquess was standing in front of her, his eyes steady. "You *are* all right," he said gently.

"Oh yes. I'm splendid."

"And fierce to boot. You gave him quite a push."

"Well, I rather think he deserved it." She took a long breath. "They meant to—ravish us, I think."

"Something like that."

His hand gave her shoulder a slight squeeze. It occurred to her that he should not be touching her. She stepped out of his reach.

He holstered his pistol. "Don't come here again, Miss Martin. Not without Colonel Lindley."

"I—" Her throat closed. "Yes. It was foolish of me."

He glanced away. "This is not England. There are different rules here."

She laughed. It was such a strange, humorless sound that she reached up to touch her lips, to make sure it was she who had produced the noise. "I beg to differ. As I've just learned, the rules here appear to be the same as anywhere."

He raked a hand through his thick black hair. The resulting disorder lent him a devil-may-care air that sat oddly with his serious expression. "What possessed you to venture into the bazaar?"

"What, am I to be cooped up in a bungalow all day, sweltering?"

"Yes." His voice was clipped with impatience. "Surely you were told what India would be like."

"I was not! In fact, that is exactly what I was discovering when I was so—rudely assaulted by those pathetic approximations of Englishmen!"

Amusement broke over his face. "Is that so?"

"Yes, it is so!" Anger, she realized. *That* was what she was feeling. "This is an entirely different country, a different *world*! Why should I be expected to pretend I were still in England?"

She looked him straight in the face. He didn't seem intimidated by the challenge; indeed, as their stare lengthened, he arched a brow. "It was a rhetorical question, was it not?"

She rolled her eyes. "Very well. Let me take advice from a man who skulks about in gardens, bolting liquor on the sly! How shall I best ignore the country in which I find myself? Would a blindfold serve?"

"Really, Miss Martin!" His voice altered, becoming softer and more intimate—*teasing* her. "Surely you shock your friends with this misplaced curiosity! India is here to be conquered, not appreciated."

"You don't believe that."

"Colonel Lindley does."

Long habit made her defensive. "And what of it? He serves the interests of Queen and country!"

"Well then," he said, laughing. "Your choice is clear. Is it to be your own priorities, or those of Britannia and the Colonel?"

She threw up her hands. "You have me there, my lord. I expect with your next sentence you'll have me bundled off to my embroidery and a life of eternal sequesterment!"

He sighed. "Better that than with your skirts around your ears in an alley."

"How *vulgar*!"

"The truth nonetheless," he said, and it was clear

from his careless shrug that he had wearied of the conversation. "I'll escort you home. You can broach to Lindley the matter of showing you around the city."

But Marcus would never agree to that, she thought. Marcus had less interest in the native culture than he did in his choice of hats. "Fine," she said, and rubbed her arms again. They were bound to bruise; she would have to wear a shawl all through supper.

They returned to the buggy in silence, the driver ceding the reins to the Marquess. Because there was hardly enough room in the back for three of them, she climbed up next to Lord Holdensmoor. He slanted her a speaking glance. She ignored it. If this were to be her last outing, she was determined to have the best view.

After a few minutes, she sighed. "It's such a lovely country."

"You should go to Almora," the Marquess said, guiding the horses effortlessly through a tangle of cows, goats, and frolicking children.

"Colonel Lindley says that no one is going this year. He says the weather's too pleasant to go to the trouble. I suppose I'll have to take his word on it; I've never been warmer in my life."

The Marquess was silent for a moment. "Damn the weather," he said then softly.

His shocking language made her remember something. "Perhaps you wish it were hotter?"

"Perhaps I do."

"Because that would promote our deserting Delhi for the season," she continued. "Yes, my intended informed me that you're trying to convince the British to abandon the city."

"Your *intended* has a devilish way of twisting my words. I want the women and children out, and I want more European troops in. You tell Lindley that, will you?"

"I don't think I'll mention this little escapade at all, actually." Emma leaned back to study him. It was coming to her now that she had been abominably rude; he had saved her from a terrible injury, and she had railed at him for it. But he had not been put out by her behavior. If anything, he had seemed amused by it. "You are rather singular, Lord Holdensmoor."

"I might say the same of you."

"Yes, but perhaps you would not mean it as a compliment."

He looked to her briefly. "But perhaps I would."

His eyes were such an improbable green. Maybe he was so unflappable because he was accustomed to people making fools of themselves when he looked at them.

Usha passed up a flask of water. Emma shook her head and handed it to the Marquess. He held the flask a few inches above his lips as he drank, his throat muscles rippling. She stared at the long line of his neck, strangely mesmerized by it. How it would feel to place one's hand there, on the front of his throat, as he drank? She touched her own neck, swallowing experimentally.

She realized with a start that he had turned back to her. His regard was searching. Color rose to her cheeks, and she looked away.

"Miss Martin, are you aware of what is happening across northern India? Are any of the ladies aware?"

She cleared her throat. "We're not witless, my lord. We've heard of the disturbances. But if the officers believe in the loyalty of their troops—"

"Native troops, Miss Martin. That is the only sort Delhi has." He leaned a little closer, and she caught the faint scent of sandalwood, overlaid by leather and soap. "Tell me why these troops should feel any loyalty whatsoever to the people who have reduced them to subjects—here, in the land of their birth."

She tilted her head. "I, of course, am not an expert on colonial politics."

"But you do seem to have common sense, which distinguishes you from most of your masculine counterparts."

She considered him for a long moment. "You really do think something's going to happen."

He nodded once, still holding her eyes. "And I suggest, Miss Martin, that you go to Almora, even if the Colonel will not accompany you."

Her anxiety had her leaning forward now too. "But if you have information, some evidence that the natives are planning an uprising, you must tell the Commissioner, and quickly!"

His long lips tilted in a half-smile. "Do you think I went to Mrs. Eversham's dinner for the pleasure of her company?"

The words felt like a slap. Surely she was mistaken; surely he was not alluding to Marcus's affair. She would not have expected such spite from him.

Her face must have betrayed her thoughts, for he prevented her next words with a quiet, "No. My apologies. That came out very badly." He began to speak again, then seemed to think better of it. His expression became thoughtful.

She looked away from him, aware that she had erred.

If one's intended was inclined to infidelity, the decent thing was to pretend innocence on the matter. But now Lord Holdensmoor knew that she was not so ignorant after all.

"You *are* singular," he said.

"Yes," she said quietly. "I'm afraid so."

At the same time, they both sat back against the seat. A sudden blissful breeze from the north caught Emma's bonnet, lifting it off her head and sending it spinning off behind them. She turned to follow its progress. A child of five or six years ran out into the lane, grabbing the hat and cramming it over his tiny ears. The sight drew a laugh from her, despite her mood.

She felt the weight of the Marquess's gaze. "Shall we go back for it?" he asked.

"No, let it be." She laughed again, taken by the ludicrous image of the boy in the frilly hat. "I didn't like it anyhow." She faced front again, tilting her chin up. It was quite pleasant, this sensation of warmth on her scalp. "They don't want to lose this place," she said. "If there's a danger, they'll be sure to act."

"Do you speak of the British, or the Indians?" the Marquess asked. "For on either count, I fear you're correct."

Three

Emma awoke with a gasp, sitting bolt upright in bed. The lamp in the far corner had guttered out, and furniture and carpeting melded into one indistinguishable mass, looming fuzzy and dark through the green mosquito netting.

Good Lord, that dream. The water roaring. The ship rearing up above. Would it never go away?

She clawed for the break in the net, then slipped to her feet to open the curtains. The Residency grounds bordered a broad street that marked the perimeter of the walled city. The lane seemed eerily desolate in the blue light of dusk. A balmy breeze whispered through the trees, carrying with it the creaks of rickshaws and muted cries of street vendors in the bazaar a quarter mile away.

A few hours yet until Marcus came to fetch her for

dinner. He had been gone to Agra for five days, and would expect a cheerful countenance. She thought she might be glad of his return, if only for the opportunity to escape the Residency. Lady Metcalfe had been ailing, and Emma had not dared to strike out on her own again. If not for her sketchbook and the new charcoals Sir Metcalfe had given her, she would have gone mad from boredom. Even so, the walls felt as if they were beginning to close on her.

With a sigh, she turned back to consider the room. The blue bottle on the dresser caught her eye. It held laudanum mixed with quinine; Lady Metcalfe had given it to her after Marcus had remarked favorably on its calming effects. Privately Emma had hoped that it would stop her nightmares. So much for that. But it *was* soothing.

She measured out a tiny bit, splashing some onto her sleeve as she lifted it to her mouth. Then she set down the bottle and looked into the mirror. A pale, oval face stared back, dominated by eyes that were shadowed with fatigue. Not sleeping well. Sweat had turned her hair a limp brown. With fingers loosening under the spell of the opiate, she smoothed a lock from her brow. No one would ever count her as more than passably pretty, but usually she didn't look *quite* this bad.

A parrot flew away from the sill, making her heart flutter as hard as his bright green wings. She put her hand to her chest and rubbed.

On a sudden decision, she reached for her shawl, tying it quickly about her shoulders as she slipped out of the room. As she paced down the Turkey leader in the corridor, a breeze came through the open shutters, carrying the scent of oleander and the metallic sharpness of the heat.

She realized as soon as she opened the library door that there were people inside. But it was too late—the conversation stopped at the squeak of the hinges, and she had no choice but to make herself known.

Lord Holdensmoor and Sir Metcalfe were standing at the far end of the room, a map rolled out on the desk between them. Sir Metcalfe looked relieved to see her; the Marquess smiled as well, but turned immediately back to the map.

"Miss Martin," the Resident said. "You are well?"

"Very well. I did not mean to disturb you."

"No, no, we are done here."

The Marquess looked up, a peculiar expression on his face. "We are hardly done."

"I will go," Emma said quickly, but Sir Metcalfe waved a dismissive hand and yanked at the bellpull.

"Nonsense. I've already been waiting above a quarter hour for the servant to bring the tea. Where is he? I'll be back directly."

Sir Metcalfe moved past her with uncharacteristic speed. When the door closed behind him, the Marquess said, "He is running from me."

"Oh?" She approached the desk. "But why? What is it you're looking at there?"

He hesitated, then sighed, pushing a sheet over. The laudanum was unfurling through her; she had to blink a few times to bring the numbers and names into focus: Seventh Dragoon Guards; Queen's Army, 23,000; 58th Native Infantry. "Stations and regiments," she said, bemused. "But why in the world would you need these maps? Surely you aren't involved with the military." Marcus would have been sure to complain about it.

"Do you see these numbers?" He pointed to a figure written in a cramped hand at the top right corner. "Three hundred thousand and fourteen thousand. Three hundred thousand men in the Indian Army." His finger traced over the number. "Only fourteen thousand European."

"A small number," she said uncertainly. "But natives have always served in the Indian army."

"Three Indians for every Englishman two decades ago," he agreed. "Now six for every Englishman."

"Surely you can't be against that. You, yourself, are . . ." She trailed off, blushing, and he shook his head.

"I take no offense at the mention of my heritage. It is my better half, I think." He smiled. "Or better quarter, though that lacks a certain ring. My concern is for the peace. While I firmly believe that England has no place in India—" Her huff of shock made him smile again. "Well, and I *am* part native, Miss Martin."

"And also an English peer, a future duke!" She knew she was sputtering, but she had never *heard* of such a sentiment!

His eyes could become weapons. They focused on her now with alarming intensity, seeming to become greener as she stared into them, hopelessly pinned. "I will be the Duke of Auburn," he said, and she had the strangest thought that he was not pleased by that eventuality. "But it is an English title, you know. It gives me no claims to Indian soil."

Emma shook her head. "I've never encountered such talk."

He was considering her in turn, his expression pensive. "No, I don't suppose you have. How are you, by the way? I had planned to leave a note inquiring after your health."

"Oh—you mean from the other day?" She shrugged. "Recovered, thank you."

"Yes?" With an upraised brow, he reached for her wrists. Unprepared, she let him take them. He turned her around, lifting out one arm, and then the other, to examine where she had hit the ground in Chandni Chowk.

If Sir Metcalfe returned now, it would be very awkward. But lassitude had fallen over her, so she held still, remarking her concern only by a pointed glance to the closed door. "Harmless scratches," she said.

"Healing nicely." His palms slid up her arms, his fingers skating lightly over the tender skin of her inner elbows. She caught her breath and cast him a startled glance over her shoulder.

His eyes came up to hers, and his hands let go. He stepped back, a look of surprise on his face.

"I beg your pardon," he said. After a moment, he turned and bent to retrieve a satchel that had been sitting by the table. "This is for you." He pulled out a slim, gilt-edged volume.

She took it and turned it over in her hands. The tooling on the leather was very fine. "'Wanderings of a Pilgrim in Search of the Picturesque,'" she read aloud slowly. She would not have taken the laudanum had she known so much reading awaited her!

"Yes, a volume by Mrs. Fanny Parkes. She toured all over the subcontinent in the twenties and thirties. I thought you might find her account of interest—although I regret to inform you, she also suffered the curse of male chaperones."

Emma laughed despite herself. It came out husky and slow. "You shouldn't be giving me gifts. Marcus would have your head."

He frowned a little at that, as if she had puzzled him, although his mouth was still smiling. "You may say you found it at the club."

"What a clever idea. I think I will." She opened the book at random, to a plate entitled *Lachchmi, Goddess of Beauty*. Her finger traced the outlines of the goddess's voluptuous figure. "Thank you. She looks as if she might step out of the page and come alive."

"You're welcome." He paused. "I would not recommend that you follow Mrs. Parkes's example, of course."

"Oh?" She looked up.

"She dabbled in opium." He was watching her very closely now. "Nasty stuff. Addictive, after prolonged exposure. Of course, no one smokes it anymore, that's fallen out of fashion here. But I've seen several memsahibs form an unhealthy attachment to their laudanum bottles."

She shut the book around her finger. "I would never—"

"You can always tell by their eyes if they've been using it," he continued casually. "Some women look quite terrifying, with those huge, enlarged pupils. Others . . ." He smiled, and reached out to brush a thumb across her cheekbone. "Others look quite charming. Nevertheless, it's not a look one should cultivate."

His finger left a trail of warmth across her cheek, like the passing of a sunbeam. "I see," she said faintly, and had enough sense to bite down on the next words that came to her: *Would you touch me again?*

"I do hope so. And now, since it appears the Resident has run away for the evening, I must take my leave."

As she watched him go, her fingers brushing back and forth along the tooled cover of Mrs. Parkes's book, it came to her that he might have said yes, if she'd asked.

The moon was climbing overhead, pulling shadows from their hiding places as it rose. With slow, muffled steps Julian's mount picked through the ruins, her head low to the sandy ground. Above, the Qutub Minar glowered against the dark sky. For six centuries the sandstone minaret had presided over the Delhi hinterland, trumpeting Islam's eastward advance.

Julian drew rein and dismounted a few paces beyond the column. Its original cupola had been destroyed by lightning fifty-odd years before. Major Smith's replacement struck a precarious, unlikely balance. The British addition to the column was bound to topple; wise visitors took note, and did not linger in its shadow.

Which was a good metaphor for the whole bloody country, Julian thought. Alas, that wisdom seemed in short supply. Commissioner Fraser and his ilk refused to heed "idle rumor." Into this category they conveniently lumped both back-alley muttering and the aborted mutinies at Barrackpore and Meerut. Meanwhile, as they smoked their hookahs and shuffled papers, commoners were murmuring of a prophecy, made after the Battle of Plassey a century before, that Britain's raj would end in a hundred years' time. "But we all know these natives are a superstitious lot," Fraser had told him with a laugh during their conference at the Probate soirée. "Humor their little beliefs, by all means do. But God forbid one should take them seriously!"

The Resident, in turn, thought Julian an alarmist—to be humored and placated, but ultimately ignored. If it hadn't been so unforgivably stupid, it would have been comical. In London they accused him of ennui. In Delhi, they thought him hysterical.

"Huzoor!"

Julian looked up with a grimace. No matter how many times he had asked Deven to call him otherwise, his cousin persisted with this subservient address. "Over here," he said, and came to his feet.

The boy emerged from a dilapidated arcade. He looked to have come from a wedding; he was dressed formally, in a turban and long robe. The silver threads of his *sherwani* sparkled in the moonlight; it had once been a very fine gown, although now there were threadbare patches at the hem and elbows. "I am late," Deven acknowledged. "Huzoor will forgive me. A party of soldiers stopped me by Quwwat-ul-Islam Masjid."

"Search you?"

"No." He briefly dropped the submissive façade and spat onto the ground. "Yanked off my *pagri* and tied it around a cow." His hands rose to check the folds of his turban. "I stopped to retrieve it. Such a noble culture your people bring to mine!"

Julian held his tongue. He could not defend the English, not now. Even ten years ago, such an episode would not have occurred; or, had it been reported, the soldiers would have faced a harsh reprimand from their commanding officers. But whatever amount of wary respect had once existed between Britons and Indians, contempt was taking its place.

Julian felt the change himself. His mixed blood had always provided fodder to the wags—after one rather reckless adventure in his youth, the papers in London had dubbed him the "savage noble." He did not much care for the name, but Rousseauian witticisms were preferable to the suspicion he increasingly encountered in so many quarters of Anglo-Indian society. More and more he felt that news was discounted simply because it came from his mouth. Even Emmaline Martin had heard gossip about his seditious tendencies, and she had only just arrived in the city.

The thought of Miss Martin further frayed his temper. If Lindley could not attend to her better, then someone needed to attend, not so gently, to Lindley.

Collecting his thoughts, he asked his cousin, "Did you happen to catch the soldiers' names?"

Deven's teeth flashed. He took a seat on a toppled pillar and stretched into a lounging attitude meant to communicate indifference. Julian suddenly recognized, with brief amusement, that Deven had picked up the pose from him. "And what if I had, huzoor," Deven said. "Would I tell you?"

"You tell me nothing, and I'm sure you feel very clever about that. But I am telling *you* that if you have a care for your grandmother and sisters, you will take the money I offered and go away for the hot season."

"Where would huzoor have us go? Mussoorie only? Simla? Calcutta itself?" Deven's smile was mocking. "Does Huzoor forget that these places are also in Hindustan? Or that these humble natives, to whom huzoor would give his protection, have skin as brown as their neighbors'? It would be better for huzoor to fear for himself."

Julian regarded him narrowly. If he had thought there was no one more bloody-minded than government officials, then he had forgotten about the existence of seventeen-year-old boys. "Stay, then. But take the money. You may have need of it."

Deven lunged up. "We have one need only, and that is for the *Angrezi* to go! Your people grind cow bone into the meal, to damn our souls and force us to convert!"

Sweet Christ. That was a ghoulish new twist on the rumors. He drew a breath, thinking carefully. "You don't believe it, I hope. After all, it would take money to realize such a plot. The British would fain waste their blunt on a little thing like religion."

Deven eyed him sourly for a moment, then shrugged.

Julian could sense the boy's increasing restlessness. Staying much longer would seem, to Deven, to be intolerably accommodating of the blight on his family tree. That he had come out here in the first place had been a victory itself. And so Julian pulled out his trump card. "If you do not take the money, I will be forced to go and give it to Nani-ji myself."

His cousin's face lit with rage. "She has told you not to come back."

"I will have no choice."

A sneer corrupted Deven's mouth. "You will shame us so?"

Shame. Was that what his existence now signified to his grandmother? He thought of the house at Ajmeri Gate. Three small rooms, set around a simple courtyard;

he remembered them very well. At one time, as a small boy, they had spelled home to him, and safety—this, despite the constant shortage of food, the struggle for subsistence waged daily within those walls.

Now his very presence there made Nani-ji despair. She loved him, yes; but how would she marry off his girl cousins if he were seen visiting?

"Take the money," he said tiredly. "Take it, and I will never come again."

Deven hesitated, scowling. "Do you swear?"

Julian touched his throat, a gesture used to signal a formal, binding vow. "*Kasam khaata hoon.*" I swear.

Deven pointed to the dirt between them. "Set it down there," he said. "And then you will walk away and I will watch. I will take pleasure in watching the Englishman leave, because it will make me think of the time, very soon, when all Indians will see the same."

Julian tossed the bag into the dust and turned. In the moonlight, his shadow stretched long and faint before him, preceding him out of the ruins.

The evening's entertainment was in full swing, women in sweltering gowns twirling on the arms of men in full uniform. The orchestra was cranking out a fast, slightly disreputable version of the waltz. Emma paused at the top of the room to make acquaintance with her hostess, a large-boned, sweaty woman in the latter years of life. Mrs. Cameron clucked sadly at their introduction, and took Emma's hand in a painful grip. "Heard about the shipwreck. A shame about your parents, my dear. Thank the dear Lord you had someone like the Colonel waiting for you!"

"Indeed," Emma murmured. "Colonel Lindley is too good to me."

The woman continued to stare, her clammy palm dampening Emma's glove. "And how long were you floating in the water, dear? You must forgive my curiosity; we're all simply fascinated. It's the most exciting thing that's happened to us in ages."

Emma stared back, mildly astonished to learn that her own tragedy had happened to all of British India. Marcus had to clear his throat twice before she blinked free of her trance. "Ah—a little less than a day, I believe."

Mrs. Cameron gasped. "All alone in the water! With every soul on that ship beneath you, dead on the ocean floor!"

"That is one way to think of it," Emma said faintly.

"And the shipmaster who found you—an Irishman, I believe?" The woman leaned forward, her lorgnette slipping from her nose to swing over one arm. "Were you forced to share quarters with his crew?"

Marcus's arm closed protectively around her waist. "Met the chap myself. A decent fellow to give up his cabin to her, but he wasn't so hesitant to accept a reward."

Mrs. Cameron leered at the Colonel. "Money, eh? Well, any amount's worth having your lady love delivered to you."

Marcus bowed agreement, and their hostess released Emma with a pat. As they walked away, Emma attempted to straighten her glove. The woman had twisted it halfway off. "That was the most horrendous gossipmongering I've ever witnessed."

"Well, she's telling the truth when she says nothing happens around here to speak of." Marcus reached over to take a glass of punch from the corner table. "Here you go. And all in all she's a good woman, quite popular with our crowd."

"The Lord forfend that I should disagree with your crowd," Emma said tartly, sipping at the punch as she glanced around. Her passing gaze seemed to signal a bevy of women to detach themselves from the far corner. As they approached in a froth of pastel ruffles and ribbons, Marcus gave a discreet tug to his jacket.

"Best behavior," he muttered. "These are the Vice-Regent's daughters' friends."

She nodded and smiled gamely as he made the introductions, but the girls ignored her, preferring to twit Marcus about some game of cricket that he'd lost. Emma found herself grateful for it. She had nothing to contribute and quickly gave up trying to follow the conversation. She was idly chipping a piece of wax that had fallen from the chandelier onto her glove when the hushed tones of a conversation behind her caught her attention.

"She's being dreadfully foolish," a woman was saying. "He'll never give her a second look."

"Oh, he might," a catty voice rejoined. "He might give her a good deal more than that, but he'll *never* give her a ring."

"Letty! Are you implying—"

"The man's an absolute rake, Margaret. They say he goes through women like a fish through water. Why, just last week, Teresa March saw Mrs. Lake leaving his bungalow at *ten o'clock in the morning!*"

"No! And her husband just back from Simla!"

Emma braced herself with a deep draft of the punch.

If they were talking about Marcus—if he were carrying on with not just one woman, but two—

"You think Mr. Lake doesn't know? Of course he does! But he dursn't do a thing about it! Why, the Marquess is famed on three different continents for his marksmanship."

The Marquess? Emma smiled. What an exhausting life Lord Holdensmoor must lead. It seemed he had his finger in every scandal the world could provide.

"But he's not in the army—"

"No, you know they'd never give him a commission, even if he wanted one. How could they trust him with the natives? He's practically one of them, after all."

There was a short silence, and Emmaline looked up, smiling at the people around her. They hadn't seemed to notice her inattention, so she took a small step backward.

"—*is* sinfully good-looking, and going to be a duke to boot. I can't *blame* her—"

"But the blood, Letty! Surely you wouldn't want to soil yourself that way, to wed a blackie—"

"Oh, and what do *I* care, if Her Majesty doesn't? It's all very legal, anyway."

"I don't know. The way he looks at a woman—always as though he's secretly laughing, as if he knew some naughty secret—"

"I've always *liked* a little danger in a man. It merely adds to his charm."

Now laughter, followed by: "Poor George, then! He's not got a flying chance!"

"Indeed, no. Why should I settle for a family that probably made their fortune hawking tinware in Essex?

Though I do feel bad, because George simply adores me. Do you know, just yesterday he said—"

Losing interest, Emmaline turned back to Marcus. Most of the little ring had melted away, leaving him and the blond girl on his arm in deep conversation. Perhaps he was already plotting his next peccadillo. "Colonel Lindley, if you'll excuse me?"

The two glanced over in surprise. How flattering: they had forgotten she was there. She should feel hurt, she supposed. But all she could muster was a slight irritation at their gape-mouthed expressions. "Would you like more punch?" Marcus asked.

She held up her half-full glass. "No, I'm just stepping out. I'll be back in a moment."

He bowed, and she slipped away, heading out the door and up the stairs.

It was very quiet in the powder room. Only the muted overture to a waltz penetrated the floorboards, its voyage upward warping the music into an otherworldly melody. Coconut-oil lamps flickered in the four corners, and their temperamental light cast odd shadows onto the wallpaper, strange figures dancing to strange music.

She sat down. The solitude suited her. She had known the room would be deserted; it was too early for damage to have been done to dresses and gloves. Later, women would crush inside, anxiously pacing the floor as their ayahs struggled along behind, patching ripped hems and scrubbing at stains. The charm of the shadows would fade, and the music would be drowned out by snapped complaints and snickered gossip.

"And this is my life," she whispered. This was what she had fought so hard to survive for when she had floated for endless hours on the breast of the ocean, the sun cracking her skin and settling salt beneath her fingernails. With, yes, every soul of that ship lying lifeless beneath her. What a dreadful, horrible image. Her feet, so small, bare and pale as they paddled, churning the water far above her mother's staring eyes . . .

The sound of her own sob made her flinch. She pressed her palm into her trembling lips. How strange that she should cry now, when her eyes had stayed dry for so long. And yet . . . "Mama," she whispered.

Mama had wanted this life for her—but why? She had said that marriage was not about love, but how could she have believed that? She had loved Papa, had laughed with him and cried with him, nursed him when he was ill. She had shared with him something precious and rare—and yet she had pushed Emma into this match with Marcus, knowing that her daughter would not have the same. How was that fair? How could her mother have done such a thing?

Perhaps Mama had simply not cared whether she would be happy.

"Enough!" The sound of her own voice startled her. After a long moment, she drew a breath, rose, and crossed to the mirror. Her cheeks lacked color. She pinched them hard, then stepped back to inspect herself.

Her eyes were bloodshot. One glance and they would all know that she'd been crying.

On a sigh, she smoothed down her hair. Her mother would have said she looked beautiful anyway. No matter what, Mama had always said that. She herself had never cared about her looks. If one was betrothed already, what did it matter if one were pretty?

What *did* matter? Was this all there was to life?

Her lips began to tremble again. Digging one gloved fist into them, she yanked open the door and stepped out. For a moment she was disoriented, and made the mistake of turning left instead of right. At that very moment, a door opened down the hall, spitting out a woman in a state of disarray.

"You bastard!" the woman snapped to whomever remained in the room. "You can't simply—*take* me and then throw me away like rubbish!"

Mortified, Emma turned to leave—but the next words arrested her in her tracks.

"Indeed. Particularly since I never took you in the first place."

Emma's jaw dropped at the sound of Lord Holdensmoor's voice. Not quite believing her own shameless intentions, she ducked into an alcove to eavesdrop. It seemed to be the theme of her night.

The woman hitched up one drooping sleeve. "My husband will have your head for this."

A burst of laughter floated out. "For rejecting his wife's advances?"

"Ha! For *forcing* yourself on me!"

The silence that followed was painfully tense. And then, in a voice so low that Emma could barely make it out, the Marquess said, "Lies have a nasty way of rebounding, Mrs. Lake. I'd advise you to remember that."

Emma hugged her arms to her chest. There was a threat in his voice, and the woman retreated a step.

"Then how about a truth?" she challenged. "I'll write Lord Mason about how you cuckolded him not three weeks after his wedding!"

Lord Holdensmoor appeared in the doorway. "And I suppose in the midst of this admirable fit of truth-telling, you'll also be inclined to inform your husband about O'Malley?"

The woman froze. "You wouldn't. You have more honor than that!"

"A lying hypocrite has no claim to honor," he said calmly. "Now get the hell out of my sight. And if you call at my home again, I'll tell your husband myself."

The woman stalked past—so close that Emma could smell the lemon verbena sachet in her reticule, and feel the air kicked up by her brushing skirts. The powder room door slammed.

Slowly Emma exhaled. Her eyes fixed on the spot where Julian Sinclair lounged against the door frame.

He seemed to be contemplating the flower print of the wallpaper, but when he was finished fastening a button on his cufflinks, he turned to her. "Miss Martin," he said, cat's eyes cutting unerringly through the shadows. "Having a pleasant evening?"

"I—" Heat burned up her throat and face. "I didn't mean to—"

"Come now. So far you've been refreshingly honest."

"I just—" She swallowed, stepping into the light. "I'm sorry; it was unforgivably rude to listen."

He gave a graceful, one-shouldered shrug. "She was making quite a scene. One wonders if she wanted to be caught." Linking his hands behind his back, he strolled toward her. "And you? Perhaps you've found out the answer to your question?"

"What question?" she asked breathlessly.

He stopped only inches away, and leaned forward to

whisper the answer in her ear. "What, exactly, my reputation is."

She jerked back a step. "Oh, I've heard all about it now," she said shakily. Her hand rose of its own accord, to touch the singed spot beneath her ear. He watched her do it, a smile playing across his lips.

Then the smile vanished. "Been crying, have you?" One gloved finger reached out to brush her cheek. "Is Lindley being a boor again?"

She stiffened. She did not want to discuss Marcus with him; she did not trust herself on that topic. She started to move past, but he caught her hand.

"I apologize," he said quietly. "Why are you upset?"

Her fingers moved nervously in his. She meant to say something light and witty. But his manner was so sober that it undid her; she opened her mouth and what came out was: "I cannot bear it."

Instantly she regretted it; heat flooded her face and she wanted to sink through the floor. She was unfit for polite society!

And yet his face did not register the outlandish nature of the remark. The pressure of his fingers remained firm. "Yes," he said. "I know how that is."

She bit her lip. She did not know how to recover the conversation. The urge was on her to reply, *Do you really understand?* But what a mad impulse. If only he would not look so concerned—*truly* concerned, his brilliant eyes sympathetic on her face. Something in his steady regard called the tears back. Marcus never looked at her like this. He never asked what she was thinking, or feeling. He simply assumed he knew. Or maybe he assumed she didn't think at all.

She breathed deeply to calm herself, then came up with a wry smile. "Forgive me. I am . . . fatigued, perhaps. I don't like balls very much."

He nodded. "Dreadful bores, aren't they?" His fingers began to play lightly with hers. "I don't know why I come, myself, since no one seems willing to listen to me."

She laughed weakly. Both of their hands were gloved, but the heat of his touch came through the cotton, and she had a sudden vivid image of his naked hand in hers. Their fingers intertwined. His hand tightening over her wrist.

You are absurd. Pull your hand away.

But she left it there, in his. "What do you expect, my lord? Cassandra is never a popular guest."

He smiled. "Ah, yes. I suppose I *am* the prophet of doom for this Troy."

Against her will, her eyes moved over his face, the strong, chiseled lines of bone and flesh, translating them to an imaginary page in vivid hues of black and gold and green. If only he could pose for her. "Why did you come tonight, then?"

He drew her toward him, and for no reason she could fathom, she let him. His other hand came to her waist, fingertips light as a ghost's as he turned her in the beginning steps of a waltz. "I like to dance?" he ventured, one brow rising as she let herself be guided a few paces down the hallway.

She laughed at the ludicrous answer, at the spectacle of him dancing her down a deserted corridor. His eyes sparkled in return. "Don't you?" he asked.

"Yes," she said, and gasped as he pulled her faster, in keeping with the music floating up the stairs. His movements were seamless, and she closed her eyes, feeling his hands firm around her. She didn't need to count, didn't need to concentrate; she was flying, and if she stumbled, his hands would be there, strong enough to catch her—

She opened them again as he came to a slow stop at the end of the hall. His expression was solemn. "Feeling better?"

Her throat thickened. Perhaps it was his kindness that undid her. He owed her nothing, or less than nothing, really: she was a woman whose future husband showed him only contempt. "Yes. Thank you."

"No thanks necessary." He gave her a strange smile. "You know, you must really pity them, the Cassandras." His hand came up to cup her face, his thumb stroking across her cheekbone. Her heart skipped a beat. "By nature, they are distracted."

"Are they?" Her thoughts were scattering under his touch. "Yes, of course they are. How frustrating it must be for you."

"All doom and gloom, Miss Martin. No time whatsoever to pursue pleasanter ideas."

The gentle mockery in his tone puzzled her. "I think I am missing the joke."

His soft laughter raised goose bumps along her arms. He shook his head, as if chiding her for refusing to laugh with him. "You *are* the joke, dear heart."

Stung, she moved to pull away—and his arm around her waist tightened.

She saw the kiss coming. She could have pulled away. She did not.

Her eyes closed as his lips brushed hers. Warm, soft. He tasted like mint, and fennel and cardamom. She stepped into him, her skirts belling out behind her; he was tall, his back broad, and her hands slid up it to his shoulders. It would be lovely to be so strong, to be unafraid of what the world might throw in one's path. His mouth gently shaped her lower lip, and then began to withdraw; her fingers dug a protest into his skin, calling him back. The kiss resumed, firmer now. She opened her mouth to breathe, and his tongue touched hers, startling a small sound from her.

Laughter and talk somewhere nearby jolted them apart. Their eyes met. His breath was coming fast. She could not decipher his expression. Certainly he did not seem to share her surprise. If anything, there was a grim cast to his features, as if he had just realized something unpleasant.

"I must go," she said. She did not know who she was, with him. It was a different sort of strangeness than she felt with Marcus. With Marcus, there was a pattern—a tiresome, predictable pattern. But if she stayed here in this hallway with Lord Holdensmoor, she did not know what she would do. "Back, I mean. Downstairs."

"Yes," he said, and drew a visible breath. Then stillness fell over him. In an instant, he went from disheveled to completely self-contained. It was a neat trick, and she envied him for it. The knowledge that his eyes were on her made her legs tremble all the way down the hall.

four

At midnight, Mrs. Cameron led the way in to supper. Emmaline found herself escorted by a balding, rotund man by the name of Cooper. He was, he informed her pompously, the assistant to the regional head of the treasury, a flawlessly managed arm of the Company government. "And you?" he asked, squinting. "You'll be the Colonel's intended?"

She nodded, waiting for the bearer to finish serving her before she responded. "I arrived here quite recently, not even a month yet." As she shifted in her seat, something hot came up against her foot.

"Ah. From Calcutta, I suppose? Or Bombay."

She straightened from peeking under the tablecloth. There were lamps set on the floor—she had almost kicked one over!

"For the mosquitoes," Mr. Cooper said. "Draws 'em away."

"Oh, really? How ingenious." She tucked her feet safely beneath her chair and reached for her wineglass. She was tempted to drink it straight down. The Marquess was seated three chairs away, and she could not look at him. Could not think of him without flushing. "Yes," she said, when Mr. Cooper prompted her. "Bombay is where I landed. It's very different from Delhi, isn't it? So many more Englishmen. And the weather is milder."

Mr. Cooper made a glum noise. "Of course you'd say that," he said, staring into his own glass. "But when the monsoons start up in a week or two, it will be wretched. I was positioned there for a while, but thank God! They transferred me." His shudder seemed a touch overdone. "Water up to your waist, I tell you. Ungodly climate."

"Mmm." Marcus had turned to cast her a narrow-eyed glance. Checking up on her. She was tempted to make a face at him.

"They're even odder there, the natives." Mr. Cooper considered his claret against the light—a shockingly rude thing to do—and then drained the glass to the dregs. "Worship some confounded elephant god, with a human body and the head of a beast. Heathens they may be, but they've got the devil of an imagination."

She stared at him. "An elephant-man? But why?"

He shrugged and turned back to his plate. "Can't say as I ever asked. Don't want to humor their ungodly ways. Say, you ever seen the pictures of those god-dess-ses?" He pronounced each syllable distinctly, as though the very word were nonsensical. "Bare-chested, with six or seven arms coming out of their backs." He guffawed at the idea. "Imagine one of *them* in your bed!"

"Mr. Cooper!" she gasped.

"Ignore him," the Marquess said from down the table. He smiled as he spoke his next words. "You're very drunk, aren't you, Cooper?"

Emma choked on her wine. "Sauced," Mr. Cooper agreed, and toasted Lord Holdensmoor with a forkful of pheasant.

With great care, she set down her glass. This was not an exchange for which Mrs. Clements' volume on Anglo-Indian etiquette had prepared her.

The Marquess met her eyes, and his smile widened. Fair enough; no doubt she was a comical sight, with her eyes as round as moons—and now her cheeks red to boot. "We try to create a miniature England here, Miss Martin, but no one claims to have succeeded."

"Indeed," she said faintly.

He smiled again, then turned back to the ravishing brunette at his side. She, however, was staring at Emma, with a nasty little smirk on her lips. Emma glanced at her, glanced away, and then looked back, raising her brows in civil inquiry.

"Miss Martin?" the woman repeated, pursing her white brow. "You're the famous fiancée, then."

Emma hesitated. She felt as though she'd fallen through a mirror into some strange parallel world where good manners were the very inverse of those in the place she'd left. "Famous, Miss . . . ?"

"Miss Crowley." The woman reached up to pat her

hair, calling to attention a prodigious display of bared bosom. "Perhaps Colonel Lindley has told you that he was stationed with my brother, Lieutenant Crowley, in Lucknow two years ago. We became very good friends there. I wonder, do you find it surprising that an officer might befriend an unmarried girl of good name? But that is station life, you know. In India, habits from Home so often make those who cling to them look . . . foolish."

As Miss Crowley gave this little speech, silence spread through the people around them. It contrasted markedly with the other end of the table, where the conversation continued as boisterously as ever.

Another one of Marcus's histories taking her unawares, then—and, judging by the reactions, a sordid one to boot. What did the woman expect her to do? Swoon? "How lovely to hear that you are friends," Emma said. "It does seem that he is blessed with a great *many* friends in Delhi." Without another word, she turned back to Mr. Cooper.

Her dinner partner was staring morosely at his plate, which was very nearly empty. She ran an eye over him. "Are you quite all right, sir?"

From Miss Crowley's other side, a pallid, poetic-looking gentleman spoke up. "Cooper old boy, it's a party! No call to look so gloomy!"

"I'm thinking of the accounts, Hawthorne," Mr. Cooper muttered. "If we have to buy new cartridges, I don't know how we'll manage it next year."

"Stuff and nonsense," Mr. Hawthorne said. "We'll just break them of this superstitious nonsense. A man can't be a soldier if he's afraid of a little pig grease."

Miss Crowley tittered. "How impressive, Mr. Hawthorne. You plan to convert the whole of the Indian militia to Christianity in the next seven months?"

They were speaking of the Meerut incident, Emma realized. In April, more than one hundred soldiers had refused to load their guns after realizing the act would involve biting bullets rumored to be greased with cow and pig fat—a problematic task, seeing that Hindus were forbidden to touch beef and Mussulmans could not eat pork. Emma cleared her throat. "Why don't you just grease the bullets with something else?"

Mr. Cooper's whole body jerked. "Good God, woman!" Bits of wine rained across her bodice as he spoke. "Do you know how much money that would cost?"

The Marquess spoke up. "Indeed. Have some sense, Miss Martin. Far cheaper to have the whole army refuse to fight."

"Balderdash," Hawthorne said. "They wouldn't dare. They know who their masters are."

"Quite right." The Marquess's voice was dry as dust. "They have a very good grasp of whom to shoot. Mangal Pandey, if you recall, missed Sergeant Hewson by inches."

"And I expect you cried into your pillow over that," Hawthorne muttered.

Mr. Cooper harrumphed in disapproval. The Marquess's eyes bored into Hawthorne; after a moment, the man colored and shifted in his seat.

"I don't understand," Emma said. "You are simply assuming that they will learn to accept the cartridges?"

Silence was her reply.

She could not help but glance at the Marquess. His

eyes were already on her, and the realization made her stomach dip—a queer but not unpleasant sensation. She arched her brows, and he turned his palms up in an expression that said, *You see? They will not listen.*

"Well, gentlemen?" he said to the table at large. "Can no one muster a platitude to soothe our brave memsahibs?"

"I need no soothing," Miss Crowley said. "I have full faith in our army, and I sleep soundly, I assure you."

"And why not?" Emma added. "Until, of course, these soldiers overcome their scruples and decide to use the bullets on the people who would force them to commit sacrilege. Which appears, Miss Crowley, to be *us.*"

Hawthorne chuckled. "That's quite a mouthful, Miss Martin. I say—do you read?"

She stared at him. "Do I what?"

"I don't mean those silly Waverley books; you didn't get your learning there. My, but it's so rare to encounter an educated woman. I'm not sure I like it."

"Hawthorne." The Marquess's tone was soft and sharp. But Emma beat him to it.

"I'm not sure I like *you,*" she snapped.

A bruising vice clamped around her shoulder. She glanced up to find Marcus standing over her, his jaw hard as stone. "If I may have a word with you," he said.

"Of course." She came to her feet, and the men rose too, making her feel all the more conspicuous. Her eyes touched the Marquess's as she withdrew, and she looked quickly away from his frown.

Marcus shut the pocket doors to the dining room with extreme care, then wheeled so abruptly that she stumbled back. He glared at her for a moment, then snatched her wrist, dragging her down the corridor and into a sitting room.

This door he did not shut so quietly; she flinched again as it cracked against the wooden frame.

In three long strides, he was before her, his breath harsh and rapid, his face mottled with color. "*What* do you think you're doing?"

Emma stepped backward, out of his grip, and her skirts collided with a settee. Pushing down her crinolines and straightening her spine, she lowered herself into the seat. "The man asked me if I knew how to read, Marcus. It was utterly insulting."

"You're a *woman,* Emmaline!"

"And?"

Save the furious working of his jaw, he was absolutely still as he stared at her. Then he exhaled sharply, clenching his hands behind his back in proper military fashion. "My father always said your father was a damned fool for educating you."

Emma gasped. "How dare he! My father would never have dreamed of maligning yours!"

"Your father was an addled old bat. He wouldn't have known a rock if it had hit him."

Emma lunged off the sofa. "My father was a wise, caring man! He—"

"He raised a daughter who isn't fit for company!"

"He taught me more than *you'll* ever know! I can read three languages, I can paint, I can—"

"Do everything except the *only* things a woman is good for: looking pretty and keeping her mouth shut."

"You pig," Emma breathed. "What has happened to you here? You were never like this before."

"Indeed? Perhaps I was not aware that my intended had worse manners than a workhouse orphan!"

"*You* agreed to this marriage!" She was shaking now, she was so angry. "And, unlike me, you were old enough to know what it meant. *You* were the one—"

"Little did I imagine you were going to turn out like this!" He pivoted, pacing the carpet in a tight circle around her. "Do you know how ashamed I was to hear you at the table? Challenging the assistant treasurer about his knowledge of the natives? You know nothing of these things, Emmaline! Nothing!"

She narrowed her eyes. "I know that none of you are even *considering* the possibility that the natives might mutiny! How irresponsible is that, Marcus? So many civilians depend on your clear thinking—"

"There you go again! How do you know we haven't considered the possibility? How dare you presume to know—"

"I know you're not even listening to Lord Holdensmoor!"

Silence fell like a funeral pall. She bit her lip.

"When have you been talking to the Marquess?" His voice, like his face, was without expression.

Emma drew a long breath. "Well, he visited the Residency yesterday."

"He visited you?"

"No! That is—we chatted. I had run into him in the bazaar while I was sketching—"

"The bazaar!" He took one step towards her. "Sketching in the bazaar with Holdensmoor!"

"Not *with* him, Marcus, he simply appeared and—"

"That scoundrel! That piece of filth! The man's

a blackguard, Emmaline—a blasphemous, treasonous *scourge* on the face of society—and to think that *you*—sketching is bad enough, it's a trollop's art the way you do it, you're determined to draw the most disgusting and lowest forms of human life—but with *him*! God almighty, are you determined to finish off the shreds of your reputation?"

"I don't think any of those activities constitutes a breach of my honor." She said it with difficulty, because his enraged look was beginning to alarm her.

He ran a hand over his mouth. "Of course you don't," he said cuttingly. "Because you have no idea what honor means, do you? You, who managed to save yourself by playing the ship doxy for a freighter of Irish peasants."

The wave of shock that swept over her blotted out all sound, leaving only an odd, whining buzz in her ears. "The crew of that ship knew more about being gentlemen than you ever will."

"You'll forgive me," he said conversationally, "if I don't take advice on etiquette from a whore."

"Funny," she said, a touch of hysterical humor taking hold of her. "That's rather how I think of you—well, that and a low-down preening coxcomb."

The blow caught her off guard. She fell to floor, the entire side of her face numbed by his fist. When she drew her hand away from her lips, her blurred vision focused on blood.

"Jesus Christ," she heard him mutter. "I didn't mean to do that." His hand closed on her shoulder, and she wrenched away.

"Don't touch me." Her lips felt thick and hot; the words came out fuzzily.

"Don't be foolish, Emmaline. Let me help you up."

"No, Marcus." She shut her eyes briefly against the spiking pain in her jaw. "You've lost the right. This engagement is over!"

He sounded impatient now. "Don't be silly. You're overreacting. All couples have their fights."

She raised her head so she could meet his eyes. "You *hit* me. I'm bleeding. This is the *end* of our connection!"

He lunged to his knees, grabbing her chin in his hand and yanking it high. "It is *you* who do not understand, Emmaline. I have waited fifteen years for your money, and I will not let your pathetic dramatics ruin my plan."

Emma pulled her knees to her chest to separate them. "Very frank of you," she said. "But I'm afraid you can't have it unless I give it to you!"

His laughter was brutal. "Let me be even more frank. I am now your guardian. Your bank accounts are in my control. You can't leave without money, so you'd best reconcile yourself to marriage."

The door clicked open. A female voice trilled, "Oh, I'm so sorry to interrupt!"

"Mrs. Eversham," Marcus said. He rose from his crouch. "I was just about to seek you out, my dear."

Willfully blind or malicious, the woman led him out with a laugh. Emmaline set her forehead on her knees, absently counting the drops of the water clock on the mantel. Three weeks until her twenty-first birthday. He couldn't mean to force her to the altar before then, could he? Surely Sir Metcalfe would not allow it.

Finally she found the strength to sit up. Blood was smeared over her peach silk skirts. She had to find a way to clean herself.

* * *

After dinner, Julian did what he had once sworn never to do: he went chasing after a memsahib.

Her seat had remained empty through dinner. He nursed a growing sense of absurdity all through dessert. His concern for her was misplaced. She was to be married to the idiot, and he had no cause to believe her unwilling. He rather doubted anyone could force Miss Martin to behave against her will. She kissed very sweetly, yes; but even devoted hearts could be swayed by a misplaced attraction. And perhaps some sort of obscure understanding existed between her and the Colonel. That was often the way of it in love; contentment between two people did not necessarily look, to outsiders, like happiness.

But then, Miss Martin did not seem content, either. And in the hallway upstairs, beneath his hands and mouth, she had not felt like a woman who shared an understanding with someone else. She had felt like a woman who shared an understanding with him.

And so, while he mocked himself with every step, he paced down the corridor, testing doorknobs. He nearly ran into Lindley as the man came around the corner, Mrs. Eversham on his arm. Like a sullen schoolgirl, Lindley made a great show of putting distance between them as he guided Mrs. Eversham past; but something in the lady's backward glance spurred Julian to a renewed purpose.

He finally found Miss Martin in the little parlour. She was crouched on the floor, staring into her skirts. Blood stained her mouth, and her jaw was purpling.

He must have made some noise. She looked up. "Lord Holdensmoor. What a dreadful expression you're wearing. Do I look so awful?" She put one hand to the arm of a chair to push herself up. He crossed to help her rise. Her wrists felt impossibly small in his hands. In contrast, Lindley's fist was as thick as a forehock. Not unbreakable, though. With a certain grip, not so difficult to form while casually shaking a man's hand, one could snap several bones at once. An additional twist and the wrist would shatter entirely.

"That bad?" she asked softly.

He shook his head.

"No, I quite agree," she said. "It is very bad. I need to clean my face."

He led her into the hallway, using his body to block her from view as they passed the portal into the long salon where the guests were dancing. When they reached the next door, he gestured her inside, then slid shut the bolt.

"No need," she protested. "I can do it myself."

"I'm sure you can." He crossed to the closet and rummaged inside for a length of gauze; then, after wetting it in the washbasin, dropped into a crouch and began to swab at her lip.

She stayed very still beneath his attentions, her large eyes curiously calm. "Perhaps I was stupid to provoke him."

He had to pause to collect himself before replying. "Perhaps he's a brutish bastard who should be kept five miles from the nearest woman."

She smiled slightly. "I like that interpretation better. Nevertheless—next time I choose to tangle with him, I should like to be armed."

He resumed his ministrations, trailing the swab up her

cheek to trace the slope of her swelling jaw. What was it about her that took him off guard? On the surface, she seemed typical. Tightly laced, primly erect; even her scent was quintessentially English—Rowlands' Kalydor soap and rosemary shampoo. But there was something else beneath it . . . something sweet and dark . . . and it pulled strange things from him: the urge to strip her down to that essence. To pull away these outer trappings. To lay her bare, and force her to show herself as she truly was.

It was not a gentle impulse. Nor entirely sexual, although it was certainly that as well. He drew a long breath, wondering at himself.

"You look very fierce right now," she murmured.

"I beg your pardon."

"Oh, no, I find it reassuring."

Only because she did not know what was in his head. "Tell me," he said. "Was it his charm that won you to him?"

"My parents, rather. They thought it would be an ideal match. His family is highly respected in Devon, but lack funds. So . . ." She shook her head, then winced. No doubt she had a bloody bad headache.

He smoothed her hair back from her face. She leaned into his hand like a cat. He would have called it an excellent sign, had he been wondering what she would be like when she was naked in his bed. But the moment did not call for such speculation. He pulled back, schooling himself. "They were on the ship with you?"

"They were."

It came to him that she might still intend to marry the bastard, out of some misplaced duty to her parents. "So what do you wish to do now?"

"I told him the marriage was off," she said, and he felt an amount of relief that unsettled him. "But he seems to want my money very badly."

"An heiress, are you?"

She sighed. "Immensely, shockingly wealthy." He was startled into a laugh; she smiled back at him. "But he is my guardian. So even if I wished to go . . ."

"Don't worry about that. I can arrange for your departure."

She drew back, looking affronted. "Really, my lord. I can't take your charity!"

And there it was again: the visage of the proper memsahib, flickering over her true face like the projection from a camera obscura. She could not quite decide who she wanted to be. Or perhaps, he thought, she simply did not know she had a choice in the matter. "I could charge you an immense, shocking interest rate," he said. He slid his hand around the back of her neck, beneath the heavy weight of her chignon. He could not help himself; he wanted to startle her out of propriety. "Or some other arrangement. Something even more interesting."

Her eyes widened, then narrowed. "Do you find me amusing?"

"Yes," he said, and laughed. "Among other things."

A rattle sounded at the door. Reluctantly he released her. "If you're to leave, you should go straightaway." At least he would succeed in delivering one person from this city.

"Yes, I suppose. Although I can't imagine he would really try to force me to marry him. I'm perfectly safe at the Residency." She hesitated, watching his face. "That's not what worries you, is it?"

He inclined his head in silent response. She had been at the table tonight; she knew very well what his worries were.

"I suppose I could accept a temporary loan," she went on slowly. "My birthday's in three weeks; you won't have to wait long."

He tossed the rag into the sink as he rose. "There's a palankeen caravan to Calcutta leaving tomorrow afternoon, if you can be packed so quickly." She nodded. "Good. I'll make the arrangements tonight. You must be packed and ready by noon; I'll come to fetch you then." Calcutta would be safe, he thought. Well situated, the seat of the government; plenty of European troops for defense. On alert after the disturbance at nearby Barrackpore. If she could not manage to book immediate passage on a ship, it would be an excellent shelter for a few weeks.

"Will I not see you again, then? After that, I mean."

The question pulled him out of his reverie. He turned back to her, studying her for a moment. How young she looked, suddenly. He tried to picture her in the London he knew—throwing dice and sipping Champagne; trading *on dits* at the theater; clapping at the races. But it all felt very distant, almost surreal; he could not even picture himself there anymore. And what came to him instead was a vision of her as she'd been in the Evershams' garden: haunted eyes, alone in the dark. A hot wind sweeping over her.

A chill lifted the fine hairs at his nape. He rubbed a hand across his neck, impatient with it. He did not believe in premonitions. "I hope so."

His tone must have given something away, for she

frowned. "Why don't *you* leave Delhi? If you think it's so unsafe here . . ."

He shook his head. This was not a conversation he could have. "I'll go fetch the Metcalfes for you." And then he was going to find Lindley.

five

Breakfast was a repulsive array of mutton chops, curry puffs, poached eggs, and kidneys on toast. The Resident's other late-dining guest, a Mr. Barclay Hosegood of Mhow, was blunting his taste buds with generous helpings of claret. Emma had never seen someone drink before noon. Apparently neither had the two servants, for they kept exiting only to return with new companions, who would do something useless like rearrange the sugar bowl before disappearing in a stifled fit of giggles.

Then again, she might be the object of their amusement, for every entry elicited from her the same question: "Any chits for me?"

"*Nahin,* memsahib," the most recent arrival said solemnly, wiping imaginary crumbs from the tablecloth while she flicked surreptitious glances at the gentleman across the table. "Early, memsahib, very early for chits."

"Yes, I know," Emma murmured. Silly, to feel so uneasy.

Against her will, she put her fingers to her lips. Would he kiss her again before he saw her off? The possibility that he might refrain made her distinctly anxious.

A door crashed open in the distance. Mr. Hosegood, in the process of refilling his glass, knocked the bottle over with a jerk. They exchanged a glance of surprise, then turned as one to the door. From the hallway came the rapid ring of boots. Just before the footsteps reached the morning room, she recognized Marcus's voice, pitched low in a curse.

She came to her feet. What was he doing here? Monday morning was parade rehearsal at the camp!

He opened this door with equal brutality, then paused on the threshold, his harsh breathing the only sound save the rhythmic dripping of claret from tablecloth to floor. His red military uniform, usually so immaculate, was covered with dust; his hands were clenched into fists at his sides. Someone had hit him hard across the face; one of his eyes was black, and his nose was swollen and bruised, perhaps broken. His bloodshot eyes darted about the room in frantic fashion, fixing on nothing.

Cold slid down her spine. Something was terribly wrong.

She lowered herself back into the chair. "Well, good heavens." Her voice sounded queer to her, comically prim. "Can't you see we're having breakfast?"

He glanced at her, as though just now taking note of her presence. "Where's the Resident?"

"At the government office, I suppose. Where else would he be?"

Marcus nodded, still out of breath, and looked to Mr. Hosegood. "You," he said, and tossed him a pistol. It splashed into the puddle of claret, and Emma flinched—braced for a discharge that did not come. "Ride like hell to the Joint Magistrate's. Tell him I can't find the Resident and he needs to close the bloody gates."

"But . . . but . . ." Mr. Hosegood sprang up, backing away from the table and gun. "Really, sir, who are you, and why—"

"I'm an officer of the Indian Army and if you do not go right now, I'll hold you responsible for the deaths of hundreds of British citizens."

Mr. Hosegood gaped dumbly. Marcus snarled and lunged a pace toward him. The man snatched up the pistol and scrambled to the door.

Marcus stood there for a moment longer, stuffing his hands into his pockets and tilting his head. When the sound came of the front door slamming, he nodded and fell into a seat. There followed a short silence, in which Emma held herself still, not daring even to breathe. Then his eyes lifted to hers; they gleamed so strangely, she wondered if he had been drinking, too.

"Well then," he said, and then continued, in the casual tones of someone describing the plot of a mediocre novel, "A large contingent of mutinous soldiers is attempting to cross the Jumna river into Delhi."

"Oh?" The response of a dedicated nonreader, designed to discourage further conversation.

"Yes. It may be too late to shut the gates."

"Indeed," she said politely. "So Mr. Hosegood is on a fool's mission, then."

He shrugged. "I couldn't say."

Emma laced her hands together in her lap, squeezing hard to channel a tumult of foreign emotions. "Shouldn't you be mustering the troops?"

"Good God!" He shoved to his feet and began to pace. "Come to reality, you stupid little girl. The troops are native. They will not fight their own countrymen!" His own words seemed to stun him; he lapsed into a brooding silence. Last week, in this very room, he'd boasted to the Resident of his regiment's loyalty. Apparently something had happened at the Ridge to change his mind.

She swallowed hard. "Then we should flee." She rose, her thoughts painfully lucid. She could not wait for Lord Holdensmoor to come. She could not assume he would be able to come.

"No." He yanked down his jacket and rounded on her with grim focus. "I'll not flee. That yellow milksop won't have fetched the Resident. I'll go myself."

"All right, just let me change into my riding habit and—"

His laughter cut her off. "Idiot. You would only slow me down." He strode to the door, paused there. "Oh, yes." He extracted a knife from his boot, pivoting to set it on the table. "If the natives come, don't dishonor me. Slit your throat quick. The wrists are too slow. Though knowing you, you'd probably enjoy being plowed by them." He hesitated, considering her. "Well, it's immaterial. If you do live, I'll come for you. Remember that. I promised your father I would watch over you, and I do keep my promises. There will be no use hiding from me."

The door slammed behind him, making the breakfast dishes rattle.

She stood in a daze. Bright streamers of sunlight were unfurling through the windows, shedding sparkling detail over the silver breakfast plates, and Mr. Hosegood's flask, and the hilt of the knife.

Emma stretched out a tentative hand. The hilt was warm to the touch. She snatched the weapon to her chest and hurried into the main hall.

The house was deserted. Servants nowhere to be seen now. Lady Metcalfe had gone to Mrs. Durham's after their morning walk; Usha had left for the market not an hour before. She was alone.

The heavy teak doors stood open to the front porch. She ran through them, tripping once on her skirts, and caught a last glimpse of Marcus as his horse galloped through the gates.

For all his cruelty, she had known him forever. And there he went. Not even a backward glance.

But wasn't it a lovely day, so pleasantly warm and bright. A brainfever bird hooted in the eaves, and the verdant lawns of the Residency stretched out before her, rolling down to the high hedges that blocked the view of greater Delhi. She looked up. There was not a cloud to be seen in the brilliant blue expanse. She realized that she was having a particularly vivid dream.

Thunder rolled through the sky.

The distant crack of gunfire followed it.

She retreated to the doorway, gripping the knocker as she searched the horizon.

Silence fell again, deceptively profound. Then, all of a sudden, a wild ringing of bells. The alarm sounding at St. James's Church.

This was no dream after all.

And there was no one coming for her.

That decided it. A riding habit was all very well when one planned to go sidesaddle, but war called for better balance. She clawed for the hem of her skirts, pulling them up until she found the tapes. A slash of the knife, and the cane crinolines clattered to the porch. Next the petticoats, falling to the ground. On a small, hysterical laugh, she turned to her remaining skirt. Hacking off the gown's extra material was easier said than done. By the time she finished, her face was wet with sweat, and the occasional burst of thunder had turned into a steady, pounding din. Was it her imagination, or was it becoming louder, nearer?

Wrapping the knife in the excess fabric, she stuck it in her pocket and raced for the stables.

She had expected to get lost. But she hadn't foreseen that the general panic would make getting directions impossible.

A gun exploded nearby, and her horse spooked, bucking hard. She fought to keep her seat, slapping her mount's flanks with a sharpness provoked by fear. The stupid nag had nearly trampled a child.

Shaken, she slowed the gelding to a walk. Crowds of natives and Britons were swarming the broad, sunlit street, their wan faces lifting every time a blast sounded in the distance. Somewhere in the city, people were dying; they were afraid they would be next. But no one seemed to know in which direction to flee, and the commotion was turning ugly. Already a man had tried to wrest the reins from her. An Englishwoman clutched at her ankles and begged for news. When she shook her head, the lady scurried onward, a baby and a scrapbook clutched to her chest.

A gunshot rang out behind her, greeted by a chorus of high-pitched female screams. Another whizzed by, so close she could hear it pass. Were they shooting at *her*? She spurred her mount into a canter, her lips moving in a silent prayer as she negotiated animals and people. *God, don't let me hit anyone.* There was no end in sight to the melee, but up ahead, she saw the opening to a small alley. She headed for it.

It was another lane lined with havelis, much like the one she had explored with Usha. A weird quiet encapsulated her as she entered it. Scattered shafts of sunlight fell, illuminating aimless drifts of dust. The horse sneezed, startling her. She pulled him to a trot.

Ahead, a woman stepped into the darkened street, her sari a vivid mélange of purple and gold. She waved at Emma, motioning for her to go back. Emma ignored her. The woman's motions grew more violent as she neared.

"Jaaiye laut jaaiye vo maar daalenge aapko!"

She swallowed nervously, uncertain what to do. Was she being warned, or threatened? No matter, for she could not return the way she'd come. Urging her horse onward, she galloped past the woman.

No one else appeared as she thundered down the crooked street. After a minute or so the alley widened, dumping her into another great commotion of people.

By the time she caught sight of the Jama Masjid ahead and realized she had blundered directly into the heart of the Old City, near the spice market, it was too late. She was penned in by the crowd. Men—mostly Indian, though she saw two or three English faces—were climbing onto whatever heights they could find, screaming words that were completely inaudible. The sweet smell of incense floating out of vegetable stalls was mixing with the acrid tang of gunpowder. Across the plaza, the vibrant paintings of the blue-skinned gods, the paintings she had so admired during her visit, had caught fire. A group of people fought, sobbing and screaming, to put out the flames.

The frantic jostling forced her forward, in the direction of the Jama Masjid. The great striped minarets of the mosque gleamed in the morning light. Around her she began to spot wounded, British and Indians as well, bloody and smoke-stained from battle. Blast it, where were they coming from? Lacking a choice, she speeded her progress toward the mosque, spying as she neared it a sizable group of Englishmen who were sheltering beneath the high sandstone archways.

A man cried out as he sighted her, stumbling down the steps as he clutched his arm. It was the Commissioner. "Mr. Fraser!" Emma hauled back on her reins and threw herself down from the horse, grabbing the man as he stumbled. "What happened to you?"

"I tried," he said wearily. "The first breach was at Daryaganj. We shut the Delhi Gate—but they went around to Raj Ghat. They'll be inside the city at any moment."

Raj Ghat was not fifteen minutes away. "Lord above!"

She turned to cast a desperate glance over the chaotic crowd. "We cannot stay here, Mr. Fraser!"

He took her hands, pressing them in his own. "Pray my telegram went through to Ambala," he said, staring into her eyes. "Pray with me for reinforcements."

"I will pray, but you must leave with me. Two can sit my horse. Come." She tried to pull him toward her mount, but he resisted, looking behind her. "You were right!" he panted, and pulled from her grip. She glanced down, shocked to find her hands coated in blood. "You were right, my lord! The troops have turned on us!"

She turned. The Marquess was mounted on a huge black steed, and his face was smeared with soot. He looked astonished to see her. "What in *hell* are you doing here? Why did you not wait for me at the Residency?"

"There's no time for this!" Sir Fraser yelled. "Holdensmoor, they're shooting their own goddamn commanders!"

The Marquess's mount shied, skittish as hordes of people milled around them. He reined the horse in a tight circle, saying as he came back around, "Get out of the city, Fraser. Don't go back for your possessions; just get out!"

The Commissioner drew himself upright. "I need a surgeon," he said bitterly. "Damned blackie near took my arm off. But first I'm going to see the Emperor, and make clear that if he doesn't settle down his people, I'll have them all blown to hell."

As if to punctuate his words, a mighty explosion rocked the earth beneath them, momentarily casting the world in tones of fire. They all wheeled, and from behind her Fraser gasped, "The magazine! Some fool blew up the Expense magazine! That's all the artillery we have inside the gates!"

"Likely one of your men," the Marquess yelled over the uproar. "It's too close to the river; the troops would have gotten it."

"Holdensmoor, it's *finished* here!"

The Marquess nodded. "Is this your horse?" he said to Emma, as he reached out to grab the gelding's reins. "Get back on it."

"But—the Commissioner—"

"Go with him!" Mr. Fraser bodily lifted her into the saddle. "I must try to speak with the King!"

"No, please, Mr. Fraser—" But Lord Holdensmoor's horse lunged forward, pulling hers along with him. Emma twisted to look back, but the Commissioner had already been swallowed by the throng. She faced front again. Dear God. The fire was not contained to the magazine. Natives with torches were spreading out through the street; before her eyes, the government building went up in flames. The torchbearers' wrath seemed indiscriminate, for even Indians were spilling from the buildings, clutching what valuables they could to their chests as they watched the rest burn.

At the entrance to the Chowree bazaar, Lord Holdensmoor drew up. "I don't think it's safe," he said to Emma, as he stared down the crushed lane.

She pivoted in her saddle, looking behind her. The street was now a virtual wall of flame, and as she turned away she saw from the corner of her eye a turbaned man reach out and grab a British woman by the hair, yanking her from her husband's side to the ground. "Oh my

God!" She reached out to clutch the Marquess's arm. "That man—"

"Shah Bahadur ki jay! Shah Bahadur ki jay!" The chant seemed to grow out of thin air, escalating into a blood-rattling roar. The unruly mess of Britons and natives—who, just moments before, had been consulting each other in mutual terror over the explosion of the magazine—now seemed to coalesce into a sudden horrifying semblance of order. The women in saris and veils shrank to the sides of the street, grabbing their children by the wrists before ducking down the tangled alleys. The British—mostly women who had come to seek their husbands at the Civil Service office, though there were a few men here and there who were screaming in broken Hindustani and English to be calm, *be calm*—froze before the oncoming mass of chanting natives, all of whom were garbed in full military uniform. One of them reached out and smashed a window front. An Englishman stepped forward, gesticulating wildly. The sepoy swung his rifle from his shoulder and drove the bayonet through the man's heart.

Emma screamed as someone dragged her off her horse. Hands spun her roughly, shaking her. It was the Marquess. He dragged her into the shadows of a building, holding her against him as violence seized the crowd.

Some terrible, base instinct compelled her to push away. She had to look.

The sepoys had broken formation, and were scattering with blades upraised. Emma saw a girl roughly her own age viciously gutted by a soldier's knife. Her morbid curiosity died. She shut her eyes again and pressed a fist to her mouth.

"Miss Martin. Emmaline!"

She looked up to find the Marquess crouched before her. In his hand was a knife, offered hilt first. "You *will* use this," he said forcefully.

She drew a shaking breath and took it carefully from his hand. It was larger and sharper than the one Marcus had offered, but it sat well in her palm. She curled her fingers around the hilt, swallowing hard.

The Marquess was loading his revolver. "Five shots," he said, and then glanced back to the street. "We're trapped if we stay here." His eyes met hers, intensely green. "On my mark, run into the bazaar."

The utter calmness of his manner was more jarring than a scream; it made the chaos around them seem like some awful hallucination. She met his eyes, panting, dizzy—and nodded.

They burst out of the alley.

No time to think. She acted on instinct, darting left and right as the mass of bodies clashed and parted around her. The sound of screams and curses and the rasp of her own panicked breath prevented any coherent thought; only her eyes could help her now, straining wide to spot openings in the bloody clash. A matronly woman stumbled into her, blue eyes fixed in shock, her nose dripping blood as she caught Emma's arm. When she collapsed, she nearly dragged Emma with her; only the Marquess's arm around her waist saved her from being trampled. She stumbled back to her feet, nausea knotting her throat as she stepped on something soft and warm. Dear God . . .

A soldier rose up before her, bloodlust in his eyes. Sobbing, she lashed out with her knife, but he knocked it from her hand with the butt of his rifle, spinning the weapon around in order to thrust the bayonet toward her. She jerked backward at the deafening report of gunfire over her head, thudding directly into the Marquess as the sepoy slumped to the ground.

"Go!" he screamed, pushing her forward again as he primed his pistol. But from the periphery of her vision, Emmaline spied another soldier hauling his rifle to his shoulder, taking Lord Holdensmoor in his aim. A scream burst from her as she hurled herself forward, her hand stretching out to knock the rifle away. It discharged over their heads, and the sepoy drew his saber, slicing it down toward her. Time slowed as she watched it descend.

Lord Holdensmoor seized the man's wrist. The saber shot up. A brief struggle. The Marquess yanked the man into his body—belly first into the pistol. The gun barked. The man's eyes shot wide; blood bubbled up at his mouth. He thudded to the ground.

She turned to the Marquess in disbelief. His eyes met hers in the split second before a great weight slammed into her temple, and the world went black as pitch.

Six

EMMA TURNED HER HEAD UP TOWARD THE LIGHT. NO air—*must have air*—she fought against her skirts, breaking to the surface on a deep, ragged inhalation. Her mother's face swam before her. Mama was screaming. Oh God, another wave was coming—

"Miss Martin!"

She gasped and hauled herself upright. An exquisitely brutal pain lanced through her head. With a groan, she fell back to the ground.

"Miss Martin, you cannot fall asleep again. Miss Martin. *Emmaline*. Answer me, damn it!"

"What?" Was that really her voice? She sounded intoxicated. Licking her dry lips, she tried again. "What? Who's there?"

The voice sounded distinctly alarmed. "Now, Emmaline. Open your eyes *now*."

She blinked, disoriented. She was flat on her back, and the Marquess sat over her, gripping her wrists at either side of her head to keep them still. The nightmare again. Always that same nightmare. "My lord," she said shakily.

His hands slid down to her shoulders, gently forbidding her to rise. "Shh, easy. You've had a knock to the head."

Of course. It all came back to her in a nauseating rush. Cautiously, mindful of the throbbing in her skull, she turned her head to take in their location. Not Delhi. Someplace else. Safety? A river flowed musically not five yards away. The sun was low to the ground, reddening the waters and limning the squat trees atop the riverbank. Hours had gone by, then. "Where are we?"

"A few miles outside Delhi. Opposite direction of Kurnaul. No other options. The troops started closing the gates."

She shuddered involuntarily. A chorus of aches and twinges answered. Gingerly she catalogued them, stretching out each limb with measured care. Her arms—that would be from gripping the pommel. Her shins and ribs—jostling amidst the crowd. Her head pounded like the dickens. Any number of possible reasons for that. Obviously she had committed some terrible sin to deserve all this abuse, but what it might have been was a puzzle.

As she sat up, the throb of her jaw demanded special note. She touched it. Definitely a fresher insult than the one Marcus had delivered. "Someone hit me."

"He regrets it."

The cold, flat tone caught her attention. The Marquess

did not look so well either. Raffish, in fact. His black hair was tangled, and an oncoming beard shadowed his jaw. Somewhere along the way he had acquired a bloody slash from cheekbone to chin. But it was his eyes that gave her pause. They were feverishly bright—at once alert and exhausted. He looked as if he were burning up from within.

The chaos of Chowree Lane flashed back over her. She wondered what he had done to get them out of the city. "You saved my life."

The line of his throat moved as he swallowed. His face turned away. She did not know how to read his mood—whether he was in shock, or struggling to master himself, or simply impatient with formalities at such a time. But when he turned back to her, his lips moved in the barest of smiles. "No thanks between us," he said, and lifted his hand to her cheek. "You saved mine as well."

His touch conjured another image—his hand smashing away a blade, wrapping around another man's wrist. Making a shield for her of his flesh and bone. She swallowed hard, and her hand rose to cover his.

Then a rustle from above them had him pressing down against her, his palm firm against her lips for silence. As she strained to detect any other noise, she became aware of the feel of his body. He was a solid wall of coiled muscle, but fine, passing tremors racked him, as if something inside him were fighting to break out. It came to her of a sudden that he was as dangerous as anything else she had faced today. She drew herself as small as possible, and held very still beneath him.

"No," he said. "I don't think it's anything. I'll go

check." He lifted himself off her and moved up the bank, silent as a shadow.

She lay there, staring upward. Long crimson clouds stretched across the lavender sky, as though giant claws had laid open the innards of heaven. A new moon wavered and blurred at the corner of her vision. Ah, God. If there was one thing these last few months had taught her, it was that tears were utterly useless. Strength and courage were the qualities that mattered, and she had enough—*yes,* she did—to see this through. She was no chit fresh from leading strings, to whimper at the prospect of being left alone in this empty place as a bullock lowed mournfully in the distance. She had braved greater loneliness when she had faced the sea. She would make herself stand up now and climb the bank. She would learn whether their hiding place had been discovered.

She stifled a groan as she rolled onto her knees, panting in determination as she grabbed at roots and rocks to haul herself upward. As she crested the rise she bumped into the Marquess, who caught her by her wrists to steady her.

"Did you tire of the vista?" he asked.

Strange, that his humorous tone could give her as great a shock as anything that had come before it today. After a soundless moment, her lips finally managed to spit out the words. "What was it, then?" She glanced beyond him, seeing only an endless expanse of scrub.

"Likely a monkey." He drew her back down the bank, to the water's edge. She thought to sit, but her knees gave way. She made a controlled collapse into the dust.

His small sound of mirth drew a sharp glance from her—and the resulting pain was stupendous. With two trembling fingers, she touched her temple, where small, rhythmic daggers seemed to be stabbing a tattoo. "What's so funny?"

"Nothing. Christ—nothing at all."

"Then what?"

"Oh . . ." He lay back against the bank, folding his arms behind his head. "You never fail to surprise me."

She could not follow his line of thought. But in these circumstances, she supposed that surprise must be accounted a good thing. Certainly she was surprised to be alive still.

He seemed content to lie there, so she let the silence settle. After a few moments of watching the current, she dipped her fingers into it—and immediately withdrew them, shuddering. The river felt warm and viscous, as though clotted with some foreign substance. She did not like to think of what it reminded her of. She backed away a little.

"You don't like water."

She cut him a speaking glance. Nor would he like it, had he come to know it so intimately.

From across the bank came the whirring of a lone cicada. Then, as if on a signal, a chorus of them started up. Dusk was deepening. She readjusted her skirt over her ankles. "Shouldn't we . . . do something?"

"Not until full dark," he said. "That's the Grand Trunk Road up there. Main corridor to Delhi. There's bound to be dacoits and stray sepoys along it."

"And then what?"

"I don't know." At her answering expression, he sighed. "I'll deliver you to a safe place. Sapnagar, I think. I have friends there."

"You'll *deliver* me."

"Yes."

She took a deep breath. "And where will you go?"

"Back to Delhi."

"Delhi!" He still wore the blood he'd shed during their escape! "Have you run mad? You can't mean to go back. Not until it's recaptured!"

"*If* it's recaptured," he said softly.

"If?" His insinuation astonished her. "You actually think we'll let the natives keep it? One of the largest stations in the raj?"

He rolled onto one arm to face her. "I am not sure *we* will have any say in the matter. The Indians appear to have already taken *back* their imperial city."

She felt unaccountably embarrassed—and then angry for it. Here they sat in the middle of the wilderness, bruised and beaten and cowering at the sound of monkeys in the brush, and he took her to task for wishing it were otherwise? "Am I to understand that you're upbraiding me for espousing the English view? Pray tell, *my lord,* after what we have been through today, do you still take some other position?"

He sat up in one fluid motion, and instinct had her lurching away. The reaction seemed to startle him as much as it did her. He went very still. Then, in curiously formal tones, he said, "Forgive me, Miss Martin. I can see I have upset you. I fear my mood is . . . uncertain."

She had backed toward the river, and dampness was creeping up her skirts, trickling over her ankles. The sensation set all her nerves on edge, but advancing seemed equally dangerous. "And your loyalties—are they uncertain as well?"

"You are safe with me," he said. "Can you doubt it?"

"That is not an answer."

"No." He exhaled. "Come out of the water, Emmaline. Please. It was not my intent to frighten you, and I'm very sorry for it."

Never looking away from him, she pushed herself forward just enough to clear the current. "You do not frighten me. You *alarm* me."

A hint of humor flickered across his face. "An interesting distinction. Perhaps you would like to explain it."

"I am more interested in your explanation," she said stiffly.

"Fair enough." He paused. "My mother's family lives in Delhi. I can only assume they remained in the city today. They would have thought it safer than fleeing."

"Your mother's . . . " She realized he must be speaking of his Indian kin. "But—surely the rebels will not harm them? They are not English."

"True enough." He looked down to his fingers, splaying them apart to make a brief study. Then, as if dismissing whatever significance he found there, he rubbed his hands together and shook his head. "I have visited them recently. It drew attention. Not to me, you understand, but to my grandmother's household." A wry smile appeared. "The English are not the only society with a horror of mixing the races. In fact, in my grandfather's time, the objection was far more likely to come from the Indians."

He fell silent. At a loss for the proper response, Emma waited.

"I was rather foolish," he said at length. "I continued

to press my attentions on them, even after they warned me against it. I thought my connections, my resources, might be of some benefit. It was naïve."

"It sounds generous."

His look was sharp. "Hardly. Were it not for them, I would never—well, no matter. Anyway, it has occurred to me that the rebels may decide to root out British sympathizers. And my actions will ensure that they are mistaken for such."

She considered this in silence, finding implications in it that chilled her. "You think the rebels will hold Delhi. That they will hold it long enough to . . . do such a thing."

"I think it's very possible," he said. "Perhaps, in the chaos this morning, you did not hear. But those sepoys did not come down from the Ridge. They marched in from Meerut. Which means the uprising began before today—and who can say where it *did* start, or how far it has spread? I had it from Sir Metcalfe that the telegraph wires have been cut in all directions."

"Sir Metcalfe? He's all right, then?"

"I don't know. I ran into him on the way to the Residency; he was looking for his wife."

"You came to the Residency? But when?"

He arched a brow. "We had agreed to meet there, had we not? I suppose I arrived shortly after you left. The point is, there may have been news of other disturbances which did not reach us."

"Lord above." This nightmare could spread to swallow the whole of India. "If *all* the sepoys decide to mutiny—"

His smile, so unexpected, startled her into silence. "Then it would no longer be mutiny. It would be a revolution."

"But . . ." It was too much to take in. "India without Britain?"

"The Americans managed it. I don't see why the blackies couldn't as well."

She recoiled at his sarcasm. "That wasn't what I meant!"

"I beg your pardon, Miss Martin; what *did* you mean?"

"Just—" She dug her fingers into her skirts, twisting the material hard. "Well, we simply can't drop everything and run away, can we?"

A warm wind kicked up, ruffling through his thick, dark hair. Very softly, he said, "I see. Is this where you preach to me of how English civilization will save the savages?"

She hated this, *hated* the way he was suddenly looking at her—as though she were some unfamiliar specimen whose novelty was rapidly losing interest. "Be fair, sir! All I meant was that we've created a society here. Laws, a justice system, a—postal service . . ." The argument sounded weak even to her own ears. "I simply mean that to leave those things behind would hardly be simple."

"Not simple, no. Few things are."

She looked away from him, to the water. "True enough."

After a moment, he murmured, "Emmaline. I am sorry. I am . . . overwrought." His laughter was unsteady. "And there's a phrase I've never used before. At least not in reference to myself."

An unwilling smile curved her mouth. “I hope you won’t swoon. I don’t carry smelling salts.”

“No,” he said. “I wouldn’t have imagined you did.”

When the darkness settled, they left the Grand Trunk Road behind, cutting across the flat, scrubby desert. The heat did not ebb, and Emma quickly exhausted her stamina. Her stabbing headache was making her dizzy. Her feet felt like lead blocks. Sweat glued the tattered dress to her legs, impeding every step. The Marquess too must be suffering, but he showed no signs of it. He moved steadily onward, pausing only when she stumbled over exposed roots and rocks. At one point he tried to take her arm to steady her, but she shook her head, gritting her teeth and forcing herself to keep to his pace.

When the moon was at its zenith, they came across a waterhole at the base of a hillock. After splashing her face and taking a few bracing sips, Emma laughed, giddy. “I was dreaming of water,” she said. “With my eyes open! And for once it was not a nightmare.”

The Marquess wiped his mouth with the back of his hand. “You dream of the shipwreck?”

“Every night.” She sobered and sat back. “Perhaps now I’ll dream of Delhi instead.”

After a pause, he said, “This is a good enough place to stop for a bit. You could try to nap.”

“Are we safe, then?”

“Soon enough. We’re headed for a village I know, on the outskirts of the district that Sapnagar rules. It’s another few hours’ walk.”

“So what would you do while I sleep? Stand watch?” She shook her head. “Just let me catch my breath.”

He shrugged and looked past her. The moonlight rendered his face a chiaroscuro of shadows and highlights; his eyes were pools of shadow as he stared out at the silvered plain.

"You are thinking of your family, my lord?"

"Julian," he said. "Julian is my name."

She hesitated. "If you only intend to go back for them, why run in the first place?"

He gave a small laugh. "How noble it sounds when you put it thus."

"You know I didn't mean it like that. But why not find them before you left?"

"I might have done, but they would have refused to come. And there was the small matter of your wanting so very badly to get out." He cocked a brow at her. "If I'm not mistaken, you even stole a horse for it."

"Why—gracious, I suppose I did! But surely the Resident will not mind. That is, if the Resident . . ." *If the Resident even survived.* She shook off the unfinished thought. "If you are saying you left to see me to safety, I'm very grateful."

"Oh?" He ran both hands through his hair, then held up his arm to inspect a cut he had managed to bandage. She recognized the fabric with a start: it was fashioned from a strip of her skirt.

He glanced to her, and perhaps he saw the realization on her face, for his smile slid into a tease. "You're not meant to be grateful, Emma; you're meant to be flattered. And perhaps a small bit flustered, if you can manage it. That would give me the advantage. I seem to need one where you're concerned."

She eyed him warily. "You're being silly, I think."

"Silly, she says?" He heaved a sigh. "Not a becoming assessment, for a man so widely accounted a rogue."

His mercurial mood bewildered her, but she was willing to match his tone, if he wanted to persist with it. It seemed far preferable to dwelling on the day's events. "You do not strike me as a Lothario. You're far too serious for the part."

"Oh? I did give it a small try, if you recall. And your mouth tasted quite sweet. But perhaps I was too subtle?"

From an airy exchange of quips, he had suddenly moved onto solid ground. Having his attention so fully focused on her made her feel peculiar, as if air were in short supply. "You're a skillful flirt," she managed. "I will give you that."

"And you're no flirt at all. Come, give it a try. Tell me how a rogue charms a woman, if not through sober, industrious application."

Her lips twitched. "That sounds like the factory brand of roguery. But all you need do is attend to a woman's vanity, I suppose."

"Ah, yes. Of course. It comes back to me now; I've been going about it all wrong. The first thing I should have said is that you are the most beautiful woman I've ever seen."

She laughed despite herself. "That's a clever sort of compliment, seeing as it reserves you the right to change your mind with the next woman you meet. As well you should, with me in such a state!"

He leaned forward a little. "Would you like me to remove the qualification? I'd be more than willing to oblige."

"No, that's all right. My looks aren't where my vanity lies."

"But you are beautiful," he said. "Don't you know it? A very rare kind of beauty, Emmaline. Your spirit is as lovely as your face."

That was too much. She dropped her eyes.

"And now I should kiss you again, I think. Isn't that how it's done?"

Startled, she put her hand to her lips. But their rough, cracked surfaces made the very prospect seem ludicrous. "Yes, I suppose—in a gothic romance. But if you kissed me now, no doubt my lip would split open, and I'd bleed on you."

His shout of laughter was quickly restrained. "Well, all right. Since you put it so romantically. Someplace else. Shall I be adventurous?"

This was too ridiculous. They were marooned in the desert, bedraggled, on the run for their lives. And he was having a bit of fun with her. It was clear from the amusement on his face, the carefree curve of his mobile lips, that she should not take him seriously.

But her heart had lost track of the game. "This is absurd."

"Indeed. So much is absurd. For instance, where are your crinolines?"

Her hands pressed flat against the thin muslin draping her thighs. Before today, she had never stepped into the world so lightly. Feeling the breeze as it flirted under her skirts seemed very close to being naked. "You are unkind to notice."

"I do try not to," he said softly. "And it seems as if it should be easy. But it isn't."

From somewhere inside, a place that trembled and ran hot and cold all at once, she found the courage to meet his eyes. "You are not joking," she said.

"No, Emmaline. I never said I was."

She inhaled as he leaned toward her. "I said my lips—"

"So you did," he said against her ear, and she closed her eyes as his teeth gently trapped her lobe.

"That is not a kiss," she gasped. Her voice sounded as if it came from a distance, barely penetrating the thunder of her pulse.

"Do you want one?" He spoke it against her skin; his tongue flicked over the tender rim of her ear, drew a line down the edge. "I thought it was not advisable."

She would have laughed, if she had not felt as though every bone in her was dissolving. "You *are* a rake," she whispered.

"My dear, how unoriginal." His mouth shifted to trace down her cheekbone, skating very lightly over the swelling bruise. His eyelashes flickered up as he passed, giving her a momentary glimpse of some unreadable thought. Then, pausing where her jaw met her neck, he sipped gently, and then again, harder now, as if trying to draw her heartbeat to the surface.

Her hand rose of its own volition, curving around the very same spot on his own jaw. His skin was so warm to the touch, the stubble a strange and pleasing texture under her palm. "This isn't a kiss either."

"No," he murmured. He pressed his face fully into her throat. For the space of several breaths he remained like that, breathing deeply against her. Her hand moved up to grip the back of his head, threading through the softness of his hair. A strange impulse to grip him harder, to cradle him fully, had her biting her lip. The urge was animal. Unnerving. Entirely out of her experience.

But how right it felt. Perhaps that was what unbalanced her most.

He spoke against her neck. "*Have* I kissed you, then?"

"Not yet," she whispered.

"Then you should be content."

"I am certainly awake."

He pulled away a little, just far enough to show her his appreciative smile. "Shall we walk?"

"By all means," she said, and gave him her hand.

Seven

A BELL CHIMED IN THE DISTANCE, A MELODIOUS ACCOMPANIMENT to a chorus of voices raised in song. It lured Emma from sleep, drawing her upward through half-formed dreams. Her eyes opened. Dusk glowed lavender on the white walls of the small room, and past the open archway, in the courtyard, shadows were welling.

She'd slept the day away, then. Fair turnabout for the hellish trek they'd endured. They had come upon this village shortly after dawn, alerted by the bright voices of young women gathering at a well. The well water, fed to her from a dipper by a girl with amber eyes, had tasted impossibly sweet—divine ambrosia, life itself. Warm hands had drawn her away from the Marquess, patting her shoulder, guiding her to this small hut where a stooped, wrinkled woman laid down a tray of lentils, spinach, and butter-fried bread. Emma had eaten with her fingers, finding no shame in it as the grandmother nodded encouragement.

The song outside drew her out of the hut now and into the lane. The village of Sukhpur was clean and peaceful, a curving line of thatched, whitewashed cottages bordering a tree-lined lane. Fading light filtered through the peepul leaves, dappling the dusty path. She started in the direction of the large white banyan tree at the foot of the village; its ten or fifteen separate trunks rose beneath a single united awning of leaves. As she rounded the turn, she glimpsed the source of the music: a stone building topped by a gleaming pyramidal canopy. A Hindu temple.

She took a seat beneath the banyan and spent a long moment studying the geometrical patterns drawn in rainbow chalk on the houses' packed-earth walls. A group of monkeys, tails cocked upright, jumped off a roof nearby and strutted past her. She smiled, her eyes following them until they disappeared.

From inside the temple came a chorus of bells. She stepped up onto the banyan's protruding root to peer inside. A large group of women and men sat on the floor, facing a table at the very front. On the table rested a small statue of a six-armed, blue-skinned flutist. She knew very little about the native religions, but it seemed safe to assume that he was the god they worshipped.

A man in white stood, holding a silver tray upon which jars of oil burned. While he waved the tray, drawing smoke rings around the statue, a younger man next to him rang the bell she'd heard from her hut. How mysterious.

The bell stopped just as the singing did, and then

everyone stood and approached the man with the tray. He smeared something on each of their foreheads, between the eyes. The Marquess, she saw with a shock, was one of the first recipients.

She was ducking back down when he turned and saw her. Someone had given him a change of clothes. His calf-length tunic and loose trousers were in the native style, made of simple homespun cotton with no ornamentation. His hair was freshly washed, rippling black and thick to just below his ears, and the red dot on his forehead called attention to his eyes, an impossible greener-than-green. If Marcus had reviled him before, he would have been apoplectic now, for Lord Holdensmoor looked anything but English.

When he reached her side, he said, "You look as though you've swallowed a frog."

His feet were bare! She raised her eyes to his. "You're Hindu, my lord?"

He came to a stop. "Please, it is beyond ridiculous at this point."

She surrendered a small smile. "You're Hindu, Julian?"

"My mother's mother is Hindu. I honor her beliefs, when I am asked to do so." He drew her up by the hand. "You look much better. But Kamala-ji said you wouldn't accept the clothing she offered you."

"My hostess? Oh, was she offering me that clothing?" There had been a pile of clothing shown to her during dinner, but since she'd had no clue what the woman was saying, she had simply nodded and smiled and continued to eat. "I thought she was asking if I thought they were pretty."

His mouth quirked. "And did you?"

"I did actually, yes." She smoothed a hand down the single braid the old woman had made of her hair the evening before. This talk of clothes was making her acutely aware of her rumpled state. Her skirts were soiled beyond repair; what had been rose was now, for the most part, brownish-gray. "I hope she hasn't retracted the offer. I'd like a change of outfits. And a bath, if possible." She gestured toward the temple. "Was the entire village there?"

"Only the Hindus. The Mussulman services are at the prayer wall, about a mile away."

"Why so far?"

He shrugged, propping a shoulder against one of the tree's trunks. "Invading armies would erect them wherever their forces camped. The villagers have probably been using that wall for five hundred years now."

She tried a smile. "Habits are hard to break."

"In some cases." He ran a hand up his forehead, shoving away a thick handful of hair. He looked tired.

"What's wrong? Didn't you sleep?"

"A little." He sighed. His hand dropped back to his side. "I've had some bad news."

Her tenuous peace evaporated. "It's not just Delhi and Meerut, is it?"

He shook his head and took her hand. "This entire area seems to be in an uproar."

"Then where will we go?"

"Sapnagar is still the plan." He looked down to where her hand rested in his, and smiled in some private amusement. Twining his fingers in hers, he overturned their hands, and studied the paleness of her palm. "Some believe your fate is written here," he said, tracing the long line from her middle finger to her wrist. The touch had a disproportionately strong affect; a bolt of heat shot through her stomach. His fingers moved to bracket her wrist, rubbing lightly over the creases that ringed the base of her palm. "These, here, signify great good fortune. And here"—his caress shifted back to the long line dividing her palm—"is your life line. You'll live a long, healthy time."

What poppycock. And yet—she supposed that the fact she still lived might be considered good fortune. She had a fleeting glimpse of herself, old and bent, battered but still surviving. Everyone she had known, gone. No one and nothing remaining but herself. It seemed a ridiculous thing to wish for. She did not like to hear that it might be inevitable.

She withdrew her palm. "A bath," she said. "Please."

The pond stood within a grove of peepul trees at a slight remove from the village. Peacocks roamed the fragrant bushes of tuberose and jasmine, and the surface of the water formed a perfect mirror for the violet dusk above. Julian had noticed that she had an eye for beauty, but she stiffened as she came into the clearing. When she reached out to catch his arm, he realized he had expected this. Had been waiting for it.

"I thought—" Her fingers worked convulsively into his skin. "I don't know what I thought." She let go of him and sank onto a rock, fingering her braid. "Go ahead. I'll wait here."

He lowered himself to her side. She had no talent for hiding her thoughts; her eyes always gave her away.

They lingered now, anxious, on the pond. "I wish I had my sketchbook," she said. When he did not reply, she turned to him inquiringly.

He made a pointed survey of her, toes to head. Ah, and there came the color back into her cheeks. He was developing a rather perverse taste for making her blush; no doubt it was related to his curiosity about how far down the blush actually traveled.

"What?" she said. "Why are you looking at me like that?"

"You said you wanted to bathe. This is where the villagers come for it. I had to make a special request that we be left alone for a bit." He leaned forward, placing a hand on her knee; her breath audibly caught as he slid a finger down her soft calf. It occurred to him that his motivations might not be as noble as he told himself. A great deal of him simply wanted to get her down to her shift.

Ah, well. He'd made no bids for sainthood. "You would not believe how many villagers are curious to know what a memsahib looks like out of her skirts." He felt terribly in sympathy with them on that account. "There's a rumor that English mems must be deformed. Why else would they need to disguise their limbs with such strange conical contraptions?"

She shot him a laughing look, evidently trying to determine whether or not he was serious. The crests of her cheeks were scattered with new freckles. It was not a look generally sought by Englishwomen; he wondered if they would change their minds if they knew how tempting such sunspots could be. Like a map bidding a man to trace them with his lips, his tongue.

He pressed forward. "Emma, you do realize that if you want to return to England, you'll have to travel by ship?"

Her laughter faded. He felt the loss of it physically, like a muscle pulled in his chest, as she turned away. She ripped a flower from the ground and began to pluck away the petals. "I have nightmares. I admit that. And I would not feel at peace in the water any longer. But it doesn't mean I can't board a ship."

"It's your choice to swim or not," he said. "But better to face it here than in Calcutta."

She lifted her chin. "Why on earth do you care?"

There was a smile rising up inside him now; he let it touch his lips. "A good question." He lay back on his elbows and made a show of contemplating the clouds.

"You'd—" She exhaled slowly. "You'd come in the pool with me?"

"Of course."

"But—I'd ruin my shift."

"Kamala-ji has clothes for you."

"This is silly. I don't need to do this."

"I beg to differ," he said dryly. "You are perfectly filthy."

"Thanks very much!"

He rolled onto one elbow to face her. "More to the point, you aren't the sort to let your fears have the best of you."

She narrowed her eyes. "I'm not afraid. I said it was *silly.*"

"And God *forbid* we should be so unchristian a thing as silly."

She closed her eyes. "All right," she whispered.

"Good girl." He rolled to his feet and pulled her up by one hand, leading her down to the water's edge. She paused there to kick at the surface. The ripples radiated out, disappeared into the depths. Then, on a jerky move, she reached for the hem of her tattered dress and yanked it over her head. "Don't look," she said in a muffled voice.

That was bloody unlikely. Nevertheless, he made a show of inspecting the treetops as she shuffled into the shallows. He heard the whispering slide of laces, and then, a few moments later, the snick of a steel busk being opened. Ah, the depravities of modern fashion. Greatly to be regretted, that one could undress oneself.

A splash announced the end of the corset. "I saw them drown, you know." He glanced at her. Her face was pale again, her freckles pronounced. "I saw their faces as the wave swept them under."

"You loved them very much," he said.

"I still do." She shook her head. "This is stupid; we should just—"

"They must have loved you as well, to accompany you here, to want to see you safely arrived."

She blinked. "I suppose. Sometimes—sometimes I doubt it. I think of all the things I did wrong—that I still do wrong. I was never the dutiful daughter. Always in trouble. I couldn't sit still, I wasn't obedient—"

"You were theirs," he murmured. "You were perfect because you were theirs."

She tried to smile; he saw the effort. But her lips were trembling. She covered her mouth with one hand. "I suppose."

"You know."

"I know," she said softly, and took one large step forward before coming up short.

He saw her flinch; it registered through her whole body. It took immense restraint not to draw her back out. She bit a finger and shook her head. "Ridiculous," she muttered, and her eyes began to shimmer with tears. He had never seen her cry when Lindley was not involved; he felt, suddenly, like the worst sort of bastard. "This should be just like stepping into a bath," she said. "Shouldn't it?"

He stepped up so he stood at her side. "I used to swim as a boy in the lake outside Auburn Manor. Drove my grandfather mad, trailing muddy water over the carpets. For all his pretensions at playing the duke, he'd have made a more convincing housekeeper."

"But there *is* a difference," Emma said distractedly. "One can drown in a pond, you know. One doesn't drown in the bath. In fact, it's very likely, odds are, someone *has* drowned here. Did you ask about that in the village?"

"No."

"But don't you think it likely? If they use it so regularly? If it's the only place they bathe? It's very easy to overestimate one's strength, in the water. . . ."

"Not your strength," he said.

"I can't—" She bit her lip, gnawing furiously. She took another step. Again he followed. The water was now up to his calves, and the tops of her knees.

"One wonders," she said.

"What does one wonder?"

Her voice was very soft now. "Who's at the bottom."

He took the lead this time, stepping in front of her.

"Personally, I always liked to float on my back," he said as he turned back to her—and like a fist to the gut, the sight of her knocked the wind from him. The shift, oh, the shift was a piece of wickedness, thin enough to reveal the shadows of her breasts, and the darkness between her thighs. She was beautifully formed, and the fabric was so thin that if he touched her, he would feel everything—the pebbling texture of her nipples; the heat where he would make her wet. "It's . . ." He cleared his throat. "It's remarkably easy to do. I'm sure you've done it before. I would make monsters out of the clouds." Christ, what was he on about? "Clouds, yes. It was a sight more interesting than my Latin lessons."

"You—know the classics?" she gasped. She had been inching forward steadily as he spoke; he watched her lower half disappear beneath the surface with an utterly unconscionable sense of regret.

"Well, and I did go to Cambridge," he said. "Actually took the double first, though I repented for it later. It made my grandfather too damned pleased with himself."

"The double first!" She turned to stare at him. "In mathematics *and* classics!"

"Let me guess. You know Latin?"

"And some Greek. And calculus—" She took a sideways step, and then thought better of it, retreating to shallower ground. She was soaked up to her armpits, and it had a brilliant effect on the chemise. He knew exactly what she would feel like now, in his hands, beneath his mouth; what she would look like, when he pulled off that ridiculous excuse for a shift and—

Hell. This had not been his brightest idea.

"Shall we float?" he asked. She glanced at him in surprise; no doubt she was wondering why his voice had dropped a bloody octave.

"Very . . . very well." She held her breath as she tilted onto her back—then shook her head violently and splashed back to her feet. "No. I cannot."

"Let me help you." He moved through the water to her. No illusions of virtue now remained to him. He simply wanted to touch her.

She closed her eyes as his hands pressed around her waist. Such a beautiful thing, this fleshly curve; corsets had clearly been invented by monks. Schooling himself with deep, even breaths, he slid his hands up to her shoulders, then around to her shoulder blades as she lowered herself toward him.

When the water came up to her ears and cheeks, her eyelashes fluttered wildly. He stood above her, waiting. It would be a better sign if she would open her eyes, but if she did not choose to, then who could blame him for failing to restrain his own? He drank in the sight of her, wondering at himself as he did. Like a green boy.

Her throat moved as she swallowed. "You've got me," she said.

"I do."

Up came her lashes.

"See any clouds of interest?"

She frowned. "Medusa, I think. Those twigs coming off the main section are the snakes." She lifted her arm to point, and the movement unbalanced her. It would have been an easy recovery, save that she gasped and started to thrash in panic.

He grabbed her under her arms and hauled her to her

feet. His hand closed on one breast—by accident, please God; he did not think he was so depraved yet as to take advantage of her fear. She froze beneath his touch, and he immediately made to pull away.

Her own hand came up and held him to her.

His turn now to inhale in surprise.

"Let me try again," she said quietly. For a moment he could not make sense of the words; then chagrin hit him. She was only trying to gather her courage.

Her head came around, and she met his eyes over her shoulder. The fear was still there, but something new accompanied it: something that had his entire body tightening, in a primitive promise to meet her tease and raise her one. She smiled slightly, and sank down out of his grasp, back into a float.

Damn this climate. Even the water was not cold. With a laugh at himself, he slid down next to her, so they were floating side by side.

She was still not entirely at peace; he could follow her journey through the peaks and valleys of fear by the rhythm of her breath—now rapid and shallow, now long and slow. After a few minutes, he decided it was enough. "Can you bear it now?"

She turned her head to look at him. "More and more, Julian." And she reached out to take his hand in hers.

As they came back over the rise into the village, a wave of cries went up from a group milling outside the temple. Emma tracked the focus of their attention to the far end of the village.

A group of horsemen was thundering into the town.

Julian uttered a short and very graphic word. He grabbed her hand and drew her back behind the tree. "Sit down," he said sharply, and then, when she failed to obey immediately, shoved her to the ground. He joined her there, his fingers steepled at his lips as he followed the band's approach.

The three men wore the bright red jackets of the British infantry, and while two of them sported saffron turbans, the third carried his black shako beneath his arm—like a head, she thought, some horrible hunting trophy.

As two women ran out to meet them, the Marquess exhaled. "They've come to see their families."

Her heart was beating a drum roll in her throat. "What should we do?"

"We wait."

"But they'll kill us!"

"Not all the sepoys are taking part in the killing. Besides, they could be deserters. But the first thing we must do is get you into Indian clothes. Right now you stand out at a hundred yards."

"But they'll see us!"

"No," he said. "Look, they're going into the temple. Come on."

The clothes offered to her the night before were still sitting in the hut: a loose, short-sleeved blue shirt that fell below her hips, a long red skirt that fastened by way of a drawstring, and a matching length of red material that she supposed was meant to serve as a head covering. The cloth was light and coarse, easy to put on; she had just yanked the shirt over her head when her elderly hostess rushed inside. She babbled at Emma, then threw up her hands. Grabbing Emma's wrist, the woman pulled her out into the courtyard.

The Marquess emerged from one of the small rooms. "*Kya baat hai?*"

He listened intently as the elderly woman answered, then nodded once. The woman gave Emma a shove toward him, and raced back outside.

He looked at her and sighed. "Come, we're to hide on the roof."

She followed him to the rickety-looking ladder set in one corner of the courtyard, hiking up her skirts when he motioned for her to precede him. "Are you sure?" she asked as she began to climb. "Isn't this the most exposed place in the house?"

"Not where we're going." His tone was resigned. "Stay down on your knees," he added, as she stepped onto the flat, whitewashed roof. She sank down, watching as he pulled the ladder up after him.

He led her to what she initially assumed was a chimney, although of course houses with open courtyards wouldn't need such a thing. In fact, it was a large, flat-bottomed receptacle for rainwater. Thanks to the dry season, it stood empty, but it was barely big enough for the both of them. Emma tucked her knees as far into her chest as possible. The Marquess's legs were considerably longer than hers, and after a few moments' struggle to accommodate her position, he settled his hands on her ankles.

"Emma, I'm sorry," he said, sounding thoroughly

amused, "but you're going to have to put your feet on my lap."

"You can't just squeeze?"

He laughed. "I'm a flexible man, but I'm not going to *squeeze* any further unless I break a few bones first."

She lifted her feet. He slid down beneath them to the ground and crossed his legs in the native fashion; even so, his knees brushed either side of her hips, and her bottom pressed against the juncture of his calves. She reached out to yank down the hem of her skirt.

"We won't be up here long," he said. "Just until they go to dinner."

"You think this is funny?"

"More like absurd."

She nodded and closed her eyes. But, robbed of vision, she became aware of new sources of disturbance. He had a distinct smell: sandalwood and something darker, mysterious and unmistakably male. It pulled at her stomach, like the scent of baking bread when she was famished. It made no sense. She wasn't hungry at all. Yet the sensation intensified every time he shifted slightly, thigh muscles moving beneath the thin soles of her slippers. It made her feel shaky.

His hand on her breast had been hot and firm. She could still feel it cupped around her.

She opened her eyes to seek new focus, and found he was watching her. His face revealed nothing save the genius of an unfair God, who had squandered so much beauty on a single man.

Perhaps her eyes were better shut after all.

"Is it hard," she began, and then stopped, appalled at

what she'd been about to ask. *Is it hard to be so handsome?* She must be sun-addled! How he would tease her if she asked that!

His brows lifted in question, and when she only shook her head, he sighed, tipping his own head back against the wall. The movement exposed a long length of throat. His hair was startlingly black, his skin a deep gold against the white of the wall. If she were to paint his portrait, she would use only those shades to capture him—along with a touch of the purest, brightest green for his eyes.

She made a faint, impatient noise. This was ridiculous. She had always admired his looks. That they should suddenly become so singularly *fascinating* struck her as absurd. She'd do better to worry about surviving the next hour.

The sun had gone down entirely now, but their enclosure blocked the breeze, so it was dreadfully hot. The braid from last night was still in place, and almost fully dried; she reached back to lift the heavy mass, twisting it around and tucking it between her skull and the wall. A bead of sweat snaked from her temple down her throat, and she caught it with a finger, wiping it across her collarbone. For some cool water, she thought wistfully. Dear God, for *ice.* At least she was no longer in English clothing.

"It will be difficult to get used to wearing a corset again," she whispered.

"So don't."

She rolled her eyes. "Wouldn't that be lovely. Alas, I'd never be able to set foot in society."

"Yes, and I'm sure you would miss that terribly."

His words arrested her. There was no judgment in them, only a gentle sort of mockery, as if he thought—as if he knew—that she did not, in truth, care a fig.

"Tell the truth," she said slowly. "Wouldn't you be shocked?"

He gave her a lazy smile. "Try to shock me, Emma. Go ahead. I promise you I would enjoy it." His voice pitched lower. "The way you're looking at me . . . I rather like it. No, no—don't look away. What a delicious blush. I must say, it does the most charming things to your skin."

Voices! She slammed a hand against his mouth and jerked her head in the direction of the noise. He inhaled sharply, making her acutely aware of his lips against her palm.

The voices sharpened in apparent dissent. She removed her hand and looked to him anxiously. His eyes were shut, his head cocked in concentration. As he listened, a frown tightened his brow. Not a good sign. She wrapped her arms around her torso, rocking slightly to vent nervous energy.

"Oh, bloody hell," he whispered. "The sepoys are trying to get the priest's blessing to fight the British, but he's refusing to give it. So they're going to prove to him that the stars are aligned in their favor. They're looking for the ladder to the roof."

"What!" She started to rise, but he dragged her back down. The voices were nearing.

They had found a way up, then. They were on the roof.

She was not ready to die. She didn't feel she was meant to, not after all she had survived already. But it seemed that Julian had misread her palm. She stared at him as he pushed her as far down as possible, wondering if this would be the last sight she ever saw. He met her eyes, but his attention seemed inwardly focused, his expression blank.

And then he focused on her, and he smiled.

It carried the force of a physical slap, that smile. It shocked her to her bones. He had shown her a great many smiles since she'd met him—enigmatic, amused, mocking; cheerful, mischievous, grimly determined. But this one she had never seen. It stole her breath more effectively than fear. An angel's curve of lips, this: a gentle benediction, a silent understanding. An acknowledgment of the strangeness of a God that would lead them to such an end. Most inexplicably, a sweet reassurance that he would not complain of having had to share it with her.

They stared at each other, and his expression changed yet again, the smile fading before a new intensity. She recognized now the message it held. She leaned toward his kiss.

His mouth on hers defeated her alarm. This slow, heated exchange of lips and breath and tongue brought out something else entirely—a strange exaltation—as though her heart, sensing the end, had spread out through her veins. Her inhalation was deep and startled, and his tongue traced the passage of her breath, tasting her with thorough and increasingly ungentle care.

"Are bhai chalo chalo jaldi dekho! Tum! Angrezi! Niklo vahaan se! Haath uthaao!"

Julian exhaled, drawing back from her and raising his hands above his head. She lay there for a moment, dazed, and then raucous male laughter registered in her consciousness.

"Get up, Emma." He was not looking at her, but at the sepoy who pressed a bayonet directly against his heart.

Eight

She stood, her legs shaking so badly she had to grip the sides of the well to remain upright. There were only two sepoys on the roof. The one threatening Julian backed away a pace, motioning for them to step over the wall.

She scrambled over, and the other soldier grabbed her, dragging her away. The armed man said something which caused his companion to burst into laughter.

The priest spat out a sharp word. Reaching down, he yanked off his shoe. With a bold stroke, he knocked the bayonet aside and slapped the armed soldier in the face with the slipper. The sepoy snarled, a guttural expression of rage.

Emma glanced quickly to Julian, who looked on with seeming dispassion as an argument appeared to ensue between the priest and sepoy. The man holding her tightened his grip, clearly distressed. He interjected something in a high, rapid voice. When the armed soldier ignored him, he spat, barely missing Emma's foot.

The one with the rifle snatched the priest's shoe and raised it over his head.

Silence fell, unmistakably tense. The priest held out his hand in an imperious command. The sepoy shook his head; he would not return the shoe. He said something very softly, and then hurled the shoe at the old man's head.

The soldier who'd been guarding Emma shouted; at the same time, Julian lunged. He took the sepoy with the bayonet to the ground. They rolled in a tangle of limbs, Julian emerging on top. He landed three punches in the man's face. The crack of bone against bone rang in the air, sickeningly distinct. Then he wrenched away the gun and leapt up, pressing the point to the throat of the man on the ground.

A knife bit into her neck. The sepoy holding her barked out a warning. Julian did not look their way, but the line of his jaw abruptly tightened.

"Don't move," he said to her.

She opened her mouth to answer, but the knife dug deeper. She felt a warm trickle of blood pool at the base of her collarbone. One little bit more, she thought. One bit.

The priest clutched his head with his hands and wailed something long and despairing. Julian shot back a string of rapid words, then placed his fingers over his brow, next to the mark he'd been given at the temple. On the ground, the sepoy rolled over and then up to a kneeling position. He asked something. After a hesitation, Julian nodded, gesturing briefly to the cut down his cheek.

The kneeling sepoy laughed—a strained sound. He waved to Emma for the benefit of his companion. "*Angrezi mem unki hai,*" he said.

Angrezi. It was a word Emma knew: *English.* A chill moved through her. What did Julian think to do here?

She looked to him. He conducted a brief dialogue with the man on the ground. His voice, low and husky around those foreign syllables, barely seemed familiar. Something he said seemed to amuse the sepoy; the man grinned, revealing teeth stained crimson. Marcus had written to her once of this strange phenomenon, so she knew it was the effect of some herbal mixture called *paan,* which was chewed and spat like tobacco. Still, in her agitated state, she fancied it the stain of blood. A bad omen—no need to look to the stars.

A hysterical laugh threatened to rise. She choked it back. It would only force the blade deeper into her throat.

With sudden cheer, the sepoy pushed to his feet. He strolled toward her, as over his shoulder Julian met her eyes. She could read nothing in his expression, but he looked at her fiercely, the force of his regard holding her still as the soldier came up to examine her.

After an agonizingly thorough inspection, the longest seconds of her life, the soldier gestured for the other sepoy to release her. "*Theek hai,*" he said to the Marquess. "*Pandit-ji ko bandook de dijiye.*"

Julian handed the rifle to the priest.

The sepoy took her arm in a rough grip, pushing her back to Julian's side.

"Thank God," she muttered. "How did you—"

"Quiet." He put his palm on her shoulder, wheeling her around so her back pressed into him. The sepoys stood together now, watching avidly. The priest clutched the rifle to his chest, but the anxiety in his wide eyes afforded her no comfort.

She felt Julian's hand tugging on her braid. He leaned forward to murmur into her ear, "For your life, trust me." Out of the periphery of her vision, she saw his hand rise. He motioned to one of the soldiers.

Who stepped forward to hand him a knife.

Shock sheeted over her like ice, blurring the scene, filling her ears with an odd, high buzz. She shut her eyes, swallowing hard. What . . . what . . .

But what she felt was not the bite of the blade. With steady pressure, he pulled down on her braid, and then—with one sharp, confusing tug—she was free. The sudden unbalancing rocked her forward. He caught her by the elbow and pulled her back to her feet.

She did not understand what had happened, but the soldiers were grinning; the one with the rifle cackled and stepped forward. Julian tossed something over. Her braid. Dear God, he had cut off her hair! Her hands flew to her scalp. Her head felt so light; why hadn't she noticed immediately? Her hair, her *hair,* he was handing her hair to that scoundrel—

The priest threw the rifle to Julian. He caught and cocked it in one unbroken move, but did not aim it at anyone. "*Jaa,*" Julian said to the men. "*Ghodon ko chhodkar jaa. Theek hai?*"

Emma felt her legs give way. As she sank to the ground, the sepoys climbed down the ladder.

* * *

They took the sepoys' horses. Apparently the men felt in charity with Julian. He had told them that she was his captive and, in the spirit of camaraderie, they had offered the spare mounts of the Englishmen they'd killed, so he might better evade British patrols.

She never did remember much of the ride that followed. A resignation had fallen over her that fear and curiosity could not penetrate. When death seemed imminent, one simply did as one must.

At moonrise, they drew up at the crumbling remains of an ancient edifice. Emma hooked her horse's reins over a broken pillar and wandered through the toppled slabs. The rosy sandstone was ghost-pale in the starry dark. The night wind sighed through the ruins.

Finally she spied a small niche in a collapsed wall that suited her purpose. She sank down into it. Her shoulders barely fit, but the stone embrace halted her tremors. She felt for the remnants of her hair, the ends that trailed raggedly at her shoulders, and clenched them hard.

Time passed—a minute, an hour, maybe centuries. She could not be sure, not in this strange land where barren desert concealed the sprawling skeleton of a mighty palace. Where night did not edge gently upward from the land, indigo to violet to fading lilac, but plummeted all in an instant from the flaming sky above, pitching the world into a darkness striated with countless stars.

The sight was somehow painful. Crossing arms over bent knees, she cradled her head in her own private darkness.

How alone she was here. She could sense the oppressive immensity of the barren plain, stretching out empty in all directions. Once these ruins must have been the center of something grand. Some sparkling world—unable, in its splendor, to conceive of its own end. The laughing men and women who had reigned here would have gasped at the audacity of their soothsayer, did he foretell the anonymity with which time would punish them. *Your world will be violently, irrevocably destroyed.*

Everything fell away, in the end. Everyone, as well.

"What," Julian murmured, "can you possibly be thinking?"

She raised her head. He was too big to join her between the fallen stones, so he sat at the opening, his legs crossed and drawn inward before him. Not an English pose. But he'd had no difficulty convincing those sepoys of his native blood. They'd believed she was his captive. That he, too, had killed Englishmen during these wild days of anarchy.

What was she thinking? "That I don't know you," she said softly.

The moon was clouded over, the starlight too weak to reveal his reaction. Only a faint suggestion here, a shadow there, suggested he faced her at all. But what use was vision when appearances proved so misleading? He could not be defined by his looks, or his name, or by the moments she had shared with him. Even his current silence held a quality strange to her. She had never known someone who could seem so still.

But it served no end, did it? No matter how unnoticeable Julian made himself, he would still draw others' attention. Some people were like that; they could not escape criticism, because they never quite managed to convince themselves of the role everyone believed they should fill.

She searched her heart. It did not disgust her, this foreignness about him. How could it, when it had saved her life? But it unnerved her all the same. It made her feel, in an immediate way, just as this entire country did on a vast and impersonal level: hopelessly weary, terribly obvious, horribly helpless. Exposed, yes, and vulnerable. His eyes saw more, even in the darkness, than she meant to reveal.

"How can I say you know me," he said steadily, "when you know best what you feel? If I seem a stranger to you, then I am."

She pressed her folded hands to her lips, taking comfort in the hard dig of her nails. "Could you not have made this easier? Could you not say, 'Yes, Emma, you do know me; I am in this trouble alongside you; and what I did, I did only to save your life, that's all.' "

His sigh was the barest hint of breath. "Because you already know that. That's not what you mean when you say I'm a stranger to you."

Her hands fell away. "What *do* I mean, then? When you behave the way you do—what else *could* I mean?"

No one would have attributed his laughter to amusement. It was cold, horrible to hear. "Do you really want me to read your soul for you? Do you want me to explain why it horrified you to see me deal with those sepoys? Why it would have been easier for you to watch me kill them, than to see me hand them your hair?" His pause was mercilessly precise. "Or do you want to hear me wonder whether your opinion would have been different if it were white men we talked of killing?"

She slammed her palm against the rock. "No! *That is not true*!"

"Then don't make me wonder," he said. "Tell me yourself."

The air burst from her lungs, a breath she'd been holding for perhaps forever. "I don't know what to make of you! One moment you're the man I met in the契vershams' garden, and the next, you're someone else entirely!"

"I see." At length, he said, "If you must *make* something of me, the days ahead won't be easy for you. I am *not* just an English aristocrat, Emma. I was born in this country, and for many years of my childhood I knew only two words of English—my first and last name." His words gained speed, took on a sharper edge. "And I must say, if you think I have changed for the worse, that I have somehow *lost my way,* you are badly mistaken. The man you met in Delhi, the one you think you know—the fucking Marquess of Holdensmoor—*he* is the act. He is what I was forced to become."

His voice softened. "Of course I did what I did to save your life. Do you think I had a particular desire to chop off your hair? But they wanted to humiliate you. I might have fought them before letting it come to that—I thought of it. But the odds were against me. And if they had taken me down, then what? Perhaps they would have killed you. Perhaps they would have raped you. But above all, you must understand that they wanted to do to you what has been done to them. Emma, this land has been *crushed* by the English. Its wealth stripped, its honor trampled. You are not dealing with penny-dreadful villains here; you are dealing with embittered human beings who have been robbed of their dignity, their autonomy, their sense of self-worth. And *that* is what this mutiny is about. Not animal grease on bullet cartridges, or any of that nonsense. It is simply the inevitable result of everything the British have done to India."

In her shock, she could grip only one coherent thought. "*You want them to win.*"

He sighed. "Emma. What I want has nothing to do with bloodshed. And as for the mutiny, it won't end in Delhi—but I do not think it will succeed. The native populace simply doesn't have the resources, organizational or material, that they'd need to defeat the British."

The British. As though he weren't one of them. God, what a fool she was! He had all but *said* he wasn't one of them! And so had Marcus, she remembered.

She moistened her lips, struggled to find her voice. "You're Indian then. You don't consider yourself English. You are Indian."

His tone was dry enough to burn. "What nice, convenient labels. If one works for you, by all means, don't mind me. Few ever do, in that regard."

She peered blindly into the darkness where he was sitting. His words were so bitter that they curdled the air. Yet prevalent in her mind was not distress, but sadness. There were worse things than being alone, she saw now; there were terrible sorts of intimacy as well. "I have failed you. Or . . . disappointed you. You think I'm a narrow-minded fool, just like the rest of the memsahibs."

In the silence of the desert night, his inhalation was audible. "No," he whispered, and somehow, with his cat-eyed vision, found her hands. "Never that. Come out of there, sweetheart."

Boneless with relief, she let him pull her forward, into the open air, into his lap. And in this wild darkness, in the middle of an empty earth, she grieved for both of them—indeed, for every human in this wretched world, who must face the trials life offered, negotiate the changes wrought by time. There was so little joy to cling to, so few certainties. Yet humans continued to endure. Continued to hope. The undeniable compulsion to survive powered them onward, like Sisyphus on his mountain.

When many minutes had passed, she asked, very quietly, "When does the price of our survival become too dear?"

He spoke into her hair. "That is not the sort of thing you decide until you've also decided to die."

She turned her face into his shoulder. His fingers closed over the back of her neck. She mistook it, for a second, as a gesture meant to comfort. Then his grip tightened slightly, and he held her harder against him, and she realized it was something else entirely. Possessiveness? That was the closest she could come to naming it. His touch said that he was taking the right to do this: to hold her to him, even if she wished to go.

She could not resent it. It actually seemed rather wondrous. His hands had performed miracles. Her life had rested in them, balanced in their capable grace. And now they rested on her, and their grace infused her as well.

Overwhelmed by the thought, she reached up to take his palm, to study the callused surface, the elegant, tensile length of his fingers. She traced the faint groove he had called the life line. He drew a sharp breath, his fingers closing abruptly over her own.

She looked up. The shadows veiled him from her, but she could feel his presence all along her skin. Heat, and vibrancy, and that restrained, careful power. She had seen how the Anglo-Indians in Delhi watched him as he passed through their drawing rooms, how their manner swung between sycophancy and contempt. He would have to be restrained around such people, especially when he could—if he liked—crush them so easily.

His face lowered to hers, so close that she felt his ragged exhalation against her lips. "Emma, you can trust me with your life. But I am not your brother. You cannot trust me in this."

"I have no brother," she said softly. "Nor mother, nor father, now. If I trust you with my life, I trust you with everything I have."

Something changed in him—a sudden focus to his silence, or the abrupt suspension of his breath. "Oh, you foolish girl." He carried her hand to his face, placing it against the rough stubble on his jaw. Caught by that intensely masculine sensation, she barely noticed as his hair brushed by her chin. And then he laid his lips into the curve of her neck.

He sucked lightly there for a moment; and then his teeth scraped up the underside of her chin, and conscious thought collapsed.

His mouth felt lightly up her jaw, shaping the outline of hers. As she inhaled, his tongue just barely entered her, teasing the sensitive flesh, tracing the corners. Yes, this was what she wanted. Enough of thinking, and analyzing, and mourning for a future that would not come to pass. She wanted *this*. Each flickering taste created its own dream of the future, luring her to yearn for something more, something . . . harder, more fierce. His lips were gentle, but she did not feel gentle; she felt alive, furiously alive, and his warmth and solidity called to her. Her hand slipped into his hair, pulling him fully against her.

If he read her thoughts, she was not surprised. Either way, he gave her what she wanted. His mouth fully opened on her own, gifting a hot, deep kiss as he pressed her back into the dirt.

The fabric between them registered in flashes across her mind. It seemed at first a slight annoyance, as she imagined how hot he would be to the touch. Then, in brief, tantalizing episodes, it translated to her—and then denied her—the flexing of his abdomen. The dig of his ribs. The push of his breath as he inhaled. She wanted it gone. It concealed too much.

He grasped her face in his hands to slant her head, to give him deeper access, to fill her. *Yes, do it,* she thought, *consume me, swallow me whole.* Odd feelings with no root tore through her. She felt frenzied, almost angry, ready to jump out of her skin. He would take her before she went. How would she go? Would she die? Would she face the water again? Could anyone keep the promises she suddenly wanted from him? The questions fluttered up through her mind; then his hand was under her skirt, tracing a pattern on the back of one thigh, and they scattered like startled birds. His fingers slid down, gripping her a few inches above her knee, as his mouth ran down her throat.

His sudden pause brought her eyes open. He held

himself over her, breathing hard, and as the moon finally emerged from the clouds, it revealed some complex and impenetrable thought on his face. For an unnerving second, she felt the space again, the immensity. It seemed to open *between* them. She became aware of the silent weight of the ruins, the broken pillars towering in shadow beyond his head.

And then he backed away from her and came up on his knees to strip off his tunic.

He was beautiful. Broad-shouldered, with a musculature carved in shadow and moonlight. Her hands jumped ahead of her mind, reaching out to explore the new territory; he accepted her sweeping strokes with closed eyes. Easy to pull him back down to her. To slide her palms lower and lower down his back, past the indentations at the base of his spine, to the swell of his flexing buttocks. He lifted himself on one arm to nuzzle into the cloth over her breasts.

She said breathlessly, "Take it off."

His surprise registered as a sudden hesitation, and then as a laugh against her shirt. "Not so proper now, are we?"

"I was never good at it," she said. "Take it off."

"As my lady bids," he murmured. He slid her shirt up over her stomach, pausing twice to press a kiss against newly exposed flesh. She grew impatient, and pushed him away. With a twist and a wriggle, she had the shirt over her head. The warm night air felt like another caress along the skin she had bared. She laid her head back on the crumpled shirt, watching him look at her, watching his eyes on her breasts.

He glanced back up to her face. "God, you are beautiful."

She did not feel anything so boring as beautiful. She felt fierce. But she held her tongue, because he would not understand it.

Perhaps he saw it, though. He smiled at her before he lowered his head.

The sight of his lips closing around her nipple took her breath away. She had never looked at herself; it was discouraged, it was sinful. But here she was, bare to him, sucked by him. Sucked like a candy, with the appropriate small noises of pleasure. Her free nipple peaked sharply; she saw her body did not know propriety either. It had been made for this. Oh, the things she had not known! That the soft, sucking noises would make heat build between her thighs. That he could use his teeth—lightly, then not so lightly—to make a slight pain an even greater pleasure.

A lifetime of training in comportment meant nothing when one's knee was touched just so. One's legs fell apart so effortlessly to let a man settle between them.

He was hard and thick against her. "Emma." His mouth opened, but no words came; he seemed to have trouble getting them out. He swallowed. "Here . . . like this . . . Are you sure?"

"You invited me to shock you," she said.

In answer, his thumb dragged roughly over her bottom lip. She caught it between her teeth and bit lightly.

He gasped, and then used his thumb to pull her lip down, to open her to a rough kiss. Rougher and rougher. She liked it. She had always suspected there were other rules, rules she might understand better than the ones she'd been given. She rocked her hips into his; he pulled away and moved down her body, back to her breasts. It dislodged that part of him that had been pressed up against her. She missed the other. "Tell me what to call it," she said breathlessly.

He looked up, his teeth holding her nipple between them. He gave it a delicate flick with his tongue before releasing it. "What?"

As her hand slid down his abdomen, ridged and hard to the touch, the light rasp of her nails drew a broken sound from him. A narrow trail of hair guided her fingertips. She closed her hand over the pulsing length at his groin. "This," she said.

It took him a moment to respond. His voice was soft. "Vocabulary?"

"Yes. The improper sort."

His weight shifted off her; and then his hand was at the waist of her skirt, loosening the ties. She arched up so he could draw it off her, rearrange it under her naked body. His hands spread apart her thighs; she looked down to see him watching himself as he did it. "Your quim," he said, and his eyes caught hers as his fingers slid into her folds. His thumb pressed on a particular spot that made her whole body twitch. "Wholly improper," he said, and gave her a dark smile before bending down.

She gasped as she felt the wet heat of his tongue. It delved into her, now rubbing, now stroking; long, generous licks, as if he were hungry, and she were his sustenance. Unbearable bliss. Her knuckles were at her mouth; she was biting them. She needed something. She needed something more.

His fingers pressed against her entrance. *Yes.* That was it. She lifted herself in a silent plea. His hand pushed slowly inside. He stretched her. Wider now, two fingers and then three. And still his tongue worked steadily, aggressively. Devouring her.

The sensation built, from an inconstant flicker to a steadily mounting hum. And then all at once it was everywhere, distending her nerves until they snapped, ricocheted, pleasure careening, her hips spasming. He held her still as he continued to work her.

"Stop—stop; it's too much."

His mouth pulled away; he rose back over her. "Oh no," he said, breathing unsteadily. His mouth was wet. "You threw down the gauntlet."

"Yes," she said weakly, for now they were face-to-face again, and he fit against her perfectly, and her . . . her *quim* pulsed where the male part of him prodded it. "I did."

"But I'll stop," he said, and laid a kiss under her ear. The spot seemed to interest him; he started to pull away, then reconsidered, leaning down again to explore it further. His teeth closed gently around her skin as his hips pushed into hers.

"Oh! That . . ."

His broken laughter was husky in her ear. "More vocabulary."

"Yes." She moaned as he did something with his hips, which caused the length of him to rub against the spot still sensitized from his mouth. "Your . . ."

"Cock," he murmured. "Yours if you want it." His breath caught as she squirmed. "But—ah, Emma, God above! Decide, if you please."

"Yes," she whispered. "I want it."

His mouth fitted to hers. Slowly he began to push inside her. The sensation was strange; so much thicker than his fingers—delicious—and suddenly—*painful.*

He paused. "This may—"

"Hurt," she said, and dug her fingernails into his buttocks. Yes. It seemed fitting that it should. A sweet hurt, atop so many bitter ones. "Go on."

She bit down on his shoulder as he pressed forward. It was too much—it was not going to be possible—it was . . . done. She inhaled in startlement. He was inside her. Such a feeling of fullness. As he withdrew, she cried out a protest—and then he pushed back in, and hot currents rippled down the backs of her legs, bringing tears to her eyes. He paused inside her—*inside her*—and put his thumb to the corner of her eye.

"Emma," he said quietly. "Are you—"

She pushed her mouth into his blindly, brutally; her hands came up to knot in his hair, her knees curling up to his sides to hold him to her. He made a noise, a rough exhalation, and began to move again. The rhythm called forth something within her; there was no space between them now, nothing in her mind but silence and this beating, pounding rhythm; and the sound of her own muffled moans, and his low gasp as she slid her foot down his calf. His thrusts grew stronger, faster, and her heartbeat and breath kept time. She arched into him: weightless, set free; and helplessly pinned, a delicious conundrum, with no choice but to submit, to yield to him, to lick the sweat from his cheek and let go of everything else. Everything but him.

She cried out and seized around him. He met his end, his body shaking violently beneath her hands.

Perhaps she was shaking as well. She could barely feel where the difference might lie.

He kissed her again, and she opened her eyes to the stars. Infinite and uncountable, bright and cold and distant. They brought her back into her skin. She ran a hand down his damp back. "My God . . ." he whispered.

Behind Julian's head, the ruins were looming, darker than the darkness itself. The earth was so dark, and the ruins so small, compared to the stars.

His head rose, blocking out the sight. He leaned down to kiss her. "Everything in your face," he murmured. "Emma, come back to me. I'm here with you."

Yes, she thought, so he was, and felt something inside her turn over, an old grief or a new hope—the sensation so sharp that she sobbed. It might have startled him; she could not tell by his face, for he was already pulling her up into his lap, his arms wrapping around her as he rocked her.

"I'm here," he said into her ear, as the tears came faster. "Emma, I'm here with you now. Listen to me: I will always be here."

Always, she thought. He said "always," but he had forgotten to say finally. *Finally you are here*. Thank God, finally at last.

Nine

Early the next morning, they drew up before a rocky plateau that burst vertically upward from the plain. Geologically, it seemed so unlikely as to have been dropped there by some wandering giant. A honeycomb of dwellings clung to the bottom slopes of the tableland, whitewashed walls gleaming in the sun.

"Sapnagar village," Emma guessed.

She was riding pillion on Julian's horse; hers had drawn up lame, and was on lead behind them. Julian caught her hand where it sat at the front of his waist. "Fort," he corrected, rubbing a thumb over her palm. "Look again at the plateau."

All morning he had touched her like this, casually and constantly. She felt slightly drunk from it; laughter came up in her throat for no reason. She shaded her eyes with her free hand and squinted through the haze. "Good

Lord! Those are walls at the top, aren't they? They're carved out of the mountain!"

"The fort hasn't been taken in two centuries. And the Maharajah is an old friend of mine. It's the safest place I can imagine."

The winding path led them up through the village. At the top, the entrance to the massive stone fortress was sealed by iron doors, taller than three men put together; they were greening with age and boasted several rows of lethal-looking spikes—to repel an elephant charge, Julian told her.

"Of course," she said. "The Indian equivalent of the log."

His answering laughter—he had laughed a great deal as well this morning—was lost in the scrape of metal. A smaller portal, which she had missed amidst the ornate working of the doors, opened to disgorge two guards dressed in white tunics and saffron turbans. They traded a few brief words with Julian, and then one of the men sent up a shout. The doors groaned inward.

Julian nudged their horse forward, up a sharply twisting flagstone path that was flanked by high stone walls. Fortress, indeed. Also, Emma thought, a rather effective prison, should the owners feel so inclined.

The grade was too steep to allow for anything but a very slow walk. Tired, she let her forehead rest on Julian's back.

The path widened as it topped the plateau, becoming a road that followed the crenellated bastions and ringed the main compound. They dismounted, and a contingent of guards escorted them through a courtyard and garden studded with fountains and statuary. They emerged into a vast marble arcade. The long walk was bisected by a shallow canal dotted with rose petals. Emma inhaled deeply; it smelled delicious.

Julian had been speaking with their escort; now he turned to her, smiling as he beheld her gaping over the water. "It cools the palace," he said. "Emma, it seems we're not the only English guests; the survivors from a nearby station are sheltering here. Will you be comfortable meeting them, and resting a little, while I speak with the Maharajah?"

She was not eager to be parted from him. But she nodded, speculation narrowing her eyes as she watched him move off down the hall. He was flanked by the remainder of the guard, all of whom wore swords at their hips.

Julian, she thought, *I do hope you know what you're doing.*

Her own escort gestured her into a smaller passage. Mazelike paths branched off it. Indeed, the entire architecture bespoke a playful mind. Rounding corners at her guard's heels, she found herself passing balconies that overlooked the rest of the fort: the outer gardens and temples, the dusty yards in which soldiers were training and merchants hawked their wares. Sometimes, from behind screens that permitted light to enter through complex cutouts of flowers and vines, she glimpsed the plain below, stretching out to the burning blue horizon. Occasionally the walls themselves fell away, and she was led through courtyards scented with blooming frangipani and ginger lilies.

She sincerely hoped she would not be expected to find her way back to the entry hall.

They stopped in a small square enclosed by three stories of latticed marble windows. With simple signs, the servant indicated that hers was the entrance on the far side of the patio.

She entered to discover an apartment filled with light. Someone had thrown open the wooden shutters, permitting ingress to the breezes roaming far above the desert floor. The walls were painted in vivid murals, and a large Persian carpet covered the floor. On a low table by the window stood a small copper pot with slits to hold sticks of incense. Otherwise the room seemed to have been designed with British guests in mind. There were English chairs and tables, and a grand canopied bed in one corner.

"Oh, thank the Lord! You must have news!"

Emma turned. She had visitors: two women, one a silver-haired matron, the other an extraordinarily beautiful young girl, with a heart-shaped face and eyes a luminous violet beneath her tangled yellow hair. The girl came forward to grab her hands; there was surprising strength in her slim grip.

"Is it true?" she asked. "Have the troops mutinied? Where did you come from?"

"Anne Marie," the older woman said repressively. "Forgive her, madam; we are very eager for the tidings, but she forgets herself. I am Mrs. Thomasina Kiddell, and this is Miss Stringer."

"Miss Martin," Emma said. "Late of Delhi."

"I see. Bikaner is our station, but we were on our way to Ajmer to join Miss Stringer's father, who had finally sent for her. The Maharajah's men intercepted us en route and insisted we take shelter here. They did tell of a mutiny, but you will understand our doubts, as we had no verification from a *reliable* sort of person." She ran an eye down the native clothing Emma wore, and her upper lip twitched. "As to that, I fear your appearance is answer enough."

"Indeed," Emma said. "The Maharajah spoke truly. The troops in Delhi have mutinied; and in Meerut, too. I know it has spread further, but no more than that."

"Oh!" Anne Marie released her and took a small step back. "Oh—no!" Her eyes flew to Mrs. Kiddell. "They shall *kill* us!"

Mrs. Kiddell looked very pale. "Calm yourself, child."

"*Calm* myself—!" On a muffled sob, the girl fled to the far window. Her narrow shoulders began to heave.

Mrs. Kiddell cast a glance at the chaise longue. "If . . . if I may, Miss Martin."

"By all means." Emma took a seat herself. "I am sorry to be the bearer of bad news, but at least we are safe here. The countryside is very unsettled at present."

"But we *aren't* safe!" Anne Marie turned back to them, her face blotched. "There is a dreadful girl who comes to taunt us—I can't imagine where she learned English, it's very queer—and she tells us that the ladies of the zenana are angry with us being here. They want the Maharajah to throw us to the wolves!"

"I am afraid it is true," Mrs. Kiddell said quietly. She began to pluck at the pilling on her skirt. From the grave dignity about her, Emma gathered that this idle gesture betrayed anxiety in the extreme. "Worse yet, she also says the crown prince of this little kingdom nurses a great hatred of the English. We are trying to introduce a Resident to the court, I believe, and he opposes that. At present he is hunting in Kashmir, but word arrived yesterday that his return is imminent."

Emma shook her head. "But there is no need to worry. I am assured of our safety by a dear friend of the Maharajah himself."

"Yes?" Mrs. Kiddell shrugged. "That may be so, my dear. The Maharajah has been nothing but kindness. But being somewhat familiar with zenana politics, I would be hesitant to rely on his word. A maharani and a crown prince, contriving together, are a formidable power indeed."

Anne Marie's noisy sobs were one thing, but the older woman's carefully contained fear was beginning to disquiet Emma. "You do not understand; Lord Holdensmoor escorted me here with the express idea that it is the *only* place he could ensure my safety."

Anne Marie gasped. "The Marquess? But he is *one* of them! You cannot trust him for an instant!"

"I trust him with my life," Emma said.

Mrs. Kiddell shook her head. "Miss Martin, he is infamous. Even in Bikaner, we have heard rumors—"

Emma came to her feet. "I will bid you good day."

Anne Marie whimpered. Mrs. Kiddell hesitated a moment, then rose. "Come, Anne Marie."

At the door, she turned back. Emma raised her chin beneath the woman's narrow-eyed inspection.

"I do not wish to know what has led you to such a state," Mrs. Kiddell said stiffly. "But I fear it was horrible indeed, and so I will make allowances. Should you wish for more . . . proper . . . attire, you may apply to us. We were traveling in full state, and have our luggage with us across the courtyard."

Emma inclined her head, but made no other move until they were gone from her doorway.

Then her hands fisted at her sides, and she sank back into the seat. There was food laid out on a sideboard; she'd not noticed it before. She stared at the silver dishes. She'd been hungry this morning, but her stomach could take no food now. It was too full of dread.

Emma was curled up asleep on the bed, still wearing the tattered *chanya choli* from Sukhpur. "She needs clothes," Julian said softly.

The woman at his side nodded. "*Haan.* I'll bring them."

He waited until Kavita had gone, then crossed to the bed with the intent to wake her. But at the last moment, something caught him. His fingers curled and withdrew. He drew up a chair, running a hand over his mouth as he considered her.

Emma slept like a child: arms crossed, hands tucked to her sides. Her mouth fell open slightly. Beautiful mouth. Rosy, plump lower lip. But he liked the upper one for its freckle. He could lean over to kiss it. Very gently, so her waking would be gradual. Confusion in her eyes, and then desire. He had the right to touch her now, and he intended to make use of it.

But instead he found himself staring at her hair. The rough ends at her shoulders. His own hand had accomplished that.

A tightness formed in his throat. He could not risk her out there. Not again.

He scrubbed his face. The exhaustion was stupendous. How long since he'd had a full night's sleep? His conversation with the Maharajah still circled through his mind. Rathore-ji was troubled, rightly so. *This hatred of the British burns fiercely, Julian. Even in my own kingdom, there is tinder to burn. But you need not fear. I am not such a fool, to play with a fire that would consume us all.*

And what of Delhi? The Maharajah's men could gather little news. They knew only that the Mughal emperor, Bahadur Shah, had lent his blessing to the mutineers. The city was controlled by them now. The British, in turn, were regrouping in Kurnaul, planning a massive attack.

Strategically, Ajmeri Gate would be an ideal entry point for their forces. One brief, concentrated siege to break through the gate. The houses beneath it would pose little impediment to British mortar and gunpowder. Did his young cousin see that now? Did Deven look at the rickety walls that sheltered his family, and consider how far Julian's gold might take them? Nani-ji would press him to listen to Julian's advice; she had promised as much, in her last letter to him. But age had settled on her heavily, and she was too frail to overrule Deven. Did he imagine, with his naïve, seventeen-year-old pride, that Delhi would stand?

There was no choice, Julian thought. He had to leave Emma here; he had to go.

She murmured in her sleep, and he tensed, ready to wake her from her nightmare. But no, she seemed peaceful; she was only turning over. And perhaps, he thought, perhaps that had been his name she'd spoken, just now.

He moved onto the bed to sit beside her. He ran a

gentle finger over her elbow until she sighed in her sleep and let her arms fall to her sides.

There was a minute, silvered scar at the base of her chin. He had never noticed it. It made him feel ignorant. Impatient as well. There was so much to be said and asked between them. Being with her felt like charting the sea: there were marvels beneath, and they lured him, and he wondered whether he ever might reach the bottom.

"Emma," he said quietly, and pressed a kiss to her parted lips.

She stirred, small twitches and movements. Soft, sleepy noises. He kissed her again, more deeply this time, and ran a hand down her side, to the swell of her hip. Her eyelashes fluttered up; color came into her cheeks. He smiled against her. Fairy tales were wasted on children. Until this moment, even he had not fathomed the power of waking someone with a kiss.

Her arms came around him, and she arched. "Julian." And then, abruptly, her body stiffened. "Julian," she said, in a different voice altogether, and he moved back to let her sit up. "Did you know—there are Englishwomen here—across the courtyard, and they say it is not safe, that there are people in the palace who are plotting against the English."

He opened his mouth, then thought better of his first impulse. The women had obviously frightened her. Bigoted, birdbrained, and no doubt hysterical; God knew what they must have told her. "Emma, they are wrong. The Maharajah has sworn to your safety. But I will speak to them, if you like, explain that their fears are unfounded."

Her hand tightened on his arm. "But it is not the

Maharajah they—" Her eyes shifted past him and she fell silent. He turned.

"Clothes," Kavita said, holding out a silk-wrapped bundle.

Good to see that she still had a talent for poor timing. "Emma," he said as he rose, "this is Kavita-ji."

"Wife of Yuvraj," Kavita said with a smile.

"The crown prince," Julian clarified.

"Oh." Emma still looked distressed. She shook her head slightly, then came to her feet to make a curtsy. "You . . . speak English, Your Highness?"

Kavita laughed. "*Na, na,* Emma *behin,* we are like sisters. Actually, you must call me Kavita only, as *bhaiyya* does when not so formal. *Aur haan,* I am speaking English very well, isn't it?"

"Very well," Emma murmured.

"Hmm. In the zenana they think me smart. But I tell them it is all because of my teacher, Julian *bhai.* I was this high"—she gestured toward the floor—"but *bhaiyya* was very patient. And also I read your English books. *Robinson Crusoe,* yes? *Vaah vaah*!"

"She is too modest," Julian said. "I did start her on the path several years ago, when I was in Amanpur for the summer—"

"My father is Amanpur *ke* ruler," Kavita put in.

"But I cannot take credit for her unique patois."

Kavita laughed. "You make fun of me, *bhaiyya*! It is lucky my family loves you, or I would tell Yuvraj you are mean to me!"

"The crown prince," Emma murmured. She looked dazed. Kavita did tend to have that effect.

"Yes, yes, my husband. Oh, but it is too bad Yuvraj

has not returned from *shikaar*! If he does not come back this week I will be very unhappy. *Aur agar vo aapki mahila se na mile to bahut nakhush honge.*"

Emma took one large step toward him. "What does that mean?"

Her sharp tone caught his attention. Christ—she was not dazed, but . . . afraid? More so, even, than before Kavita had entered the room. What was this? "It means he will be unhappy if he doesn't get to meet you," he said slowly. "Kavita, perhaps you might be kind enough to have someone arrange for food? I believe the dishes are grown cold."

"Oh—*haan*! But while I am gone, you must put on the clothes I have brought. They are for tonight, you know. Tonight there is dancing!" Kavita clapped. "A celebration in honor of your arrival!"

"Thank you," Emma said. "I will try them."

"But—*bhaiyya,* if the servants are to come, I must ask you to leave." To Emma she said, "I am very sorry, I hope you will not mind that we must keep Julian separate? I know your English ways are not so . . . strict. But *nahin to* the servants will talk, they would say there is no honor in our court. Because Julian is my brother, it is very important for him to show *tameez,* to show, how do you say—"

"*Izzat,*" Emma said softly, surprising the hell out of him. "Yes, I have heard of the idea."

Kavita beamed at her. "Yes, very good. Now come, *bhaiyya.*"

"One moment." At her impatient moue, he said more firmly, "I will join you in *one moment.*"

He took Emma by the arm, but did not have to ask; as soon as Kavita disappeared, she said in an undertone, "Julian, that woman—I see she is a very good friend to you, but the ladies across the courtyard—they spoke of her."

"Did they?" It did not surprise him that Kavita had sought them out. She would have few opportunities to practice her English, what with the strict purdah in the palace. Only because he was her *rakhi* brother, and had known her since she was little, did the Yuvraj countenance their connection.

"Yes. They said she has been making threats against them."

The idea was so absurd that it startled a laugh from him. He regretted it immediately; she pulled out of his grip and her eyes flashed an accusation. He retrieved her hand, ignoring her muttered protest. "It must have been a misunderstanding. Emma, you heard her yourself; her grasp of the language is not always . . . precise."

"But it is good enough," she said. "And they spoke as if it had happened more than once, not just one slip of the tongue. As if she had been tormenting them."

"Then they are lying," he said flatly.

"How can you know that? You have not spoken to them!"

"I have known that girl since she was a child. She is whimsical and occasionally thoughtless, but she is not cruel." He did not like the way she was staring at him. He had thought they were past this. "Emma, do you think I would take risks with your life? After last night, can you doubt it? I would do anything to keep you safe.

But I can tell you, on my life, that Kavita is sincere when she calls you her *behin*—her sister."

"And her husband?"

"What of her husband?"

"They said—" She glanced to the door. "They said her husband is no friend to the British," she finished rapidly.

"True enough. But he is well under his father's thumb." When she looked unconvinced, he sighed. "Very well then. I will speak with the Maharajah, I will suggest that he detain his son in Kashmir until the unrest has died down. The roads are not safe, after all. Especially for the scion of a court known to favor the British."

Unease drew a line between her brows. "You know better than I," she said. "But if you think he would listen . . ."

"What's more important, I think it would give you peace of mind." He leaned down to press a kiss on her brow.

"*Bhaiyya!*" Kavita stomped back inside. "I know the meaning of 'moment,' and this is too much!"

Emma's hand dropped away. "Go," she said.

"Emma—"

"Go." Her eyes met his. "I trust you, Julian. I do."

"Why looking so sad, *behin*? Are you not excited for the dancing?"

He arched a brow at Emma. She gave him a smile, but it was not wide enough for his taste. "I will speak with the Maharajah during the *durbar,* and then I will come to you."

Kavita made a noise of protest. His look silenced her. So, there really was a first time for everything.

* * *

Emma nearly tripped on the heavy, gold-encrusted skirts that Kavita had lent her.

"*Bechaari!* It is tricky, *na*? But it's important to look very good for these events," Kavita said, steadying her before continuing on down the stone passageway. Two guards armed with scimitars trailed them. "Of course, no one will see us—but even so, it is important."

Emma ripped her eyes away from the walls of the tunnel, which were decorated with highly detailed paintings, and embedded with mirrors that amplified the light from the torches set on either side. They were beautiful. They were also windowless. Anything could happen in here.

Kavita is sincere when she calls you her sister.

She drew a breath. She trusted him. "What do you mean, no one will see us?"

"The entire court will be present. So we will be in *purdah*." At Emma's expression, Kavita laughed. "It's not bad, I promise you. *Matlab yeh hai ki* we will sit behind one of the *jallis* on the edge of the courtyard. Usually I sit with Maharani-ji, and all the women push each other to see better, and it is most dreadful. But Maharajah-ji has made a section just for us, so we will have the best view." She led Emma up a stairwell to their left, and they emerged into the cool of the evening, taking seats before a tall, intricately carved screen that looked out onto an immense marble courtyard.

Over a hundred men were seated there on large silk cushions, their brightly colored turbans making them appear like a flock of bobbing parrots. At the far side of the courtyard, Emma could just make out through squinting eyes the Maharajah and Julian, seated on chairs above the rest of the crowd. The entire group flanked a rectangular pool, in the middle of which rose a large sandstone dais. As she watched, four men in white pajamas scurried forward, two of them jumping into the pool and submerging themselves up to the chin. Their companions passed them a thin stone plank, which they settled against the dais before climbing out of the water.

"The nautch girls, the dancers, will perform in the middle of the pond," Kavita said. "The musicians are across from us, in that balcony. Below are the Maharani-ji and her court, though you cannot see them."

"Rajkumari-ji?"

They both turned. A slender woman in a diaphanous silver sari held forth a tray with two jewel-encrusted goblets. Kavita handed one to Emma, then sat back and waited as the woman sipped from the other.

She caught Emma's glance as she then took the goblet. "She tastes it for poison." Her eyes fell to Emma's cup, and she smiled. "Would you like her to try yours too?"

"Do you think it . . . necessary?"

Kavita's smile deepened. "It is always possible that only one cup would be poisoned. But why? Your enemies would not be sure that you would choose the right cup." She laughed suddenly. "*Haay Ram,* your face! Do not worry, *behin.* Here, I will taste your drink myself." She reached for the goblet, but the servant gasped and snatched it away.

Kavita scowled and said something sharp to the maid, who bowed lower this time. After a tentative sip, the woman returned the glass to Emma and moved off. "Suchitra has clumsy manners," Kavita said to Emma. "Her heart is good, though. Now try your drink before it melts. It is sherbet soaked in liqueur—very naughty, and very tasty."

Emma took a sip, wincing at the strength of the alcohol. But it left a pleasant aftertaste in her mouth, and was deliciously cold. She tried it again, and decided she liked it.

"Oh!" Kavita leaned forward, watching eagerly as the dancers paced gracefully into the courtyard. "*Bahut sundar hain, na?* Very beautiful!"

The women were wearing bells on their feet, and in the sudden silence, their very steps seemed a sort of dance, the jingling melodious and harmonized. They were lovely in their bright silks, their shoulders thrown back and their chins held high, the kohl around their eyes making them appear like princesses from an exotic fairy tale. She saw Julian lean over to whisper in the Maharajah's ear, and wondered for a moment whether she did not look very pallid and unattractive by comparison.

A sound cut across the stillness: high and sweet, similar to that of a violin. And then, to a mighty flourish of drums, the nautch girls lifted their hands over their heads, spinning across the thin plank to the dais with such speed that Emma was sure one of them would topple into the water. As they belled out in a circle in the center of the pond, a man rushed up to remove the plank, pulling it out of sight.

"They remove the plank so the nautch girls cannot

reach the Maharajah," Kavita whispered. "Two generations ago, a maharajah was knifed in this very *aangan* by a traitorous dancer, so we take no chances."

Emma nodded distractedly. The women moved like water, their arms seeming boneless as they bent and twisted in fluid, curving arcs. One of them moved to the front of the stage, stretching out her hands in supplication as she began to sing.

"She sings of a love that was not meant to be," Kavita translated. "Of her beloved, whom she cannot even look at for fear of the Emperor's wrath. Her heart pounds, and sleep will not come to her—" Kavita turned to look at her. "Are you in love with *bhaiyya*?"

The alcohol had hit Emma's brain of a sudden, or the question had scattered her wits. "I—I beg your pardon?"

Kavita smiled. "I am forward? But I feel very comfortable with you, *behin*. Perhaps we knew each other in a past life. Surely you must have been Hindustani, for how else could you have won Julian? He is not so stupid to give his heart to one of these cold, goatlike Englishwomen. Like the two Maharajah-ji saved. You met them, no? So they told me. Such arrogance, such disrespect! *Ulloos*. Sometimes I think these Englishwomen do not deserve our Maharajah-ji's kindness."

A dreadful girl comes to taunt us. Emma looked out. The distance across the courtyard to Julian was very great, and the stone screen was as effective as steel bars. Behind her, one of the guards shifted, his sword scraping along the wall.

"My question makes you unhappy," Kavita murmured. "But I would not sneer at the idea of being

Julian's woman. Many women have tried to make him their own. He is rich and handsome and *bahut dilwaale,* very courageous. He has stalked a man-eating tiger with nothing but his shadow and his blade, and Maharajah-ji thinks of him as a son. All men respect him, even if his blood is soiled by his English father."

"I do not sneer," Emma said softly.

"Then you are afraid. I was afraid too, with the Yuvraj. But the fear will pass. Here, have some more to drink. We shall have a toast, as you English put it." She placed Emma's hand on the abandoned goblet, then raised hand and goblet both to tip against her own. "To overcoming our fear. And—to Hindustan."

"To India," Emma said quietly, and took a sip. Over the rim, she met Kavita's eyes.

"Whomsoever's it may be," the princess murmured, and then looked back to the dancers.

Kavita would not be denied on the matter of the sherbet. Hemmed in by sword and stone, Emma could see no use in antagonizing her. Thus, by the time Julian appeared, she had been successfully urged to toast a litany of wonders: the dancers' grace and dexterity, the Maharajah's generosity, the fine evening air—even the maid's promptness in delivering each new round. After a while the liquor began to blunt her nerves. Shortly thereafter, it blunted her balance.

"What has she done to you?" Julian asked, catching Emma as she stumbled into him upon rising.

"We had a sherbet," Emma said carefully. She had never been so glad to see him. She almost said so, and pressed her fingers to her mouth to stop herself.

"It was that honey liqueur Yuvraj likes. And now I will fall asleep from it." Kavita yawned. "Surely Maharani-ji will forgive me if I retire without bidding her good night."

"I'm sure she will." Julian's amusement was evident. "Would you like me to walk you to the zenana?"

"*Haay Ram!* The *tamasha* that would cause! No, the guards will take me." Gathering up the folds of her skirts, Kavita staggered off, weaving dangerously around the corner and out of sight.

Julian laughed. "If only her father could see her now."

"Julian," Emma began, then grabbed his upper arm as she swayed again.

"Careful," he murmured. His hand came around to the small of her back, causing his bicep to bunch beneath her fingers. And suddenly the words in her mouth fell away. He had been inside her. This body had been pressed flat against hers, part of him *inside her.*

Her mouth went dry.

"Shall I take you up to the roof?" he said softly. "No one about to see us. It's quite a view."

"What a shplen—*splendid* idea." Her motives, she thought, were not *strictly* base; if there was no one to see them, there would be no one to hear them, either.

He pulled her down the corridor, then helped her up a steep staircase leading onto a small, flat roof. Ah, but it *was* a fantastical scene. The moonlit plains stretched out in all directions, and above, the moon was riding low in the sky, a bright, swollen yellow. "A hunter's moon," she breathed.

His hands came around her waist as he placed a kiss

at the base of her neck. "And what might *you* be hunting, up here on the roof?"

She turned to him with a smile, and then another answer occurred to her. "I think—I am more in the way of the hunted, actually."

His fingers flexed at her sides. For a long moment, she held still beneath his scrutiny, willing him to see that her next words would be carefully considered. When he leaned down, his forehead settling lightly against hers, she murmured, "I respect your faith in our safety here. I do. But I cannot share it."

He sighed. She closed that last small inch and kissed him softly. "I am sorry," she said as she drew away.

He shook his head. Then his gaze shifted beyond her, to the sight of the plains beyond them. "Emma, I'm leaving for Delhi tomorrow."

She jerked backward, out of his grip. "What!"

"I'm going back. The Maharajah's runner returned tonight. The mutinied troops are laying siege to the British encampment on the Ridge, and the army is gathering in Kurnaul, preparing to march on them. I'm going to help with the negotiations."

"You can't go back! When I've just told you—and Julian, you could be killed!"

"Emma, *listen* to me. I spoke with the Maharajah. He will keep his son in Kashmir. He—"

"It's not the son I'm worried about, it's the bride! That woman—"

"Emma, I am in love with you."

Her mouth opened, closed. "You—" She was windless. "What?"

He smiled a little. "You heard it aright. And this is the

only place I know that is safe enough to leave you. I am going to leave you here *because* I love you. And if that cannot secure your faith . . . God, Emma. Then I don't know what else I can say or do."

"Take me with you," she said instantly. "Take me to Delhi."

"No."

"Why not?"

"Christ, Emma!" His rage startled her; she took a step backward, and he swung away, paced over to the wall. Shoving a rough hand through his hair, he turned back. "Do you know—I killed *three men* to get you out of that place. Perhaps more. The bazaar was—" He shook his head. "Do not mistake me; I have slept well ever since. But you want me to take you *back*? Back *there*?"

"Then stay here! Let someone else take care of it! You're not in the army—no one expects you to help!"

He threw her a glance. "True enough, that."

She flinched. Belatedly she realized that the pain she felt was her own nails, digging into the hollow at the base of her throat. "Julian, don't you *dare* try to prove yourself to those people. They aren't worth it, they—"

"Those people *are* my people. Both sides," he said. "British and Indian, I owe something to both of them. It's almost my . . . my *duty* to help end this bloodshed."

"No," she whispered, because it was clear to her, suddenly, that argument would not sway him. The set of his face . . . the ticking muscle at his jaw. *I will deliver you to a safe place.* That had been his original promise, on the banks of the Jumna. He'd planned to leave her all along. How had she forgotten that?

But, God above, so much had changed since then.

The entire world had changed. He *loved* her. "Julian. I can't—" *I can't lose you too.* "Julian, if you go, I will never . . ." *Will never forgive you.* She touched her lips. Did she mean it? Would she say it?

"And there is my family," he added tonelessly. "I must at least try to make sure they are safe, whether they want my help or no."

No. She would not say it.

Her eyes burned. She turned them toward the coolness of the moon. It did not blur in the night sky. Did not waver.

"I'll come back for you," he said. His voice was very close suddenly. "Emma—must I even tell you that? I vow it to you on my soul. I vow it on *you.* You'll stay here until the fighting's ended, until the countryside is settled. And then I will come back for you."

She drew a deep, unsteady breath. Squaring her shoulders, she faced him. "Of course you have to go. How silly of me to try to stop you. It is brave of you to go; noble of you. I admire you for it."

His words were low and hoarse. "Don't look at me like that. I will come back for you. Damn it, say you know that."

"If you survive, I'm sure you will." The words seemed to singe her lips as she spoke them. Her mouth twisted, beyond her control.

His hand closed on her arm. "Of course I will survive. I will survive for this."

His kiss was not gentle. His lips moved over hers roughly, bruising, authoritative as they laid claim to her. She tried to break away, but his grip tightened, painful now. He would not let her go. But *he* would go. They all went from her, the ones she loved were all washed away eventually. She felt a sob twisting up in her throat, and she fought it down with her anger, with fingers stiffened like claws, anchors that dug into his shoulders as she kissed him back.

And then she shoved him, and he did release her, taking a step back, his breath coming fast and quick.

"Go," she said. "Go then."

She would say no prayer for him. She had tried them before. They did not work.

Ten

Kavita pressed a glass of lemonade into Emma's hand. "It is not so bad, Emma. This war will be over very soon, and Julian will come to fetch you."

Emma ripped her eyes away from the design she'd been doodling in the sketchbook Kavita had gifted her. For a second she stared blankly at the lemonade. "What? Oh, thank you." She took a sip, flinching backward as one of the attendants swiped her face with the long feather fan he was waving.

"Hey! *Kya kar rahe ho!* Watch it!" Kavita snapped. The boy muttered an apology, and the princess bent another smile on her. "But I know how difficult it is to be separated from one's beloved. I am waiting breathlessly for my Yuvraj."

"Yes," Emma murmured. An entire week now with no letter from Julian. Was he still alive? Had he managed to lure his headstrong young cousin out of the city? She rubbed her chest. In the daylight, love felt like a stone on her heart, crushing the breath from her body, leaving her listless. But at night, in bed, she relived what had passed between them in the ruins, and she could not sleep. For want of his hands, his voice, she paced the length of her room.

"And when he does come back," Kavita added, "I will beat him with a shoe."

Emma smiled. The Maharajah had kept his word; four weeks now, and the crown prince remained in Srinagar. Kavita was quite put out.

"Yes, a smile! Very good, *behin*. You must leave off these long faces. You were starting to remind me of those *ulloos* down there." Kavita nodded to the parterre below, and Emma glanced down to discover that Anne Marie and Mrs. Kiddell had mustered the courage to emerge for a walk.

The women would not speak with her. She did not know why. Perhaps Kavita had said something and they'd taken it amiss. In the last few weeks, Emma had come to realize that Julian was right; there was no cruelty in the princess, only a youthful enthusiasm that occasionally suffered disastrous mistranslations into English. Her scorn for the women, Emma suspected to be a show, meant to disguise her hurt feelings at their rebuffs. Kavita was accustomed to being loved by everyone, after all. And after so much time with her, Emma knew why. The princess was very winning, in her peculiar way. Canny, playful, and wholly irrepressible.

She gave Kavita a rueful smile. "Let's give it one more try," she said, and leaned over the terrace wall.

"Mrs. Kiddell! Anne Marie! How do you do! A lovely day, isn't it?"

Anne Marie managed to sniff loudly enough to be heard on the terrace. "I think we decided not to speak to her, didn't we, Mrs. Kiddell? Some people are remarkably thick."

Emma raised her brows, looking back to the princess. "I am thoroughly blackballed."

Kavita snorted. "Stupid goats, the pair of them. Perhaps I should stick them and Suchitra in a small—" She cut herself off at the sound of trumpets, twisting in her seat to look toward the main fort gate.

Emma stood up, shielding her eyes against the sun with her sketchbook as she followed the progress of a pack of approaching horses. "Dear God, those aren't sepoys, are they?"

"*Nahin,* no, Emma *behin,* those will be the Maharajah's men. It is tax time, you know, and he sent them out to the villages a week ago to collect his tributes." Kavita's grin was wicked. "That is how he pays his tithe to the British—by bleeding dry his loyal subjects."

Emma looked to her hands. "I'm sorry, Kavita. That's not right. I begin to wonder if any of it is right."

"Perhaps you shouldn't, though," Kavita said gently. "I know you are trying to be fair, *behin,* but we are only women, and thinking too much is dangerous for us. The men make the decisions, so let them also take the responsibility."

Emma grimaced. "A sad state of affairs, isn't it?" Shrieks from the garden made her stand again, and she laughed despite herself as she saw Anne Marie and Mrs. Kiddell lapsing into hysterics at the sight of the

Maharajah's tax collectors striding down the lawn. Anne Marie had collapsed to the ground, and Mrs. Kiddell was trying unsuccessfully to drag her inside, screaming for help all the while.

Kavita joined her at the wall, laughing too. "Such fools!"

"You know it's very unkind of us to make fun," Emma said after a moment. "Mrs. Kiddell!" she yelled. "Anne Marie! It's all right! Those are the Maharajah's men!"

Mrs. Kiddell whirled, craning her head up to Emma. "Oh, thank God! Are you sure?"

"Yes, I'm—" Emma paused as Kavita put a hand to her arm. "What is it?"

"Those men," Kavita said slowly, her face paling. "I don't recognize—guards!" she screamed. *"Oe bachaao!"*

Emma pivoted back to the scene below. Mrs. Kiddell was still looking up at her, eyes wide and expectant, when the first man reached her. He did not hesitate in his task, drawing the knife from his belt and slitting her throat in one unbroken gesture. Her head lolled back brokenly as she slumped to the ground, and Anne Marie let loose an unearthly, bloodcurdling scream.

Emma staggered back, her hands fisted to her mouth as she watched while the girl was dragged into sight, one of the men slitting her dress down the front with an expert sword hand. "My God—dear God—God in heaven—"

"Emma!" Kavita shook her roughly. "*Behin*, you must run!"

The man suddenly looked up, and for the split second

they stared at each other, Emma had a glimpse of hell. Then the knife slashed again. *Her breasts.* He had cut off her breasts. As Anne Marie tumbled to the ground, he cried out, pointing up to Emma with the bloody blade.

She pivoted, grabbing Kavita's wrists. "If Julian comes back—when he comes back—tell him I—"

"*You* tell him!" Kavita dragged her forward to the double doors of her apartments, pulling Emma inside and chaining the portal. "Quickly, *behin,* rip down the tapestry. *Haay Ram,* where are the bloody guards?"

Emma raced to the other side of the room, jamming her sketchbook under her arm so she could yank off the heavy draperies. They collapsed on her in a cloud of dust, and she pushed her way free, coughing violently.

"Push the candles into the niche!"

Emma shoved herself against the iron candelabra until she heard a sharp click. Kavita lunged to the opposite wall, pushing on one of the plaster panels until it seemed to break. It swung inward to reveal a musty passageway, and the princess grabbed a torch from the wall, shoving it into Emma's hand.

"It lets out by the stables. Give them—" She searched the room frantically, and then glanced down at herself, yanking an ornate gold ring from her finger. "Give them this, and take one of the horses. Ride in the opposite direction of the sun, and you will encounter British troops. Go, *behin*!"

Emma kissed her on the forehead, hard, and then ducked into the passageway. By the time the door slammed shut behind her, she was already down the first flight of steps.

* * *

She rode as she had never ridden before. She rode alone, with the desert wind scalding her cheeks and the sun beating down like a punishment. Her mind was blank. She could not bear to think. It was not conceivable—not possible—humans could not *do* such things. She pushed it all aside, and she rode. Kavita had said to ride away from the sun, and so she did.

It was when she encountered humans again, when she began to pass through deserted villages, burnt and mangled, some littered with native corpses and still afire, that she emerged from her torpor. At first she assumed it was the work of the sepoys as well—blood upon blood upon blood—and then it came to her that this made no sense. It was the first logical thought she'd had in many hours, and with it, her mind began to click into working order.

Why would the soldiers burn and murder their own? This had to be the work of the British. A breath caught in her throat. Yes. The British marching through, on their way to Delhi.

She should be relieved at this evidence that she was near her own countrymen, but instead she felt an equal terror, one that made her cling to her beleaguered horse's neck and weep soft, senseless tears. They were all the same, British and Indian alike, those men who could commit such horrible acts of violence against the innocent. She wanted none of it, none of them. She battled a brief, powerful urge to slow her horse, to drop to the soft, beckoning sand and wrap herself in its warmth. To lie there until a decision was made for her—the ultimate and most final way to avoid the bloodshed enveloping the world. But Kavita had told her to ride.

When she finally sighted a band of horses, and realized through her blurred, gritty vision that they were not British but native, she felt nothing. Relief, perhaps. She had done as told. Now it would be finished.

She pulled her horse to a walk as she approached them. For some reason the urge took her to pull herself straight, to tilt her chin up proudly. It was not in her nature to be weak, even now. That, at least, was something to be proud of.

She had laughed at them. She had laughed at Anne Marie and Mrs. Kiddell, seconds before they died.

She choked on her sob, gritting her teeth as the sepoys rode up to surround her.

"Memsahib," one of them said, so respectfully that her nerveless fingers twitched in astonishment. "Memsahib, where are you coming from?"

"Sap—Sapnagar," she stammered. Their grave demeanors, their stillness as they flanked her, made no sense. "They—they killed—"

"Memsahib," the man sighed, reaching out for her reins. She flinched, waiting for him to draw his sword, but he patted her mount's nose, lifting prematurely aged eyes to meet hers. "Do not fear. My regiment has not turned. We will escort you to the British camp."

In a daze, she let him pull her mount around and lead her into the sunset.

The town of Kurnaul was in chaos. Its winding streets had been converted into a maze of sagging, hastily assembled tents, with wearied soldiers loitering in clumps by the shallow cooking pits as they waited for orders. A recent rain shower had turned the dust to mud, and the entire scene was mired in grays and browns, perfectly reflecting the mood in the air.

The sepoy whose regiment had escorted her here had vanished into the mess some time ago, supposedly to locate a room for her amidst those of the officers' wives. But after enduring a half hour of curious glances and sly insinuations from passing British soldiers, Emma finally dismounted, walking with directionless purpose into the encampment.

She felt eyes on her as she passed, whole groups of men falling silent to follow her progress down the makeshift lane. Perhaps they were staring because of her native dress. Or perhaps it was her hair, its abbreviated length perfectly evened by Kavita's maid. Likely it was simply more of the same speculation she had overheard while waiting for the sergeant. Was she a fallen woman? Had the mutineers ravished her?

She did not care what they believed. A reputation seemed the most ludicrous concept to her now. Good, bad, tarnished, destroyed—what did it matter? She was alive. So many were not.

"Hey there, miss."

She turned slowly to face the man who had addressed her. His cheeks reddened under her inspection.

"What is it?" she asked quietly.

"I'm dreadful sorry to say this, miss, I can see you've been through something or other nasty. But this here is the officer's section of the encampment, strictly no civilians allowed. Maybe I can escort you to the ladies' quarters?"

She glanced over his shoulder, pondering the tents behind him. "Who are the officers in charge?"

"Oh, I'm sorry, are you here to see one of them, ma'am?"

She hesitated as an unlikely possibility occurred to her. "Colonel Lindley wouldn't be here, would he?"

"Why, yes, he is, ma'am, that's actually his tent right in front of you there. But he's just been called out unexpectedly to make a survey of the neighboring villages. We're trying to keep law and order around Kurnaul, you see, ma'am, and we heard rumors there was trouble brewing up north. He's gone to crush it."

"How admirable," she said flatly. Was the destruction she had witnessed Marcus's work? Did that fit his definition of law and order?

"Lieutenant Ripley!" someone bellowed from nearby. "Do you want to be debriefed or not?"

The lieutenant grimaced. "Wait here just a moment, ma'am, and I'll find someone to show you back." He disappeared into one of the tents, and Emma stood there in momentary indecision. But the thought of confronting a flock of proper British memsahibs nauseated her. Shoving her doubts aside, she splashed across the muddy street and ducked inside Marcus's tent.

The flap swung shut behind her, and she held her breath, waiting to see whether someone was going to raise a hue and cry. When the squelches and muttering outside continued unabated, she backed up into the blessed stillness of the tent. Alone. And, for the time being, safe.

A small laugh escaped her. Safe. *Oh, Julian, you were wrong.*

She struck the air with her hand, shoving the thought away from her.

The interior of the tent was bleak. Portable desk. Chair. Inkwell. A pile of rolled maps in the corner. The bed was neatly made; Marcus always had been immaculate. She debated the merits of a short nap. But she did not want to lie on his bed, and anyway her mind was too full; it felt swollen to bursting with the things she had seen, horrors etched on her brain in the colors of scalding sunlight and blood. Her fingers clenched. Yes, drawing would keep her sane, would keep these terrors at bay.

She crossed to the desk, picking up a pen and pulling her sketchbook from the depths of her pocket. Dirt crumbled off the cover, and she stuck her hand back in her skirts to turn the pocket inside out. Assorted bits of filth and sand rained onto the floor.

She sat on the chair, pushing aside a letter written in that thin, flowing script the natives called Urdu. The script was soothing. Gentle, sloping curves, to contrast the jagged edges of her thoughts. She found herself tracing the words with her fingertips. What delight she had felt when she had first set eyes on the language, that day in the bazaar in Delhi. How long ago that seemed. Even today felt as though it had lasted an eon. Perhaps by tomorrow her hair would have turned white, and she would have lines around her eyes. Anything was possible in this country.

The script blurred before her, dancing suddenly, like the nautch girls at Sapnagar. She blinked, and the lines shifted again. Now they suggested waves, the march of the ocean. How strange. Perhaps the script was the key to it, then. The key to everything.

Alarm touched her. Her thoughts were not making sense.

She exhaled shakily and shoved the letter away. Turning to a fresh page in her drawing pad, brushing off the sand and dirt, she put pen to page. The pen jerked; a bold line streaked off the parchment, jumping down to continue along her skirt.

She shook out her trembling hand and tried again. This time the pen obeyed. It rendered along the dirty page a line worthy of any language: the curve of Anne Marie's flawless cheek.

She blinked a few times to orient herself before hauling her face off her hand. Her neck ached from being twisted at such an odd angle; how had she managed to fall asleep? She looked down at the paper, sucking in a breath. Dear God, it was too horrible. It was exactly right. She closed the book on a shudder.

Her arms were stiff. She rose, stretching them over her head as she turned. A man stood at the front of the tent, watching her in thin-lipped silence.

"You been sleepin' awhile," he drawled. He had papers in his hand, and he slapped them against his thigh. "I been watchin' you."

She swallowed hard. "I was waiting for Colonel Lindley to return."

"I'm sure you was."

"I am his betrothed," she said more sharply. "He is expecting me."

His smile was slow and ugly. "You done fooled me with that one once before—you and your blackie friend the Marquess. Now I know that ain't the truth." He took a step toward her, and as she recognized him from that day in the bazaar, she heard herself whimper. "I saw you ride in with them natives. I heard what happened to you. A terrible shame. I always thought that proper ladies'd die before they was dishonored. I expect you was hopin' to die, you just didn' have the strength to do it yourself."

"You are wrong," she said, as loudly as possible. "And if you do not back away *this instant*—"

He lunged forward, his dirty fingers clamping over her mouth. "I'll make you clean," he whispered in her ear. "I'm as English as they come. You won't even remember what those filthy blackies did to you."

She struggled to breathe, casting her hands back behind her for a weapon. Her fingers fumbled over the sketchbook, knocking it to the floor, and he pushed her down so hard her head cracked against the ground. She moaned, her hand slipping off the desk just as it closed over a letter opener.

"It won't take long," he promised her, his mouth wet on her ear. "Just one—"

She spiked the letter opener into his temple.

He gurgled low in his throat, his eyes rolling wildly. "What—the—" His voice wobbled into distortion, and then he toppled off her, his body spasming violently. She hugged herself as she watched him die, rocked as she felt her own mind tremble, her eyes seeing instead Mrs. Kiddell's panicked face, upturned in a plea. She heard her own high laughter as she called, *"It's all right! Those are the Maharajah's men!"*

Her breath sounded funny to her. Short, wheezing, sobbing little noises. She reached out—*shaking, shaking like a leaf, Emma*—for the drawings that had spilled from her book. Her fingers trembled too violently to sort out her own papers from those the dead man had dropped. They would think someone had stolen them. They would think her a thief. A thief as well as a murderer.

Dear God.

She lunged up and raced from the tent.

Cawnpore stank of burned flesh and gunpowder. The lieutenant left Julian to wait at the edge of the old parade ground. He leaned against a wall, the ground vibrating beneath his feet. Half a mile away, near the building where Nana Sahib's men had slaughtered scores of British women and children, the army was strapping mutineers to cannons. Blowing them apart in steady, rhythmic explosions.

The lieutenant had looked rather green, escorting him into camp. "Newly transferred from Calcutta. Not used to it yet," he'd admitted. "But give me a few days, and I'll do. Had a letter from the missus in Shropshire, and she even told me to kill one for her. The papers at Home are full of it, she says. Hey, you seem to be holding up pretty well."

He'd already seen it before. In Delhi and Meerut. Lucknow, Jhansi, Benares, Agra. Also countless smaller towns, too inconsequential to remember. He had been looking for a very long time now, and everywhere he went, the sounds of vengeance had already arrived. The steady bark of cannon fire. The creak of the noose. The shrieks that from a distance sounded neither Indian nor British—only human.

Cawnpore was too far from Sapnagar. She could not have made it here. Knowing what had happened in this place, he might have been glad for it. But it had been too long now for any gladness. Months since he'd touched her, listened to her laugh. Since she had disappeared.

Kavita said she had told her to ride away from the sun. And so he had gone east, slowly, methodically searching. First British stations. And then, retracing his steps, small villages where she might have sheltered, where someone might have taken pity on a woman in need, a woman wearing a ring of the house of Rathore. Nothing. Vanished.

This place was his last hope.

She had asked him not to leave her, hadn't she? And as she'd spoken, there had been tears in her eyes that she refused to shed. And his voice, as he'd promised her safety—he could hear it so clearly, the unforgivable fucking arrogance as he'd promised her she had nothing to fear—

"Holdensmoor! A surprise indeed!"

He looked up. Lindley was striding toward him, jaunty, cheerful even. Julian put a finger to the corner of his own eye, and then to his mouth.

"Ah?" Lindley turned to the aide at his elbow, who nodded and produced a handkerchief. "Dirty work," he said, scrubbing the blood from his face. "What can I do for you, then?"

The courteous manner was unexpected. It bumped his

pulse into a rapider speed. Perhaps . . . "I am looking for Emmaline Martin."

Lindley, turning to hand off the handkerchief, paused. Julian studied his back, looking for any sign.

The Colonel turned, frowning. "Here? In Cawnpore?"

"Yes."

Lindley studied him. "I see. Well, I know there is bad blood between us, cousin, but to taunt me about Emmaline—" He paused, as if suddenly struck by something. "But the bad blood is all yours, of course. Indeed, how it must chill you! To walk into a camp filled with good English soldiers, baying for native blood. Does that not make you slightly *nervous*, my cousin?" His head tipped to one side. "But no, you seem quite unmoved. Remarkable!"

The chatter was making him impatient. "You haven't seen her. Or heard anything of her."

"No, and I can't imagine why you think I might have done. That is, yes, we were contracted, but the last I knew, she was in the Residency, digging in her heels and refusing to come with me. I expect she must be dead now. A pity! She was to have inherited a good deal of cash, and I might have used it. Then again, after my services here, I expect I'll be set up nicely no matter whom I wed. Perhaps even a knighthood. Do you think?"

"Aim even higher," Julian said quietly. "Try for my circles. I will keep you very close by."

Lindley laughed. "Oh dear. Is that a threat? How unwise. I *am* commanding officer of this little station, Holdensmoor. Say, I heard rumor that you were in Delhi during the assault. Is that so? Manage to protect your *darker* kin, did you?"

Go, his grandmother had told him, as he had backed away from Deven's funeral pyre, torch in hand. *You have fulfilled your duty to this family.*

Felled by a single British bullet. As deaths went, it must have been relatively painless.

Pray God Emma had been so lucky.

He turned away from Lindley and began to walk back the way he'd come. He was not as strong as Emma. When the tears came, he could not check them.

Part Two

Eleven

London
May 1861

THERE WAS NOTHING TO SEE OF LONDON OUT THE window. They were moving through a yellow haze reeking of sulfur, jaundiced with coal smoke. In the interior of the carriage, the darkness was complete. It required a tight grip on the strap to stay seated, for they advanced in fits and starts, halting often with no warning. The driver was fearful of collisions, perhaps. Some minutes before, in a sudden brief clearing of the fog, they had passed an accident. An omnibus had smashed into a carriage. One of the horses was dead, the others screaming and fighting the traces; bloodied passengers had milled about in a daze. Bystanders flooded from the shops—gawking, shouting for help.

Emma had taken no interest in it. As the coach jerked forward again, she had spotted a man crouched a little ways off, his shoulders wrapped in a gray blanket stamped *The Lady Danforth Relief Fund.* He was laboring over the pavement with a piece of chalk, trying to repair the damage the crowd had done to his drawing. It was a passable rendering of the head of Napoleon, subtitled with a clumsy scrawl: I AM STARVING. So, she had thought, here was London's first lesson to her. She was not the only one who survived through art.

She might have thrown him a penny, but it was a passing impulse. And the window was bolted shut.

Back into the murk. Over cobblestones and granite setts the fog spread, subsuming buildings, warping sound. Here and there came the glow of gas lamps, disembodied haloes that loomed from nowhere. A carriage rumbled by, unseen; traces jingled, a whip cracked. Now a sudden ball of red light, and another and another, bobbing wildly—and a cry distorted by the fog, so it seemed at one moment to come from right at the window, and then abruptly from a great distance: "Links! Links for a sixpence!"

Across the bench, her cousin was pressing a handkerchief to her mouth to filter the air. Emma watched her for a moment. Then, experimentally, she drew a breath through her mouth. The air tasted thick and burnt, and it seemed to take on weight at the back of her throat, a bitter clot that could not be swallowed. She did not know why anyone would choose to live in this city, but perhaps there was something to it. Breathing felt like choking here. And since one could not go without air, there was no choice in it, which made it comfortable. She pulled in an even deeper breath. Yes, there was no respite for it but to submit. Then it grew easier.

"You will make yourself sick," her cousin said.

She turned back to the window. She was not in charity with Delphinia. The question of the paintings loomed between them. *Burn them if you like:* that was what she'd said a year ago. Or was it two now? Perhaps she had not meant it; she hadn't been well, at the time. But certainly she had told Delphinia never to show them to anyone.

How merry this coming interview would be. *Indeed, sir, yes. This painting is of a charming scene I beheld whilst in India. It made me scream at the time, but my fears were unfounded; I did not die by the man's hand, he was killed first. Here is another, of a moment in Alwar which has lingered with me particularly. I am so pleased you find my technique commendable. Had I not experimented with the Italian style, I would not have been able to furnish the depth and vividness required by the subject. I would not have been able to finish it, and instead it would have remained inside my head, and perhaps if you wished to interview me, you would have had to call at Bedlam, or someplace like it—but nicer, I expect. I could afford better.*

The carriage slowed to another halt. A soft touch at her shoulder called her back.

"All right," Delphinia said. "We are here, coz."

Once indoors and settled, Delphinia asked Lord Lockwood's man to light a fire. The air in the drawing room quickly became as thick as the fog without. A maid brought tea, but Emma could not sit for it; she paced the edge of the carpet as her cousin poured. "Surely you are not nervous to meet the Earl?" Delphinia asked.

Emma shrugged. She had thought she was ready for London. But with every passing hour, Durringham's allure grew stronger. If she were in Devon, she would be taking an evening walk right now. A stroll through the fields at Gemson Park, after a long day of painting. Perhaps she would be frustrated—all her newest work seemed mediocre—but at least she would be at peace.

"Perhaps you are melancholy," Delphinia said more sharply.

The temptation to remain silent was powerful, but in this matter alone she could not taunt her cousin. Delphinia had witnessed some very black moods in the last few years, and she had borne them without complaint. "Not at all," said Emma. "And not for some time, so there is no need to worry on that account."

"Are you vexed with me, then?"

Her steps paused as she considered the question. She did not know what exactly was in her: anger, or nerves, or exhaustion. But that did not surprise. Her mind had something in common with the fog outside; what she ought to feel often came to her in unrecognizable forms. With another shrug, she said, "If I am vexed, there is good cause."

Delphinia shot to her feet. On someone larger, the effect might have been impressive. But Delphinia was as petite and pink-cheeked as a china doll. "It is bad of you to hound me for it, Emma! You know I'm already feeling quite guilty."

"And so you should," she said wearily. "I gave you those paintings on the express understanding that you would not show them to anyone."

"But I didn't mean to!" Delphinia cast a glance to the door. "I had them hung in the green salon, and you know that *no one* ever goes in the green salon except family, but then Gideon gets on so *well* with Lord Lockwood, and so I received him there, and—yes, he *saw* them, Emma. And he fell in love with them! He said they were *beautiful*!"

"I would watch out for him then. He is clearly perverted."

Delphinia wrinkled her nose. "Yes, I did think it a *bit* odd. But do you know what I thought then?"

"I cannot imagine. I hadn't realized you had thoughts so very frequently."

"I thought, why, the Earl of Lockwood is famous for finding new talent! If he showed your paintings at his next ball, he could make you the talk of the town!"

"The target of the town, more like." Emma resumed her pacing. "Delphinia, you know I intend to make a name for myself." It was all she planned for, really. "But these paintings are not the way to do it."

"Well, what other paintings have you got?"

Dear coz. As subtle as an ax. "I *will* have more. That is the point. After I come back from Italy—"

"I don't understand why you need to travel so far to learn to paint more pleasantly."

"*After* I come back, I'll have work fit to show. But if my name has already been ruined by these paintings, no one will be receptive."

"Which is why I told Lockwood he cannot reveal your identity." With a pleased smile, Delphinia retook her seat. "Now do sit, Emma, and have some tea. It's oolong, perfectly lovely."

A sudden thought arrested her. "Your story has changed, Delphinia! In the letter, you said Lord Chad showed Lockwood the paintings while in his cups."

"Oh. Did I? Well, you know how confused I can be—"

"You are not this jejune." Emma felt suddenly light-headed. She lowered herself into a Queen Anne chair. "Tell the truth. You deliberately showed them to him!"

Delphinia's eyes fell to her teacup, which she was turning around and around in her hands. "Really, coz. Your theory casts me in a very unflattering light."

She shook her head. Even a year ago, this would have destroyed her. "Confess," she said grimly. "They say it is good for the soul."

Delphinia looked up. "They also say blood is thicker than water. Or a small promise broken. Is it?"

"It was not a small promise. Not at the time. You have no idea!"

"No, I do not, for you will not *explain* to me! You never have done!"

Emma looked away, to the fire. She would like to explain. She had often pondered doing so. But where to begin? Avignon, perhaps. Some months after her return. "You *must* get out of Durringham, coz. You are *frightening* me." And so she had faced the water again, and landed in a world of summer beauty. She had tried so hard in Avignon, so hard to be content with flowers. She had piled her palette so full of lavenders and greens that she'd dreamt of choking on the colors.

She would have gone mad had she stayed there.

And so back to Gemson Park, for another one of her fits. Feverish weeks closeted in that small studio, where the sunlight itself, streaming through the windows, seemed ironical—such a cheerful illumination for the growing darkness on the canvas, the oils she corrupted into scenes that would scare a child from his sleep for months.

When it was over, she had wanted them away from her. *What an idiot I was.* Imagining that she was done with it. There had always been more to paint, in those first couple of years.

One painting, *one,* without blood. She had started it during that miserable voyage homeward. It had been her sanity when the waves grew restive, when they had leapt up against the porthole as though calling her back to them. But she had never completed it. She had painted his expression to show love and hope and faith, and once on land, when the enormity of her mistake became clear, she could not figure out how to undo it. She did not look upon it now. She did not think of it.

Prettier scenes were the order of the day. She had several paintings started. Little girls, village celebrations, winter landscapes. And they were, she thought, terrible. Lifeless. Perhaps *she* was the one whose nature was perverted. Surely it was an aberrant talent that excelled only at depicting violence.

"I am sorry," Delphinia whispered. "I thought it for the best. Can you forgive me?"

What else was there to do? She pressed her lips together and nodded.

"Ah!" Brightening, Delphinia retrieved her teacup and leaned forward. "Very well, then, yes, I showed him the paintings. Something had to be done to pry you out of that hole! You've been hiding there for too long—"

"I was not hiding, I was painting. It is what artists *do.*"

"It's unnatural!"

"It was a compulsion," Emma corrected quietly.

"Hmmph. Did you not always say as a girl that you wanted to be a famous artist?"

"Famous, you note, not notorious."

"Really, Emma, you must take a chance when it is offered. I know you're afraid of running into Marcus—"

Emma was surprised into a laugh. "That toady? Don't be absurd."

"New titles." Delphinia rolled her eyes. "So gauche. And broke to boot, if you believe the gossip; he gambles terribly. But you needn't worry. Lockwood can't stand pretension. I'm sure the Viscount won't even be at the ball!"

Emma shut her eyes. Her cousin spoke as if it were already decided. "Delphinia, those paintings aren't—pleasant. The idea of presenting them at a *ball* seems perfectly mad."

"Allow me to disagree, Miss Martin."

She rose in unison with her cousin. "We did not hear you enter," Delphinia said.

Lord Lockwood bowed. "I am sorry to have kept you waiting. Countess, looking lovely as ever." He lifted Delphinia's hand to his lips before turning his attention to Emma.

"My lord." She extended her hand. He was remarkably handsome, somewhere in his mid-thirties, with sun-striped brown hair and striking amber eyes. They ran over her very thoroughly. He put her somewhat in mind of a tiger, sizing up his prey.

"Miss Martin." He offered her a wide smile. "If I look discomposed, it is because I did not expect you to be so young."

In fact, he did not look discomposed, and she suspected all at once that he rarely found himself so. "My cousin said she had told you—"

"Of course she did. But if you'll permit the observation, your paintings reflect a certain degree of . . . experience . . . which I find impossible to reconcile with your lovely face." He bared his teeth in another smile. This one had a wild, uncaged quality that made her uneasy. She wondered what it was that he saw in her work—if her paintings disturbed him or, God forbid, excited him.

He seemed to sense her discomfort, taking a step back and—perhaps she was imagining it—toning down his effect. "Forgive me for overhearing," he continued, "but I must say, I believe a ball is *exactly* the place to display your work. When I saw them, it came to me that *here* are the things we tend to forget in this cloistered little world of ours. The things that make life worth living, worth fighting for. Indeed, the things that make evil worth fighting *against*. I wish to remind society of it, if you'll allow me."

An odd speech, but delivered very smoothly. Had she not been watching so closely, she might have missed the way his hands fisted as he spoke. "You feel very strongly about them, Lord Lockwood. Do they speak to you personally?"

"How could they not?"

"They are very violent," she said bluntly.

"So is the world."

"That may be. But I do not believe they are the best way to begin a career. And forgive me if I sound ambitious, but a career is my aim."

"I admire your aim. I plan to help you realize it."

"I am flattered to hear it. Perhaps, then, you would care to see other work—work in progress. Paintings more suited to display."

He considered her for a moment. "Let me show you how I've arranged them. Perhaps that will answer your concerns."

She would have put an end to the farce then and there. But she was thrown off by a growing sense of familiarity with him. Strange; she knew she had never met him before. "Very well," she said slowly, curious to see if she could work out whom he reminded her of. "But I must warn you, I don't think I'll be swayed."

He inclined his head. "If you'll follow me."

They trailed him out of the salon and across the oak-paneled floors of the ballroom. The adjoining gallery was high-ceilinged, long and narrow. He gestured to the walls. Her paintings had been arranged expertly. Each occupied the precise amount of space needed to create its own impact without distracting from the next. Turning around and around, staring at works she had never seen save in the harsh light of her studio or the amber tones of Delphinia's gaslit salon, Emma experienced a visceral thrill. It was close to fear, but felt more like . . . awe.

These were *real.* Dark, dynamic. Each figure within was caught in a precariously balanced moment in time, twisting in the exquisite heights of emotion: bloodlust, terror, agony, exultation. She wrapped her arms around herself. She had been possessed by these images. *These memories.* And yet here they were—apart, separate from her. Mounted on a wall, with no sign that her blood and tears had ever had anything to do with them.

"You have a genius," Lord Lockwood murmured, as Delphinia drifted on down the gallery.

So strange to hear him say this, and to know it, for once, to be truth. To *feel* it as such. Not nightmares, not some sickness of the mind, but art. Why, *why* could she not realize this mastery in her lighter work?

He spoke again. "I must ask, the lines at the bottom of these—do they have significance? Are they messages of some sort? I have puzzled over them."

She might have said, *They are evidence and admission of my sin. I killed the man who first wrote them, you see.* "The Countess calls them 'unintelligible captions to scenes of incomprehensible horror.'" She slanted him a glance. "You will find that my cousin is never short of words, or theories."

"As theories go, it's rather a good one. Do you subscribe to it, Miss Martin?"

"I am only the artist; I leave the intellectual exercises to others."

"Somehow I doubt that. These works are the products of an athletic mind."

She smiled. "All the same, I cannot show them. They are—good, yes. For what they are. But they are also . . ." She shook her head. "Not for display."

"So you believe that art is meant only to be decorative?"

He could not have picked a more precise rejoinder. She bit her lip. "Let us be frank, sir. They would think me mad."

"I admit I am surprised to find you remarkably sane. But there you have it. It was a demon who held your eyes open, and an angel who gave you the strength to bear what you must witness."

"You should not make poetry of it."

"Then what use is art, Miss Martin? Should we paint only country scenes?"

She glanced back to the paintings. "I would like to paint something happier. I have started to do so." She decided suddenly to continue with honesty. "Unfortunately, it seems I can't manage it with nearly the same skill."

"Perhaps you must first surrender these," he said gently. "Once they belong to the world, their claim on you may weaken."

Still she hesitated. "They would not thank me for showing their war heroes thus."

"And that is exactly why you *must* show these. No one else will do so." His voice dropped, for her ears alone. "So few have justice. So few have the means to exact it. These scenes deserve to be witnessed."

Ah. Something in his tone made it clear to her suddenly: what she had recognized in him was a quality in herself. The gravity imparted by suffering—and perhaps, she thought, the wildness as well. "You know these," she said softly. "You understand."

"I do," he said. "And such is the power of your art, so will all of London. Those who have the souls left to see it, anyhow."

Delphinia came sweeping back down the hall. "Marvelous!" she cried. "Isn't she a genius, Lockwood? I have been thinking of pseudonyms—what say you to Aurora Ashdown? It has a certain ring, does it not?"

"I have not agreed," Emma protested. But she could feel herself being converted. She had already felt that it was time for a change. This was not the form she had envisioned for it, but a delay in her travels would not be hard to arrange. And besides, if she meant to be done with the past—truly done with it—then a prolonged visit to London should not unnerve her. Indeed, she should be most indifferent to the prospect of running into . . . reminders, of that other time. "And no one will know it is I?"

"Not from my lips," Lockwood said.

"Or mine," Delphinia added. "Oh, do not look at me so, Emma; this time I *do* mean to keep my promise."

"And you are offering to become my patron," she pressed Lockwood. "To facilitate showings, when I produce other work that interests you."

He bowed.

"Splendid," said Delphinia. "It's settled, then. I tell you, Emma, London will love you! They will be shocked, and so they will love you."

"They will certainly love to hate me. Or the unfortunate Miss Ashdown."

"Ah, but isn't that even more rewarding?" the Earl said, almost to himself. "Love is so fleeting, but hate never dies."

If they had not already shared that small moment, she would have been seized by the most inexplicable urge to step back as he smiled up at the wall.

Occasionally, lately, a strange feeling would take hold of him—a sudden, unpleasant clarity, as when a sleeping man recognizes he is only dreaming. Just now, for instance, he could feel every grain of fog passing over his skin. The blotted haloes of gas lamps seemed to throb, bright and dim, in accompaniment to the beat of his heart. And in the immense silence of the dark, empty street, the sound of his footsteps sharpened, striking with the speed and impact of bullets, coming faster and faster even when he slowed his pace.

Yet Julian's routine suggested no imminent catastrophe. In the morning, as always, he boxed and fenced with Master Nagasaki. Then to estate business. In the afternoon he attended Parliament. By seven, his circle reconvened at Brooks's to debate strategy. Proper peers of the realm. Impeccable, irreproachable. After an hour and a half, he excused himself. It was the outermost limit of his patience; the temptation to smash something usually peaked just before the carriage pulled round.

Arriving home, he changed into the evening clothes his valet had laid out for him. It was the height of the Season, every night bringing another ball or fête, and Caroline thrived on such things. Certainly it was one way to pass the time. Nightly they agreed that the music, the crowd, and the decorations were rather remarkable. Occasionally she pulled him into an alcove to fuck. The novelty did not seem to pall for her. Perhaps when someone caught them, she would be forced to become more creative.

Sundays presented a small deviation from routine. Sundays he went riding through the countryside. Alone, always. Last week he'd taken an ill-advised jump and ruined his best mount, Aries. A trifle deep-chested, but what lines. What heart. Three years of earnest service, and what had he gotten for it? A bullet through the brain. Julian had instructed his valet to burn his riding clothes. He did not know what he would do this

Sunday. Obviously he was a goddamn menace to the innocent.

And then there were Wednesdays. How had he forgotten this most auspicious of days? On Wednesdays, Caroline hosted a small dinner party at Auburn House. She claimed she could not comfortably accommodate her guests at the house on Dover Street. Also, although her husband had been dead for two years, she still felt qualms of conscience at bringing Julian to the house where she had passed her married life—so she confessed, with downcast eyes. Julian recognized that he was meant to be charmed by this admission. He declared himself charmed, and opened Auburn House to her friends. The status of official hostess did not appease her; she wanted something else from him. Of course she did. But she was clumsy in her angling, and he liked to watch her writhe on her own hook.

And so these dinner parties on Wednesdays had become commonplace. She enjoyed them as little as he did, unless she was drunk, which she would not be yet, because he'd mistimed his arrival and they would not even have laid the first course.

He paused at the area railing to stare up at the windows. A curtain twitched aside, revealing a dark silhouette against the brightly lit interior. Caroline, hoping for his arrival. He had not attended last week.

What had he done instead? He had no memory. So went large chunks of his time, gone into the ether.

He sighed and started up the stairs. The door opened before he could ring.

"I thought it was you standing out there! What are you doing, on foot?"

"I wanted a walk."

Caroline brushed past the porter to clasp his cheeks. "So cold you are! What intemperate weather for May. You're hardly dressed for it, Julian; I can't think why you didn't take the brougham. And where is your muffler?"

Julian handed his hat and greatcoat to a footman and took Caroline's arm, guiding her into the front parlor. Within, the bulk of her guests were chatting over cakes and liqueur.

"Look at him," Caroline directed the room. "Dressed for a summer's day, and it nearer to snow!"

A pause. Everyone looked up. Perhaps they were marveling at Caroline's stupidity. He was her lover, not her bloody son.

The windowpanes rattled in a sudden gust of wind. Rain slapped against the glass, a dozen small sharp sounds; and then thunder rolled over Mayfair.

"Alas, I will not be able to join you this evening," he said to the room, and turned on his heel.

He was standing at the window in his bedchamber when she found him. This mist. The driving rain could not break apart the miasma. It obscured the road, and all he could glimpse were the tips of horses' ears, bobbing in and out of the muck as they pulled a carriage down the lane. Was it faith that allowed them to move forward blindly, with no idea of what lay ahead? Or sheer animal stupidity?

"You're in one of your moods," she said from the door.

"Am I?" He drew the curtains shut, turning back to the plush, fire-gilded contours of the room. His servants needed no instruction; the whole damned place ran like clockwork. He wondered, idly, how long it would take them to stop lighting the fires, if one day he simply never returned.

"I know you better than you think," Caroline said, and reached up to unpin her hair. The chignon toppled, unwinding over one shoulder in a chestnut coil. Her eyes tracked his attention to her hair, and she smiled. "Undress me."

He stayed where he was. "Have your guests requested a show?"

"I dismissed them. You rather killed the mood. Anyway, they were boring me. Will you not come here? Very well." She crossed to him, lowering herself to her knees with her back to him. "Unhook me."

He flipped the eyelets open with one hand. The dress split like a flower opening.

"Now the laces," she said. "That's it, thank you. You've been brooding for days. I know what's running through your head."

"And what would that be?"

She turned on her knees, her hands busy with the studs of her busk. "The war. It shows in your face, you know."

"And what would you know of it?" He was being a rude, childish bastard, but he could not find it within himself to care. He wondered sometimes that she stayed with him.

"Nothing, of course. But I know this, Julian. You are Auburn. Your place is here."

"Riveting insight."

"Maybe it is, at that. If you would make an effort to fix your mind on it—to let go of the other—it might be easier."

"Oh yes," he said. "Easier, indeed."

She was silent for a moment. Then her shoulders gave an impatient little roll, so the corset fell away, onto the floor behind her. Clever trick. She was garbed for battle, in carmine lace. One did not find scarlet chemises just anywhere.

When he lifted his gaze, she offered a rueful smile. "What, you see nothing of interest?"

"Did I not demonstrate my appreciation thoroughly enough this morning?"

"Oh, you're always thorough. That isn't the problem."

"If you'd care to elucidate—"

"Perhaps I shall. Does the prospect frighten you? I know you like to steer away from anything of a personal nature."

"That's hardly just," he said mildly. "We speak of many things."

"Oh, yes." She tossed her head and rose, stepping out of the gown. A few impatient flicks of her fingers and the crinoline was collapsing to the floor. "Politics, and plays, and maybe even my first marriage. But we never speak of *you*. And when I try—well, you end up like this. Brooding."

"What do you wish to know?"

"I heard a rumor—" When he looked at her, she shrugged. "I know you don't like them very much, but I'm sorry, I couldn't help hearing it. It was about you. In India, and a woman."

"I don't understand."

She kicked the discarded clothing aside with one foot. "Don't be difficult. You know to what I'm referring."

"No. I'm not sure I do."

"They say you fell in love with a woman who died in the Mutiny. And I want to know—what I want to know is—is that why you haven't asked me to marry you?"

He dragged a hand over his mouth. "Where did you hear that?"

She rolled her eyes. "I don't remember! From Lauren Pritchett, perhaps—or no, from Viscount Lindley."

"Lindley?" He leaned forward, frowning. "Lindley told you that?"

"What does it matter?"

Yes, what could it matter? There were pathways he had closed to memory, and breaking into them was painful. But—what had Lindley known? Could he simply have guessed?

"Look, Julian, all I want to know is if that's the reason!"

He stared at her, casting about for the subject of the question. Ah yes—marriage. "I don't suppose it ever crossed my mind to ask."

"But—" She looked touchingly uncertain all of a sudden; unexpected to see that emotion on a woman of such notorious experience. "But why? You're a duke now, Julian, and you have a duty to beget an heir. I suppose I could understand if you wanted a debutante to wife, someone fresh and untouched—"

He actually laughed. "Dear God, no. I'd most likely break her."

"I agree," she said instantly. "And that's why I thought—I mean, we've been paired for nearly a year now—not exclusively, of course, I know you've had other women, but you always come back to me—don't you? And that has to mean something, because everyone knows your reputation for—for flightiness—"

"Flightiness," he repeated distastefully. "Is that what—"

"Well, you are flighty," she said. "I've been keeping count. And only since Gregory died, mind you, so I can't imagine how many there were beforehand."

"Bravo, Caroline. How charming to know you kept your eyes to yourself while your husband still lived."

"Oh, God damn you, Julian Sinclair!" She came to her feet, and so did he; with a lunge to the bed, she grabbed a pillow and hurled it. He ducked. His laughter was genuine now.

"Forgive me, Caro, but it's rather funny. Had I known you were monitoring me so closely, I might have—"

"You wouldn't have done anything differently, and you know it! You've never given a damn for what anyone thinks. But *really,* Julian, even if you don't care what they all say, you *must* care about leaving an heir—don't you? And I know that I didn't conceive during my marriage to Gregory, but his wife before me was also barren, so I wonder if it wasn't his fault—"

"Enough. You don't need to defend yourself to me."

"Yes, I know." She gave him a sheepish smile. "It was just so bloody *hard,* listening to them all whisper about it. But you know all that." Her smile changed, becoming somewhat bemused. "Goodness, I say we don't talk about personal things, but I do go on about my own problems! It's just that *you* never say anything. . . ."

He sighed. "There was a woman, Caroline."

"Oh." She looked afraid suddenly, and he felt a touch of pity for her. A touch. "What happened?"

"She died in the Mutiny."

"Were you—did you see it happen?"

Christ. "*No.*"

"Then what—"

"Stop." He said it flatly, so he would not yell it. No matter how much she might wish to know the story, he could not relive that time. "Suffice it to say she died through my carelessness."

"My God," she whispered. "I didn't know, Julian, I—I shouldn't have brought this up. I should have known it was too soon."

Four years since he'd last seen her. Was four years too soon? It seemed as though a lifetime separated the person he was now from the one he'd been then, with her. He shut his eyes for a moment, forbidding himself to recall it with any clarity. Closed, gone, ended.

Dead.

The guilt was not dead, of course. Once it had gnawed at his gut like acid. He had thought it might never subside. But gradually, it changed. Now it only ached. Sharper, of course, on days like this, when the thunder in the distance sounded like cannon fire. He would not surrender to it. It had subsided; it would continue to subside.

Only, something did not subside: the sense that he was living behind a pane of glass. Reflections everywhere he looked. In none of them did he recognize himself.

"It's been four years." He spoke slowly, listening to

himself to discover what would emerge from his mouth. "It is past time, I suppose."

She made a convulsive, aborted gesture that drew his eyes back to her. A small smile moved his lips as he witnessed her attempt to rein in hope.

He heard himself ask, "Do you feel like becoming a duchess?"

Twelve

SHE STOPPED AT THE BOTTOM OF THE STAIRS TO THE ballroom. It was time. She could do this. She had vowed to see it through.

I am not a coward.

A tide of chatter was rushing down the staircase. Delphinia's hand at her back was pushing her into it. All these voices, merging indistinctly. A sea of people. Belled, bright skirts interspersed with the standard gentlemen's blacks. Lounging indolently seemed to be a London custom; the stairway was crushed with loiterers. "I'm all right," Emma said to herself.

"Of course you are." This from Lord Chad, who had Delphinia's other arm. "You look quite smart, Emmaline."

"Absolutely dashing," said Delphinia.

Yes. She would not underestimate her cousin again.

Delphinia had spent an hour closeted in conference with the seamstress. The result was a very low-cut gown with a transparent lace fichu that accented her décolletage. Fashionable and provocative. But the silk itself was a dull navy that drank the light, with sleeves that fitted tightly down to the cuffs of her wrist-length gloves. It left bared no skin that an admirer might feel safe to stroke. The dress was bold, but it also made her untouchable.

Sometimes her cousin understood her very well.

The skirts were another matter. Such excessive width was still viewed in Durringham with suspicion, and so she had no practice with it. She felt like a small moving planet. Perhaps the feeling should encourage her. She could go smashing through the crowd, her own force of gravity.

Instead she was being pulled up the stairs, her feet clumsy with fear. The sight of a dark head made her stumble.

The man turned. Unfamiliar face. Their gazes slid past each other.

Would it be like that, if she saw him here? Would he pretend not to know her?

She'd imagined it a million times, until she thought herself quite unmovable. Hardened into indifference. She would be sophisticated, cool, perhaps slightly amused. *The peccadilloes of our youth*. He would not see how he'd nearly destroyed her. How she'd argued with herself, during that slow, shuffling journey east to Calcutta, that he would come. After what she had done in Kurnaul, she'd traveled under Anne Marie's name. He would be asking after Emmaline Martin. But he would come looking, and when he did, his notoriety would cause the civilians among whom she hid to remark, "The infamous Marquess has come to camp in search of someone," and she would go to him.

So she listened, and waited, and every morning when she rose she asked whether anyone had visited the camp overnight. But no one had ever remarked on the Marquess. He had never come.

The army had moved them to Calcutta so slowly. Death everywhere, villages burning, unburied corpses, safety uncertain. And as the weeks passed, her anger had grown. *You said it was safe, you left me to die. You said you would come for me, and here I am, alone.* Her fear had grown too. *Are you dead? Are you hurt? I will wait for you.* Six months she'd lingered in Calcutta, with the blood of an English solider on her hands, in a time of war. Sick with anxiety that some old acquaintance of Anne Marie's would appear to unmask her. Willing to take the risk anyway. And then, a chance meeting with Marcus. The unthinkable news. "Holdensmoor? Why, he's already gone to England."

She had not believed him. Not until weeks and weeks later, after that hellish sea journey. Emerging from her chamber at Delphinia's country home. Her cousin's sharp-edged worry. Lord Chad's uneasy regard. An outdated newspaper column leapt up at her from the pile in the library. *The Marquess of H—, called before the Commission today in Whitehall, refused to accept commendation for his involvement in the efforts to recover Delhi.*

The date of the paper had made it plain: he'd been back in London before she had.

Things had gotten very black then.

Long ago now. She had changed. And it was very easy to think on these things in Devon. Two hundred miles from London and even farther from his ancestral seat, she could nurse a very pure scorn for him. But here, moving in her cousin's circles . . . a tremor had set up in her knees.

"You are pale," Delphinia whispered.

"I'm fine," she said, and saw Delphinia flinch. Her voice had come out very cold. "No, truly—I am well. But . . ." It was hard to accept this about herself: what a little coward she was. "Do not have the majordomo announce us, if you please."

She was glad to see the Earl as they entered the ballroom. He pressed a coupe of Champagne into her hand and said in an undertone, "It is a brilliant success, Miss Martin. All that anyone is talking about. You must go into the gallery and listen."

"Will you accompany us?"

His eyes had shifted beyond them. "I will be glad to follow, but in a moment. I see someone I must speak with first."

As he moved off into the crowd, Delphinia sighed. "Such a handsome man. I wonder where his wife is? It was a most splendid wedding—wasn't it, Gid? Several years ago now, and then they went traveling for some time in the continent. It would have been nice had *I* enjoyed such a honeymoon. Only no one has seen her since. Have they, Gideon? I can't imagine he likes to keep her in the country; it was a love match, if I recall."

Lord Chad said, "I beg you will not ask him. He's devilish touchy about it."

"Do not swear, Gideon! We are in company."

He sighed. "I'm off to find the cards."

"Gideon, wait!" As he stalked off, Delphinia stamped her foot. "He is such a *beast* at times. Well, if he does not come to see how Lord Lockwood has arranged the paintings, he will regret it!"

"I do not doubt," said Emma. Lord Chad was a master statesman, but his talent was for democracy. He had no defenses against a natural autocrat like his wife.

As they entered the gallery, the silence struck her. She longed for the fuzziness that the Champagne would impart, but her throat felt too tight to swallow any more. Here was her work, then, forced on the world. Never had she imagined that anyone would care to look upon the terrors she'd expunged in oil. Indeed, did they care? The silence offered no verdict. People clustered in small groups, sipping their negus and wine and punch, trading wide-eyed, unsettled glances. Lord Lockwood obviously had peculiar criteria for declaring this a success.

When the pounding of her heart had quieted, she began to pick out some of the murmured comments. ". . . nightmares, I tell you," one woman whispered. And then a gentleman: "Must have been there, poor thing . . . tortured . . ."

The hushed atmosphere was broken by a man in the far corner, who pronounced in shaking tones, "We should have killed the lot of them! The entire goddamned country!"

Her hand tightened on Delphinia's arm. *No.*

"That's not it at all," a woman snapped. "These paintings aren't about assigning guilt. They are about suffering. And perhaps futility. Nothing was won in that war."

Emma's eyes fell gratefully on the speaker. A tall brunette with a long, slim neck, she held herself with confident grace, as if she were accustomed to being thought beautiful. She must be of some import as well, for the first man shot her an angry glance, but did not challenge her.

At least some of them understood. And the rest were not demanding her blood, precisely because they did *not* understand. But the experience was not as rewarding as she had hoped. She felt peculiarly exposed, standing here.

"There you are," Lord Lockwood said at her elbow. "I do beg your pardon, I've just had some happy news and wanted to make my congratulations. But—ah, there she is." He waved, and the brunette who'd defended the paintings came toward them, joining the group as Lord Lockwood led them a few steps out of the gallery.

He paused at the edge of the dance floor to make introductions. After the courtesies were exchanged, he said, "Lady Edon, my very best wishes to you. I've only just heard the news."

She smiled and inclined her head. Delphinia's face brightened. "Oh, Lady Edon! Can it be? Is there a very lucky gentleman to congratulate?"

Emma bit back a sigh. Her cousin loved nothing so much as news of a wedding. The Baroness, whether she knew it or not, had just won a half hour of their time, and a pressing investigation into the details of her private life. "Yes," Lady Edon said, "he—why, here he comes now."

Delphinia turned. Emma must have turned too, for one moment she was still watching Lady Edon. The next her eyes were on him.

He stood a few paces off. Facing away from her, twisted at the waist to speak to a woman whose fan tapped his forearm. She recognized him by the slope of his jaw and the contraction of her gut and the shade of his skin, which even in wet, gray England retained a golden cast.

Shock was a peculiar sensation, like ice washing down the backs of her knees. She let out the breath she'd been holding. The test was finally upon her. *It does not matter, it should not matter.* It seemed now to have always been inevitable.

"You must come visit with me and my cousin," Delphinia was saying. "We can help you choose the flowers. I do love these little projects!"

"But perhaps your cousin does not," Lord Lockwood replied. "I daresay she looks a bit peaked at the prospect. Miss Martin?"

Did *he* hear her name? Was that why his shoulders stiffened? The lady with the fan stepped back from him; what had his face revealed to her? He was turning. She could not bear this. She would run. She would turn on her heel and run.

No. He does not deserve even that *from you.*

A memory flashed over her: Mrs. Kiddell, squaring her shoulders in the face of bad news. Dignity incorruptible. She had admired it then.

She straightened. She felt nothing; she was composed. But as he faced her, oh, it all crumbled, the scene, her resolve, and her mind understood color alone, blotches of it here and there, spreading and shrinking chaotically. Resolving into his eyes. Staring into hers. Greener even than she remembered. *I will come back for you.*

She could not do this. He looked . . . he looked as though she were the very last person he had ever hoped to see and that at any moment he might be sick all over the ballroom floor.

And she had thought he would only ignore her.

She laughed. It was a quiet, slightly unbalanced sound. Lockwood's hand was suddenly cupping her elbow. "Are you quite all right, Miss Martin?"

"I am fine," she said, turning back to the group. It was true. Thank God, she was fine. A shock of coldness, a brief windless horrible moment—that was all. Far better than some of the ways she'd imagined the scenario playing out. A small problem: she could not speak. Her tongue felt leaden. She tried a smile, but her lips could not balance it.

"Julian," said Lady Edon, "do come over here."

And now they would be introduced. Now Lord Lockwood would say, "Miss Martin, this is the Duke of Auburn." And Emma would say, "How do you do, your grace," as if nothing had ever passed between them. *He* so clearly had forgotten it—

But why would the Baroness call him by his Christian name?

"Perhaps the prospect of marriage is unsettling him," said Delphinia. "It is often so, I fear."

God could not be this cruel.

He moved all at once. He was in the far periphery of her vision; and then he was coming up to her in two long strides. He grabbed her by the wrist and pulled her around to him, the spin so fast and strong that her skirts belled out. "*Emma,*" he said. His hand ran up her arm to her shoulder, while Lady Edon gasped and Delphinia said something shocked and sharp and Lockwood said, "*Jules,* what the—"

His hand stopped at the curve of her neck. "You are here," he whispered. "It is *you.*"

She was trembling. Or was that his hand that trembled? "Yes," she said. Her lips had gone numb. This was all wrong. Something was very wrong. She had rehearsed for a different scene. He was supposed to ignore her. They were supposed to ignore each other.

His hand tightened. The pain registered but she did not really feel it. His long breath was audible. "Christ—*Emma.* What—how—"

"Julian," Lockwood said. He stepped forward. "Julian, let her go."

"Julian, you are making a *scene,*" hissed Lady Edon.

Her bewilderment was growing. His eyes wandered over her. She looked past his shoulder. Yes, people were looking, whispering. Her dress was very low-cut, after all. And her sleeves so long. There were very few places her skin could be touched. That dip at the base of her throat, just above where her collarbones joined. His hand spanned her shoulder and his thumb fit into it, as if to test her pulse. As if he had the right.

It woke her from her daze. "*Damn* you," she said. "Get your hands *off* me."

Lockwood grabbed Julian's wrist and forced it away. "Auburn! What in God's name!"

"How long have you been here?" His eyes were on hers. Burning. She would like to hit him. The urge made her shake.

"Not above an hour," she said, "and now I am *leaving*!" She turned on her heel and he lunged forward to catch her arm.

"The hell you are," he said.

She yanked out of his grip. "If you touch me again—"

Lockwood stepped forward, and Julian made a guttural noise. The Earl went very still. "All right," Lockwood said. "All right then. Let's adjourn to my study. Discuss this."

"Oh, I would like to discuss it very much," Lady Edon said. "Not with you, perhaps."

Discuss it? All sitting around in a circle and sipping Champagne? "No," Emma said, and to Julian, "Stay away," and pushed into the crowd. Swimming through it. And the room was swimming too, as if she'd drunk too much when really, she'd only just begun. *Touching* her! Somewhere in this ridiculous house was a place where she would smash her fist into the wall and then scrub his touch off her throat. She went shoving through guests, heedless of whom and where she pushed. Exclamations of irritation shot up in her wake. She did not care. Let them yell.

"Lockwood." He said it with difficulty. "Let go. Or I will break your arm."

Released, he plunged into the crowd. Not difficult to track her. Chaos lay in her wake. Spilled Champagne. Crunching glass underfoot. Guests complaining. He followed her through the gallery and emerged into the music room just in time to see her slip out the far doors. The garden. It was fitting.

This was not Delhi, however. It had been a nasty week of weather, and the night was chill and sullen with remembered storms. A strong wind slapped a spattering of rain through the tree branches as he descended the steps to the lawn. He paused to listen, senses acute, intent. If she would not come to him, he would find her.

The thought briefly pierced his trance. He would *find* her.

Then something rustled in the direction of the elder bushes, and his senses narrowed again. He moved toward it, slowly, making no sound.

She was sitting just beyond the hedgerow, on the edge of a drained marble fountain. An open magnum of Champagne rested on her knee. Her thumb circled the lip of the bottle. She raised it to take a long swallow. The novelty registered, dimly. Drinking from the bottle. Not something he had ever seen a woman do. So casually she sat there and did it.

She lowered the bottle. Her head turned. *Emma.* It was undeniably Emma. Again that sensation. A fist in his gut, clawing, twisting.

"I told you not to follow me," she said.

He stood there for a long moment. Minutes? Making sense of that. Not follow her. She was alive. *Alive.* Not follow her?

All at once, the fog in his brain dissipated beneath a mighty lick of rage. "I thought you were *dead*!"

"Dead!" Her head tipped to one side. "*Dead?* Come now, surely your grace must have a better excuse than that! Where did the Duke think my fortune had gone?

Did he imagine that money could be spent from the grave?"

Another sheet of rain gusted through the garden. A downpour, soon enough. He could not trust himself to approach her. "How long have you been in London?"

"Not long."

"How long?"

"A week."

"Before that."

"Devon."

"How long there?"

She shrugged. "Three years now? Yes, that's about right."

"Three years," he whispered. *Devon*. Bloody Devon. A day away by rail and road, that was all. While he—he had haunted London like a ghost, grieving for her, *mad* with it—"And before Devon. How did you . . . get out of India?"

Her eyes narrowed. "If you're looking for itineraries, I do not have the ship and train timings on my person."

"The devil take you," he spat. "Do you have *any idea—"*

"Will your fiancée not be looking for you?"

"Why in God's name did you not *come* to me?"

She came to her feet. "*Me?* You ask why *I* didn't come to you? I . . ." She turned away for a moment, then wheeled back. "How *dare* you, you *bastard*! You cannot *imagine* what I went through, waiting for you to—" She stopped abruptly. "No. *No*. I will not do this. I am done with this. I am done with *you*. Long done. Oh yes." The Champagne bottle waved a dismissal. "Go back inside, sir. Lady Edon will be looking for you."

"You little fool," he bit out. He did not know what to do with his fury. At her. *At her.* "Do you imagine I'm going *anywhere*? For four years I thought you dead, and now you simply—*pop* back into my life and expect me to—what? What *did* you expect? Christ! That I would *bow* to you? Let Liam introduce us as though we were strangers?"

"We are strangers," she said flatly.

"To hell with that. *You will give me an explanation.*"

"Explanation," she said, "oh *yes,* you may have this one," and hurled the Champagne bottle at him.

He did not move. It whizzed by so closely that he felt the air move along his cheek. The shatter was spectacular; small stinging droplets dampened his back. She did not look away from his face. He did not look away from hers.

"Work on your aim," he said.

"I will do."

"You knew I was alive. You were not even surprised in there. And yet you didn't—*Emma,* my God. Not a single communication, not a *letter.*"

She stepped toward him. "*You* could have been clearer. Because evidently I did not *understand* at the time. When you said you would *come* for me, I thought you meant that you—would—*come.* And so I waited. Imagine it, Julian. I waited in Kurnaul. In that mess. After escaping what—what happened in Sapnagar. I *waited.* And then, when you did not come, I waited in Calcutta. *Months.* And in every dak bungalow along the way. God help me. Who knows, I might yet be there if Marcus hadn't said—"

His hand was on her then, gripping her shoulder. *"Said what?"*

She turned her face away, breathing hard. Color mottled her skin. No freckles now. Hair a dull brown from lack of sun. Time had slimmed the line of her neck and shoulders. She was fully a woman. Beautiful. If she did not speak, he was going to *throttle* her.

"*What did Lindley say?*"

Her chin came around. "He told me you had already left India. And it . . ." Her eyes fluttered briefly shut. "It was true," she finished quietly.

Like a candle doused, everything within him went dark. He marveled at it, from the curious distance where his thoughts still worked, where he was able to direct his mouth to assemble the words.

"I looked for you," he said.

Silence.

"I looked for you for months."

"Yes?" She was not looking at him anymore. She was studying the remnants of the Champagne bottle behind him. "Pity, then. I shouldn't have thrown it. We could have toasted your efforts."

"You don't believe me."

Her shoulders moved in a small shrug. "I don't know. Perhaps I do." She glanced to him. "But it doesn't matter, does it? You still left me to die there. Oh, you couldn't have known, of course; and I don't blame you for it. After all, I didn't die. And all's well that ends well, yes? So I do hope you won't trouble yourself over it. Certainly it does not occupy *my* thoughts overmuch." Her brows rose. "Oh, I see that shocks you. What, did you expect me to still be in mourning for our . . . our star-crossed romance? The only man I ever loved, and all that?" She paused. "No answer for that, I see."

You left me to die there. The words were acidic in his ears. They settled so well into the groove his own thoughts had worn on the subject. As for the rest of what she said—if he had not had the eyes to watch her, perhaps he would have believed she meant it.

"I want to know what happened to you," he said.

She smiled a little. "Curiosity killed the cat, your grace. And now—I think I'll be off. I'm sure my cousin is ripping up the place looking for me. Do convey my good wishes to Lady Edon."

She made her retreat into the house with slow dignity. But the stiffness with which she mounted the stairs, and the small bobble at the top, gave her away. Her knees were about to give out on her.

He let her go, only for that. Only because it was very clear that she would not want him to see her collapse. London was not war-torn; she would not be able to vanish. God help her if she were foolish enough to try.

A crack of thunder sounded. As the rain began to beat down, Julian shut his eyes and turned his face to the sky. The rain was cold. His thoughts felt more lucid than they had in a long while.

He thought it highly possible that he was going to kill Marcus Lindley.

When enough time had passed, he went back into the house. Not surprising to find Lockwood waiting.

"What in bloody hell was that?"

Julian strode past. "Is she gone?"

"As though the devil were at her heels."

"No wonder you and I rub along. We have a peculiar talent for making women run."

Lockwood came up beside him. "*Careful,* Auburn."

"Indeed. Very careful."

A brief, aggrieved silence, and then: "That was a bloody *guest*. One I had to work quite hard to lure here."

Julian came to a stop. "I do not like the sound of that."

"Don't you?" Lockwood stepped in front of him. "I find it odd, but it seems we are about to come to blows. If that's the case, let's do it here rather than in the gallery."

"Afraid of an audience?"

Lockwood made an exasperated noise. "Did you perhaps notice that this entire event is meant to draw attention to Miss Ashdown's art? You are quite stealing her thunder." He frowned. "Have you seen the paintings, Auburn?"

"You are strange by routine, but I would not have thought you dense. No."

"Perhaps you should have a look at them."

"Alas, I have a prior appointment."

"And where might that be?"

"It depends," Julian said. "But I believe I will start at the East India Club. Step out of my way, or steal Miss Ashdown's thunder; it is all up to you."

Lockwood caught him by the arm, and he felt his fist curl. He had thought to save it for Lindley, but if Lockwood wanted a go first—

"Look at them as you pass, then." Lockwood was quiet but insistent. "At the least, do give them a look."

Julian threw off his arm. "Good evening," he said, and strode into the gallery. If not the East India Club, then Brooks's. Lindley was nothing if not predictable.

A woman backed into his path, her palm pressed to her mouth as she looked up. He sidestepped, but her arrested expression caused him to flick a glance toward the source of her horror.

Jesus Christ.

The Indian man was sitting cross-legged on the ground, his fingers pursed in meditative stance, thumbs to middle fingers, palms up. There was a look of peace on his face that spoke of transcendence—the sort of enlightenment saints attained through long and painful martyrdoms. His expression could make one yearn to find religion. And so it stood in shocking contrast to the bloody knife stretched across his lap, and the scene of carnage around his seat in the dirt: dead women and children, mutilated civilians and soldiers, Indian and British bodies littered like trash.

Julian took a step back from it. He smelled gunpowder. Dust and blood clogged the back of his throat. Another step. The wall pushed against his shoulder blades. His eyes moved to the next painting.

The frame barely contained the massive form of the British soldier. The perspective was from beneath him, as though the man were reaching down to throttle the viewer. His uniform was covered in dirt and blood. He looked familiar. It was not simply the death in his eyes that Julian recognized.

His gut realized before he did. The roll of nausea alerted him, lifted the fine hairs on his neck.

If I see you again, I'll kill you.

He had said that to this man. He could hear himself saying it. Where? Where had he said it?

On a breath, he forced himself closer to the painting.

The brushstrokes were harsh, long and angular and thickly layered. He could envision how it must have been done: by literally slashing the colors onto the canvas, violent downward strikes of the brush-wielding hand.

Save for the bottom. From a few feet away, it became apparent that there was delicate gibberish running along the base of the painting. A pace closer, and the gibberish snapped into focus: sloppily rendered Urdu. *The city is not secure; therefore wait.*

"This is my favorite as well," Lockwood said, startling him. "They will all sell, you know; I've already had offers. But I think I'll keep this one."

He could not imagine wanting to look on these paintings every day. Or ever again. "Not the—" He swallowed. Where was his voice? He had forgotten the smell of it, the smell of the dying; but suddenly it was everywhere around him. The blood—the texture of the oil paint served it so well—"Not the sort of thing one hangs in a bedchamber."

"You think? I'm not sure. The man has a powerful lust in his eye."

The key turning in his locked memory. *Chandni Chowk.*

"Oh yes," Lockwood said. "I had meant to tell you. Lady Edon—"

Emma on the ground.

One man over her, reaching for his belt. The other holding her maid.

This one. Yes.

"—if you could stop by Dover Street—"

There were war drums in his head as he walked down the gallery. The ground was vibrating beneath his feet in steady, regular vibrations, and all of these people, whispering and drinking and staring at the wall, had no idea. No idea at all.

As he reached the last of the paintings, his breath left him. For there was Sapnagar, its distinctive plateau detailed in miniature, as though seen from a great distance. And in the foreground, a village on fire, and a band of bloodied sepoys approaching.

And where was I then? he thought. At that very moment, rendered with such clarity that it was as if he were seeing it through her eyes—where had he been then?

Curiosity killed the cat, she had said to him, and smiled.

Thirteen

Emma sat down amidst the chaos of her room. The shattered remnants of a Chinese vase trailed across the carpet. Clothing everywhere. Spattered paint. She'd ripped the canvas she had spent yesterday stretching. She could have kept on. There were still curtains to be pulled down. Mirrors to be broken. Seven years' bad luck; she was game for it.

But her fury, so full-bodied that her hands might have pulled apart the chair on which she sat, reminded her of something. She had felt like this before, in that moment before she had killed the soldier in Kurnaul.

She shuddered, dropping her head to her knees. She was as much a monster as any whom she'd painted.

And the dream. Her parents. The shipwreck. For the first time in more than a year, it had come to her last night. Her mother's face—

Damn him. She had been done with this, finished. She could not bear to live it again!

A knock came at the door. She ignored it. Delph would go away in another minute. All day she had been knocking, and retreating, and knocking again. It would be kinder to assuage her concern, but Delphinia wanted answers to the most irritating questions—such as why the Duke of Auburn felt entitled to manhandle her.

"What is the connection between you?" she had demanded upon boarding the coach. And when no reply had proved forthcoming, she'd said to Lord Chad, "I did not know madness ran in that family. You should have seen it, Gideon. He was looking at her as though she were a ghost, and groping her, and mumbling all manner of claptrap!"

As though I were a ghost. It seemed a fitting comparison. Ghosts were also robbed of their peace, at the very time when they should have found it. Her career launched. Her paintings a success. She kicked at the newspaper by her foot. The critics were most impressed.

And the guests—they had not simply admired her work, they had wanted to buy it. She was sure Lockwood had stopped her in the hallway to tell her that, as she'd come in from the garden. She'd been in no state to fabricate happy hallucinations, so she expected that he really had said to her, "Several people have inquired about purchasing the work."

So, an all-around triumph. Ruined by him.

How effortlessly he destroyed her. Had once not been enough? She had never admitted her love, as he had done. But how she had loved him. Did he imagine that *his* declaration, so long ago, to that girl she had been, gave him the right to question her now? And yet he *had* asked. He had asked what had happened to her, and he had looked at her as though he knew her, as though he could guess the answers. How she had wanted to strike him! As if anything remained in her that he might recognize. *Look more closely,* she should have said. *See what is really here, if you can bear it. And once you do see, you will not ask me again to tell you how I made it out of that country. You will no longer wish to hear it.*

The sound of the key turning in the door brought her to her feet. "I do *not* desire company."

"I only wished to see if the bedroom was still standing," her cousin said as she stepped inside. She carried Poppet, her small white lapdog, in her arms. "It sounded as though you'd taken to ripping up my floorboards."

Emma settled back onto the chair. "Very well, then. You see the floor is intact."

Delphinia surveyed the room. "You were very angry."

"And now I am exhausted." Emma manufactured a laugh. "Dismantling bedrooms is very hard labor."

"A note came for you."

"Put it on the dresser."

"Oh, do open it, Emma." Delphinia set Poppet onto the floor. "I'm dying to know if it's from the madman."

"He is not mad," she heard herself say. "That is . . . he says he thought me dead."

"Dead!"

Emma bent down to scoop up the dog. "I wish you wouldn't let Poppet wander in here. I've got turpentine about."

"Emma, why in the world would he think you dead?"

She toyed with one of Poppet's soft ears, receiving

an enthusiastic lick in return. "He helped me to escape Delhi. I told you once that I'd had help. But then we were—separated."

"Oh!"

It was somewhat amusing to watch Delphinia struggle to restrain herself. She had tried asking about India before, in darker days; no doubt she feared a response similar to the ones she had gotten then. Hysterical tears. Or, later, stony silence.

Emma had never been able to speak of it, or him. Only paint it.

Her one painting with no blood. It appeared in her mind now. Frighteningly immediate, with his face last night to draw upon. On the canvas, his figure was complete. The rooftop was complete. And the moon was perfect, swollen gold in a soft dark sky. But the background remained blank, even though she had always been able to envision it. At first she had thought it would be a flat, gray wasteland, dotted with corpses, stretching out like a premonition behind the promise of his eyes. She'd done the first rough sketch of it in Kurnaul, while waiting, like a fool, for his reply.

Then, later, she had changed her mind. No corpses were necessary to symbolize the horrors she'd seen. She would leave the plain barren, as barren as his promise had been.

Yet she'd never managed to bring herself to finish the background and call it done.

She wondered whether he had thought her dead even as she'd sat in Kurnaul envisioning it. Or had he come to that conclusion later? He said he had searched for her. Had she somehow missed word of him? Had he come and gone, all while she sat there sketching, pouring her heart and love and sorrow into her pencil, watching his face come to life on the page? If he had found her then, it might still have been all right. Even then, she—*God,* she could not bear to think on it!

She would not think on it.

As for the present, he would not prove bothersome. No, he was done with her, quite done, engaged to be married to the lovely Lady Edon. The perfect match for a duke, was Baroness Edon—a quick glance in *Burke's Peerage* had proved it. That volume was the first thing Emma had thrown today.

What pompous little children they'd make together.

She put her fist against the sudden pain in her gut. Pounding stakes together to stretch canvas was such a physical endeavor, and disassembling them even more rigorous. All sorts of twinges resulted.

She saw that Delphinia was still waiting for her to speak. "Here, take Poppet back. Did Lockwood tell you last night? He received offers on some of the paintings."

"What a marvelous compliment! Will you sell them?"

She shrugged. Once, she had supposed that she would simply burn the paintings. That a time would come when destroying them would be the logical final step. But she hadn't even been able to burn that first sketch of Anne Marie. She would have liked to destroy it, for it lingered at the edge of her mind like a sore. She had *tried* to burn it. Two years ago, she had snatched a bottle of wine from the cellar, some bread and cheese from the kitchen, and nursed a fire in her bedroom—intending to celebrate as she watched the drawing incinerate.

But there was something of herself in the sketch—and even, perhaps, in the letters she'd snatched from the soldier—that she was not quite able to let go. A piece of what had made her as she was today. She could disown that part of her, certainly; she could leave it behind, but it would not be destroyed. And so she had put the papers away from her. All of it. The evidence of her greatest crime, and the scene of the greatest crime she had witnessed—they lay pressed together in one of the frames hanging in Lord Lockwood's gallery. Perhaps Julian had even considered the painting that held them. Surely he had seen her paintings last night? She wondered whether it had crossed his mind to speculate at who could have produced such scenes. What he had thought of them, and whether—

She pressed her fist harder into her stomach. The busk dug into her sternum, a bruising pressure, satisfying somehow. "Coz, I must go."

"Now? Where? May I come?"

"I mean, I must leave London. I am expected in Rome anyway; I can rebook my passage this afternoon."

"Oh, *Emma.*"

"And I think I will let Lockwood sell the paintings. I am done with them."

"Can you really not talk about it, dear?"

Emma gave her a little smile. "There is nothing to say."

"I don't believe that. Emma—"

"Do you know what I *was* thinking this morning? A strange thought."

"Tell me."

"I was thinking it is fortunate that Mama died before

your mother. She loved Aunt Anna beyond life itself. She would not have survived it."

Delphinia's lips trembled; blinking rapidly, she bent down to kiss Poppet's head. Aunt Anna had died the previous year of the influenza. Perhaps for the first time in her life, Delphinia had been overwrought. She had passed several weeks at Gemson Park, helping Emma in the garden, reading aloud at night. At first, her voice had broken every page or so. By the time she'd left, she had made it steadily through entire chapters. "I thought of my mother this morning too," she said softly. "Oh, Emma, I think of her every day. If only Papa lived nearer to London! I feel sure she would worry about him, all alone in that drafty house."

"Yes. It's a terrible feeling, worrying for loved ones." Emma leaned forward to take her cousin's hand. "I hope I never have to do so for you. Believe me, coz, I would rather go first. I have done enough grieving for a lifetime."

Delphinia made a small noise and launched herself off the chair. Poppet went yipping to the ground. "Do not go to Italy," she whispered as she pulled Emma into a hug. "I will miss you so."

"I must," Emma said gently. "Did you not hear me? I will go and paint. I am done with the rest."

With a sigh, her cousin released her. "I think you very foolish, Emma. But I love you all the same." She shook her head and reached into her pocket. "Here is the letter, then."

Emma took it and crossed to the credenza desk for a letter opener. "It's from Lockwood," she said, reading quickly. "That's why it wasn't marked, he thinks to keep our connection anon—"

"What is it?" Delphinia came up. "Emma?"

She lowered the letter. Her hands were shaking. "I cannot credit it," she whispered. "The Royal Academy expresses an interest in showing my work. The *Royal Academy.*"

Delphinia's eyes widened. "It is an immense honor. Why, it is the very highest, Emma."

The letter was crumpling between her fingers. Some would save this letter forever; they would kiss it and frame it and dance in celebration. "Delphinia, *I cannot stay here.*"

"Emma! If you cannot stay for this, then—then I am shocked and disappointed, and I think you are not going to Italy for your painting. I think that . . . you are running away!" Her cousin stepped forward to seize her wrist. "That's it, isn't it? But what are you running from? Is it him? Of course, it *must* be him! He helped you to escape Delhi, he—and last night—why—what *is* Auburn to you, Emma?"

"Nothing. He is *nothing* to me."

"Then why can't you stay? Even *I* know that this is the most splendid start to a career any artist could ask for!"

She shook her head. There were no words to explain this. She had not been a coward last night; her rage had made her strong. But what of the time when rage began to fail her? It surely would, eventually. Already it failed her in her dreams. And tonight? What if she thought on it in her bed before sleeping? The quiet of the house would allow his voice to sound as clearly in her head as if he were next to her. *I looked for you.*

Her heart was breaking, when she had thought it in bits already. To go through all this again, to let him smash her once more, was not a choice. It was nauseating. Literally unthinkable.

She pressed the letter onto the desktop. How slim and small her hand looked as it smoothed over the parchment. One would never guess it capable of so many things. The destruction around her. The paintings the Academy admired. Other things, even darker. There were depths in her that she could sense only dimly, that she hid even from herself. Could she rely on them?

"I don't know if I can do it," she said quietly. It felt like a confession, and a prickle of shame stung her cheeks as she looked up to her cousin. "I don't know if I *can* stay."

"No," Delphinia said, and moved forward to take her hand again. "Of course you don't. Emma, one never can know, without *trying* first."

"A hundred pounds says you don't make this next shot."

Julian glanced up from the billiards table. "A thousand."

Marwick whistled as he chalked his cue. "A thousand. Did you hear that, Adams!"

"I did," a young man said from the corner, stepping up and giving his paisley waistcoat a tug. "I'll witness, Lord Marwick."

Marwick shook his head. "All right, Auburn. As a friend, I'd protest that you're out of practice—but God knows you can spare the brass."

Julian leaned down and in one unbroken gesture knocked off the shot. The other two groaned as the ball snapped into the far pocket.

"Bloody hell, man! That should have been impossible!"

"Another game, Auburn!"

He stepped back, throwing his cue to Adams. "You play for me." Marwick was already digging inside his pockets, cursing under his breath. "Give it to Adams," Julian said. "Spending money for Oxford."

"Never play with a shark, Lorrie," Marwick grumbled, as a footman stepped up with a pencil. He bent over the table to sign the note, then handed it to the boy with a flourish. "Spend it all on women."

"Yes, sir." Straight-faced, Adams pocketed the note.

"Good. Then it'll do you for a week, tops. I say—Auburn, where are you going? Wait up, man!"

Julian ignored him, cutting across the plush lobby of the club toward the gaming room. Despite the early hour, the den was filled with cigar smoke and quiet conversation, gentlemen hunched over their cards with the concentrated dedication of connoisseurs.

He spied Lord Chad in the far corner. They briefly made eye contact, and the man's brow lowered. Something clicked in Julian's brain as he moved on—*that* was why the woman with Emma last night had seemed so familiar. A black laugh moved through him. He motioned to a manservant with two uplifted fingers. He had crossed paths with Chad and his Countess innumerable times in the last few years. And yet he had never known that news of Emma was but a word away. He could not have imagined to ask.

The ache in his shoulder reminded him of another thing he hadn't known: Chad hired footmen for muscle. His paid thugs had not *turned* Julian away from the house on Bolton Street this morning. Accuracy demanded a more forceful verb.

"Your grace."

"Thank you, Lionel." He accepted the tumbler of Scotch, downed it neatly, then reached for the second. The bearer masked his surprise well enough. Julian had not come here for play or strong drink since his return from India. It had not been a conscious decision; he'd simply no longer needed alcohol. Sobriety had felt equally numbing to him.

He was reconsidering the notion now. The Scotch seemed to rip down his throat, traveling like a tide of acid to his stomach. Nothing objectionable in it.

"Lionel," he said, "arrange a private room for me. Something in the back, facing Arlington Street."

"Directly, sir."

Adams was passing, looking very pleased with himself. Julian crooked a finger, and he changed course, amiable and loose-limbed as a puppy.

"Sir?"

"A favor from you."

"Say the word."

"Do you see the gentleman in the far corner? The one darting me the surreptitious scowls."

"D'you mean—Lord Chad?"

"Yes. Find out his plans for the evening. Be subtle, if you please."

With a cheeky salute, Adams ambled off in the direction of Chad's covey.

Corrupting the youth. A novel pastime. His conscience did not twinge; it was otherwise occupied.

He bolted the last of the Scotch, and the indubitable Lionel appeared like clockwork with the next round. Very good; the man learned quickly.

"Note for you, sir," Lionel said, and held out a letter along with a large brass key. "Also, sir—your room."

He took the brass key and used it to split the seal of the letter. Caroline, importuning him to receive her. He felt bad about that. He would have to deal with her. No apology, of course. That was the best thing about Caro: she did not set precedents that she didn't wish to follow. Fidelity, jealousy, judgment—none of these appealed to her. If he disappeared for days on end, doubtless she would pout, but she would not *castigate* him when he returned. Her expectations were adjusted to the lowest common denominator; one simply couldn't disappoint her. It was a comfortable and convenient attitude, provided it was genuine. As it was, with Caroline.

You left me there to die. You couldn't have known; I do not blame you for it.

She damned well should blame him, Julian thought. She should have thrown more than the Champagne bottle at his head. She should have found a pistol and blown his goddamned head off.

"Sulking in the corner, old boy? Masters told me you made a poor showing last night. Staggering about Lockwood's like a boy who'd filched the keys to the liquor cabinet."

Julian bolted his drink and pushed himself up from the table. "Lindley. I've been waiting to run into you all day. There is a matter of great import we must discuss. I require your . . . advice."

"Is that so?" Lindley seemed to inflate. He cast a look around the room, no doubt to gauge the number of witnesses to this gratifying request. "Very well, Auburn. I am already engaged, but I will gladly make time to advise a cousin."

"Excellent. Lionel has arranged for a room for us."

Lindley trailed him down the hall. At the door into the study, key turning in lock, Julian looked up and asked, "Have you seen Miss Martin since her return to town?"

The smirk on Lindley's face faltered. "Emmaline?"

Julian opened the door and pushed him inside. Lindley swung around, his hand moving to his waist.

Julian locked the door behind him. "You forget you are no longer in the army, Viscount. You do not wear a pistol."

Lindley flushed. "What is this about, Auburn? You wanted advice?"

"Yes, indeed. I am contemplating the benefits and drawbacks of a certain proposition—one to which I find myself most ardently inclined."

Lindley stopped his backward retreat. Confusion, and perhaps relief, lightened his face. "Lady Edon," he said. "Is *that* what this is about?" He laughed. Yes, definitely relief. "Well, her reputation isn't quite the thing, of course. But if you don't mind the tales, then certainly, as a member of the family, I will give my approval. Her lineage, after all—"

Julian waited a moment. But nothing more was forthcoming. "Go on," he said. "I believe it just occurred to you to remark on my bad blood. I see no reason for reticence. At one time you were quite expansive on the matter."

Lindley glanced uneasily around the room. Bookcases against the walls, and a few wing chairs that bordered a low, scrolled table. Little of interest, less of use. The single, small window was set high into the back wall, and the milky haze outside was not taking advantage of it. Put out the lamps and it would be very dark. Julian strolled forward.

"Bygones," Lindley muttered. "I let bygones be bygones."

"Curious. My proposition is directly inspired by one such bygone. Would you like to hear it? No," he said gently, as Lindley's startled eyes came back to him. "It does not concern Lady Edon."

"I didn't know." Lindley's voice was suddenly higher. "Believe me, Auburn, in Cawnpore *I did not know.*"

"And later, it did not occur to you that I might find her reappearance to be . . . interesting news?"

Lindley's lips moved soundlessly. And then he advanced a pace himself. "Damn you, Sinclair! You filthy, rutting beast. You had her, didn't you? I thought so; when you showed up in Cawnpore, I thought—"

His words ended in a wheeze, as Julian lunged forward and took him by the throat. Back, back, the man's boots scrabbling between his feet, until he slammed Lindley up against the bookcase. Books thumped down around their shoulders. Lindley's throat, pinned beneath his hand, worked convulsively. A pleasant feeling. "Here is my proposition," Julian said, and stepped on Lindley's ankle to forestall a kick. "I will kill you. The drawback:

I will be tried for your death." He put his whole weight into his hand as Lindley began to claw at his fingers. "Benefit: *You will be dead.*"

"Au—burn—" Lindley went for his eyes. Julian shifted grip, yanked him forward, and pulled him into a chokehold.

"Benefit," he said in Lindley's ear. Not so calm now. The urge to snap the bastard's neck was cramping his hands. He could do it. So easy. "The world will be rid of one pompous, spineless, vicious, murdering son of a bitch. Drawback—why, Viscount—I cannot think of another one."

"Emmaline—will—"

A slight readjustment of the arm around Lindley's neck, just a bit more pressure, solved that annoying tendency he had to talk. As if anyone cared. "She might not like it," Julian said. "That is true. I have thought of it. Then again, the marvelous thing about Miss Martin is that one never can be sure. She may be *thrilled* by it."

"Ha!" Lindley jammed up his shoulders. "Thrilled? By *you*? Like it or not, you abandoned her, you—"

He slammed Lindley forward into the bookcase. Lindley's head cracked against a shelf; he went down on his knees.

"Get up," Julian said. "Let's do it properly."

Lindley hauled himself up by the shelving, then in one continuous movement turned and threw a punch. Julian sidestepped, but did not see the next one coming. The fist glanced across his cheek, throwing him back a step.

The following jab was too obvious. He caught Lindley's fist and twisted it around, yanking it back behind the man's torso and twisting until the bone cracked. On an ear-splitting shriek, Lindley fell away from him.

"Yes, that will hurt," Julian said, as the man clutched his arm and rocked on the floor. "You may never be able to draw a gun again. Pity you don't still have access to the cannons."

The door closed behind him without a sound. They kept everything marvelously well oiled around here.

Fourteen

"Do you enjoy Verdi?"

His voice, very soft behind her, made Emma flinch. Suddenly she violently regretted the whim that had led her to the edge of the drawing room for a better view. Miss Tietjens was singing the final aria, and the audience was rapt; Delphinia, somewhere in the middle of the crush, would be no help at all.

Well, she did not need help. She kept her eyes trained on the soprano. "You were not invited to this event."

"Asked after me, did you?"

"Only to make sure to avoid you."

"But there is Champagne, and a garden. You could practice your aim."

She bit her lip. He would go away in a moment.

"Very well. At the least, you must tell me where you learned Urdu. And such interesting Urdu, at that."

At that, she turned. "*What?*"

Julian was directly behind her, his arms crossed, the long, elegant fingers of his right hand looped negligently around the stem of a wineglass. She had forgotten the tricks of his eyes, the way they turned such a luminous green-gold in candlelight. "Shh," he said, and set his glass onto the floor. "You will disrupt the mood."

"It is already disrupted. *You* are here." She could not believe it. Lord Lockwood had told him her identity. Ashdown's real name. Knowing it was she, Julian would have seen too much in those paintings.

He jerked his head toward the door. She cast one last glance in her cousin's direction, then followed him out into the antechamber. The air was better out here. She drew a deep, bracing breath. "He promised he would not tell anyone."

His smile was sharp-edged, a little mocking. "Do you imagine he needed to tell me?" He leaned back against the wall, considering her. The white wallpaper set off his dramatic coloring, black and gold and green. She had thought him like a fever dream the first time she saw him. It came back to her suddenly. She had thought him so beautiful. She could not do this. "Sapnagar and the soldier," he said. "I recognized both."

"You—" Oh, she was a *fool.* But Sapnagar had been so small, so inconsequential in that painting. And the soldier; how could she have known he would remember?

Inside, the crowd burst into applause. The doors opened to disgorge a handful of guests. As they passed, their heads turned toward Julian, and she heard a gentleman among them mutter something about "Auburn" and "the cheek." Julian took no notice. "I must congratulate you, Emma. Your artistry is exquisite. And the Royal Academy—a great achievement."

Her stomach knotted. "Continue thus, and you will unmask me."

"Only if we are overheard."

The implication startled a scoff from her. "You cannot seriously think I will accompany you anywhere."

He shrugged. "You seem to value your anonymity very highly. I can't say I blame you. Your paintings are powerful. They are also . . . provocative. I wonder if you know the extent of it yourself."

He was confusing her. This conversation, trying to fend him off, felt like dueling with a moth. She did not like it. It was crucial that he not discompose her. "We have nothing to talk about."

"Then perhaps we can share a moment or two of truth."

She did not want to know his truths. The ones he'd already given her were enough to ruin her sleep. "Why in the world should I care to do that?"

He smiled now, though not pleasantly. "I am beginning to find this routine absurd. Unless, by chance, you are suffering from a peculiar amnesia concerning what has passed between us."

"Four years ago," she said. "Water under the bridge!"

"Then a very stagnant river."

More guests were exiting the drawing room now. Again, they seemed to evidence a most unusual interest in Julian. "Auburn," called one young man, "you should go over to the Turf Club, I think. New, yes, but it's already got a promising reputation for poor *ton.*"

Julian turned at that. Emma could not see his face, but when the gentleman looked into it, he paled and hastened from the room.

"What are they talking about?"

Turning back, Julian shrugged. "It seems I am about to be blackballed from my club."

"For what?"

"Ill temper. Shall we walk?"

She had no idea what to do. She clenched her fists, started to turn away, then wheeled back. "Why won't you just *leave me alone*? After all, you were so very good at it before!"

He exhaled. "And there you have it," he said, and took her wrist. "Come with me."

His fingers were hot on her skin. He still smelled the same. The scent wrapped around her as he led her down the hallway: sandalwood and bay soap, and the subtle musk of his skin, the scent of the body that had pressed into hers, once. The lights seemed to brighten and dim. Her head felt very light, as though it were swimming off her neck, toward the ceiling. She could not believe she was following him. Did she have a choice?

He stepped ahead to open a door. "No," he said, and with his hand at the small of her back, urged her forward again. The next room suited him. "Splendid." He guided her inside.

She moved away from him, across the teal and taupe carpet, Axminster it looked like, very fine, and her arms were wrapping around herself for comfort because she did not know what to do. "You must leave me alone," she said, staring at nothing. There was a giant globe, as big as a carriage wheel, standing near the desk. It was startling and unusual, and she recalled suddenly having heard of it: the Ardsmores' famous globe. She stepped forward and put one finger on England. How small it looked, how defenseless, against the vast waters of the world.

His hand closed on hers. "No," he said, very close, his lips brushing her ear. The passage of his breath called up goose bumps from her skin. She could feel the heat of him all along her back, only an inch or two separating them. She inhaled, heard the way it shook. Her throat was seizing. He murmured, "Let's go back, shall we?" And his hand moved hers across the surface of the orb, applying pressure to give the globe a spin, so her finger came to rest on the shape of the Indian subcontinent.

"Where were you?" he asked quietly. He moved her finger to Delhi. "Here you were. Almost four years ago, exactly. And I found you in the garden, with your face turned to the breeze."

Don't do this. She shut her eyes. His hand tightened on hers.

"Open them," he said savagely. "If I can bear it, so can you."

Her next breath sounded like a sob. She felt his reaction to it; it was communicated through his flesh, his arm pressing along the side of hers, the way his knuckles whitened.

"You were in the garden," he said. "You did not like the wine. It was awful, you were right. We spoke here, for the first time, in Delhi. And we touched here for the first time, as well. It was sweet, Emma. So sweet." His lips turned in to her neck. It was not a kiss. Merely a—touch. It had nothing to do with the other, in that hallway in Delhi. So long ago. "Do you remember?" he said, shaping the words against her skin, so the memory that broke over her was not visual, but physical. He had brought stars out in her stomach that time. She had liked it then but now it made her want to scream; it was soft torture, the drip of a water clock when one had a migraine; it exacerbated the pain she already felt. Pain she had been done with, which she *should not have to feel any longer.*

She shook her head.

His head lifted slightly. "And then," he said after a long moment, and there was nothing she could read in his voice, only a hard, quiet resolve. "Then the war came. And you were here." He moved her hand up a small fraction, to a shaded region labeled *Rajpootana.* "Did you know that? Did you ever look to see where you had been? Once you'd come back to this country, did you look to see where Sapnagar could be found?"

She fought to swallow. It was important to swallow, to clear her throat. She wanted to make her voice as hard and fierce and clear as his. "*No.*"

"Kavita still remembers you in her prayers, you know. She mentions your name in every letter. She still calls you her *behin.*" He paused. "I will not tell her you did not look for Sapnagar. I do not think she would understand it."

Damn him. A tear slipped, hot and burning, down her cheek. "Good," she said. "I do not care. Tell her. Or don't tell her. Your decision."

"I'm not blind," he said, very low. "Words are not the only way we communicate, you and I. They never were."

She pushed back against him, trying to break away, to run. But he was ready for it and he stepped forward, the length of his body pinning her against the globe. "You are the second person I have held down today," he said at her ear. "I will be more gentle with you, but I will not let you go. Do you understand?"

She slammed her heel onto his foot. He laughed softly against her hair. "Yes. He tried that too. It works better when you're not wearing slippers."

"I *will* hurt you," she said.

"I've no doubt of it, Emma. But first things first." His voice hardened again. "We have you in Sapnagar. Then where were you? You mentioned Kurnaul." He forced her hand down and to the right; she was fighting against it. "Perhaps we need a calendar to complement this endeavor, for I went to Kurnaul as well. I went here." He pressed her finger hard into the surface. "Is that where you were? Kurnaul, Emma? *Is it?*"

Something in her snapped. "I will show you," she said in a hoarse, ugly voice. "Take your hands off me and I will show you."

The pressure of his grip eased. "Show me, then."

"Take your hand off."

His hand lifted. But he did not step away from her.

"Here," she said, and slammed her finger against the spot marked *Kurnaul.* "Yes, I was here. It rained incessantly. Half the civilians were sick from the cholera. I waited for you there. Weeks. And then they moved us southeast." She moved her finger an inch. "Here. Bar— Bart—"

"Bharatpur," he whispered. "Yes. I looked—"

"Outside of Bartpur. The Maharajah was friendly to

us, they said. I waited for you there. But our camp was not safe. A man rode in. His arm nearly severed. The—the tendons. He'd run into a band of mutineers—and we were only civilians. They could not spare many soldiers. He warned us. So we rode again. All night, well into the day. By that time I was sick. I'd caught something in the camp. And then we were quartered here." Her finger landed on Alwar. She could not speak the name aloud. She had seen terrible things in Alwar. Terrible.

His sigh made no sound. But she felt it all along her cheek. "God, Emma. Alwar, yes. I was there too; I was there twice. *How* did I—?"

"There was a woman I was quartered with there. Her child had been killed. Before her eyes, I expect. She did not stop screaming. Day and night, she screamed. One day she found a pistol. The officer was having his tiffin. He had laid it down beside him. She took it. She took it and she used it on herself in our tent."

His grip had fallen away. She turned around, raising her face to his. If you understood madness, did that mean you shared it? For she had known why the woman could not keep from screaming. And never better than at this moment, for if she began to scream at him now, she knew she would also never stop. If she kept going, if she told him all of it, she would only be able to do it in a scream. So what if his face was clouded, if his expression was haunted? She was sure she looked worse, but she did not care. She put her hands against his chest and shoved him two paces back. "You want my whole itinerary? *I will not give it!* I have given you *enough!*"

"Alwar," he said. "Bharatpur. Kurnaul. Lucknow?

Agra? Where else? Emma, I was there. I looked at all of those places for you. I was *there*."

The breath went out of her. *These* were the things she had not wanted to know. Because—"I wish that you had found me. God above, Julian, I wish you had found me! But—" She found air again. "You didn't find me." He thought he had found her now. It was so clear in his face. But he would never find her. That girl he'd looked for was well and truly gone. And what remained—no one would want it. *She* did not want it. She pushed out the breath she was holding. "And the journey I took then, it's simply . . . too late for you to follow."

"Emma, you are not the only one who took that damned journey."

"No," she said after a moment. "I am sure you suffered too. It's a very lonely path, isn't it?"

"Yes, but—"

"And sometimes one acquires a taste for the loneliness. So it seems."

"You are afraid," he said. "And angry. I understand that—"

"No," she said, sharper now, because he was looking at her as if he knew what was coming, as if he could not be surprised by anything she might say. Did he actually believe that? Did he really think that this could be as simple as listening to what she said, and giving a nod of acceptance? His intense, unwavering regard promised things that he *could not promise*. He was so sure his opinion would be unaffected by anything she told him. But he could not know what was in her head. What was in *her*. And he would not like it. He would recoil and she would not be able to bear it. Seeing him leave again.

"I'm not angry," she said. But suddenly she was no longer sure of it. An awful pressure was building in her chest. It could as easily be anger as grief. "I will admit to being afraid, though. Yes, I am a coward. And I beg you will leave this coward *alone.* I really—I can't tell you strongly enough that I don't blame you. It is an impulse, to be sure, but not a fair one, or logical. And everything else—" She shook her head. "It is too late."

A long silence passed between them. She leaned back against the globe, watching him. The racing of her heart, the nauseous anticipation in her gut, suggested that she feared something else—she did not know what it might be, but she was ready for it, ready to defend herself.

But when he spoke, his question surprised her. "And your paintings?"

"What of them?"

"What is the Urdu, Emma? Where is it from?"

He had a gift, didn't he? Unerring aim. "It is no concern of yours."

"And so we are back to our fundamental disagreement, for I think it is. The Urdu is rather peculiar. I would like to know where you learned it."

"From a dead man." It was more than she had ever admitted. "And now, if you will once again permit me the pleasure, I will leave *you.*"

"Again and again," he said. "If that is your desire."

"No, thank you," she said as she passed. "I am fond of finality."

Crossing the threshold of the room, she could not prevent herself from glancing over her shoulder. His back was to her. He was staring at the globe. As she reached out to pull the door closed, she saw his hand come up and across his body, a sudden violent backhand. The door shut soundlessly. The click of its latch was lost amidst the sudden crash in the room beyond.

Julian threw open the door, taking a vicious pleasure in the way his valet's face paled. It caused him to glance in the mirror as he passed through the closet, and he laughed harshly at what he saw there. Good. Bloody well and good. He looked drunk and enraged and also as sulky as a boy. Exactly as he felt.

He pushed into the bedroom, and Caroline burst up from his sheets. "Julian! Finally! You would not believe the tales I have been hearing—Lady Fitzgerald said you have crippled Lindley! She said she would no longer receive you, but I told her it could not be true!"

"What are you doing here?"

She came up on her knees. "My God—it *is* true, isn't it?"

"Caroline." He took a slow breath. "I would like to be alone."

"Incredible! I defend you to a crowd of people who think you should be prosecuted for assaulting a national hero, I don't even *ask* for an explanation of the *humiliation* you put me through at Lockwood's, and this is how you—" She shook her head. "Look here. You obviously need to talk to someone. What's going on?"

He eyed her for an exasperated moment, trying to resolve her two heads into one. Finally he gave up. He turned to the small liquor cabinet for a reinforcement, and saw that his outstretched hand shook. No. He made a fist and stepped back. This was not the way to do it.

"Listen," he said, turning back around. The bed was rumpled; she had obviously been waiting for some time.

The sky-blue peignoir was new, and there was a bottle of wine decanting on the low table beside the bed. She had taken great pains. "Caroline, I am sorry. I am . . ." He lowered himself into a wing chair and pressed his face into his hand. Her scent was still on him. He could smell her on his skin. Had he pressed his own smell into her? Christ God almighty, he hoped she tossed in her bed tonight thinking of him.

Caroline made some noise, and he looked up. Her hair was loose; a lock slipped suddenly off her shoulder. Otherwise she was quite still, her expression impassive. Waiting.

"Caro, this is not going to work."

He had seen her eyes take on that light at the gaming tables: hard and calculating. "It's that woman," she said.

"Not precisely."

"You want to be with her."

He looked back to the liquor cabinet, then down to his palm. His fingers closed, obscuring the lines. *Some people are engraved into your palm, child; from birth, they are with you, know it or not.* So long ago, his grandmother had told him that. "I was wrong, Caro. I thought certain . . . things . . . did not matter to me." He looked up. "Perhaps you should think of aiming higher as well."

She scoffed. "Higher than Auburn?"

"Yes. You could do better than what we have here."

She gave him a little, disbelieving smile. "Do you mean, I could look for romance and true love and undying affection?"

"Something like that."

"Well. I never thought I would see the day." She shook her head a little. "Geoffrey offered that, Auburn. And do you know what? It smothered me."

"Perhaps he was not the one for you, then."

"Do you hear yourself? What an absurd schoolboy you sound!" She leaned forward, her eyes intense on his. "*Think,* Julian. Our marriage would be perfectly civilized. Devoid of ugly scenes—like this one. I would not trouble you with nonsense. I would not nag if you failed to return home at night. I have tried that already, and it does not please you. And do you know? It does not please me either! I am sick of playing the mother for my lovers. If you wish to pass the time in other company, very well—that is your decision. Stay out all night at cards; I'll say nothing. Flirt with other women if you like. This girl? Have her! What difference to me? I like you too much to push any rules on you. And I know you like me a great deal too. Don't you?"

"Yes."

"Well then, think of it! We could be *free* within this marriage. Don't you see?"

"I see you would be most understanding," he said gently. "But Caroline—it occurred to me tonight. I am no longer twenty. And perhaps that sort of freedom has palled for me."

"Oh ho!" She fell back against the headboard, laughing a long, forced laugh. "Julian Sinclair, *wanting* the spurs laid into him! This must be quite a girl." She reached for the decanter and poured herself some wine. He waited, watching. A little sad.

With an elegant flip of the wrist, she tipped the glass to her mouth and drained it in one swallow. Her knuckles came up to wipe her mouth. "Is she the one, then? From India?"

"She is not the subject of this discussion."

"I see. Have you had her yet?"

All of a sudden, his head pounded. "Caroline, I am rapidly becoming unfit for company. I think it best you leave now."

Her tone grew ugly. "What, she would not have you, then?"

He stood. "No, she will not have me. And I am coming to believe she never will have me. Perhaps that will give you some comfort. Certainly it proves that my decision here has nothing to do with the question of freedom."

"You are a *fool,*" she said. But her eyes were tellingly bright. He sat down on the very edge of the bed, so he could touch her cheek.

"Caro," he said. "I pray to God that one day you will also be lucky enough to feel this foolish. But I wish you a happier ending. That is all."

Her face turned away. "I must dress," she said, barely audible.

"Yes. I'll wait outside."

Fifteen

THE CLIPPED REPORT OF BOOTS ON MARBLE DIStracted him. Julian turned in time to see Lockwood rounding the corner. "Auburn, there you are. Jolly good of you to disappear on me like that!"

Julian's lips quirked. Ever since Liam's return from Australia, he'd been making a point of aping the English gentleman. It was getting to be a bit much, however, if he insisted on maintaining the pretense in his own home.

"You're quite taken with that painting," Lockwood said, coming up to his side.

"Yes." Julian looked back to the looming soldier. He hoped it was only a recollection of that day in Chandni Chowk—but the background did not look right for it. Had Emma run into the man again? Good God, he would drive himself mad with these questions. And he could not bring himself to force them on her again.

The look on her face in the library . . . it would not leave his mind. "I'm glad to see you reconsidered the bedchamber."

"Well, and I may still put it there. Just like old times."

"I beg your pardon?"

"Shared a room with ten or twelve like him in Botany Bay. Even killed a few, when the going got rough."

"Yes, I see the appeal, then. What a lovely thing to be reminded of in the morning."

Lockwood's manner was suddenly sober. "Forgetting is the danger, Jules."

Julian cast him a glance. They'd been friends since their salad days, drinking and pranking at Eton and later, at King's College in Cambridge. But since his return from the penal colony, Lockwood was a bit of an enigma. Mellowed, and frighteningly cheerful. Yet occasionally Julian got the unnerving sense that when Lockwood took his leave, grinning and joking and smiling, he left to go find something to smash.

"You're slightly deranged," Julian said. "Do you know it?"

"Yes, of course. Is that a sign of greater or lesser madness?"

He shrugged. All things told, being hit over the head on one's wedding day and tossed without explanation onto a hulk could give a man cause for madness. Society, thanks to Lockwood's clever insinuations and Julian's own small comments, believed he had been traveling with his wife these last few years. Julian knew better. Perhaps Lockwood's wife did as well. That was a question yet to be resolved, since the lady had not emerged from the woodwork since Lockwood's return eight months ago.

"It almost burned last night," Lockwood continued. "Some damned fool left a lamp burning in the music room. You know it, it's at the other end of the gallery, lets out onto the garden. Well, it *did* let out on the garden. Gone now. We caught the flames right in the corridor."

"Dear God."

"Curious that a lamp was burning in the first place. The staff knows I don't use that room."

"None of them could account for it?"

"No."

Julian considered the painting again. *The city is not ready.* And the Sapnagar painting: *Our intention is to enter through Kashmir Gate.* He wished to hell he had examined the other paintings more closely, that night when they'd all been assembled here. But he'd been in no state for clear thinking. "Are the others already at the Academy?"

"Yes, apart from the few they couldn't accommodate."

"And those?"

"Sold. You would not believe how quickly they moved. Why?"

"Perhaps nothing. Only . . . this Urdu. It seems to be military instructions."

"Curious."

"Yes. If only she would explain it."

A moment of silence passed. Then Lockwood said cautiously, "You have met Miss Ashdown, then?"

"I imagine you did not miss it at the ball."

He could feel Lockwood's scrutiny. "Do you know,

apparently she is weighing a trip to Italy. Any idea as to why?"

Every muscle in his body tightened. Running away, was she? "I can't imagine. You'll have to ask Miss Martin herself."

"You know her from India, then. How, I wonder?"

"I wonder how your wife fares. You do still have one, yes?"

Lockwood's brows arched. "Drink?"

"By all means."

As they headed for the closest cellaret, Lockwood began to laugh. "Just like the old days. You as wily as a cat when I asked about one of your women!"

"She isn't one of my women."

"So I've noticed. Does that mean I can have her?" As Julian turned on him, he grinned, holding up his hands. "Well, that answers one question. Though it raises several more."

"I could say the same to you," Julian said evenly.

They cut into the formal salon. Julian grabbed a decanter of whiskey from the sideboard.

"Come now, Jules, if I can't have her, why won't you? She's a lovely girl, and I think we'll both agree she's quite talented."

Bloody idiot. "She's not interested," he said, and splashed himself two fingers.

"She can't be that uninterested. I saw her face that night."

He contemplated the depths of the glass before downing it in one go. The look on her face, as she spoke of the war . . . "So did I," he said quietly. He would not put that look on her face again. He would leave her alone; he was resolved on it.

"So that's it? You're not pursuing her?"

Julian settled on the settee as Lockwood helped himself to brandy. "Were you always so quick, Lockwood?"

"You're done. Despite the fact that you came after her that night her like a cat after cream."

"Christ. What a poet you are."

"What? Should I be more crude? You were watching her like you were plotting out how best to tumble her down and spread her—"

"No," he said calmly. "I was not. I was watching her like I thought she had come up from the grave."

"I see." Lockwood set the decanter on the table between them, then sat down opposite. "Your pardon. Perhaps I was confusing my own healthy lust for yours. She does have a very nice set of—"

"Enough!" He slammed down the glass. "You are speaking of a lady!"

"And we both know that means nothing. Most ladies have their skirts around their ears before you so much as crook your finger. What you mean is that we are speaking of Miss Martin."

Julian shrugged. Lockwood thought he was approaching a point. Best to let him get done with it.

The man threw one booted foot over his knee. His fingers drummed against his thigh. "Look, Auburn, you've not been yourself these last few days. Thrashing your fellow clubmen. Jilting your fiancée. I hear you even smashed the Ardsmores' globe."

"I've commissioned a replacement."

"But it's poor form. Keep it up and no one in London will receive you."

"Horrifying thought."

"Oh, come off it, Jules. It's most unlike you. I can only credit it to your run-in with Miss Martin. It seems your fixation—"

"*Fixation—*"

"Quite right, your *mania,* then. If you want her, Auburn, by all means have at her! But I beg you, do stop making scenes, and do try not to scare her away to Italy. Whatever you're doing, it's very clumsy. And, as the lady's patron, I find her contemplation of a prolonged tour abroad very . . . annoying."

He inhaled slowly, releasing his breath in a rush. "Listen. I have done nothing to her."

"Then may I suggest you try the opposite? Because this—"

"She will not have me."

Lockwood sat forward, his hands folded beneath his chin. "Have you actually laid out the cards and let her decide for herself? I understand the lady's hesitance. But for all your infamous shortcomings, you certainly could offer her a wild ride."

Julian gave a short laugh. "You have this all wrong. There is a history between us."

"Mmm."

"And for whatever reason, she feels she cannot acknowledge it. She is determined to remain unattached."

Lockwood shrugged. "Then do not offer an attachment. Perhaps she will enjoy herself enough to change her mind."

Julian mulled it.

After a moment, Lockwood spoke again. "The key, as I said, is to avoid chasing her off. Another drink?" He reached out to pour one for himself.

"Yes. And a suggestion for you."

"My breath is bated."

"If your wisdom regarding women is so great, you might try applying it to your own bloody situation."

Lockwood took a sip. "Ah, it doesn't get better than the forty-six, does it?"

Julian laughed.

Emma spent the morning ripping open crates that had arrived from Devon. It was a nasty business—nastier even than her mood. Delphinia's lady's maid, who for the time being was doing for Emma too, had lodged a strong objection to the prospect of manual labor. "Miss Martin, your hands will be ruined. You *must* let me fetch the footmen." And something in Beckworth's disapproval had reminded Emma of her mother, who had always fretted over Emma's hands, so chapped from turpentine. "I will worry for myself," Emma had snapped. The woman's upper lip had quivered in affront as she took herself off—no doubt to tattle to Delphinia.

Churlish behavior, Emma thought now. For Beckworth was right: by the time the crates were fully dismantled, one of her hands had started to bleed and the clock was chiming midday. To make it worse, she paused on her knees, eyes closed, to catch her breath, and when she looked up, she found her paintings ringing her like bogeymen—all leering eyes and open mouths, hands stretching out in pleas for help.

These were the paintings she had not dared send to Delphinia. The ones she had not thought her cousin could bear to see. But the Academy had requested to see them. And Lockwood had insisted.

She could not wait to get rid of the lot.

And then there was that dratted portrait of Julian, smirking at her from her elbow. She had forgotten to instruct that it be left in Gemson Park. She hauled herself to her feet and dragged it to the wardrobe. Painting was such a cumbersome art. She should have taken up the flute. Transporting it didn't make one sweat.

A knock came at the door. "A visitor, madam."

She took the card from the footman. Lady Edon. What in the world? "I will be down directly."

The Baroness rose as she entered the morning room, then resettled onto the sofa in a crunch of lace and stiffened silk. "I know we're not formally acquainted," she began, clasping her hands before her and fixing Emma with a measured look. "But I've come to believe we have reason to know each other."

Remarkable that Lady Edon's stupendous looks only improved with proximity. Her French perfume was another matter. Emma sneezed.

"Oh, dear, are you ill?" Lady Edon offered a handkerchief. "Would you like me to ring for something?"

Emma had taken the handkerchief with a polite smile, but at the rest of the offer, more fit for the hostess than the guest, she lowered it to her lap. "How kind of you. If you'd like something, Lady Edon, do not hesitate to ask for it."

A brief downward flicker of the Baroness's lashes registered the barb. "Yes, well. In fact, I hope this will be a short call. I think we have very little in common as it is, and I hope to lessen that to nothing by the end of our talk."

"Blunt of you," Emma said. The woman laughed.

"Yes! So it is. And if you'll allow me to be even more blunt, Miss Martin—I have figured out who you are."

"Indeed?" Emma leaned back into the seat. She had the advantage of the Baroness, for, when she was working, she did not wear a corset; her posture, then, could communicate indifference so much more effectively. "And who am I?"

"Fine, if you really wish me to elaborate: I know you were with Julian in India."

He had *told* her? The anger that moved through her brought her up straight again. "What of it?"

"Well, Miss Martin, forgive me if I say this happens all the time. Girls are always losing their heads over Auburn, and usually we do our best to ignore it. However, you've been plaguing him in more than the usual manner, and so I have come to warn you. You see, he tries to conduct himself honorably, but if you tease him overmuch . . ." Lady Edon inched to the edge of her chair, her hazel eyes widening. "He just may *bite.*"

Emma lifted her brows. "Indeed? Bite what, my lady? I have baked no cakes for his grace, I'll have you know."

"Very funny, miss. You think you're the one to save his grace from his dark past? I've seen it a thousand times—young misses guided by their overeager mamas to try to rescue the poor, misguided duke from his sinful ways. But Julian is not a boy, and you, like all the rest, will find that he has willingly chosen his path."

"What path would that be? It occurs to me to wonder if we are speaking of the same man. Yours sounds rather depraved."

"Excellent, your good sense is reasserting itself. He would hardly spare a thought on devouring you, little spinster that you are." Lady Edon's wine-colored lips stretched into a nasty smile. "And you would hardly be a cake, my dear. Perhaps a pastry puff, gone in one bite and just as easily forgotten."

"My goodness." Emma wished she had a fan; she would have snapped it open and made a show of cooling herself. "What a graphic image. I must ask, do you make it a habit to warn off each of these thousand misguided women, or am I a special case?"

"Hardly special," Lady Edon said tightly. "But you're more persistent than the rest—"

"Remarkable, seeing as I—"

"—and I won't see Julian bothered on your account."

How could Julian take up with such a dreadful woman! "Forgive me if I observe the tension in your manner. You must be unused to Julian breaking from your side to run after other women."

"You had best address him with the respect his esteemed personage decrees," Lady Edon hissed back. "No one has given you the right to use his Christian name!"

Emma smiled. "Indeed?"

After a moment, a dull flush appeared on the lady's cheeks.

"But yes," Emma continued, "that *is* what they say about the familiar address. Thank you for reminding me. May I return the favor? Calls before three o'clock are very gauche. Insulting one's hostess, even more so."

Lady Edon rose slowly, with that innate grace Emma had so admired at Lockwood's house. How deceiving it had proved. "You think you're very clever, but I'll tell you this: you would never be able to manage him. Your silly, simple country girl charms will not hold him. You will wear your heart on your sleeve, and every time you turn, you will find it bleeding and sore. His infidelities will destroy you."

Emma came to her feet as well. "I begin to wonder if you know him at all, Lady Edon. He does not strike me as the sort of man to be unfaithful."

Lady Edon rolled her eyes. "Then I change my mind; it is not Auburn who is a threat to your heart, but any red-blooded male. You'd best sequester yourself in a convent if you're not willing to face that fact." She re-adjusted her wrap and swept out, brushing past Delphinia on her way.

"What—" Delphinia turned to track the Baroness's departure. "What was *that* about?"

"I have no idea," Emma said. "I could not think how to stop it, once it had begun."

"Was she blaming you for her falling-out with Auburn?"

"Falling-out?" Emma's stomach contracted. "What do you mean?"

"Didn't I tell you?" Delphinia's head tipped, her expression curious. "People are saying he broke it off with Lady Edon. Almost directly after they became engaged. Very odd. I think the man is quite unhinged, coz. Did you know, he has been thrown out of Brooks's for attacking Marcus? They're working very hard to keep it quiet, because they can't prosecute him, you know; the party needs his vote too badly, and besides, he could bring down the Bank of England if he liked. But if it were to hit the papers that he'd maimed the Avenger of Cawnpore? Why, I believe there would be rioting in the streets!"

Emma snatched up Lady Edon's discarded handkerchief. She saw now that it was monogrammed with Julian's initials. Of course. The Baroness must have regretted her failure to notice it earlier. She stuffed it into her pocket. "Have the carriage sent round. I am paying him a call."

"Oh! Are you mad? Did you not hear what I just told you?"

Emma gave her a sharp look. "You must stay out of it, coz."

Very queer to be in his home. He left her sitting for a half hour in his drawing room, so she had a good deal of time to reflect on it. She could not say what she had expected—something lofty and intimidating, perhaps. But while the house, from the outside, certainly managed to impose, her most immediate impression of the interior was warmth and whimsy. The floor was a patterned marble, typical of Mayfair. The delicate wooden screens lining the walls, the carved teak doors, and the Turkey rugs might have been lifted from Sapnagar. The only fault she could find was the darkness. It needed a skylight in here, like the one she'd installed in her studio at Gemson Park. He would like more sunlight in the house, she expected. It must have seemed unbearably gray to him as a child, coming from the brightness of India.

The bench on which she sat was made of fragrant sandalwood, inlaid with ivory. She fingered the delicate pattern. Was his bed made of sandalwood, too? That might explain why he always smelled of it.

She should not be thinking of his bed.

The footman finally appeared to escort her into the study. Julian was seated at a desk at the far end, beneath a mullioned window that shed cold light across the mahogany appointments. He did not rise as she approached. "Emma. Alone? What a surprise. Do come sit."

The greeting threw her off. She paused for a moment, then drew herself up and crossed the broad expanse. He was working in a ledger. Bookkeeping. She had never imagined him as a man of business. Politics and war, yes; they were complex and fierce enough to suit his temperament. But something as tedious as accounting? It did not square.

As she took her seat, she said, "You don't look like a man who's been on the tear."

He laid down his pen and raised his head. "What does such a man look like?"

She saw now that she had not been precisely correct: there were shadows beneath his eyes, as if his sleep were poor as well. The sight made her uncomfortable, and so she let her gaze wander. It seemed Marcus had not gotten in a single punch—unless that shadow at the edge of his jaw was slight bruising, and not some trick of the light or oncoming beard. He was dressed very casually, a white shirt beneath a slate waistcoat and jacket. His four-in-hand tie was loosened. He could have quickly fixed that. But evidently he felt that her presence occasioned no formalities.

Her unease increased. "You have broken off with Lady Edon."

He merely looked at her for a moment. Then he smiled a little. "Hmm. You know, I never thought to see you here. Particularly not after our little scene the other night."

"And I don't want to be here," she said. "But—"

"But here you are. Never say someone forcibly delivered you? I'll send round for the police."

Difficult not to feel foolish. "I felt it imperative that I make clear my feelings once more."

"Good God." He leaned back. "Have pity on a man's vanity, Emma. What next, an advertisement in the *Times*?"

She gritted her teeth. "It simply occurred to me that if your broken engagement has anything to do with me—"

"Whyever should you think that?"

His face was too striking to effect true blandness. He would never be able to temper the vibrancy of his eyes, or the dramatic planes of his face; these were inbuilt. But he was doing a very good job of aping mildness, and she found it provoking. "I don't see the point of this. The other night, you implied I was a hypocrite. Now you're the one who's being disingenuous."

"Am I? Nevertheless, humor me. Why should it concern you?"

"The Baroness seems to think it does."

The leather armchair creaked as he settled back. His fingers tapped together in a steeple, thoughtful. "She told you so herself, did she?"

"In fact, yes. She came to see me today."

"Ah. Well, I'm sorry for the inconvenience. She

misunderstood me." His voice was pleasant to the point of rudeness. It might have been anyone sitting across from him, if not for that loosened necktie, and everything . . . else.

She waited. He did for a moment as well; and then, with a small shrug, he retrieved the pen and bent back over the accounts. An irritating scratching noise announced his progress down the page.

"You have more faces than a pair of dice," she said.

His brows arched, but he did not look up. "Which is your favorite?"

"This one, I suppose. It is the most remote."

"Did you come especially to see it?"

"I told you why I came. I—"

He stood suddenly and came around the desk, tossing down the pen as he advanced. She made to rise but his hands closed on the arms of her chair, caging her as he leaned down to speak. "You must make up your mind, Emma. At the Ardsmores', you told me to leave you alone. Now it seems you come seeking my attention. Although you might have picked a better way to get it. Think back on India; perhaps you'll remember a few of the things I taught you. Though"—his glance flicked down her—"You are not dressed properly for it. Too many clothes."

She felt her upper lip curl. "You are crude."

"I am busy," he said, and his eyes slammed up into hers. "And you are prying into matters that are none of your concern." He straightened and withdrew.

"Excellent to hear it! I will be going, then."

"By all means." He leaned back against the desk. "Or say why you're really here."

But suddenly she no longer knew why she had come. The news that he had broken off from the Baroness had seemed very alarming at first hearing—proof that he intended to keep pursuing her. For why else the sudden break? And then there was the other news from Delphinia—and all she had been able to think during the ride here was, *You mustn't let me do this to you, you mustn't. It is all for naught; you are chasing a ghost.* But now, under the weight of his cold, measuring stare, she felt the biggest idiot. Pompous, even. For he was perfectly well. Composed as a block of ice in Norway. No danger of a melt.

She made to rise.

"I can tell you this," he said suddenly. "We are no longer engaged. And I do admire your conscientious impulse; had I indeed tossed her over for you, I suppose it would be very good to know that you remain uninterested."

She hesitated, then sat back down. Despite this callous routine, she simply could not believe him. "I *do* think it unwise. You should take her back."

"What an odd conversation we're having," he said softly. "The oddest yet, I think."

She willed her face to yield not so much as a twitch as she stared at him. "I simply thought to warn you. To caution you. As a—*friend,* if you like. Not to be hasty or reckless. That is all."

"A friend." He smiled. "Charming. Are we to be friends now?"

"I—we have been friends in the past, I think."

"Oh, but the *past,*" he said. "Water under the bridge, and all that."

There was a trap here, and she had not only walked into it, she had fashioned it. "I should not have come."

"But now that you are here, you must not run away so quickly. After all, we are *friends*. Delightful!" He shoved the ledger aside to sit down on the desktop. "So tell me," he said, his eyes moving over her face, "what has my *friend* been doing today? Aside from receiving calls from Lady Edon."

He was different, she thought. Time had worn deeper grooves around his eyes; she did not think they had come from laughter. And this jaded quality—this easy talent for mockery—it had not been there in India. Had it? "I have been uncrating paintings," she said. "And thinking of starting another one."

"Excellent. Full of blood and guts and gore."

"No, in fact. As I told you, I'm done with the past. I am seeking a fresh start."

"Ah. So, flowery bowers and whatnot?"

These casual little stabs were dizzying. She could not track why she should feel so hurt by them, and as she tried to puzzle out the cause of one, she was already smarting from the next. "Something like that. If I can manage it. I'm not very good at it yet."

"Perhaps the subject matter is lacking. It is not very exciting, after all. Or . . ." He paused. "Perhaps what's lacking is your imagination."

She narrowed her eyes. "You are angry with me."

He shrugged.

"Very angry," she said, and rose. "I understand. As I said, I should not have come."

"No, you should not have done. But I am touched by your earnest little concern for me."

"It was not *you*, it was your connection with the Baroness—"

"Your concern for Caroline, then. How good of you to care."

Caroline. He spoke her name so familiarly. She clenched her fists. "You are—"

"If it soothes your conscience, I can say that my connection with the Baroness had been deteriorating for some time. Long before you popped out of hiding."

That word again! "I was not in *hiding*."

"She wanted more than I was willing to give. And I felt bored, and rather—smothered by her affections."

She took a step away. "That is very cold!"

He shrugged again. "It is my nature. I prefer things to be simple."

She could not help but laugh. "Simple? Yes, of course. You are the simplest man alive. Julian, I do not know what you think to achieve with this charade, but good luck with it. I am leaving."

"As you came," he said, flicking his fingers in the direction of the door.

She took two steps, then turned back. He was still leaning against the desk. She could read nothing in his face.

"You are the talk of the town," she said.

"I often am."

"The talk is not flattering."

"Again, I do not perceive the novelty."

"Don't you care, Julian?"

"Why should I?" He glanced back to the ledger. Flicked to a new page with one finger. "Did you know me to mind it before, in the time that shall not be named?"

"But it wasn't *true* then."

He made no reply.

"Very well," she said sharply. "If you will make me ask—is it true now?"

"Is what true?"

"What people are saying!"

He sounded bored now. "Oh, I don't know, Emma. What *are* they saying? I will need details; I do not keep track of every *on-dit* about me."

"So many of them, are there?"

"So it seems, to bring you flying to my door."

"She implied you were *unfaithful*. That you were a rake!"

His long lips curved in a smile. "But I am a bit of a rake, Emma."

Her breath suddenly felt shorter. "She said you were incapable of fidelity."

"And that concerns you?"

"No," she said instantly. "That is—I am no moralist."

"Ah. So perhaps that's why your art is failing you. Put a little of that self-righteous, melodramatic fervor into it and the scenes will simply come alive."

"I am neither of those things!"

"You weren't, once."

"And you weren't a cheating rakehell, once!"

He stepped forward and put a finger beneath her chin, lifting her face to the light. "You are very young," he drawled. "I do forget sometimes."

She jerked her face away. "Condescension, from your great age? All of thirty, are you? Do you know, perhaps I should paint *you*! I expect I could apply a good *deal* of fervor to it."

"You are very welcome to do so," he said. "We rakehells do love to lounge about for the pleasure of ladies' inspections." Whatever her expression revealed, it amused him. "Good to see I'm not the only one who is angry, Miss Martin."

She turned and stalked out.

He was very convincing, she thought in the carriage homeward. What to make of his act, she had no idea; at any rate, it would be much more comfortable this way.

Sixteen

"THIS WAS THE LAST EVENT I WILL ATTEND," EMMA said impatiently, as Delphinia finally joined her in the lobby. The concert hall was under renovation, and one of the walls was covered with a massive sheet; a group of young swells was poking it with their canes and raising an enormous amount of dust. "I have a great deal of work to do, and that was the most inferior rendering of Mozart I've ever heard, and if they continue to thump that sheet, I will go over there and thump *them*!"

"Oh, don't look so put out, Emma. It is the Season, what can *I* do about it?"

She was sick of the Season. It made a large city feel remarkably small. She was sick of running into Julian. He was in attendance tonight, and had been seated in the box opposite with a blond woman, Mrs. Someone-or-other, who had touched his arm freely and at length. Was it her imagination, or had someone in the crowd hissed when he had entered? She would like to tell London what sort of man they chose to idolize in Marcus Lindley, but then, she lacked the vocabulary to accurately describe such an extreme combination of viciousness, cowardice, and arrogance.

"The maids could scrub the floors with that scowl of yours," Delphinia said.

"I do not enjoy these events."

"Oh, hadn't you made that clear yet?"

"Well then, you can stop haranguing me to join you. That's what you can do for me. I've had enough of this."

"Look here, it is not my fault if your mood has been sour all week! Now stop complaining. Gideon will be along in a moment, and we will leave. I say—is that Lockwood's *wife*?"

They both turned as Lockwood made his entrance. In tow was a tall, curvaceous redhead whose unfashionably freckled countenance bore signs of acute displeasure. Perhaps she was irked by the inhumanly swift pace at which the Earl was dragging her forward.

"My lord," Delphinia called on a laugh. "Is it not rather late for an entrance? The third act has begun."

"You know me," he said carelessly, and came to a halt before them. "Fashionably late or nothing."

"Nothing would be preferable," the woman next to him muttered.

The Earl's usually congenial features tightened in a scowl. "Miss Martin, Countess, allow me to introduce my sist—"

"His wife," the redhead said, sticking out a hand so forcefully that Emma saw her cousin flinch. "Anna Wint—Devaliant, I suppose."

"Just barely," the Earl said moodily. "More like a sister."

Lady Lockwood grunted. "I think not. God is too kind to saddle me so permanently to you."

Emma gave Lady Lockwood's hand a shake. A very strong one. That was what it turned into, by the lady's own choosing. "I am very glad to meet you, Countess."

The woman offered her a wide smile, and the pale, heart-shaped face which moments before had been overshadowed by that blazing red hair seemed to light her up from within, dazzling all of them into a momentary silence.

Then Lockwood snorted. "Good God, Anna, are you still using that trick?"

She didn't so much as spare him a glance. "It's no trick, Devaliant, it's my bloody *smile.*" Her fiery brows drew together as she considered Emma. "You'll be the artist, then, the one he's promoting?"

"Shh!" The Earl of Lockwood looked around frantically. "Damn it, Anna, that's supposed to be a secret!"

"Oh, was she unaware she painted?" The Countess patted her arm, all sympathy. "Are you also a victim of selective amnesia, then? My husband knows all about that; perhaps he can suggest a remedy, as he seems to be able to dispel it at will."

"That's quite enough!" Lockwood took her arm and pulled her off. Emma exchanged a marveling look with her cousin.

Delphinia whirled after them to call,"Do come visit, Lady Lockwood!"

"Can't, I'm off to Paris tomorrow!" the woman yelled back.

"The hell you are!" the Earl snarled, and that was the last they heard as he dragged the Countess around the corner.

"Highly irregular," Delphinia said excitedly. "Do you know, the last time I saw them, they were cooing at each other like turtledoves."

"Time does change all," Emma muttered. The crowd of boys with canes was growing by the minute. Blast it. "*Where* is Lord Chad?"

"Waylaid by Viscount Palmerston." Delphinia sighed. "I saw the man lurking about when the curtain fell. They'll be out in his carriage, plotting strategy. I do wish the Prime Minister had a more gentlemanly concept of social occasions."

"I'm going to wait outside, then."

"I'll come with you," Delphinia said, gathering up her skirts. But Emma waved her off just as Lady Mablethorpe appeared, running up to ask about some charity event Delphinia was helping to plan.

They would never get out of this place. With a sigh, Emma ducked out the door.

Her headache lessened instantly. The weather was finally holding clear, and the night breeze was cool and soft, hinting at the summer to come. Save the crunch of horses chomping at their bits, and the distant weary coughs of coachmen who had been waiting hours now for their masters' returns, all was quiet. She did not see Lord Chad or the Prime Minister.

Footsteps caught her attention. Someone was advancing down the street, his top hat jerking with the force of his stride.

He lifted his head, and she realized it was not Lord Chad. Their eyes met, and he quickened his pace. He was bounding up the pavement now. Toward her. Odd. Not—reassuring. She put her hand to the door, but it was stuck. She put her whole weight into the tug. He was lifting his cane—with her free hand, she rapped the knocker—where were the footmen? Where was—

Something flashed at the bottom of his cane.

It was a blade.

"Go away!" she yelled. Stupid, stupid. Her hand, clammy with anxiety, slipped off the doorknob, and she stumbled back a pace—he was not five yards away now—it was all curiously familiar. She lunged for the door again—

The huge oak panel flew outward, knocking her to one side. She turned in time to see the man pivot, tripping over and then dropping his cane in his haste to flee into the maze of coaches.

"Are you all right?" Julian ran a quick look down her, then took off into the street after the man.

Emma blinked. The light pouring from the open door was blinding her. She leaned forward to push it shut.

"Oh! Stop that!"

"I'm so sorry," Emma said, as the blonde emerged. Mrs.—Mrs.—"Mrs. Mayhew? I did not see you there."

Mrs. Mayhew eyed her narrowly, then turned without comment to the street. Looking for Julian, no doubt. Emma leaned back against the wall, looking as well. Her heart was pounding. She should never have left Durringham.

After a minute, Julian came jogging back. He paused at the base of the stairs to retrieve the abandoned cane just as his carriage rolled up, ducal seal on the door. The doorman leapt off the back perch and came up the steps. "Mesdames," he said, "may I be of service?"

"No," Emma said, her eyes on the object in Julian's hand. As he carried it up, she saw that it was one of those trick weapons, the type that Lord Chad carried when he went to Bethnal Green on one of Delphinia's charity missions. Whoever had approached her had meant to hurt her.

At the look on Julian's face, she shook her head. "I can't imagine what he wanted. It's not as if a lady carries money."

The blonde stepped forward. "Auburn, shall I—"

"A moment, if you please," he said. Mrs. Mayhew flushed magnificently. Prettier even than Lady Edon. Emma felt her own cheeks warming. It was rather absurd, wasn't it, that she'd fancied Julian set on resuming their ancient romance? He had no shortage of choices, each more exquisite than the last.

Mrs. Mayhew returned inside. Julian gave a pointed look to the doorman, who frowned, and then said, "Ah!" and slipped after her. When the door shut, Julian gave a little heft of the cane and said, "This is odd."

"Yes, it is very odd," Emma agreed. "I prefer country life, to be honest."

"No, I mean it is damned *odd*. Men with false-bottomed canes don't just lurk about Hanover Square Rooms, rushing at whomever they spot. Did you get a look at him?"

"Yes, somewhat."

"Recognize him?"

She laughed a little. "From my vast acquaintance with the criminal element? No, of course not. But—you know, I did think it strange. He might have been Indian. His complexion—" She stopped as his brow dipped sharply. "What of it? It would not be *so* unusual. A sailor, perhaps, someone who works on the docks . . ."

"Perhaps nothing. But it occurs to me to ask—do you know that your paintings are subtitled with military instructions?"

Silly to find that startling. It would make sense; they were from the letters she'd taken from the soldier. "And if they are?"

"I'm not sure," he said. "But they give me a very bad feeling."

An alarming thought came to her. She *had* killed the soldier, hadn't she? He'd been dead when she left the tent. But—what if he hadn't been? What if he had somehow seen the paintings? And, recognizing his own words, had realized where to find her? Sent a friend to exact vengeance?

But even if he had lived, how would he have seen her paintings? His accents had suggested his station to be very low; she did not think he could have advanced into the lofty circles invited to Lockwood's ball.

"I think it is nothing," she said.

"I would like to be sure of it. Do you have other paintings? Or the source from which the writing came?"

"I . . . do have some such, but I don't think—"

"Hey there!"

They both whirled, so quickly she stumbled over her own feet. Julian caught her by the arm to steady her, which served to deepen the scowl on Lord Chad's face as he bounded up the steps. Lord Palmerston trailed behind him, sending a distracted smile Julian's way.

"I say, Auburn, hands off my cousin!"

"It's all right," Emma said quickly.

Julian stepped away from her. "I was just informing Miss Martin of my intention to pay her a *call* tomorrow, Chad. Perhaps you could inform your *footmen* of my plans."

The significance of his emphasis eluded her, but Lord Chad actually colored. "Well, to tell the truth, Auburn, I don't know. Your form of late—"

"I will be at home to his grace," Emma interrupted. Julian was right, it was best to be sure of it.

She did not look for him to follow her as she turned to go fetch Delphinia. He would be off to find his blond companion, no doubt.

A scrabbling of toenails against the floorboards announced the entrance of Delphinia's dog, who went tumbling past Emma to snuffle at a discarded shawl. Delphinia herself appeared in the doorway. "The Duke is downstairs," she said. She had a printed box beneath one arm and a bouquet of roses in the other.

Emma glanced past Delphinia's frown to the clock. Not yet four. "I expected him later. Those aren't from him, I hope?"

"No, from one of your petitioners. Lockwood had them sent over. If you do not agree to paint a portrait for one of these people, London's gardens are going to be denuded. Where shall I put them?"

"The sofa will do for now. And have the Duke—"

"I was very tempted to send him away."

Emma laid down her brush. "But you quite rightly realized it was not your place to do so."

"Emma, the man is—"

"I know what he is." Or at least she had known, once upon a time. Increasingly she entertained the startling idea that time might have altered him as much as it had her. She set down her brush and untied her apron, aware of Delphinia's nose wrinkling.

"You're in no state to receive him anyway. You look a mess! Your hair is coming undone and you've got paint on your nose and—"

Emma laughed; Delphinia was patting her own chignon as though the disorder might be contagious. "Nevertheless, he is coming up."

"Here! To your studio!"

"Yes. He knows I am Miss Ashdown. He's here to see some of my earlier work."

Her cousin gasped. "The ones you would not show me? Emma!"

"I will show you as well, if you like. But afterward. I need to speak with him alone."

"No." Delphinia drew herself to her full height. "It is not proper, you being closeted up here with him—"

"Delphinia, don't be absurd. I am so firmly on the shelf that the maids are tempted to dust me."

"Nevertheless, as the matron of the house, and your hostess—"

Emma spoke calmly. "I have offered to open my parents' house, if my presence here discommodes you."

Delphinia's jaw squared. "Hmmph. You are very managing, Emma."

"It comes from my mother's side, I believe."

On a speaking silence, her cousin shut the door.

Emma tossed the apron aside. All morning, on and off, she had fought butterflies. To have him up here—but his interests were purely impersonal. The Urdu, that was all. Nevertheless, the canvas on the easel manifested her distraction. The interplay between burnt umber and ultramarine blue, so crucial to every layer that would come after it, currently looked like a child had done it—with a trowel, not a brush.

She was still studying the pathetic grisaille when he appeared at the door. "Come in," she said, not lifting her eyes from the canvas. "The paintings are stacked against the wall by the armoire."

He came to her side instead. "What is this?"

"A new painting. Or it will be." For some reason, she could not bring herself to look at him. To have him in here, looking at her work . . . There was something gratifying in it, and that alarmed her. "This is the grisaille, the first layer."

"Interesting. It looks nothing like a painting."

"No, it would not yet, even if it were better. But the grisaille is the foundation for the light and dark of the whole. Without it, the work would lack luminosity and depth. It would have no . . . dimensionality, I suppose."

"Important, then."

"Yes. And difficult. Perhaps the most difficult part of the piece." He was very close; she could hear the rise and fall of his breathing. She wondered if this might be the right time to experiment with the *impasto* style the Parisians were using. The critics labeled it a crude and regressive trend, but she suspected it might prove more accommodating of the constant distractions she faced here.

"Shall you make one of these for me, then? Or will you leave me sadly flat?"

"What do you mean?"

"I mean, when I pose for you."

She stepped around the easel to adjust one of the brass supports. "Your offer was serious?"

"Wasn't yours?"

She raised her head. He was looking down at her, from very far up, and his lips wore a faint smile. *His lips would take more time.* She had thought that once, when contemplating how she would draw his face. She had been thinking in terms of charcoal then, but it would hold true for oils also. She remembered laboring over them in the other painting. How to communicate their softness? But also the way they could turn so very firm? The way they could shape one's own lips, guide and direct them . . .

Stop it. She straightened, unnerved and irritated. "It is kind of you to offer. But I think not. Painting you would be—"

"Too frightening?" he asked sympathetically. "I've noticed my presence unsettles you. I am doing my best to put you at ease, but you must meet me halfway, Emma."

His manner was infuriating, perhaps because he did not bother to hide the condescension that underpinned it. "Indeed? How charitable. But really, Julian, I fear I couldn't do you justice. After all, I have but a small talent, and you are so very . . . *pretty.*"

His brows shot up. "Pretty," he repeated flatly.

"Hmm. But perhaps I could rely on your reputation to carry the work. Why, I could paint you as Lucifer tempting Eve. Just think! Your face could be on the walls of the Royal Academy, representative of original sin and all the troubles of the world."

He threw back his head and laughed. "Absolutely perfect! And shall you be my Eve?"

She squared him with a look. "Of course not. It must be someone who is open to that sort of temptation."

"Touché," he said, and bent down to retrieve something. "Perhaps you may use Mrs. Mayhew, then." He held up her sketchbook, which was opened to a hastily drawn portrait. "I see you have mastered her features."

"Give me that!" She lunged around the easel to snatch the pad away. She sensed his eyes on hers as she crossed to the desk and locked the sketchbook into a drawer.

"Is this how you spend your days, then?"

She glanced back. "How do you mean?"

His head tipped to the side as he considered her. "Locked in here, committing the world to the page?"

She took a step and nearly tripped over Poppet. The dog was forever nosing about. She bent down to scoop him up, chucking him under the chin as he squirmed. "I would not word it that way. But that is the nature of painting, yes."

"So that would be your excuse, then."

"My excuse?"

"For remaining at a distance. For the sake of your art, you must remain the observer."

"Don't be absurd."

"Did you even exchange two words with Mrs. Mayhew last night?"

"I believe I spoke to her; I am not sure she responded."

"And that was enough for you? Enough to know how to draw her."

"Observation does not require intimacy," she said.

"Of course." He shrugged. "Only—it seems very lonely, Emma."

Poppet whimpered beneath her tightening grip. She murmured an apology and let the dog jump out of her arms. "I imagine it would seem so to you. But you must keep in mind, I am not so isolated when in Durringham. I have a wider circle there; the village is most hospitable."

"I'm sure. The residents must be very gratified, that the lady of the manor condescends to be received by them."

"It is not like that!"

"Oh? How is it? Does the vicar's wife turn to you when she needs an extra hand? Do you drop by the milliner's for gossip in the morning?"

She rolled her eyes. "I would not like such a closeness. It would distract me. I have other things to do."

"Yes," he said. "Painting, of course. And—?"

"It's very amusing, your concern. I didn't think a rake would be so invested in the interests of community. Or perhaps—" She raised her brows. "Perhaps that is what drives *your* wayward tendencies. Are *you* lonely, your grace?"

He smiled. "No, I think you have rakes figured wrongly, Emma. The art lies in omitting the emotion. No connection other than the physical."

"A shame I am not a man, then. I should enjoy being a rake. Perhaps I would excel at it."

"Do you think so?" he asked softly.

"Look, you are here to see the paintings, aren't you? Then come look at them and leave me be."

To her relief, he followed her to the corner without argument. But with her hand on the sheet draping the paintings, she hesitated. "You have seen my other work."

"Yes, as I'd said."

She kept her eyes on the muslin. "You were not—surprised by it? That *I* should have painted it?"

She could feel his keen regard, like a tangible touch moving over her face. A few paces separated them. He still seemed too close for comfort. "It is very powerful stuff," he said slowly. "Masterful, even. But no, I was not entirely surprised that you should have that sort of skill."

It was very flattering answer, but it did not satisfy her. She wondered what she had hoped to hear instead. With a sigh, she pulled off the sheet and stepped back.

She had arranged the paintings deliberately; the first was the hardest for her to look upon. It was unfinished, the sides of the man's face fading into the grisaille. An eerie effect, but fitting. If he were indeed a ghost, then she had made him so.

"Here he is," Julian said quietly. "The other one from Chandni Chowk."

"Yes. You have a very good memory."

"Why did you choose to place them both in officers' tents?"

She shrugged. "Abuse of authority in the place of authority."

"He looks more bloodthirsty than I remember."

Her mouth twisted out of her control. "Then you don't remember him correctly."

"And you do." He eyed her strangely before refocusing on the canvas. "Curious. You only ran into them that once, correct?"

She waved off the question. "What does the Urdu say?"

"Oh, it's very entertaining. It reads—if I can make it out correctly; your handwriting is abominable—'Ten *crore* for troop movements in the following areas.'"

"Crore? What is that?"

"It's a bloody lot of money."

"Oh." She reached out to finger the canvas. How aggressive her brushstrokes had been. She remembered how her wrist had ached each night in bed. "Did the army pay its spies, then?"

"Not so well as that."

"So it must have been a joke."

"One doesn't joke about things like that. You can't read what you paint on there," he mused. "Emma, did someone write out this Urdu for you?"

"No. I found it."

"Where did you find it?" He pulled the painting back to look at the one behind it. He swore under his breath, and then read the Urdu aloud. "'If women and children are killed, all the better.'"

Her voice dropped to a whisper. "What a peculiar thing for an English soldier to say."

"A soldier? *Christ*. Emma, where did you find this?"

"In Kurnaul."

"How? From whom?"

She stared unseeing at the painting. "Why would our army want women and children to be killed?"

He gave a strange little laugh. "To have a bloody good time retaliating for it. Heroes were made at Cawnpore, you know."

"My God. I might be sick. I—oh, God, what is wrong with Poppet?" She pushed past Julian, dashing around the easel to the patch of carpet where the little dog lay twitching. There was foam at his mouth, and he was whimpering, so softly she had to lean down to catch the noise. "I *told* Delphinia not to let him in here! I told her the paints would poison him!"

She stroked his stomach and paws, and it seemed to calm him. He gave a long sigh and went still.

"Poppet! Julian, I think he's . . ."

Julian knelt down at her side. She scratched the dog's stomach, but he did not move. Girding herself, she pressed two fingers gently on his chest, then leaned down farther, straining for the slightest whisper of breath.

"Yes," she said, sitting back. "Oh, the poor dear thing! He's dead!"

Julian reached out to flick at a piece of paper. "What is this? He's been into something."

"Delphinia is never going to forgive me! Oh, please let it not have been my paints—"

"He ate this, I think."

She plucked the wrapper from his hand and held it up for a sniff.

"Stop that," Julian said sharply, and knocked her hand away. "If it—"

"It's chocolate," she said. "It's—he got into the box." She looked around for it. There it was; the dog had knocked it off the arm of the sofa, and pieces had fallen all along the floor. "Could it have been the chocolate, then?" She picked through them tentatively. "Just one piece, it looks like. But he's gotten into chocolate before. It must have been the paints. Julian, Delphinia is going to kill me!" She looked back toward the easel. Her palette sat, undisturbed, on the small side table. And she had only been working with two colors. Poppet could not have gotten to them. "But how . . ."

"Where did you get the chocolate from?"

She looked back to him, her hands clutching in her lap. "Oh God," she said softly. "You don't think—"

"Emma, tell me where you found the Urdu for your painting." His voice was very grim.

"Letters," she said dumbly. "I copied lines from them onto my paintings of the Mutiny. But surely—"

"And they were on display at Lockwood's. Christ almighty!" He came off the floor in a rush. "You put evidence of this on display for the world to see!"

"I didn't know!" She scrambled to her feet. "How could I know!"

"Someone knows," he said. His eyes fell to the small dog lying on the floor between them. "Someone is trying to kill you."

How strange that such commonplace words could be combined to signify something so hideous. "Poor Poppet," she whispered, blinking back tears. "Everyone knows chocolate isn't good for dogs."

"Emma, listen to me," he said slowly, and with a hand on her shoulder, pushed her down onto the couch. "It's all making sense. The man who rushed you in Grosvenor Square—the fire at Lockwood's—"

"Yes," she said blankly. "I see where you're going.

But—it's impossible, Julian. The man who wrote these letters . . . he's *dead.*"

"Are you sure?"

She scuffed the carpet with one foot. "Quite sure."

She knew he was watching her, but she did not look up. He spoke again. "How many of the paintings at Lockwood's had lines from the letters?"

"All of them." A laugh popped out of her. In a black, black way, it was rather funny. "And every painting I've given to the Academy."

"And where are the letters themselves?"

She looked up at him.

"Whoever saw the painting must think you understand what you've written there. That you have proof of—whatever this was. Do you?"

"Yes," she said. "Well—I know where they are, at any rate. But no, they're not . . . with me. I hid them."

His eyes narrowed. "Why would you have hidden them if you didn't know what they said? Has someone threatened you over this? Did you take them to protect yourself?"

"No. Nothing like that. They just—fell into my possession, so to speak."

His frustration was clear. "If you will not tell me how you got them—"

"I will not."

"Then tell me where you bloody hid them!"

"One of the paintings," she said, and came to her feet, bound for the desk. The red ledger lay open to a fresh page; she flipped back and ran a finger down the list of paintings. *As I Laughed.* "Oh, Julian, it's in one of the paintings I *sold*!"

"Why in God's name—"

"I did not want to see those things again!" She turned to him. "I couldn't destroy them; I tried, I did—"

"*Why?* Why couldn't you?"

She shook her head. "A Mr. M. Colthurst has it now."

"Colthurst!" He ran a hand over his face, up through his hair. "Michael Colthurst. Of course he'd be a fan of Miss Ashdown. Lockwood sold your painting to that bastard?"

"Why? Should he not have done?"

He shook his head. "Emma, the letters must be gotten back. We must know what they're about. Who wrote them."

"Yes." She stared, unseeing, at the dog. And then, shaking herself a little, she said, "I must take him to Delphinia. Poppet, I mean."

"And I will find Lord Chad."

"What!" She looked up. "Are you mad? You cannot tell him! He's a member of *Parliament*!"

Julian lifted mocking black brows. "And I am . . . ?"

"Oh, you know what I mean," she said impatiently. "If he thinks my paintings are evidence of—of some sort of collusion to let civilians be murdered, he won't let me display them! He'd fear the scandal, the repercussions for the government! There *would* be repercussions, wouldn't there? The Mutiny was so horrendous—people would be outraged—he'd *never* let them be displayed—"

"Because he'd fear for your life," Julian finished softly. "Emma, you can't display them anyhow, regardless of the scandal."

"No. I *must* have that exhibit." Her voice was unsteady; she could not help it. "It cannot be canceled now. It's the only reason I stayed. It's—look, I'll find the letters; I'll hand them to the authorities in secret. It can all happen very quietly; no one need know they're connected with the paintings. How many people can read Urdu, after all? Or think the lines are meant seriously, if they do read them?"

"Be sensible," he said curtly. "You have sold the frame in which you put them. You can't just go barging into people's houses to pry apart their artwork, much less Colthurst's. The man is not a . . . gentleman, shall we say. Lord Chad will be able to secure government dispensation for it, or he'll turn the matter over to the police—"

"The police!" She knew she was revealing herself most dreadfully, but she was beyond caring. "No! No one in the whole of England will even *glance* at my art if they associate it with something so heinous. I'll be finished! Utterly done with!"

"And you'll be alive," he said. "Dear God, Emma, you can't be putting those paintings before your life!"

She had never wanted to hit anyone so badly. How dare he make it sound so trivial, so small? *Those paintings*. This wasn't about thirty paintings! This was about her entire future as an artist—the dream she lived for, the aim which had kept her sane and helped her to survive when nothing else and no one else had. Least of all *he*!

"Yes," she said. "I am willing to take a risk in this matter. And you will stay out of it, your grace."

"And consider myself responsible when you get yourself killed?" he asked savagely. "Thank you, no, *Miss Martin*. I've suffered through that once, and I'm far too estranged from my conscience to go through it again."

"Listen to me! I *will* get the letters back. Even if I have to break into Colthurst's house to do it."

He stared at her for a long moment. And then his eyes suddenly narrowed. "So there is your passion, then. Dried into the paint."

"Yes," she said. "Very good; you are hearing me clearly at least."

His laughter was abrupt. "Your grisaille had better be damned good, then." She lifted her brow, and he said, "Dimensionality, my dear. How uncomfortable it would be, to have your love confined to two dimensions."

"But then I should never be out of my depth. Now tell me about Colthurst. Do you know the man? Are you certain he won't prove receptive to my inquiries?"

"I know him better than I would like. Do not call attention to yourself by contacting him." He turned in a tight circle, his hand pressed to his mouth. "All right," he said. "If you're determined to do this—he opens his house once a month. Tomorrow night, in fact."

"Excellent. If you will help me secure an invitation—"

"He does not accept lone attendees. We will go together."

It took a moment to gather her wits. "You want to help me? Thank you. I would be very glad of it."

"I wouldn't be so sure of that. You're going to need to modify one of your dresses. And a very heavy veil will also come in handy."

A presentiment prickled over her. "A—veil?"

"Yes." His mouth twisted into a smile. "You will pose as my paramour. At any rate, you're not bound to run into anyone in Colthurst's house that will know you."

To pose as his lover? She would not imagine what that entailed. "No. If you need a paramour, you must take Mrs. Mayhew."

"To do your dirty work?" His brow quirked. "To go skulking around the house, prying open paintings?"

She felt her cheeks warm. "Very well, yes, that's a stupid idea. So I will attend you. But not as your paramour. I will go as your . . ." Cousin? Ridiculous. Auburn was too well known to claim a sudden relation.

"Oh, what a difficult decision." His voice was suddenly all purring kindness. "Poor Emma. You cannot think of an alternative, can you? And you are wondering, how far might the act have to go? How far would you truly stoop for your career? Could you go so far as to let me put my hands on you, if the situation called for it?"

The contempt in his voice caught her off guard. Was it for her, or for himself? "I—it is—" Surely it was for her. The alternative was . . . too distressing to think upon. "You are right," she continued quickly. "I am being foolish. Of course I will do anything you think necessary."

Had he expected that? His face registered no reaction as he exhaled. He glanced down, and she followed his gaze.

"Poor thing," she said again. "Let me take him to Delphinia."

"Yes," he said. "And I will go make the arrangements for tomorrow."

Seventeen

THE CLOCK WAS STRIKING MIDNIGHT AS EMMA SLIPPED into the vestibule, past the small closet where the night porter was sleeping, to wrestle open the front door. The night air was brisk, and she drew the sable hood of her pelisse tighter around her as she picked her way down the footpath to the curb. The thick netting over her face made it difficult to see. Blindly, she put out her hand, and Julian's strong grip drew her up and into the coach.

She settled back against the banquette with a sigh of relief. "I do hope no one heard my exit. That door groans terribly. I can just imagine Lord Chad, chasing down the street in his dressing gown!"

"He won't be able to follow where we're going."

"That sounds ominous."

"It should."

She lifted the veil away to see him more clearly. He was dressed very formally, in a black tailcoat and starched cravat. "What sort of place is this?"

"A singular one."

"Do you care to elaborate? Or would you prefer me to be surprised, and give myself away?"

He shrugged. "It is a sort of informal club, for a faster set than your cousin could imagine."

"Debauchery, then."

"Yes. Don't touch the food or drink. Don't smile at anyone but me."

"Should I smile at you, then?"

"If the whim strikes you."

"How often would the whim strike your paramour, do you think?"

He gave her a long, unreadable look. "It depends on what sort of relationship we shared."

"I am thinking you would not bring a two-bit piece of fluff. It looks to be a formal affair."

"No, that's not what I meant." When she waited, he shrugged again. "Perhaps we are affectionate," he said. "But more likely than not, if Colthurst's is our destination, we share something a bit more . . . unusual."

"Again, you will have to be specific."

"The possibilities are rather broad."

"Name one."

He looked out the window. The amber light of the street lamps gilded his face, accenting the hollows beneath his cheekbones, and the firm slash of his lips. "None of them requires explication, Emma. You may smile at me or not, as you like."

A curious feeling took hold of her—amusement and

sadness, all at once. Of all the people in the world, surely he should be the last to think she needed sheltering from something as harmless as antics at a party. "I have eyes, you know. And you've already taken note that I am very observant."

"All right," he said. "Your vice could be a preference for watching others."

"That seems fitting."

"Watching as they couple." His eyes cut toward hers. She could see the quirk at the corner of his mouth; he was ready to laugh at her, and that was the only thing that prevented her gasp.

"No," she said. "A definitive *no*."

"Then I expect you would not like to be watched, either."

Now she did exhale in shock. "I cannot believe Lockwood sold my painting to this man!"

"Yes, I plan to discuss that with him."

His tone took her aback. "It sounds as though Lockwood will not enjoy the conversation."

He said nothing.

"But you should not speak to him," she said. "I will do so, if I see the need. It doesn't concern you, Julian. You have no right to speak on my behalf."

"Or perhaps," he said, "your vice can be pain. It can be your particular talent, Emma—giving pain to your lovers. What say you? No? Or I can take that privilege with you, if you please. It seems that some people enjoy it a great deal. We could make it more interesting if we switched the roles occasionally."

"No," she managed. "Some things are squarely outside my ability to dissimulate."

His eyes were steady and hard on hers. "Do not underestimate yourself, my dear."

The sudden speeding of her heartbeat made air a difficult purchase. "Is this what you want, then? Shall I act very coldly to you?"

His smile was slow and somehow threatening. He looked wolfish suddenly. A stranger to her. There was nothing in her memories of this man. "Cold? No, that would not be to the point at all. Would it? Do you forget your very intentions?"

He was trying to scare her. She did not know how she knew it, but the certainty was there, inarguable and visceral. "You make no sense."

"Shall I demonstrate?" He leaned forward. She watched his hand cross the distance between them. Felt it slip under the veil's bunching and wrap around her nape. "You do not know your own mind," he said very softly. His thumb came around to the front of her throat, applying the slightest pressure, just enough to make her cognizant of the strength in the hand gripping her neck. She inhaled sharply. "It is all in the touch," he murmured. "Do you feel it? The idea of the game is to test yourself against it. Go ahead. It's all a very delicate balance. If you ask me to push too hard, there will be pain. If you ask me to ease off"—his hand slipped away—"you will feel nothing at all."

"That would be preferable by far."

He sat back. "For some purposes," he said. "Not for the ones we entertain. Do recall our goal."

"I have it well in mind, and I would remind *you* that I never *asked* you to do anything. You offered your help!"

"And you accepted the offer. But what does that have to do with what we're discussing?"

She pulled down her veil again, so he would not see how she flushed. "You are infuriating. I am done with these games."

"Ah, the perils of engaging with three-dimensional objects. If you ask a question, I may answer back."

"My mistake, clearly."

"Yes," he said after a moment. "Your mistake."

A few minutes passed. She contemplated the wet streets slipping by. Water was churning through the gutters, and the lights from the coach threw leaping reflections along the cobblestones. So strange to be here with him, like this. Only a month before, it would have seemed like the most absurd fantasy. Nor would she have been able to guess how it would be, between them. That it would hurt so much, and yet—she drew a deep breath—that it would also afford her such bittersweet pleasure. She had waited so anxiously for his arrival tonight. The need to retrieve the letters had only been part of it, she feared.

A touch at her skirts startled her out of her reverie. "My mother had a dress this color," Julian said. She looked down; her cloak had fallen open around her knees. "This exact shade of red."

She could not remember that he had ever mentioned his parents before. She should not want to know about them. Yet the words came out anyway: "Do you recall much of her?"

"Not enough, I suppose. I was very young when she died. Four, barely five."

She frowned as she thought back to what she knew of

his childhood. "And that is when you came to live with your grandfather?"

That seemed to startle him. "Did I never tell you this?"

The question made her chest ache. "Never mind. It was idle curiosity."

"No, I'm game for answering. If not from me, then I can't believe you haven't heard it from someone else. The story used to be a London favorite."

"Would your paramour know it?"

"Yes. Most likely."

"Then you should tell me, I suppose."

A brief silence. Then he laughed softly. "Good God, Emma."

She turned back to the window. "Go ahead," she said curtly.

"Very well." Another pause. "As you know, my father died when I was very young. At the time, my grandfather had not made up his mind as to whether he should file for the title to be diverted to Marcus. Whether my parents' marriage had been valid and all that. So he left me with my mother. No plans of retrieving me."

"So you went to her family, then."

"Not at first. When my mother's mother married an English soldier, her family disowned her. But after his death, my grandmother reestablished herself in the native community. Her son, my uncle, married a Hindu woman. My grandmother lived with them. But my uncle did not like to remember his English blood, so the household did not acknowledge my mother or her English husband. My grandmother did not even know when my mother died."

"So the British took you in?"

"Idealistic of you, but misguided. You must remember at this point it was assumed that Lindley would have the title. I was only a skeleton in the closet to the Anglo-Indians."

She pulled up her veil to see his expression. "So what did you do?"

One shoulder lifted in a careless shrug. "I made do."

"Made do? You can't mean—"

"I was a street child for a bit. Had a devilish good time of it, actually. No lessons, no rules, just one long period of mischief and mayhem."

She stared at him. Living off the Delhi streets! She had seen the way those children lived—the way their clothes hung off their knobby limbs in strips, the hope in their eyes as they clustered around cooking stalls, hedging their lives against the kindness of strangers. "Your grandmother," she whispered. "She overrode her son? She found you and took you in?"

"Eventually. When word reached her of a street child with Sinclair green eyes, she grew suspicious. As you may well imagine, it's not the most common eye color in Delhi orphan packs." He chuckled at the memory. "She tracked me down and dragged me off. I was not so pleased to be civilized, but my uncle—well, he made sure I obeyed her, and in the process I think he also came to accept me. We all rubbed along rather well, until my grandfather came." His mouth pulled in a grimace. "By that time, I was not so eager to go."

She cleared her throat. "And did *he* treat you well?"

"I was his heir," he said.

That was not an answer to her question, but now he

had turned to his own window, so she did not pursue it. "It must have been horribly difficult to come here. Knowing nothing but India, I mean."

"Difficult?" He sounded intrigued by the idea. "Yes, I suppose so. Relearning English must have been tedious. I can't clearly recall. I think I was too confused by everything to really consider whether I liked it or not. And then, by the time my head cleared, it was too commonplace to question. Children are remarkably adaptive in that regard. Ah," he said as the carriage came to a halt. "Here we are."

He reached across to take her arm, just above the cuff of her glove—his manner very casual, as if he had not just recited a tale that would make a person weep for him. "I will escort myself," she said, and reached for the door.

"Wait." He held out his hand. "You said you meant to do this. If you are going to change your mind, do it here. Once inside, turning missish will put us in a bad position."

She stared at his hand for a moment. Long, elegant fingers. He should be the artist, with fingers like that.

There must be a trick to it, she thought with sudden desperation. A paramour would be touched a great deal, in her lifetime. Surely at some point, it would all start to feel the same. Anyone's skin, not someone's in particular. And the incipient emotion, the stirring in the pit of one's stomach, the temptation to speak words better left unsaid—these responses would be dulled into nothing. The client would not mind it, if her emotions remained unengaged. He did not contract with a paramour in order to know her. He cared only for the pleasure her body might provide. What was the trick?

She reached out and settled his hand onto her arm. *Anyone's.* Anyone's would tighten so, would press a warmth into her that seemed to slip down through her stomach, to wash down her spine and the backs of her knees. Give it a little time, and the novelty of the sensation would fade. "No," she said. "I will not be missish."

Julian gave his name at the door, and they were admitted without ceremony or announcement. The silence in the vestibule was marked. "No music?" she asked.

"No," he said. "One more flight up."

As they crested the stairs, they came upon a woman perched atop a table, her nude form draped in grapevines. Emma took Julian's face as her guide. He looked supremely detached, and so Emma also strove for impassivity. A young buck, on a settee at the table's edge, was plucking fruit from the vine as he conversed with a handsome blonde in very low-cut aubergine satin. He split the grape with his teeth, and as Emma watched, his hand dipped into his companion's bodice. He lifted her breast out and ran the grape over her nipple.

"You should have worn powder," Julian said calmly. "Your blushes will excite interest."

"If they call me a fraud simply because I blush—"

"No, I mean you will draw *interest.* It will be an inconvenience for us."

"I will keep my eyes on the floor, then."

"Yes, that would be better."

But she had a difficult time restraining herself. They passed through a drawing room with food and wine set out on a sideboard. People drifted from low, silken cushions to the card games scattered throughout the room. Their manner was very informal; they helped themselves to trays of comfits, laughing and talking as they raised their glasses in toasts. A few men nodded to Julian as they passed, and looked with curiosity into her veil.

"Are there no servants about?"

"No," he said. "Not unless you count the guards."

She looked back as they exited the room, and saw what she had missed before—two men, dressed very plainly, sitting by the doorway. They both wore pistols.

"Why would he need guards?"

"There was a murder here once. It drew attention. Colthurst does not like that."

They turned into a long hall. The gas lamps set into the walls were interspersed with authentic rushes, braced in iron brackets that jutted out like curling black tongues; brass urns were positioned beneath to catch the drippings. The torches spat out a temperamental light that lent the hallway the look of hell. There was a peculiar smell in the air—dark and sweet and dizzying.

"An interesting scene," she said.

"You overextend that word."

They followed the Persian leader, passing thick oak doors that transmitted an array of noises: moans, laughter, the discordant clash of piano keys . . . a cry of pain? She could not tell, and when a muffled groan was overlaid by a piercing scream, she glanced quickly at Julian. His forearm was tense beneath her hand; a muscle in his jaw ticked.

"Marwick said he saw it in the study," he said beneath his breath. "Down this way."

"You look very uncomfortable."

He blew out a breath. "I have not been here in a very long time. It was not always so . . ."

"Unnerving?"

"Only that I would not have brought you, had I known."

"It will be all right," she said gently. Her left hand was already resting on his forearm; she brought her other around to cup his elbow, so her grip encircled him. "Very easy, in fact. You've gotten me out of much worse."

His head turned at that. Under the lick of the inconstant light, his face was all gold and shadows, but his eyes glittered. They were a light of their own, and beneath them, the hall rocked a little, as if she had just lost her balance.

What was she doing?

She withdrew her hand. He was helping her. That was the end of it. They were not even friends. Not really. She did not think *she* could be friends.

"Are you all right?"

She realized she had come to a stop. She stepped back into a niche in the wall; the depressions in the carpet suggested a bench had recently been removed. "I'm just a bit . . . dizzy."

"The opium smoke, perhaps." He lifted away the veil to study her face. "You can always tell by the eyes."

"Yes," she said. "I remember that."

"Do you?" His finger curved beneath her chin, as if to lift her face—but he made no move to raise it. So she did, merely to escape his touch. It felt like sunlight on her skin; it aggravated her dizziness.

"I threw the laudanum out," she said. "Afterward. Did I ever tell you?"

"No," he said softly.

She wondered what he saw in her face. If her expression matched his, so solemn. "Are my pupils large?"

"Perfectly normal." He brushed his knuckles up her cheek and into her hair, to slide out a pin. She made a sound of protest and reached up to stop him. He shook his head. "You must look the part."

Yes, that was right. She must look the part. She stood very still as his hands moved through her chignon, submitting to the small twinges as he plucked out her pins. Her hair came down in pieces: first a lock, then another; and then the whole thing, tumbling past her shoulders. In the hallway. Where anyone could see. She should care. She leaned back against the stone wall, watching him.

"It grew out," he said.

"It took a very long time. A mind of its own."

He smiled a little. "Well, and what did you expect? It is *your* hair, after all."

A door flew open down the hall. Much squealing. Someone came racing down the hallway toward them. She reached up for her veil, and Julian leaned forward. "Just in case," he said, the barest thread of sound; and she felt his hair brush past her ear, felt his lips press against her neck.

No.

His teeth pulled at her flesh, lifting a small bit. His lips sucked on her. It would leave a bruise. *I must look the part,* she thought. That was all. If only she *were* a paramour. Last night, the old nightmare had awoken her, but she'd known her tears had nothing to do with her parents, or with the threat against her life. When she was alone, there was nothing to distract her from the truth.

She had lost so much of herself. But some things did not fade.

She opened her eyes on the darkness. A woman streaked past, her gown split to the waist; a man was hard on her heels. She was about to be caught, but she did not look sorry for it.

Julian pulled back. He pressed his thumb into her lower lip. "You've been kissed," he said, soft and matter-of-fact, as he massaged her mouth.

She wondered why he did not use his mouth to achieve the effect.

"Yes," he said after a moment. "Appropriately wanton." He pulled her out from the wall and flipped down her veil. She licked her lips and tasted the salt from his skin. She remembered this—the feeling of hunger, but not for food.

Down the hallway they went, past the huddled shadows of the man and woman. The couple was lying on the carpet, the man on top; he was whispering something into the woman's ear that made her giggle tremendously.

"Here," Julian said, pulling her around a corner to a set of double doors. The handle would not turn. He felt inside his jacket and produced a key.

"How in the world—"

"Servants can be bribed." He fit the key into the lock, and the door swung inward. "I'm locking it, but we should be quick about this. Find the lamps and turn them up."

Inside, she felt her way toward the dim glow of a lamp along the wall, biting back an exclamation when her shins collided with a table. Julian got to the other one first; the strengthening flame on his end revealed a dreadful fresco of nymphs and satyrs. She turned hers up and found herself staring at a tapestry. "No," she whispered, turning full circle. "No! Where could it be? Wait—" There was a crate resting against the credenza. "Could that be it?"

Julian went down on his knees and put his hand to the edge of the wood. The effort to pry the thing open made the veins pop in his forehead. He shook out his hand and tried again. This time the wood gave with a sharp snap that froze them both in place.

"Nothing," Emma said after a moment. "I don't hear anything. Go on."

He broke away the board, and then another and another, casting each piece to the floor. Together, they lifted out the painting. Emma ripped the brown paper wrapping away.

"This is not my painting," she said. The nude woman was lying on her back, being tickled by a small dark creature. "Good God, and it's a terrible painting, at that. But—" She looked around once more. "It's not here, then!"

"Marwick saw it with his own eyes. I can't—"

"If he's moved it—"

His palm was suddenly covering her mouth. "Shh."

She heard it too: Soft laughter from the door. A thump, followed by a curse.

She stiffened. "They're coming in here," she said against his hand.

"Colthurst," he said. "Unless someone else has bought a key."

Eighteen

Julian closed his eyes to listen. A scratch in the lock, followed by a long pause, as though the party were being distracted. *Damn it.* Emma's lips felt hot beneath his palm. Her breath moist. She smelled of soap and rosemary, and he had a sudden vivid flash of her as she had looked in Mrs. Cameron's washroom, so long ago. Her eyes still reddened with tears as she'd laughed up at him. *Do you find me amusing?*

She was looking now at the crate, disassembled on the floor. "Oh dear," she whispered.

Yes, that was the rub. It would be more than a little difficult to explain why they were breaking into the man's possessions. "Perhaps you can fit beneath the desk." He cast a look around for likely weapons. They might be able to talk their way out of it, but if Colthurst got riled, it would be better to leave him unconscious. "I will—"

"No. His guards are armed. Pistols, Julian. I saw them."

"Yes, but they're hardly going to shoot a peer," he said. "Now go see if you'll fit."

"But we cannot risk it." She swallowed. Her hands rose to his face. The lightest pressure on his cheeks. "Perhaps—perhaps they will not be surprised to find us doing *other* things in here. Perhaps it would . . . distract them from noticing. The crate, I mean."

It took him a moment to hear what she was suggesting. His thoughts snapped back from the sounds on the other side of the door. "Possibly," he said.

"Just for show," she said. "Just for a moment, until they shut the door again."

"Yes," he whispered.

She made no move, however. Simply stared at him.

Poor Emma. She really did not know her own mind.

He weighed alternatives, in that brief, fleeting moment. They would tell Colthurst the door had been open and they had wandered in seeking privacy. They might make it out of the house before he noticed the mess they'd made. Even if he noticed, they could come up with some story. But things might get sticky, and Colthurst might demand to see her face. That would not be acceptable.

Emma might never give him another chance, either. He could not trust her in this; she couldn't even trust herself.

On a breath, he leaned forward. It was such a small space to close. Such an infinite distance to cross.

Her lips trembled beneath his. Uncertain, hesitant; nothing like the sureness he remembered from her. He kissed her softly, willing the party at the door to pause, to change their minds, to think of better games; for he knew that gentleness would not convince them, and it was what she required in this. He stroked her lips with his, and her fingers went lax on his cheek, slipping down to his jaw.

He opened his eyes. She quickly shut hers. She had been watching him.

He closed his eyes again and willed her to look her fill. *Open your mouth,* he thought, and ran his tongue along the corner; and her mouth opened, and he used his tongue to trace the lining of her lower lip, to draw her out, so her breath caught and her body pitched forward and her arm came around his neck.

The taste of her: familiar and strange at once. Like falling into a dream, at last finding it real. She gave him her full weight, her breasts pressing into him; the dress, the damned dress was like tissue paper, and when he had told her to alter it she had taken him seriously; she was not wearing a corset. He did not feel gentle anymore. He put his hand to her hip—to her waist—it rose of its own accord, and the weight of her breast, cupping her, was beyond—

The key was now definitively turning in the lock. A flash of mockery, for himself alone, *yes, make sure to convince them, Sinclair.* He bent down and hooked an arm under her knees; she made a small, startled noise as he lifted her up and seated her on the sideboard. But her legs fell open; she was not averse, and as he rose, his hand ran up her calf and thigh, lifting her skirts to her waist. He stepped between her legs and his cock pressed against her through his trousers and he gasped and so did she; her eyes were perhaps open but he had shut his again, and his hands hooked behind her ears as he bore her back against the wall behind her to pin her and kiss her hard enough to forestall any protest she might be foolish enough to make.

The door latch clicked open. "Oh! I say! In here, are you?"

Julian pulled his mouth away. "The door was open. Is it a problem?"

"Auburn! No, no. Carry on."

The latch clicked shut.

He went very still above her. Her hands on his back momentarily paused their kneading. But she did not let go. Their breath mingled, harsh and rapid.

"This means nothing," she whispered.

"Nothing," he said, and kissed her again, and his hand moved back to her nipple. It peaked beneath his thumb, beneath the rasp of his nail, and she moaned. He broke away from her mouth to bite the side of her neck; and then fell onto his knees to lift out her breast and ake her nipple between his teeth, harder perhaps than he should have; she had tried to get away from him, hadn't she? Her nails dug into his scalp, and he bit her again, on the other breast. She whimpered, and he wet her, sucked her into his mouth. Her thighs trembled where they pressed against his ribs. He slid a hand beneath one, at the very top of her thigh, in the warm, damp crease between thigh and buttock. A flick of his fingers, against the moistness of her quim. *"Julian,"* she said, and her voice broke.

He reached up to press his palm over her lips as he pushed two fingers into her. Her muscles tightened around him; he looked up at her and her eyes came open as he pushed up against her passage, his thumb finding her clitoris, rubbing. "Do you want this, Emma?"

She tried to speak, and he meant to let her; but instead his palm was pressing harder against her mouth, forcing her head back against the wall as he rubbed her quim more insistently. There was a light sheen of sweat on her upper lip; all around him, the darkest base note of her fragrance, everything that was Emma, suffused the air. "Nod," he said, in a voice he did not recognize as his own; *you will scare her.* But good, he wanted to scare her like she had scared him, for years, four goddamned endless years of it.

Her head jerked in a nod. He gave her another finger, watching her face now, the small twitches as she adjusted to the feel of him, the quivers of the slick flesh around his hand. Her thighs strained apart as he touched that secret part of her, deep inside; her face said she had never known it was there; he had not showed her, he supposed, there had been no time for it back then. He put more pressure on the upward thrusts of his hand, and her eyelashes fluttered and her head tipped back, allowing his palm to trace down over her chin, along the smooth slope of her neck, as she came.

Her quim was still contracting when he bent further down and ran his tongue along the skin stretched by his fingers. Now her exclamation was sharp; she did not like it, she wanted to be done now. He closed his lips around the nub of engorged flesh, and stroked with his fingers again, ignoring her when she tried to pull his head up. It was painful, being pushed across one's limits. He knew it well enough. His free hand caught her wrists and set them to one side, holding them there. She subsided; she seemed to like being held still. Of course she would. It was not her choice then, was it? It meant nothing. She merely submitted.

Another orgasm now, weaker. He could do better. Now that he knew how she wanted it.

He withdrew his fingers, reached for her arms to pull her down. Her legs folded bonelessly as she slid down into his lap. With one hand, he freed his cock from his trousers. She looked down at it, and wet her lips; she was dazed, he thought, quiescent, purposefully so; she fell back against the credenza and invited him with her eyes to do as he liked. Her eyes offered everything to him and promised nothing. They spoke the phrase again, more clearly than her lips could: *It means nothing.*

The anger that settled over him was hot and hard. "Do you want me to fuck you?" he said.

Her head lolled to one side, taking her eyes away from him.

He reached out and pulled her face around by the chin. "Yes or no."

She stared. She could not say yes, of course. Not and remain on that floating iceberg she'd found for herself.

"Yes means no," he said. "No means yes. Do you understand me?"

Her eyes fell to his cock again. Rose, heavier-lidded.

"Do you understand?"

"No," she said. "No, I understand."

Goddamn her. "Do you want this?"

"No," she said, and lay back on the rug, her hair spreading around her face like a cloud.

He levered himself over her, reaching between them

to fit the head of his cock to her. Her breathy gasp nearly undid him. Her hips shifted away; her hands came up against his chest. With a black laugh, he let go of his cock and caught her wrists again, pinning them to either side of her head, pushing down his hips to pin her. *Ah*. There. She was so tight, so hot and so wet as he pushed into her. She groaned, and the violence of the feeling that moved through him was transmitted through his hands and his initial thrust; it brought her eyes open and he loosened his grip on her arms with a muttered curse. There was fear here. Not hers, but his. She was soft, and yielding, and hell, but he could not trust his impulses; he wanted to move inside her so hard she would be forced to throw off this sham, to cry out in some genuine way, yes, even in pain perhaps, to beg him to stop. But he could not do that to her. It was nowhere in him. So he gritted his teeth and pushed her arms down when they demanded it and tried his best not to hurt her as she was inviting him, urging him to do.

"Ah—ah—" She writhed beneath him, and everything in him tightened, from his balls to the crown of his head, and he pulled out of her just as he came.

Windless, he lay diagonally across her thighs, listening to her breathing gradually slow. He should stand up now. He should not say a word. God *damn* her.

Instead he found himself leaning over her. She lay very still, her eyes shut, her face perfectly still, pale in the gaslight. Enchanted by some icy spell of her own making. Beyond his touch, really.

"It means nothing," she said.

"Nothing, Emma." And he bent down to catch with his lips the tear that slipped over her temple.

Her face turned a little toward his. He kissed her softly on the mouth. No hedge of thorns had ever grown so thick as the cold with which she surrounded herself. With his lips and tongue he willed it to melt. *Wake up, Emma. Sleep no longer.*

Her fingers fluttered upward, brushing lightly across the back of his head. More than enough to hold him to her. He kissed her more deeply, and her mouth opened. With a little sigh, she finally kissed him back.

Once in the coach, she pulled herself back against the seat and stared out the window. Not ten words had passed between them in the last hour. Julian had cornered Colthurst and plied him with whiskey, and gradually worked out that the painting had been sold to the Sommerdons that afternoon. She had sat beside them, arranging her lips into a smile at every appropriate cue, although the veil made it unnecessary—Julian had implied very strongly that he had a taste for disfigurement, which put Colthurst's leering curiosity to a quick end. It had not occurred to her to mind the implication. Her thoughts had been in a tumult, and she was grateful for the veil. Everything had seemed too bright of a sudden, painfully loud. The violinist in the corner might as well have been bowing along her sinews, so wildly had her nerves vibrated to his tune. Her hands, hidden in her lap, had been shaking.

She could not believe what she had just done.

She wanted to do it again.

The interior of the coach was very dark; Julian had not turned up the lamp. But she could dimly make out his form, across from her. The weight of his attention pressed against her throat like his hand had done, earlier. It pushed out the words that had lodged there for an hour. "Am I one of your women now?"

He gave a low laugh. Not of amusement. "One of my women."

"That's what I said."

"Yes," he said at length. "I suppose you are."

She turned back to the window. With one finger, she followed a raindrop down the other side of the glass. Fitful little thing. Advancing in jerks and starts. Pausing without reason. The mad impulse was upon her to observe that he had lowered the bar for her. She was not resplendently blond, neither elegant nor beautiful. She could hear how her voice would sound as she said it: vitriolic, cutting. But the only one who would bleed from such a remark was she. And so the impulse bewildered her, and she repressed it.

"It was interesting," she murmured.

"A cold way to describe it."

"Is it? How would you have done?"

"But then, I told you such things did not require emotion. Perhaps you have learned it now. Often one has to experience such truths to credit them."

"Experience is a great teacher," she agreed softly. Her raindrop had left her. She slid her finger up to a new arrival.

"And yet you seem melancholy. Not quite the same thing as unmoved. Or, for that matter, interested."

Then she was a better actress than she had guessed, for there was nothing unmoved in her. Her senses would not calm. They strained in every direction, fixing on no object in particular, so that every small sensation registered as something startling. The air leaking through the window was an icy breath on her throat. The velour banquette brushed against the backs of her arms like a cat wanting petting. She sat forward, but it was no good; it brought her closer to him, to his scent, and suddenly everything in her was inclining toward him, thrumming for want of what he could give her. She had forgotten how it could feel to be so . . . alive.

"Perhaps it was not so effective a lesson," he said.

Her mind focused on his words. On what she might make of them. "Do you propose to give me another one?" She smiled as something—a small rustle in the dark—betrayed his surprise. "By your own admission, you are a roué, Julian. I could hardly expect a different response."

"Indeed?"

"Indeed," she said.

"Very well, then." He spoke evenly enough, but she had the impression that a note of mockery colored his words. "If that's how it's going to be, you must go about it properly."

"Yes? How would I do such a thing?"

"Open your parents' house."

To have him there. Her breath caught at the images flashing through her mind. She had never seen him in the light. "Yes," she said. "Yes, I had already planned on it. It will be safer for my cousin if I leave. And the light there . . . it is better for painting. There's a very wide salon on the second floor, with large windows along the walls, eastward and westward."

"I would not be interested in your salons."

"No, but I would. Is that all?"

"Of course not. You must prepare yourself for society's condemnation. No one will receive you. They will not even acknowledge you in the street."

She supposed it would be a more final sort of disgrace than what she had endured in Delhi. She expected he was thinking of that girl as he issued his warning—the one who had fled into the Evershams' garden to escape the censure and pity of strangers. He was still trying to protect that girl, wasn't he? The thought sobered her for a moment; a strange loneliness slowed her heart. She had long since cast off such worries; she had no use for such protection. She needed other things entirely. The clarity of light. The sharpness of sound. The fullness of sensation he had given her, all unwittingly, with his body and his kiss. But perhaps she could have those things from him, if in return she allowed him to give her what *he* thought she needed.

"You must help me to be discreet," she said. "I will hire an amenable companion, so as to maintain appearances."

"Excellent idea." Now he was no longer bothering to disguise his derision. It puzzled her.

"You do not believe me? You think I will not do it?"

An infinitesimal pause. "I think you will do it," he said. "Why do you ask?"

"Because it sounds as if you're having fun at my expense."

"But I am, Emma. So?"

Her fingers knotted together in her lap. "Then *you* don't mean to follow through. Is that what you're saying?"

"Oh no," he said softly. "I mean to follow through."

"Then—" She did not understand him, and suddenly

the weight was back on her chest. For a little while, she had felt so free. Reckless and fearless, unencumbered by complexities, giddily drunk on the very air she breathed. But if he forced a reckoning between them, it would all be lost. "What do you mean, then? Follow through on—on making me your mistress, yes?"

"What else could I mean?"

"Yes," she said, and felt settled again, and easy. She lifted away the veil, and his features came into focus. "Just to be clear."

"Clarity is, above all things, to be desired."

"Well, I will open the house. And the painting—shall we go to Sommerdon's to get it?"

"I will make inquiries. He is a great collector, and a loud one; it should not be difficult to find out the details."

"You will let me know, then."

"Yes."

"And I will let you know. About the house, I mean. It should not take long."

"You will let me arrange for the staff. And guards. You will need those."

"But—you just said—"

"Surely it is the least I can do." Again, mockery.

They were pulling up at the house. She put her hand to the door, but he caught her wrist and pulled her over to his bench. She let him do it; only the brush of his fingers over her skin, and it was as though roman candles were sparking in her blood. But when she settled onto the cushions beside him, he did not lean forward to kiss her. Rather, he sat back and turned up the lamp. His eyes roamed her face. So beautiful, he was. She was tempted to reach out and stroke his cheek, but it would not be in keeping with her role.

Would he not kiss her again before he left?

When he smiled, impatience finally took hold of her tongue. "What?"

" 'Half-sick of shadows,' " he said softly. "It's all right there in your face."

"What do you mean?"

He shook his head. "I would tell you, but you would not like the answer." Leaning forward, he threaded his fingers through her loose hair and pulled her into a brief, hard kiss. When she would have opened her mouth, he pulled away. "Go," he said. "I'll wait until you're inside. I know you like to be the one to do the leaving."

Breathless, she slipped out of the carriage and up the walkway. The latch slipped off the gate soundlessly, and she had just managed to fit the heavy brass key into the lock when the front door opened beneath her hands.

Delphinia stood there, clutching her wrapper to her throat.

Emma looked past her into the hall. No sign of Lord Chad.

"He's sleeping," her cousin said. "Well, come in, Emma. You'll wake the servants. Unmarked," she went on, with a jerk of her head toward the carriage, now pulling away from the curb. "That's something, at least." She reached past Emma, and the door thumped shut. An ominous sound.

"Delphinia—"

"Come with me."

Her cousin set a rapid pace down the hall, her shoulders determinedly square beneath the frilly white wrapper.

Inside the morning room, all the lamps were lit, and a book and knitting needles lay on the chaise. "You were waiting for me," Emma realized. "Did you hear me leave?"

"No. I couldn't sleep. I was thinking of Poppet and—well, *you*, actually. I came by your room and found you gone. Beckworth was sleeping, so I was very afraid you had . . . gone off alone, I suppose. Although now I think of it, perhaps that would have been preferable. Oh, take off that ridiculous veil and sit down." As Emma tossed the hat and shrugged out of her cloak, Delphinia gasped. "Good lord—your dress! What have you done to it? No, don't tell me. You were with Auburn, weren't you?"

"Yes."

"Emma, are you . . . *consorting* with that man?"

"It's late. Perhaps we should discuss this in the morning."

"Emma, listen to me! You will *ruin* yourself."

"I understand your concern," Emma said. "You cannot have me under the roof, behaving like this. I have decided to open my parents' house."

"No, you do *not* understand. You are scaring me!" Delphinia began to pace the boundaries of the chaise. "I thought you were getting better. I thought you *were* better. But this man! He has thrown you *backward*! Your moods of late—and such behavior! No better than a twopenny trollop! No respectable woman—"

"You forget yourself," Emma said sharply. "I have not been respectable for a very long time. Not since that freighter—"

"I am *sick* of that line. Do you think anyone remembers it? You are an heiress, Emma. If only you would circulate, you'd find that money has a way of weakening the memory. People would be willing to forgive a great deal of you, if only you made it possible for them to do so!"

"Oh, how generous of them. To accord me the respect I can purchase! Why, it gives a whole new color to the idea of a *sterling* reputation, doesn't it?"

"Emma!" Delphinia suddenly looked teary. "Oh, Emma—why must you be so difficult! Don't you see? This is your *life* we are discussing! No one will receive you if you continue to gallivant around like this! It's all right for Auburn—he's a *duke,* dearest, he's a *man*—but it's not all right for you! You must not let that man seduce you!"

Emma bit back a sigh. How to explain to her cousin? One could hardly say, *You're right, it is my life; and it is for my life's sake that I am seduced.* Delphinia, for all her sympathy, was fortunate beyond measure. She would not fathom how the prospect of feeling—really *feeling,* after such a long, blank, white stretch—might outweigh any sacrifice of name or station. And so, carefully, Emma said, "The life you lead is not the one I would choose. If it's my happiness you're worried about . . ." She could be cruel now, and put an end to the conversation by saying that her chances had been ruined the moment she was forced to come to London. But that was not even true. Gemson Park had been peaceful, but also, increasingly, stifling. Hence the plans for Italy. Yet, now the idea of leaving London . . .

She could not lie to herself. What troubled her was the idea of leaving *him.* She wondered, suddenly, what her pupils looked like. For he, too, was a sort of drug.

Only a mere taste of him, after so long, and it was enough to . . . stir her so . . .

"And what of marriage, Emma? Has Auburn even spoken of it? Or is he perfectly happy to ruin you?"

He was not happy in the least. He looked at her as though she were a puzzle he meant to solve. Julian was anything but stupid. If she kept him intrigued, all the better. It would lure him back to her, at least until he managed to crack the riddle. And then—well. So what if he turned away? Affairs ended. Indeed, their impermanence was their defining quality.

"No, coz," she said. He had never spoken of marriage. Not even in Sapnagar. Why was that?

"Oh Emma. Think of it! To spend your whole life alone!"

She should be grateful for it. What she wanted from him was the opposite of marriage. There was no reason to resent his failure to offer what she would not take.

Strange, then, that she should find the failure noteworthy.

"It would be no easy thing," Delphinia said. "No nursery, no one to love . . ."

She feared suddenly that she knew what Julian had seen in her face. His eyes had always seen too much. She came to her feet. "I am to bed," she said, and her voice was not steady.

"Emma—"

"If you want to continue this, we can do so in the morning." But at the door she recalled something. "Delphinia. 'Half-sick of shadows.' Do you know that line from somewhere?"

Delphinia bent over the chaise to gather up her

knitting. "It does seem familiar. Let me think." With jerky movements she wound the tail of the yarn around her needles. "Oh, yes. What a heathen you are, Emma! It is Tennyson. 'I am half-sick of shadows, said the Lady of Shalott.' Why do you ask?"

She dimly remembered the poem. "It's about a curse, isn't it?"

"Yes. The lady is locked in a tower, and not allowed to look directly on Camelot. So she spends all her time weaving, and singing, and watching the world outside through a mirror. The line about the shadows comes when she spots a pair of young lovers and realizes she is lonely."

"And she dies," Emma said.

"Yes, Lancelot comes along, preening, and she cannot resist looking down on him. So the mirror cracks, and she leaves the tower, and dies. Very dim-witted of her to go floating down the river; I would have gone by foot, myself."

"Or not have looked down in the first place."

Delphinia huffed. "No, in fact I would have looked much sooner, or have gone mad from weaving all day. But then, I forget who I'm speaking to—the hermit who had to be pried, kicking and screaming, from Durringham."

It was a sharper blow than she had been braced for.

"Oh, Emma—no, I'm sorry, my temper is *awful*, I didn't mean—"

"No, it's all right." She turned away. Delphinia simply knew her too well; even by accident, she managed to strike at the heart of the matter. One *did* need to be a little mad to hold oneself apart from the world so strictly.

And her cousin had every right to say it; after all, she had seen firsthand evidence, in these last few years.

But on the stairs, her feet paused, and her hand clenched over the balustrade as the realization struck her: it had not been *Delphinia* who quoted the poem to her.

She lay abed in darkness, but sleep did not come to her. When the grandfather clock in the hall rang three, she rose and slipped down to the library. There were three books of Tennyson on the shelf; she chose Moxon's volume, and it opened beneath her hand to a print of the lady herself, tangled in the threads of her own weaving.

Quickly she scanned the poem. She had read it in the schoolroom, of course. It had not seemed so terrifying to her then; indeed, she recalled thinking the Lady of Shalott everything that was glamorous. Only now did she see it clearly: the poor lady was wretched. Possessed by fears she could not even name, driven by them to obsession. *She knows not what the curse may be, / and so she weaveth steadily, / and little other care hath she.*

Emma's fingers traced the plate. No wonder the people of Camelot had been afraid when her body floated to shore. Who wished to look upon the face of madness? Only Lancelot could see her beauty, and even then, his admiration was tempered by pity.

She shut the book on her finger, staring into space. Save the slim sphere of light from her candle, the library was dark. No fire to warm the air. The carpet felt chill beneath her feet. This could not be how Julian saw her.

If it was, why in the world would he care to associate with her?

Oh, it was only a poem. Quoted, no doubt, off the top of his head. She shoved the book back into the shelf and exited into the hall.

But her feet did not take her to her room. Rather, they ascended another flight, to the salon Delphinia had allotted as her studio.

She turned up the gaslight and stared at the unfinished grisaille. As bad as she remembered. Her fingers felt so clumsy around the brush these last few months. The space in her mind where paintings were born felt as flat and infertile as the desert outside Sapnagar. *Blood and guts and gore.* The nightmares that had fueled her earlier work had lost their grip now. But while she longed to paint, to drown her uncertainties in color, there was nothing to put on the canvas. She did not care about flowers. She could not be passionate about a bowl of fruit. The very concept of a "still life" baffled her. There was nothing *still* about life. Even the Lady of Shalott, despite her best efforts to resist, had been swept up in the current.

The girl she had been would never have inspired Julian to think of such poetry. That girl had been so eager for life that she would have broken the mirror with her own hands. Thrown open the tower door before a day of imprisonment had passed.

Did he see her like this? So remote and fearful and obsessed? So altered from that girl? Did he see her like this, even as he bent down to kiss her?

Now she felt it building in her. Like an itch in her veins, this need to create. And yet it was different from the fevers of Gemson Park. His mouth had pressed upon her earlier tonight. He had touched her so softly. How was it that the merest brush of his lips could spread sensation through her entire body?

She crossed to the wardrobe. She watched her hand open the latch. The frame was cumbersome. She could not lift it onto the easel unaided, so she dragged it over to lean against a bare patch of wall. His eyes were perfect; she had done very well with them. This, her first painting after her return. Amazing, that the technique had already been in place. No blood or guts or gore necessary. He seemed to be watching her, and she felt something turn over in her chest.

You are not the only one who took that journey.

The background was so blank. It was not right. She could see it suddenly—how it must be. Not barren at all.

She returned to the closet, her hand passing over the tubes of already mixed colors. They were wrong for this. Nothing so dark was called for. She took up the jar of linseed oil, and a packet of mitis green pigment. It would be spring in the desert. Yes: everything coming alive. Plants with deep roots, that had gone underground for winter, would be rising again through the soil. She had always loved him, after all. And perhaps he knew it. Perhaps he saw more than she had suspected. And despite it, he did not look away.

Nineteen

The next morning, she took the short walk to her parents' house. The air was mellow on her face; the sun flirted over her wrists as she waited for Delphinia's footman to unlock the door. Strange to be here again. As a family, the Martins had been fonder of the country, so Emma had never spent much time in London—a few winters as a child, and also that single Season, the year before they had sailed to India. She found no ghosts lurking in the formal sitting rooms, no sad memories to dim the radiant sunlight spilling through the long windows of the westward-facing salon. And yet, as she crossed through the vestibule and lifted her skirts to negotiate the stairs, she found herself pausing, caught by a recollection.

Yes. The swish of her debutante-pale skirts, as she had tripped down these stairs, had thrilled her. She had felt beautiful, and full of hope. Her first ball! How generous of her parents to give her a Season, even though her marriage had been finalized in the schoolroom. How gratifying to see their smiles as they waited below—their expressions proof of what the mirror told her: she really *was* beautiful. "You'll be the belle of the ball, Emmaline!" This from Mama, her eyes shining with tears. "If you will do me the honor, daughter?" That from Papa, his arm outstretched, making a perfect crook for her gloved hand. How adult she had felt, on his arm.

She caught hold of the balustrade and pulled herself up the stairs to her bedroom. The door opened too forcefully; it cracked against the wall, swinging back at her, and she caught the rebound with the flat of her palm. A smarting pain, well deserved at that. She was very stupid, she feared.

Julian had sent a note this morning. And along with it came a charming sandstone carving, small enough to fit into her palm. She had taken it at first for an elephant, until she had noticed the human feet and hands, and the pouting little belly. His note read:

You may recall Mr. Cooper's remarks on the elephant-god at a long-ago party. I do not believe he ever explained how Ganesha came to have an elephant's head. He was guarding his mother, who was taking a bath in a pond. His father, Lord Shiva, who had been absent since his birth, returned unexpectedly, and wished to see his wife. Neither Shiva nor Ganesha recognized the other, and Ganesha, in protection of his mother, would not step aside to let Shiva pass. In a rage, Shiva struck off his head. As you may imagine, this did not please Ganesha's mother. Shiva restored his son to life by supplying him with a new head—from an elephant. Despite his somewhat unusual new form, Ganesha found himself all the more beloved after his resurrection.

I enclose him because he is renowned to expedite the removal of obstacles. I am meeting Sommerdon this morning, and hope to have the pleasure of delivering the letters to you shortly thereafter.

She reached down now to her pocket, to finger the surface of the carving. It was a small shock to her, every time he came back. But he did come back. Even her basest conduct seemed only to amuse him.

She looked around the room. It seemed likely that she would lie with him here, on the mattress. It would need to be aired. She would have the rugs beaten as well. He had taken her on the floor, in Colthurst's study, and she had not even noticed how the carpet felt. But she would notice here. She had the feeling that she would not miss a single detail anymore.

A peculiar feeling twisted her stomach. Nerves and anticipation all at once. She crossed to the corner of the room; one yank and the sheet that covered the mirror was collapsing in a cloud of dust. She discovered herself in the glass, looking back. Her lips were twitching. She released the smile, watched it curve across her mouth. He was wrong, then. She liked what she saw in her face. She would tell him so, when she saw him next.

Next, to the curtains, which years of stoppered sunlight had faded from bronze to a dull yellow. As she hauled them apart, a movement in the street below caught her eye. Of all people, Marcus Lindley was stepping out of a coach, and into her yard.

He looked up. She stepped back, but too late—he had seen her; he lifted his hand in greeting. She frowned and came out into the hallway. Downstairs, the footman was opening the door to him.

"What in the world," she said as she descended the stairs. "What are you doing here? How did you find me?"

"I had to speak with you." He seemed more subdued than she remembered. The beginnings of a paunch stretched his mauve waistcoat, and burst blood vessels dotted his nose. His arm was in a sling. "I am contemplating a certain proposition," he said. Something in his words seemed to belatedly amuse him; he gave an odd little laugh. "I should like to discuss it with you, if you please."

"You may call on me at Lord Chad's. I am not at home to you here."

"Ah yes. I do remember that about you, Emmaline. You recall propriety, but only when it suits you."

She traded a look with the footman. His brows lifted slightly, an offer of support. "Leave or I will have you thrown out," she said.

"Even though I come in memory of a certain soldier, last seen in Kurnaul?"

A rushing filled her ears. It resolved into the voice of the footman, saying, "Miss? Miss?" He had stepped forward, his hands outstretched as if to catch her.

"No," she said, through lips gone numb. "No, I am quite all right. Viscount, if you will follow me."

It was the longest walk she had ever taken, down that

empty hall. So much of her furniture was in Gemson Park; there was nothing to absorb the echo of her footsteps, or the sharp ring of his boots on the marble behind her. He had come running through the Residency, that bright sunlit morning, and she had thought then that he would be gone from her life forever. *How could he know?*

The air in the front salon was musty from disuse. She drew the curtains, hoping it would give her thoughts time to clear; but when she turned back, there was only the pounding of her heart, and a panicked denial repeating in her head.

He was leaning against the door. She drew a breath. "All right, Marcus. Explain yourself."

He tilted his head. "You must be confusing me with someone else, Emmaline. I have never taken orders from you." He paused. "You have paint on your sleeve, you know."

She did not glance down. "Yes, I've been painting this morning. You always knew I painted. What of it?"

He shook his head. A lick of blond hair fell over his eyes, and he flicked it back impatiently. It struck her suddenly that he was not as calm as he appeared. His gaze would not focus on hers; it wandered around the room, latching onto nothing. He had visited her parents here, before. Perhaps their memory would recall him to decency.

But when his gaze returned to her, his smile was very ugly. "Your little talent has grown even more vulgar than I could have imagined. Those paintings! They are atrocious, fit only for burning, *Miss Ashdown.*"

She had sensed it coming. She hoped her face did not betray her. "Again I ask, what of it?"

"I will tell you *what of it*. You have written lines from a military communiqué all over your paintings. That communiqué was entrusted, by me, to a man who was found dead in my tent in Kurnaul. Curiously, the letter had been stripped from his corpse. I therefore have no alternative but to conclude that *you* were the one who took the letter, and *you* were the one who killed him."

She looked away. The oak leaves brushing against the window were very green. The color, she thought, of Julian's eyes. "I have no idea what you're talking about."

"That will not fly. You see, I have made inquiries. Do you remember that portrait of you, the one your parents sent to my mother? It prompted a former lieutenant of mine to recall your presence in camp. He says you asked after my tent. There are other eyewitnesses to place you there as well—coming into the camp. *Leaving* the camp, shortly before my aide's body was discovered."

With every word he spoke, her thoughts grew strangely clearer, and her pulse slower. "He attacked me. I defended myself."

"I find that difficult to credit. You knew I was there, but you did not turn to me. Rather than seek my help after *defending* yourself, you chose to run. That is not the action of an innocent woman. I think the court would agree."

Why *had* she been so foolish as to run? It seemed very distant to her now. "I did not know what to do," she said. Her voice sounded very flat to her ears. She could not find the appropriate emotions within her; they seemed to have withdrawn from the scene.

"Well, I have come with a proposition. I am in financial straits. And it's a seller's market for art, I fear."

"You bought my paintings?"

"Yes, to protect you," he said impatiently. "Of course, it's all up to you. If you prefer to hang, you are welcome to it. The murder of a soldier during wartime—it's no small crime. But if you chose differently, it would be of benefit to me. I could make use of your fortune. And your parents intended it for me anyway, you know."

She looked to him. "You can't be proposing—"

"We will wed. I will have your money. And no one ever need know you killed the man. Otherwise, the noose. Your choice, Emmaline."

"You are mad. You cannot prove I killed him."

"Indeed? Tell me how *you* would prove your *innocence*. So many witnesses to place you in Kurnaul. And others, I'm quite sure, from Alwar all the way to Calcutta, who will remember you by the name Anne Marie. I told you I made inquiries. The East India Club is a hive of information; you cannot imagine the number of people who recognized your portrait."

She looked down to her hands. Her fingers were twisting together, a fleshly puzzle that looked very painful. Her knuckles were white.

"If not for yourself, Emmaline, then think of your family. Lord Chad's career certainly would not thrive, after your execution. Your cousin's life would be ruined. Your estates would be confiscated. A terrible waste."

The silence was immense. Uncanny. The clocks, she realized. The clocks were wound down. She had not considered how one depended on the sound of them. "No," she said. She could not go back. Not now. "I will not do it."

The carpet, dusty as it was, muffled his footsteps as

he approached. "Then perhaps you will consider this: there is more than your own guilt written on those paintings. There is proof of Auburn's collusion with the rebels."

It was too absurd. She laughed.

"You doubt me? Did he never tell you of his cousin, then? The boy was one of the civilian ringleaders of the Delhi uprising. My aide chronicled Auburn's visits to the lad's house. Giving him money, counseling him. You have quoted from that dispatch, too."

"*No*. He was only trying to help his—"

"I do not care what he was *trying* to do. It looks very bad. I had not wished the thing to come to light, for the sake of the family name. To have Auburn hauled up on charges of treason? It would blacken us for generations. But there you go; I am willing to make that sacrifice."

His hand filled her vision. He was waiting for her to take it. The left hand, she saw. Julian had snapped the other. So rumors claimed.

Pity it had not been his neck.

His grip closed on her fingers. Her bones ground together as he drew her to her feet. "Come," he said. "You need more convincing? I will show you how thoroughly you have damned yourself."

Sir Eastlake, President of the Royal Academy of the Arts, was a thin, nervous man with a patchy halo of graying hair, the dimunition of which he monitored with a gentle pat every few minutes. He seemed nervous about Julian, and apart from the occasional narrow glance, kept his regard fixed on Lockwood.

At one point, when Eastlake was waylaid by an

employee, Lockwood leaned over to remark on it. "Perhaps there's a priceless globe somewhere about. Could explain it."

Yes, he could do with smashing something. He'd spent the morning fencing with Sommerdon at the Athletic Club, letting himself be beaten into the ground by a man in his sixties with a bad case of gout. All for nothing, it turned out: he'd finally broached the subject of the painting, and Sommerdon had confessed ignorance. He had heard of Miss Ashdown, yes; but he was not in the business of supporting untried artists. If the critics commented favorably on her show at the Academy, he might give her a look.

Afterward, at the Park Club, Julian had found Colthurst engaged in deep play. Up and down, the man swore to his story: Sommerdon's man had purchased the painting, for a rather spectacular sum. Cash, no less.

On then to Lockwood's, where it became apparent that all of Miss Ashdown's paintings had been purchased by third-party representatives. "It's normal enough," Lockwood had said. "But that they all paid with coin—well, under the circumstances, yes. I should like to make some inquiries."

Lockwood had other uses as well. The man was very well connected with the seedier parts of the city. Invitations had been sent to St. Giles and Tiger Bay, interviews conducted, and men dispatched to loiter, discreetly armed, near Lord Chad's townhouse. His own third-party representatives, Julian thought.

Eastlake turned back to them. "Where was I? Oh, yes. Naturally, when I was asked to be the director, in fifty-five, I was hesitant to accept. One must focus one's energies, you know, and art is the most demanding of mistresses."

"Indeed, Eastlake? Then you're choosing them wrong." Lockwood clapped a hand to the man's shoulder. "Come out on the town with me some time; we'll fix you up all right."

Eastlake choked on a cough. "Ah—yes, yes. My lord, you are humorous. But, as I was saying, the honor was very great as well, as great as the duty. And so I examined my constitution, and was pleased to discover—"

"Just show us the bloody paintings," said Julian.

Eastlake's mouth thinned. "Indeed. I must emphasize how irregular this is. But after consultation with the board members, and because Lord Lockwood has been so generous in his support of the National Gallery's construction—"

Julian strode past. He could hear Lockwood behind him, nattering on about how appreciative they were.

And there were her paintings. Some were already mounted; two men were in the process of hanging another. The rest stood propped against the wall.

He moved down the row, reading silently. *The aim is not to avoid casualties. You will meet at the northernmost point of the ridge. The signal will be three lamps filled with ghee. You should send the money with my man.* And—"Bloody hell," he said softly. *He sends money to the house at Ajmeri Gate.*

"There is more than one author to these letters," he said as Lockwood came up. "And one of them seems to . . . know me."

"Oh? How can you tell? Did she include their signatures?"

Julian cut him a look. "You are too damned amused by this."

"Not in the slightest. If I look cheerful, it's because Eastlake headed the other way."

"I can tell because one of the writers uses the third person plural address. *Aap*. His grammar is sophisticated, and the vocabulary is heavily Persian. The other uses a very informal mode. *Tuu*. And it's bazaar language, there's no finesse to his diction or his constructions. Classic Addiscombe College hodgepodge, so I would guess he is British. But for the first . . . oh, Christ."

"What is it?"

"She used this line before. 'Ten *crore* for troop movements in the following areas.' But she omitted the rather important bit preceding it: '*Nana Sahib is pleased to offer.*'"

"Nana Sahib? The—what do they call him? Butcher of Cawnpore?"

"So it would seem."

"Ah, a little treason in the afternoon. Not on the syllabus at Addiscombe, I expect."

Julian shook his head. "He's an officer, whoever he is. Here he's addressed as *afsar saahib*. And here . . ." He heard the laugh escape him. Of course. What a sweet, sweet surprise. "Here they call him *colonel*."

At Bolton Street, Emma was not at home. But, to his surprise and displeasure, Lady Chad insisted on receiving him. She was settled into a horsehair chair in the front salon, looking uncomfortable in the extreme. Her companion, an older woman who was knitting a bootie, took his appearance as a signal; without a word, she came to her feet and slipped out.

"I do not want witnesses to what I must say," Lady Chad told him. "I trust you have no objection to the irregularity?"

"None at all," he said. "But I cannot stay long. Lockwood is in the coach."

"It will not take long. Tea is already coming."

Emma's absence was making him very uneasy. She would be followed by his men, of course, but it occurred to him that she had not responded to his note this morning, either. Why was that? What a damnable new etiquette they were forging. He wondered, as he took a seat across from Lady Chad, what she would think if he turned to her for advice. *I would like to marry your cousin. She would like to make me into a kept man. It is a novel conflict. I welcome your thoughts on the matter.*

"You seem distracted," Lady Chad said.

"I am wondering where Miss Martin might be. I have some rather urgent news for her."

"Indeed." Lady Chad eyed him for a moment. Her hands in her lap were fretful—toying now with a handkerchief, now with a fold of her muslin skirts. He was going to have to proceed very carefully here; the lady was clearly in no mood to be forthcoming.

He drew a breath and schooled himself to patience. "Allow me to offer my condolences regarding the passing of . . . Poppet."

Her hands stilled. For such a tiny thing, she had a gimlet stare. "I understand you were in the room at the time of his demise. I wonder if you have any details to contribute."

Hell. He'd stepped right into this one. "I understand that chocolate is highly toxic to canines."

"Indeed? It never was so, before."

He would accept the blame for many things, but not for the death of her damned lapdog. "They were not my chocolates, you understand."

She sniffed. "Yes, of course I know that. Oh, never mind. As you may guess, I wished to speak with you about my cousin. I understand that you helped to save her life in Delhi."

Oh, this was interesting. "She speaks to you of that time?"

"Well—no." Lady Chad frowned. "Not exactly. But she has acknowledged your help in escaping the city."

So it was all bottled up, then, save what emerged on the canvas. "You've never pressed her?"

The color came up in the Countess's cheeks. "Of course I have pressed her! How could you imagine otherwise? But you don't know what she was like after she returned. I . . ." Lady Chad lapsed into silence, staring into space.

"Feared for her," he finished softly.

"Yes. Very much."

"She was so bad, then?"

"You cannot imagine. Almost—mute. But the tears, they were ceaseless. Sometimes she could barely breathe for them. Gideon even spoke of the asyl—" The Countess shot him a glance—startled, he thought, by her own indiscretion. "But of course it was just talk," she continued hastily.

"I am glad to hear it."

He did not bother to veil his contempt, and the Countess's color deepened. "Only talk," she repeated sharply. "And only in passing. She was very distraught. But Lord Chad recognized that it was natural, after what she had been through. Anyone would be the same."

"Yes."

"And I *did* think, if only she would talk . . . But she never would do. She is terribly stubborn, my cousin."

The tea arrived. They waited for the servant to leave, and Lady Chad poured. He realized he was drumming his fingers, and flattened his hand against his knee.

She considered him curiously as she handed over a cup. "I wonder what *you* might be able to tell of it. At least in connection to Emma's escape from Delhi. I will not offer you sugar, by the way."

"I would not ask for it. Yes, I could tell you the story. But I think that is for Emma to do. Don't you agree?"

"You should not speak of her so familiarly."

He shrugged and picked up his own tea. A sip confirmed that he still did not like the stuff. Ironic, since the one thing Britons and Indians inarguably shared was a love of the leaf. "That is how I think of her," he said.

She slammed down the teapot—an expert temper, he noted; all the spray came in his direction, a tiny scalding rain across his knee. "But we have gone off track," she said sweetly. "My *point* is that I offer you my gratitude, as her loving cousin, for whatever aid you afforded her in that time. But that does not mean you have any right to *exploit* that debt by abusing her so! You are very lucky I have not taken this matter to Lord Chad; he would be sure to call you out for it! Luring her out at all hours to God knows where, playing fast and loose with her good name!"

"I believe she would manage it even without my help," he said dryly.

She sat back and clicked her teaspoon against the saucer as she stared at him. There was a vaguely martial rhythm to it. "Then we disagree," she said flatly. "For I can trace all of her recent—*behavior*—directly to the events at Lockwood's. Since that night, she has not been herself." Perhaps she saw the encouragement that gave him, for her voice hardened. "She is sleepless. Ill-tempered. Distracted and generally sullen. And now, Lord above! Wholly irrational. Those are not the sort of changes one wishes to inspire in a woman—even, or perhaps especially, if one is a rogue, a debauchee, and a scapegrace nonpareil."

It was amazing, what one would take from a woman. Any man who'd characterized him thus would know to reach for his pistol as he said it. But Lady Chad, seeing her hit take effect, merely sat back and sipped her tea. She had Emma's spine, no mistake there. He smiled at her; he rather liked the woman. "Point taken."

"Yes," she said. She put down the tea and resumed her drumroll with the spoon. "So I wish to make it very clear to you now," she said, punctuating each word with a sharp rap. "You may think that your title and your wealth will protect you, but I warn you, Duke: I have my own ways of extracting revenge. The hand of a woman may be soft, but her reach is long. And its subtlety does not make it any less effective!"

The saucer shattered.

She glanced down at it, then gave a little shrug and tossed her spoon onto the table.

"I am duly chastened," he said. "But you have noted yourself how stubborn she is. She would open the house regardless of my actions."

"The house! The house is the least—"

"And perhaps, since we are speaking so frankly, I might also observe that her recent melancholy is but a small deterioration—if that—from the state in which she previously found herself: namely, isolated, lonely, and damnably resigned to it."

The Countess blinked. "Why . . ." She shook her head a little. "Do you—*care* for her? But you hardly know her! You . . ." Lady Chad's eyes shifted past him, narrowing in thought. "You knew her," she said slowly. "You did not merely help her escape Delhi. Were *you*—could *you* be the reason she broke off from Marcus? She would never tell me the whole of it."

"No," he said. "That was her own doing. Although I may have privately cheered her decision."

"As did I," the Countess said softly, her brow knitting. And then, with a little shake, she seemed to recall herself. Her regard returned to him. "Four years ago now. And you thought she was dead."

"Yes."

"And then you ran into her at the ball. And you—and she—" She leaned forward, and her voice dropped to a whisper. "Why—are you in *love* with her? *Have* you been, all this time?"

He studied her in return. "She is not the woman I knew in Delhi, Lady Chad."

She sat back, disappointment clear on her face. "What do you mean?"

He shrugged. "Simply that had you asked me to characterize her then, I would have called her bruised, but ultimately . . . unscarred. She had a joy for life that was rare. It illuminated her; the shipwreck had not destroyed it."

"Yes," Lady Chad murmured. "I remember. Such a laughing, vibrant girl."

"But not now," he continued softly. "That is what you are thinking; do not bother to deny it. And a stranger, looking upon her at present, would not be nearly so charitable. What would he see in her? Fatigue, yes. Fear. And a failure of hope. Those are not attractive qualities, Countess."

Lady Chad's scowl would have broken a weaker brow. "How *dare* you—"

"And to come to the point we have both been dancing around, the stranger might detect a touch of mania as well. Those paintings are not the work of a restful mind."

The Countess was on her feet now. "You are a loathsome, devilish—"

"But to answer your question, yes."

Her mouth snapped shut. She considered him for a moment. "Yes?"

"Yes."

"Despite all of—what you just said?"

"Perhaps even because of it," he said quietly. "I am perverse that way, I fear."

After a long moment, the Countess sat back down. "So," she said. "You . . . do love her. I must say, you look *peculiarly* resigned to it."

He shrugged. "It is not fresh news for me."

"And for Emma?"

"Neither welcomed nor openly acknowledged."

"But acknowledged all the same, you believe."

"Perhaps," he said. "I cannot know. Not anymore."

"Not anymore," she repeated slowly. "Well. My, my! But there is an easy way to tell her: you must ask her to marry you."

Now he laughed. "Madam—no, no, forgive me, I do not mean to make fun. But do we speak of the same woman? The one who planned to run off to Italy to avoid me?"

"Yes," she said thoughtfully. "There is that. For all her bold claims, she is very set on remaining unattached. Why, she even told me she would rather—" She shook her head. "The silliest things. Oh, Emma." She sighed and reached out to touch the teaspoon. "I do apologize. I seem to have become a bit . . . overwrought."

"I had not noticed," he said, and she gave him a look, and laughed.

There was a knock at the door. The footman brought over a note to him. He took it with some surprise. Lady Chad arched a brow as he broke the seal.

It was from one of the men he'd dispatched to watch over Emma. As he read it, his blood went cold.

"Where is Emma?" he asked, and his tone was such that her frown returned.

"At her parents' house. Why—what is it? What's wrong?"

But he was already on his feet, headed for the door.

Twenty

Emma tasted grapes in the back of her throat. The bowels of the warehouse were saturated with their scent. From far above came the rumble of passing carriages and carts. She picked her way down the aisle, the sawdust soft beneath her feet. On either side rose stacks of casks—port or sherry or burgundy, she could not be sure which; the red lamps hanging every few feet from the ceiling did not provide enough light to decipher their labels. Ahead, Marcus carried a lamp affixed to a long stick. She would have liked the extra light, but she refused to walk at his side.

The clerk upstairs had seemed to know him quite well, and had handed him a stack of letters that Marcus had withdrawn into an anteroom to read for some minutes. That was odd. Why would he receive mail here?

Indeed, that he should have stored her paintings here was curious in itself.

"I have had some peculiar news," he said now. "Auburn has been needling the board at the Academy, trying to secure a private showing of your paintings."

Unease prickled over her. Had he been spying on Julian? Did he intend to take revenge for his arm? "Strange," she said.

"I wonder—you did not tell him you were Miss Ashdown, did you?"

"Of course not."

The floor of the warehouse abruptly sloped upward. They crossed under an archway, and he unlocked a door which opened onto a warmer, dryer space. The air here smelled different, green and raw like broken saplings. Bales of unidentifiable produce were stacked shoulder high to her left. "One moment," he said. "Hold the lamp, please."

She took the stick from him, grunting a little with the effort of balancing it. A key scraped into a lock. His hand at her shoulder pushed her to the right, into a large, hot room. A cot stood in one corner, stacked with what looked like cheesecloth. Next to it, a shelf held empty jars of various sizes. Along the wall to the left was a huge stove, with two chimneys rising into the ceiling; a copper kettle hung suspended over the unlit coals. There was a familiar, sickly sweet odor ghosting through the space. She recognized it from Colthurst's house. Opium.

Like a finger scraping down her spine, presentiment made her shiver. Even aside from the obvious, there was something very wrong here.

"All right then," he said. "Here they are."

She dutifully lifted the lamp, and the light spread across her paintings, strewn haphazardly across the floor. They were marked with boot prints, as if someone had paced across them, again and again. She moved the lamp in a slow arc across the jumbled pile. He had bought so many of them. Almost all of those she had sold. As she reached the end, she sucked in a breath. Anne Marie's crumpled form. The blood spilling from her throat. *As I Laughed.*

The painting was not with Sommerdon after all.

"You see I have more than enough of them to make my case," Marcus said. "Even without the parade of witnesses."

"Yes," she said numbly. How could he have bought the painting from Sommerdon so quickly? Or—had Sommerdon ever had it at all? But what reason could Marcus have to purchase it under a false name?

"What will it be then?" he asked. "Your family's ruin, and my own? Or marriage, and your life?"

Her breath was coming shorter. Everything in her body was registering an immediate danger, only her brain could not puzzle it out. Why would he want to hurt her?

"Or perhaps I can make you an even better gift," he went on. "We will burn them. Would you like that?"

She licked her dry lips. "It would make no sense for you to burn them. They are evidence, aren't they? With which you may compel me."

"True. But as far as evidence goes, they are grotesque, and cumbersome, and draw too much attention. Auburn poking about—it unsettles me. So I have another solution. The letters from which you took these lines. You will give me those, and they will serve just as well."

She was grateful for the dim light. It concealed the way the blood drained from her head. The paintings damned her; they were the work of her own hand, dated by her own brush; they evidenced her possession of the letters to the year. But the letters alone—they were proof of nothing. Except whatever strange conspiracy the Urdu hinted at. "I destroyed those," she heard herself say.

"Hmm. But surely these paintings could not have been completed all at once? How did you recall the script so well, if you did not have examples before you? You do not *know* Urdu, do you?"

"No," she said quickly. "But—once I was finished with all the paintings, then I burned them."

A short silence fell. "I do not believe you," he said then, softly. "You see, it occurs to me that there is reason for you to lie. You take a perverse pride in these atrocities. You think them worthy of the Academy, no less. And so you do not wish to see them destroyed. Well, listen to me, Emmaline. I will give the paintings to you. Those which are not too damning, at least. Withdraw them from the Academy, and we will store them away in a place of your choosing. Provided, of course, you give me the letters. And if not . . ." His shoulder lifted in a shrug. "I can burn them now." He bent down, and his hand closed on *As I Laughed*. "It will not take long to light the fire."

"All right," she said instantly. "The letters are in Gemson Park."

"Excellent," he said. "We are speaking honestly now. It is a solid enough foundation for a marriage. And you may keep the works from the Academy, but I believe some of these must go. Hand me the lamp; I will light the coals."

She acted on instinct alone. With a mighty swing of the stick, she brought the lamp into the wall.

A loud crash, then absolute darkness. His curse was startled. She inched backward. A wooden frame cracked, and then another; his boots thumped over them toward her. She took a leap in the direction they had entered, and the stick still clutched in her hand caught against the door frame, slamming into her gut. Windless, she threw it behind her and darted out.

"I find it curious that you would run," he called. He sounded very calm, which frightened her more than anger would have done. "Unless someone has *read* those letters for you."

Oh God.

Suddenly the suspicion churning her stomach crystallized into words: *He* was the one whom the letters damned. That was what this was all about.

To the left, in the distance, was a dim red glow: the lights from the section through which they had come. She hauled up her skirts and ran.

The laces seemed to constrict around her ribs. The breath squeezed from her in raw, pained gasps. She made it through the archway, and the smell of grapes was upon her again; she stumbled down the slope into the cellar and his hand hooked into her chignon.

Her feet went out from under her. Backward she fell. Her torso hit his knees, and he came down under her on a curse. She threw her elbow back toward his arm, hoping to hit the sling.

A cold pressure jabbed into her spine. "I will shoot you," he said hoarsely.

She froze. The rasping of her breath she could not control. "Then you will not have my money."

"Turn around. Are the letters really at Gemson Park?"

She met his eyes. "Yes."

He slowly wriggled out from beneath her. Now the cold metal rose to kiss her forehead. Just between the eyes. He could not miss such a shot, even if his left hand gripped the hilt awkwardly.

She swallowed and wet her lips. "What would you gain from it? I have told you where the letters are. And you have so much evidence against me."

"Whom else have you told of the letters?"

"No one."

"That does not account for Auburn's interest in the paintings," he said flatly. "Damn the bastard! It should have been mine. *You* should have been mine." The regret in his voice chilled her; she heard her death in it. "Your parents always intended your fortune for me. If you hadn't been such a bloody—do you see, Emmaline? You gave me no choice."

"I don't know what you mean," she whispered.

"Oh, I think you know well enough. Otherwise—well, this whole farce. I had to have that money from Nana Sahib. A little exchange of troop movements, a friendly deal. The debts were piling up—what else was I to do?"

A click sounded: the hammer being drawn back.

"The letters are *not* at Gemson Park," she said.

"Then I will be gone from England by daybreak."

A gunshot rang out.

He fell away from her.

She sat there. Her trembling fingers rose, hit against her nose. She traced up to her forehead. Whole and smooth. Covered in a film of cold sweat. Not dead, then.

"Emma."

She flinched at the sound. So unexpected. The hand on her back was gentle.

"Emma," Julian said again. He bent down to settle his gun on the ground. "Are you all right?"

"Yes," she whispered. She took Julian's hand and let him pull her to her feet. His arms came around her; she hugged him back, fiercely. Then she realized he was not hugging her; his hands were making a rough, quick survey of her arms and torso. "I *am* all right," she said, and saw over his shoulder Lord Lockwood, standing at a few steps' remove. It recalled her to the moment. "We need a lamp," she said. Her voice was jerky. "Colthurst's painting. It's here. The room down the corridor."

"Good," Julian said, and pulled her into a real embrace this time. She set her face into his shoulder, breathing in the smell of him. He was shaking, she realized. She ran a hand along his back, making a shushing noise. Against her neck, his lips turned into a smile.

"He was a traitor," she whispered. "The letters indicted *him*."

"Yes," he said. "I know. It's all right now."

Lockwood cleared his throat. "Shall the body disappear, or should we go about it properly?"

Julian pulled back from her. "Properly. Let the letters go to Whitehall."

"Copies for the newspapers too, I should think. No editorials on fallen heroes that way."

"Quite right. No mourning; save the world some bombazine."

"No!" She caught Julian's arm. "You mustn't circulate those letters. God, why do you think I came here with him? Marcus said the Urdu would prove you'd colluded with the mutineers!"

His brows arched. "And you *believed* him?"

"No, of course not! Only, if your cousin was involved, and the letters mentioned your gifts to him—"

Lockwood lifted a lamp off its hook and moved past them, down the corridor.

Julian took her face in his hands. "Emma. It's *all right.* General Wilson knew I was visiting Deven. Hell, it was his righthand man who showed me how to slip into the city." He sighed, and suddenly he sounded very tired. "If Marcus was paying his spies to catch me out, his money was wasted."

"Oh." There was so much she still did not know of that time. And so much he did not know, as well. A strange sound came out of her throat.

His hand turned, so his knuckles brushed her cheek. "Lockwood can handle the rest," he said. "I will take you home."

The thought of facing Delphinia's bright questions made her shudder. "No," she said. "Your house." At his look of surprise, she mustered a weary smile. "It is time we talked, I think. You see, Marcus is not the only one those letters will damn."

* * *

In the coach, her nerve began to fail her. Perhaps he sensed it, for he asked no questions, but drew her up against him, and held her head to his chest. It was the way he would hold a child, she thought, if they were to have one. If her words did not end every possibility his eyes offered her.

Once inside, she led the way, past his startled porter and into the drawing room. Some senseless part of her brain was seeking an advantage. The high ground from which to conduct this sad little confession. Her heartbeat was starting to speed, the same way it had done when Marcus's wits fell apart before her. But now the person she feared was herself. The things she must say now, and the price they might exact, were as frightening as a gun to the head.

When he entered after her, she saw that he meant to come straight to her, and she raised a hand. "No," she said. "*Wait.*"

His footsteps halted. He had always listened to her, hadn't he? Had always *heard* her. "All right," he said, never taking his eyes off her as he tossed his greatcoat aside. It slipped off the side of the divan onto the floor.

She considered him in return, and the panic within her began to subside. The painting was so *right*. Thus did he look on the canvas: grave, steady, patient, warm; prepared for anything, really. "Julian, I must say I do not like Lancelot very much. He seems vain. The Lady of Shalott deserved better."

It took him a moment to reply. "Yes. True. And I dislike the reapers as well. Sad shows, listening to her sing and taking no action. If any of them had known his fairy tales, he would have seen the proper course was to climb the tower. Remove the lady before the curse took effect."

She smiled. "A much better ending." But how to go on, how to get there, she had no clue. Her eyes dropped to the coat on the floor. "Your valet will be angry with you."

He said nothing to that.

"Yes," she said. "All right, then." Her lips were dry. She licked them. "I must tell you I have done things," she said, and yes, that was good, that was in the right direction. "I have done things for which I would have been hanged in England."

No reaction. His perfect face blank as he regarded her. Then he gestured toward the sideboard, asking her permission to move. She nodded, and he crossed to take up a decanter. She mustered a thin smile as he splashed two glasses full of it. Looked that bad, did she?

"I have never told anyone," she said. "I—" Her lips felt too weak to hold the words. She bit her knuckles, waiting, waiting. Yes. There it was. "About the man I killed. Or what I did in Sapnagar."

Slowly he approached, to set the glasses on a long, low table. "May I sit?"

"Yes," she said. He took the seat across from her, drawing it up so close their knees almost touched.

The beveled glass was slippery beneath her fingers. Her palm was sweating. She took a sip, and choked.

He leaned forward—a convulsive, aborted movement that her eyes caught, and warned him against. Slowly he sat back.

"Surprised me," she said. "That's all. It burns like seawater." She took a deep breath, then tipped the glass back. She could take the rest, one long swallow. The flame spread down through her. When she lowered the glass to the table, she saw how hard he was trying. But his expression would not be schooled. That telltale tick in his jaw. He knew it, and he did not look away from her; he let her see his struggle.

She was not so brave. She did not want to cry in front of him. But then, she did not think she would. Even if she had never spoken the story aloud, she had relived it in her mind a thousand times; and now, as her mouth opened and she finally began, she heard how her voice reflected the familiarity of the tale. So did schoolchildren speak, when reciting an old and much hated lesson.

Sapnagar. That was where it had started. That bright, sunny morning, four years ago. She spared him no details. She told him that she had been thinking of him. That Kavita had warned her not to look too deeply into men's affairs, that the British justification for ruling India had nothing to do with either of them. She told him of spotting the sepoys from far off, of how they had assumed it was the Maharajah's tax collectors.

She told him how they had laughed at Anne Marie and Grace, and how her own hasty words, the false comfort she'd called down to them, had stopped them from fleeing the sepoys.

She told him what she had seen the sepoys do to the women.

He made a noise. She looked to him, and he reached out to take her hand, pressing it firmly within his own as he lifted it to his lips.

"Go on," he said quietly, settling it on his thigh.

She recalled that horrid ride through the desert, when

she had not cared whether she lived or died. Such strange thoughts she'd had. The sand, like an endless ocean. Memories of Kurnaul were blurry, too. Perhaps she had been in shock. Could that be it?

"Yes," he said. "Yes, Emma."

In retrospect, she wasn't sure why she'd gone to Marcus's tent. Perhaps she'd wanted to see a familiar face. Despite his betrayals, she still associated him with home—the simple happiness of Gemson Park, and girlhood. But he hadn't been there, of course. She'd fallen asleep—

"No," she corrected herself, voice thickening. "I'd drawn a very horrible drawing, of Anne Marie. And then I fell asleep."

She'd dreamed the drawing, dreamed it was real. That it was all happening again, but to her now. And then—when she'd woken—

Julian refilled her glass.

"He'd followed me into the tent. Watched me sleep. It was that man, of course—the man from the bazaar. You recognized him in my painting. The unfinished one. I do wish you'd just shot him then—when you were pointing the pistol at him. Unkind of me, I suppose. Then it would have been on your head instead of mine. Do you remember that day?"

Her words were all out of joint. Jumbled, a Bedlam poem. But he seemed to understand. He also seemed pale. It looked odd on him. "I have never seen you pale," she said.

"I should have shot him. I would gladly have shot him. What did he do, Emma?"

"Oh, he did try to rape me. But I killed him first."

Julian lowered his head for a moment. When he looked up, she did not recognize him. There was nothing to his face, nothing, only those green eyes which seemed to burn straight through her numbness, leaving her raw, unprotected against her own guilt and horror. She could not look into them. Here was what she had feared. The seed of all her freshest nightmares. She lowered her head. Her hands smelled like the liquor. They felt very cold against her face.

"Emma," he said.

And the sound of her breathing, so loud against the seal made by her palms.

"Emma. You must let it go."

The darkness behind her eyes was red. It did not have to be so. Press hard enough, and one could see stars.

"Emma," he whispered. *"Let go."*

"Oh, *God,*" she said, her voice breaking. "I killed him, I *killed him.* I p-put a letter opener through his head, his eyes rolled back, his *mouth—*"

His arms were around her now. Her face in his chest. Muffling her sobs. She was watching, from somewhere above—and then his arms tightened and she was flesh, her throat was closing, the wool of his suit scratching her skin, the air coming in jerks. Everything was coming up and out of her and the sounds of it were horrible, and his embrace was tight to hold her together, surely. She dug her head into his throat and struggled to breathe.

After a minute—or ten, or twenty—she realized he was murmuring to her. And then, with a small shock, she realized it was not English he was speaking. It was a different language, that melodic, lilting tongue that her maid Usha had used, so long ago. Like yesterday. It made his chest vibrate. It was more soothing than English, like a lullaby, nonsensical, blank. English was so heavy. So desiccated and hardened by meaning, by pain and anger and even the jests and petty quibbles, everything under the sun that obscured the basic truth. But the sound of his voice as he spoke to her now, she heard the wind in it, the stillness of the night. Stars above. The things that had kept her going. Always in her memory they had been there. That night on the way to Sapnagar. She had tried to ignore it, but she had always failed. It had always been there, quietly, as his voice was now, against her ear, against her hair.

She pulled away. "He dropped his letters. He was holding them when he came in, and he knocked down my sketchbook. I was gathering up the drawings in a hurry—I was in a panic, not thinking—and I took it all. By accident, and then I didn't know how to get rid of it. Because—well, it was proof, wasn't it? Proof of what I'd done. And the whole camp was talking. A soldier, murdered in their midst."

He stroked her hair back from her face. A strand or two stuck. She reached up to pull them away. Her cheeks were wet. His shirtfront as well, she saw suddenly.

"I—" She swallowed. "This will change your idea of me."

He took her by the chin, directing her gaze back to him. "No. You know it does not."

"But I murdered—"

"In defense of yourself," he said. "And the letters should not worry you. If you took them from him, then he was part of the treason as well. There is no question of anyone blaming you."

She exhaled in disbelief. So easy? All the reasons she should not be forgiven—could he not see them, even now? So much blood had been shed around her. The horror like a contagion, and she so hopelessly infected. And then the original sin. "Laughing at Anne Marie and Mrs. Kiddell—"

He exhaled sharply. "Sweet girl, how can you blame yourself for that? You had no idea those were sepoys."

"Their last memory—if they were lucky, Julian. It was of my laughter. *Laughing* at them. So . . . hard to bear."

"Yes. It is." He kissed her forehead, and one hand stroked down her spine, urging her back against him. After a long moment, he said, "My cousin died, Emma."

"What—oh!" She tried to look at him, but he held her still.

"Deven died," he said softly. "In the assault on Delhi. I lit his pyre; my grandmother gave me that honor. But I did it only for her. Deven would not have wanted it. He did aid the rebels, you know. He hated what I stood for; he would have died another death to know I performed that rite for him. And that knowledge . . . yes, it lingers with me. Much as Anne Marie lingers with you."

Now she did wrest out of his grip, just enough to meet his eyes. "You were trying to help him, Julian. Always. You were trying to keep them safe."

"Of course," he murmured. "And you were only trying to survive, dear heart."

Her face was so close to his now that their eyelashes tangled. "And what did I survive for, do you think?"

She felt his smile against her lips. "For art, Miss Martin?"

"More than art, I think." And then, on a deep breath, she kissed him.

His eyes closed, and he accepted the kiss, letting her do as she liked, his lips mimicking hers. Always accepting her. His fingertips slid down to either side of her waist, balancing there. As if she were the lead in this dance, and he would follow her step for step. The thought made her smile. She broke away, and he exhaled.

"You came to me," he said.

"Yes."

"Do you know why?"

She smiled. "Julian. You looked for me in Kurnaul. You looked for me in Alwar. Where else did you name? Lucknow. Agra. Bartpur. Have I forgotten any?"

"Several," he said, and his finger ran over her bottom lip. "But you know that."

"Yes. But there is one city in particular I never heard you name. You never named London."

"No," he said softly.

"I thought you had not found me here," she whispered. "Or I thought you would not want me, as I am now. But you *did* find me here. Didn't you?"

"Yes." Something moved across his face as he looked at her, and it caught her like a hook; her next breath felt painful. Her heart was breaking to look upon him, or, no, it was finally knitting together; he wore his emotions so openly before her, she could not conceive of how to doubt him. She took his jaw in hand and directed his mouth back to hers. There was a hesitance in his lips, and she eased it by instinct alone, running her tongue along the seam of his mouth, sliding her hands down his chest. When his tongue finally touched hers, she laughed into his mouth and said, "Will you not take me to bed? Or is always to be floors for us?"

His forehead settled against hers. "Emma—there is nothing I would like better. But . . . the servants."

"What of them?"

"There is only one way I can take you upstairs. And that is if I know I will have the opportunity, later, to repair the damage it does to your name."

"Yes," she said. "Take me upstairs."

Twenty-one

A FRAUGHT SILENCE GREW BETWEEN THEM AS HE LED her down the darkened corridor. On one side was a long row of portraits, Julian's English forebears. They stared haughtily toward the opposite wall, where dark Indian tapestries, embellished with gold wire and mirrors, glittered in the light from the sconces. Despite the anticipation upon her, Emma found herself wanting to laugh. The arrangement was the product of a sophisticated eye, with a taste for color as well as mood—but there was nothing subtle about the statement it made.

His fingers twitched around hers as they passed a maid coming down the hall. "Spotted," he said. "No going back now."

She smiled at him. "Did you think I meant to?"

Now his grip firmed, and his pace quickened a little,

so that she was giggling and breathless when they finally reached the end of the corridor. He drew her through a small anteroom leading into his bedchamber. His valet looked up from a pile of neckties, eyes widening as they fixed on her.

"The evening is yours," said Julian.

"Sir," the man said, and hastily let himself out.

She stepped inside. So this was where he slept. A thick Turkey carpet ran from wall to wall. Two chairs flanked a small, scrolled table by the fire. In one corner stood an overflowing bookshelf, and two doors set into the far wall opened onto a sleeping porch. The late-afternoon sun spread fingers of light through the doors' glass panes, illuminating the carved surfaces of the rosewood bed frame, picking filaments of silver from the canopy's burgundy silk swags.

Turning around, she saw that the door through which they'd entered was flanked by two handsome chests, inlaid with brass wire. She had never seen anything like them. Perhaps he mistook the direction of her interest, for he moved into her path, blocking the door.

"You took my meaning downstairs," he said.

His tone was perfectly even, but he watched her closely. It came to her that he expected her to try to bolt—and he was resolved not to let her do it.

Amusement and love and the smallest trace of sympathy took hold of her. He still thought her hesitant—and why shouldn't he? She had gone about this in the most backward way. "Yes," she said, and fought the twitch of her lips, for he was very serious. "I understood you."

But it was not enough for him. "You are entirely compromised," he pressed.

Now she did give vent to her smile. "*Almost* entirely. I look to you to complete it."

His answering grin was wry. "By marrying you, do you mean? For let us be clear: that is what we're speaking of."

The idea of it swelled up in her like an orchestra's overture, and she had to blink very hard to prevent the tears. She caught up his hand. "Take it back," she said.

"I beg your pardon?"

"You cannot say such things until I say that I love you, Julian. So let me say it; I have waited far too long to do so. I *love* you. For a very long time now. For years."

His fingers closed around hers, and he laughed, a soft, happy, slightly incredulous sound. "How hard that was for you," he murmured. "You almost look resigned to it."

"Yes, I'm a dunderhead," she said. "It's only—"

But he cut the words off with a kiss. "I'm teasing you," he said against her mouth. "And myself, a little."

She smiled beneath his mouth, and his hands slid down her ribs to settle on her hips, just below the edge of her corset. Their firm pressure made her voice go husky. "Very unkind of you," she murmured, "to tease me so."

His voice was equally soft. "You must learn to accustom yourself to it. For there is more than one way to tease, and I plan to try them all on you. Turn around."

It took a moment for the command to penetrate the growing lassitude in her brain. "Oh," she said, as his hands at her waist gently nudged her around to face the direction of the windows. His fingers played cleverly over the cameo at her throat, and on the buttons at her wrists; in another second, her jacket was slipping from her shoulders. His hands moved again, making an economical descent down the eyelets of her gown; she shivered as his mouth found her bared nape. A finger gently traced the top of her spine, playing on a sensitive spot between her shoulder blades. The gust of his breath made her shiver. He laughed softly, and then the corset was loosening, as he worked at her laces. She reached up to unfasten the busk, and he lifted the thing away.

His hands came around to settle over her breasts. Gently his palms cupped her, drawing her back into his body. He was aroused, hard and hot against her lower back; but for a long moment he simply stood there, holding her, his breath steady in her ear. Her eyes fell shut. Warmth was moving up her face: the sunlight, spreading farther into the room. She felt as if she were floating. All along her back came the heat of his body, and in front, there was the hot embrace of his hands on her breasts, the slightly callused texture of his palms.

"I am yours," he said quietly.

His thumbs brushed over her nipples—just once, the most fleeting abrasion. But it was enough to speed her pulse again, and she turned her head, looping her hand over the back of his neck to pull his mouth down to hers. Her tongue brushed against the seam of his lips; they were flavored by the brandy he had drunk. She pulled harder, and his mouth opened fully, so she could breathe him into her.

When she broke away, it was to say, "You have me at a disadvantage."

"A pleasant change," he said, and she laughed, and reached up to unwind his necktie. Next his frock coat, the wool soft and finely textured beneath her fingers. He wanted to help; she batted his hand away. Now the buttons of his black waistcoat, and the braces beneath. His trousers did not come off so easily. She resisted his effort to help, falling to her knees before him to unhook the buttons. As he lifted his shirt over his head, she pulled the trousers down.

An artist should not be shocked by the human body. But she had never seen him in the light, and sculptures lacked certain . . . details. Her body had accommodated this thickness; it was astonishing. She traced the vein that ran down from the head of him to the black curls at his base, and his sharp breath inspired her to stroke him again. It was not so frightening, she thought, and curved her hand around it, and felt how the skin moved over the hardness beneath. She glanced up; his face was hard now, set in fierce, grim lines. Startled, she said, "Oh—I didn't mean—" But when her hand would have released him, he reached down to hold her there.

"It's . . . fine," he said, and laughed a little. "Just—surprising."

She felt a flush prickle through her cheeks. His eyes traced down her. "God," he said softly. "How you blush."

His tone, so hushed and heated, made her legs go weak. She sat back on her heels, running her eyes down his length, past the planes of his abdomen and the angular jut of his hipbones, the narrow expanse of his hips to his . . . cock . . . wrapped in her hand. The sight stirred her. She could touch him here. And he would continue to look at her like this, as though she held all the answers he wanted, because nothing she did could deter him. She drew a breath and laid her free hand against his thigh, so sculpted, the muscle flexing beneath her touch. The anatomy books she had studied did not cover it. Her hand smoothed down the flare of his quadriceps. He moved as though to urge her back up, but she did not want to go. This part of him was hers as well, and she had neglected it, hadn't she? She set her mouth to the skin of his thigh, nipping lightly; his muscle tightened beneath her lips even before she heard his gasp.

She drew back a little. There were benefits to being hopelessly singular. One's imagination could conjure possibilities that might not occur to others. She moved her lips to where her fingers curled around his cock, and heard his breath catch again. From the heat of her breath on him? Only that? She hesitated briefly. He was watching her do this; she felt his eyes on her. Embarrassment and excitement felt so similar, at times. On an indrawn breath, she darted her tongue over his tip. Salty, scented with a faint musk. His strangled noise intrigued her. Had she made such noises, when he had performed a similar thing on her?

The thought made her dizzy. Yes, he had done this to her. He had put his head between her thighs, and licked and sucked her; and now she would do the same. She opened her mouth and put her lips around the head of him. There was nothing to hide between them anymore, nothing more intimate than this; he had looked into her soul and told her he was hers, and her tongue, tracing the underside of him, made him moan.

After a moment, he said roughly, "Come," and now she did let him pull her up, because her limbs were too weak to resist his hands' direction. He stripped the chemise from her, and released the tapes of her crinoline; she stepped out of her clothing. Taking her bottom in his hand, he pulled her into him again, and now they were pressed naked together, in the light. She set her face into the crook of his neck as he stroked her, broad hard strokes down her back that brought her so close that his cock had nowhere to nestle but in the space opened at the tops of her thighs. She parted her legs slightly for a better fit, and the pressure as his hardness arced up against her quim made her moan. She opened her mouth on his skin and bit him. He had done so, before, and she understood now why he had liked doing it.

"Look," he said softly, and she raised her head. He turned her so she faced the pier glass. His forearm came around her waist, the veins in his arm standing out, the muscle there flexing as his hand angled up to close over her breast. She watched in the glass as his other hand slid between her thighs, cupping her gently. He held her quim as if it were his, which it was, she thought suddenly. She was his as much as he was hers. Every part of her answered to him.

His regard in the mirror was slumberous. She met his eyes, and the corner of his mouth quirked a little, as if he had secret plans for her and the thought of them pleased him. She put her hand on top of his where it held her breast, and he rubbed her nipple lightly. His skin looked so dark in comparison with her pallor; his hair was so black against her cheek as he leaned down to swirl his tongue in her ear. She made a little noise, and his hand moved between her thighs, pressing up into her with sudden sure pressure. Her hips jerked.

In the mirror her face reddened further, and her eyes widened. She might have laughed at herself, a little embarrassed, if she had had the strength to do it, or if, as his eyes met hers again, anything in his face had suggested humor. His thumb found that spot which robbed her of breath, and he began to push upward on her from within, and his hand at her breast chafed as he sucked on her earlobe. "The bed," she said, and did not recognize her own voice—so hoarse. The sound of it heightened her agitation. She felt like a tuning fork, quivering; or a flute played by his mouth and fingers, pushed rapidly up through the scales.

He swung her around and up into his arms, turning her so her legs closed around his waist as he carried her. They tumbled onto the mattress. She found herself seated on top of him, and rose onto her knees, thinking to climb up to kiss him again. But he used the space opened between them to reach down and take hold of himself and rub the head of him in the dampness between her legs. The sensation, the idea it inspired, made her catch her breath. "Like this," she said, and "Yes," he said, and she exhaled as she felt him press upward, spreading her, forcing inward.

He moved into her so deeply that it burned a little. She doubted, for a moment, whether she could take anything more. And then his hips jerked, and she was fuller still, the loveliest dilemma. His hands grasped her waist to direct her, and as she began to move—clumsily, at first, and then catching the rhythm—the burn gone, only the sweetness remaining. The friction distracted her mind, let instinct play guide. She circled her hips, and watched his eyes flutter shut, his head tip back. The sight made her flush hotter; she leaned forward to lick the sweat from his cheek. It was the same taste as she remembered; she tasted him again.

His eyes came open under the stroke of her tongue.

"You . . ." he said, but it seemed he could not finish it. He rose up and turned her over onto her back, and she laughed and then his hips rolled and her laughter ended in a gasp. She remembered that night in the desert again, so clearly that it was as if they were back there, and the bed and its silk hangings and the rich afternoon light faded before the overlay of shadows and stars.

He took her hand and moved it down, so she could feel where he pressed into her. The sensation, the feel of their fingers tangled together there, as he moved in and out of her, brought everything in her to a keening pitch. She broke around him, and their lips met, and his movements grew fierce; she held onto his back and felt her own strength, her own resilience, as she absorbed the furor of his thrusts.

When he finished, she caught him to her and would not let him pull away.

"I will crush you," he said.

"I am not fragile," she murmured.

"No," he whispered against her breast. "Anything but." His hand came up to thread through her hair, so it fanned out over her shoulders. He murmured something else, which she did not understand. When she asked, he smiled. "It is a couplet by Ghalib, a poet I once met in Delhi. 'In love my temperament found a new taste for life: it found a cure for the pain, and a pain without cure.' "

She stroked his hair softly. "It is beautiful. But I do not wish to give you any more pain than I already have done."

He leaned up to kiss her. "Too late. I am clearly very badly off, to be reciting poetry in my own bed."

She laughed and pressed his head back down, so her hands could stroke through his hair. She felt—changed, she thought. As though the sunlight had settled inside her. The dark crescents of his lashes, the curves of his lips, made her want to kiss him again. But then she would miss the sensation of his breath, so soft and hot against her breast.

The moment seemed precious. Portentous. It was borrowed, she thought, from her future.

After a minute, he pushed up on his elbow to look her in the face. "The proposal," he said.

"Yes," she said. "You may make it now. But first—I want to tell you. I have finished a painting."

"Yes?"

"And it is not bloody, or self-righteous. Though perhaps it is melodramatic."

He laughed softly. "But not flat, I hope?"

"No, not at all. It is of you, on the roof of Sapnagar. I had drawn you once, in Kurnaul. But the plain was filled with bodies. Not so in this painting. There are no shadows behind you, now. Nothing dark. Only the future. And it is green and lovely to my eyes."

He opened his mouth, and a door opened. Emma ducked beneath the covers as he said something.

"All right," he said after a moment. "We've scandalized the poor chambermaid into her grave, but I think you can come out now."

She poked her head back up.

"You are blushing again," he purred.

"Well," she said. "I suppose the nice thing about being ruined is that a woman of uncertain reputation does not need to fret over niceties."

One black brow lifted. "Nor does a duchess," he said.

"Who's to be a duchess? You haven't even properly proposed yet."

"Let me try again," he said with a grin, and rose over her, and took her mouth with his.

Catch up with love...
Catch up with passion...
Catch up with danger....

Catch a bestseller from Pocket Books!

Delve into the past with *New York Times* bestselling author

Julia London

The Dangers of Deceiving a Viscount

Beware! A lady's secrets will always be revealed...

Barbara Delinksy

Lake News

New York Times bestseller!

Sometimes you have to get away to find everything.

Fern Michaels

The Marriage Game

New York Times bestseller!

It's all fun and games—until someone falls in love.

Hester Browne

The Little Lady Agency

New York Times bestseller!

Why trade up if you can fix him up?

Laura Griffin

One Last Breath

Don't move. Don't breathe. Don't say a word...

POCKET STAR BOOKS
A Division of Simon & Schuster
A CBS COMPANY

POCKET BOOKS
A Division of Simon & Schuster
A CBS COMPANY

Available wherever books are sold
or at www.simonsayslove.com.

17660

FINALLY A WEBSITE YOU CAN GET *PASSIONATE* ABOUT...

Visit

www.SimonSaysLove.com

for the latest information about Romance from Pocket Books!

READING SUGGESTIONS

LATEST RELEASES

AUTHOR APPEARANCES

ONLINE CHATS WITH YOUR FAVORITE WRITERS

SPECIAL OFFERS

ORDER BOOKS ONLINE

AND MUCH, MUCH MORE!

POCKET BOOKS
A Division of Simon & Schuster
A CBS COMPANY

POCKET STAR BOOKS
A Division of Simon & Schuster
A CBS COMPANY

16035